The Consequence
of demolishing a pillar

The Consequence
of demolishing a pillar

A
Novel
By
Makonnen G.igzi

Historical thriller

Cover picture: Emperor Haile Selassie I in full dress.
Public Domain
Created: January 1970
An official portrait of which b/w copies were
distributed by the Ethiopian government

Cover Design and Layout: Melena G
Editing; Author/journalist Mulugeta Gudeta

Publisher: BoD – Books on Demand, Stockholm,
Sweden
Print: BoD – Books on Demand, Norderstedt,
Germany
ISBN: 978-91-7969-363-3

Haile Selassie was Emperor of Ethiopia from 1930 to 1974. He is remembered as a defining figure in modern Ethiopian history; his contribution to Ethiopia's development, particularly in education and foreign relations, was immense. Ethiopia was a charter member of the UN and the founder of the African Union under his administration.

In 1973, famine claimed the lives of tens of thousands in the province of Wollo, and the emperor was blamed for not tackling the catastrophe as required of him. Taking advantage of this development his opponents instigated mass movement that led to the conspiracy by the army to stage a coup against him. In 1974, a group of young officers deposed him, and installed themselves as a Provisional Military Administrative Council, AKA Dergue. Shortly after the assumption of state power, the Dergue executed sixty of the emperor's officials without due process of law. The emperor's grandson, Eskinder Desta and Prime Minster Akililu Habtewolde were among the executed officials. On August 27, 1975 the Dergue smothered the emperor to death while he was under custody. The emperor was 83 years old.

Note:
The naming tradition used in Ethiopia does not have family names. A person's name consists of an individual personal name and a separate father's name. In this tradition, children are given a name at birth, by which they will be known.

Dergue: The military junta (108 junior officers) that deposed Emperor Haile Selassie and ruled Ethiopia from 1974 to 1987 is widely known as Dergue. A Geez word meaning "committee" or "council."

Zemecha: A national service program (18 months long) that drafts high school students who are supposed to raise the awareness of the rural population.

Zemach: A student (Age. 18 – 25) drafted in the Zemecha program.

Red Terror: A violent political repression campaign of the military Dergue against its opponents. The red terror was based on the Red Terror of the Russian Civil War and most visibly took place after Mengistu Hailemariam became chairman of the Dergue on 3 February 1977.

Chapter 1

The day had come.

A sleepless night had befallen him; he had fallen asleep only briefly. During that brief time, he had dreamed. As he slid out of his bed now, the dream still floated vividly behind his eyes. A frightening dream, so lovely at the beginning but absurd at the end; the girl he loved just vanished in the air while he held her in his arms.

It had been almost a year since Daniel, 19, had that strange feeling of being drawn to the girl, but he had not told her about his feelings. He was waiting for the right time; a time so perfect that when he told her, she would not laugh but capitulate.

The right time seemed to have come now. Daniel and the girl were supposed to travel to the countryside on a national mission. Last September, while Ethiopia celebrated its new year, a hundred and eight young officers claiming to represent the armed forces had staged a coup and ousted the emperor. The officers announced that they had established a Provisional Military Administrative Council to rule the country, and pledged to reform land ownership in the rural regions, apply good governance in the cities, and maintain law and order all over the country. The Council, widely known as Dergue, declared Socialism as its guiding ideology.

To implement its new ideology, the Dergue summoned the youth to join a development campaign known as *Zemecha*, a kind of a national service program that would send tens of thousands of high-school and university students out into the rural regions. Many of the students had no idea what Socialism was all about, but they were expected to explain its benefits to the people in the rural regions.

Daniel was one of the Zemachs, and among the first batch leaving today. Unlike the dream, his hope of getting a decent job and marrying his love had never been closer to coming true. The girl was also travelling today to the same region where he was assigned.

Mindful not to wake his brother, Kibrom, who was sleeping on the other side of the bed, Daniel heaved himself to his feet and walked to the window. Carefully, he opened it and let the morning air into the house.

"Daniel," a voice called from behind him.

"Yes."

"Is it today?" Kibrom asked, half-awake, his face buried in the pillow.

"Yes, it's today," replied Daniel. "Now, will you get up? It's half-past six."

Kibrom ignored his request and went back to sleep instead. Daniel walked to the toilet with a towel wrapped on his waist. He bathed his face and the upper part of his body at the backyard's running water pipe. Then he walked casually back, drying his body, and enjoying the cool fresh air. It was then that his eyes caught a sheet of paper stuck between the woods that made the fence. He reached and pulled out the paper that appeared to have been placed there intentionally. On his way back to the house, he skimmed through the lines.

In the bedroom, Kibrom was still sleeping. Concerned not to disturb him, Daniel sat carefully on the edge of the bed and continued reading the paper. The leaflet criticized the Zemecha for its poor preparations and inadequate planning and called on the youth to boycott it.

A boycott was the last thing Daniel wanted to hear. It sounded like aborting a three-month pregnancy. Besides, his conviction in the virtue of the Zemecha was too deep for anyone to persuade him to quit. He had eagerly waited for this day since its announcement three months ago. Decisively, he tossed the leaflet aside, moved forward, and opened the closet. He took out his Zemecha uniform, his shirt and cape, and put them on.

His mother, Abinet, was about to burst into tears when she saw him in the Zemecha gear for the first time. Daniel noticed her attempting to compose herself and control her voice. Yet, her voice quivered as she said, "May God be with you wherever you go, my son," her eyes blinking to deter the tears.

"It's all right, Mother," said Daniel. "I'm not alone. There are sixty thousand students; boys and girls, some younger than me."

Kibrom came yawning and stretching. In his hand was the leaflet.

"Oh, yeah! Our little soldier," Kibrom laughed, staring at Daniel. "So, you have decided."

"Well, there is nothing to wait for?"

"Did you read this paper?" asked Kibrom.

"I don't understand the politics."

Daniel was more into music and sports than following the current affairs of the country. He had been a soccer player for his school until he got injured last year, and was forced to quit. He exercised in the Young Men's Christian Association (YMCA) and often trained in the 5000 metres race.

"How could you trust this government? It's deceiving the students with promises it won't keep."

"I am a student with no knowledge to decipher the mysteries of politics and government."

"There is no mystery here. Soldiers should not be in the government in the first place. You know that, don't you?"

Daniel gave it a thought. "I know, Kibrom. But the Zemecha is an obligation we need to carry out. This has more to do with educating the people in rural areas rather than supporting the government. You know that in some places in this country babies are killed for teething on the wrong jaw. Girls are stoned for not found virgins during their wedding day. I think we can make a difference in those places.

As they exchanged these words, their mother, Abinet, was sitting bent over on a stool, fanning the iron brazier on which a teapot was boiling, listening quietly. She did not clearly understand what the Zemecha was all about, but she had not failed to grasp the subject's general idea. She knew that it was peaceful, and no harm would befall the Zemachs. What Daniel mentioned about women's treatment in the countryside was a matter of personal experience for her.

Abinet's husband had first picked Abinet's older sister for a wife. As his first choice was not found intact on the night of the wedding, the bride had to suffer the cruel punishment delivered for such misbehaviour: to be raped by the groom and his best man, flogged, and then hauled back to the family. She still remembered how the groom, now her ex-husband, and his best man came to reclaim their loss.

Abinet's father, a respected priest, had to hush up the shame that had befallen the family by offering them another wife— a little girl. At the age of 14, Abinet was made liable to save the family from disgrace. Her elder sister, the 16-year-old bride, had to flee from home.

However, there was something ugly Abinet sensed in that Zemecha and did not yet understand. Just months before, the Dergue had executed sixty-three officials of the former regime and a few of its own, including the head of state, General Aman Andom. The shock of that fateful day of November 23, when the Dergue announced the execution as a political decision, still rang in her ears.

"How is the region?" she asked, "and the people?"

"It's such a rich place and a fertile one. As for the people, you know country-people; they are all the same, harmless and friendly but suspicious," Daniel said as he strode to his bedroom.

He had packed everything he needed for the Zemecha almost a week before. Now, Daniel just needed to do some last-minute packing. He went to the closet and pulled open a drawer from which he fished out the family album. He selected some pictures of his family members and placed them in his wallet.

Sensing someone approaching him, Daniel turned and saw his mother in her Sunday dress. She appeared to have lost considerable weight. The moments of misfortune she endured at various times had left their marks on her face. There were dark rings of worry and fatigue around her eyes. Unable to utter a word that could express his feeling, he bent over and kissed her on the cheek. He, then, turned to the pictures, and put them in his wallet. Reluctantly, he also stuffed in his father's photo.

From outside, the sound of a car engine cracked. Daniel took his baggage. Abinet wrapped herself up in her Netela, a thin cotton Ethiopian traditional cloth. Even Kibrom put the leaflet aside and stood. They all went out of the house, loaded the baggage on the car, and headed north to pick Ghenet.

Ghenet's residence was not easily accessible by car. One had to drive a long way around and then walk along the footpath and into the slums. Daniel got out of the car and walked the narrow alley leading to Ghenet's residence. He jumped over a decayed wire fence for a shortcut to enter the middle of the slum where shyly barking dogs received him. The filthy alleyway was full of washing and garbage. Greeting familiar faces, he met along his way; he reached the old little shack where Ghenet lived with her mother and her siblings in a two-room dwelling.

The door was left ajar.

"Good morning," Daniel called in a loud voice, attempting to be heard over the laughter.

"How are you, Daniel? Come in please," the soft voice of a girl reached his ears. No doubt, it was Ghenet's voice. As she emerged through the door, Daniel felt his heart jump. His mouth dried up, and he muttered something inaudible.

Though he knew her since childhood, his approach was more reserved, and tense recently. As a result, he was nervous and never seemed to know what to say.

"Are you ready?" he forced himself to speak.

"Yes, mother is dressing up. Come in," Ghenet said smiling, then stepped aside to let him in. As she smiled, a dimple appeared on her cheek, adding to her beauty.

In Daniel's nervously watching eyes, Ghenet appeared to be more beautiful today than ever before. His memories must have changed his perception, and his fantasies adding to her beauty because Ghenet had not changed much. She was the same dark brown girl with slightly flat nose set between round cheeks, except that her kinky hair was longer in the front and cropped from behind.

When Daniel entered, the two little children, Ghenet's brother and sister stopped wrestling and looked at him. From their faces, Daniel could realize that the cruel hands of poverty had seized the throat of this household. The children were skinny and underfed. He approached the boy and the little girl, and kissed their bony cheeks.

"Did you come with your father? I won't go with you if he is around," the mother said flatly. She hated Daniel's father, Goytom Gobezay, for what he had done to Abinet, Daniel's mother.

"No, not him, but Mother is with us," Daniel replied.

Never had such a vast number of people gathered in the city of Addis Ababa at one time and place for the same purpose. Over a hundred thousand people had come out to see the Zemachs off. Janmeda, the largest public arena in the country, was crowded to capacity. Those who could afford it had come by their private cars; others by taxis, busses, and trucks. People from the surrounding countryside had walked to the city to celebrate the occasion. The young, the elderly, the rich, the poor of every tribe, and every religion had come. It was an event so unique that it moved everyone and touched every heart.

Even nature seemed to be pleased by the occasion. It was a bright, cheerful day. The thin, whitish cloud that hovered over the eastern horizon was diffusing toward the centre; the sun beyond seemed to be steadily following to take note of the special event.

"That son of yours, over there," Elsa pointed at the Zemachs who paraded through the stadium saluting the public, "Is he leaving today?"

"Who? Which son are you talking about?" Goytom Gobezay glanced at the beautiful young woman he married after Daniel's mother.

"Daniel is among the first Zemachs who leave today. Ah! You don't know. You came just to see your busses."

Goytom knew that students were conscripted for the Zemecha, but he had no idea that any of his sons would travel today. He was startled when he heard the news from Elsa. He turned to the parading Zemachs and searched for his son, but he couldn't spot him. Daniel was swallowed by the Zemach crowd who were now receiving the tributes of the cheering mass.

Flowers and green leaves poured down as the young Zemachs in full uniform paraded through the crowd. Flanked by the guard of honour in camouflage suits and the army band, the Zemachs were met by tremendous applause of a delighted citizenry.

As the procession came alongside the tribune, where the Head of State stood, the musicians changed the tune to one of the new songs that had caught the nation's pulse. Instantly the applause erupted again with new force, and every living thing in the area sang the song—Tenessa Terramed - a song that held tragedy from the past and hope for the future.

A moment later, when the applause subsided, a peculiar thing began taking place. Some five or six metres away from where Goytom Gobezay stood, a few youngsters began applauding and shouting a name, "Mengistu! Mengistu!" They agitated the people around to join them. As similar cheers came from different directions, the ovation spread, and, in a moment, the entire Zemach students picked it up. The people, too, applauded in rhythm. It was like a beat of a giant drum, and every blow was accompanied by the loud chant of just one word, "Mengistu! Mengistu!" It was for Major Mengistu, a prominent member of the Dergue, that they were calling.

In the early days of the revolution, though the Dergue worked outside of the public eye, deliberately wrapping itself in secrecy, Major Mengistu was said to have played a significant role in guiding the revolution as the students wanted it. He was rumoured to have been one of the Dergue members who pushed for more radical changes. He was considered the champion of change, and the youth worshipped him.

Goytom Gobezay looked toward the platform and spotted Mengistu flanked by high-ranking government officials. General Teferi, the Head of the state, stood right next to him. When people talked about a certain Mengistu in the new government, it had never occurred to Goytom that this was the Mengistu they meant. He had known this Mengistu a long, long time ago. He had never imagined that the Mengistu he knew could rise to such a height of prominence.

Puzzled and shocked, he continued to look intently at him, scrutinizing his object of concern. The man was Mengistu himself, the same person he knew; flat nose, tiny black eyes, and large lips. His small frame seemed to have grown a little bigger. Mengistu was waving his hand at the parading Zemachs, beaming down at their joyful, happy faces turned on him. He laughed and was tempted to jump up and follow them. Goytom watched him thoughtfully and uttered some expletives before shifting his eyes to the crowd.

"Zemachs! Zemachs!" the loud speakers roared.

Suddenly it was silence.

"Attention! Zemachs are requested to queue up at their respective busses," the speakers exploded again.

Two of the buses decorated with the Ethiopian flags, garlanded, flowers, and green leaves, belonged to Goytom. As the Nyala Transportation Company's sole owner, Goytom had made a good deal with the Zemecha Headquarters by assigning busses to transport his share of the sixty thousand Zemachs to various regions. He expected to earn quite a lot of money on this deal. He had a similar deal in mind for the return trip some eighteen months later.

He watched the busses move slowly in single file, cleaving the crowds into two. As the busses rolled, he saw mothers weeping, fathers fighting back tears. But soon, they gathered strength, dried their eyes, cleared their throats, and turned their sobs into applause.

Songs and chants, religious melodies glorified the entire scene. To the people, the Zemecha was the one hope left to alleviate their miseries. They seemed to believe that this Zemecha would not remain just as a hollow promise of some politicians but a practical effort that would bring betterment in their lives. This was simply because it was their children in charge this time; they knew they wouldn't fail them.

Many followed the busses, running behind them as far as their breath could last. In less than a quarter of an hour, the busses were out of sight, out of the city. Then suddenly, it seemed, as though the warmth of the city just went out.

Chapter 2

While people celebrated the Zemecha in Addis Ababa, a thousand kilometres north, somewhere in Eritrea, an unfortunate village was burning under a hail of bombs. A few hundred Eritrean farmers lived in the area that was considered as a strategic location for the Ethiopian army to control the western farmland of Eritrea. Thus, the army had built a fuel depot and distribution centre of military hardware in the middle of the village and deployed a special regiment to see its safety.

For many years, the region had been the scene of a civil war of devastating proportions. At issue were questions of self-determination and human rights that had grown increasingly complex as the war progressed. Like many Ethiopians, the Eritreans had hoped the revolution would introduce a new era of peace and reconciliation. But that was not to be; the Dergue approached the Eritrean problem no differently from its predecessor. As military men, Dergue members were ruled by stubborn pride that would not allow them to negotiate with the liberation fronts while the fronts had the upper hand over their troops in the field.

In the first week of May, before the rains came, consolidated Eritrean guerrilla forces suddenly moved to surround the village. They had acquired intelligence reports indicating that there was modern weaponry in the camp. Much out of negligence than contempt, the army had not made any effort to survey the surrounding. As a result, they were not aware of the rebels hovering over them, like vultures waiting for a dying man.

Over the weeks, the rebels intensified their siege, disconnecting the army from any possible supplies and communications except the radio. It appeared the army had no option left other than surrendering if help did not arrive in time. Realizing that its successive call to the head-quarters had come to no avail, the army decided to break out of the suffocating predicament all by itself. As a result, full-scale fighting broke out.

Since the government troops had been cut off supplies for several weeks, they soon ran short of food and water. On the contrary, the rebels were yearning to get hold of the weaponry that would play a decisive role in the struggle to come. So, they fought determinedly to win the battle. At last, the army was to suffer the humiliation of defeat. Before it surrendered, though, it had managed to transmit the final message to the headquarters to whom it revealed the imminent collapse.

Afterwards, while the rebels had been busy collecting the weapons and tallied captives, the sky suddenly turned into a stage of fire theatre. Fast-moving machines invaded the airspace and tore through the air from every direction. They dove, banked, and sored with tremendous speed. Then they began the real job: dropping bombs and explosives, killing indiscriminately anyone who stood on two or four feet, including government troops. The reasoning behind this horror was to destroy the weapons before the guerrillas could lay their hands on them.

The camp erupted in flame and explosives flared up, wrecking the entire cache of weapons. In less than a quarter of an hour, they reduced the poor village into ashes. No one appeared to be spared from the inferno.

On-board the Ethiopian jetliner that flew over the village of Awgaro on that day was Daniel's cousin, Ermias Tesfay, travelling to Addis Ababa. Sitting by the window, he was purposefully surveying the outside with a binocular. Below was the Great Rift Valley, as magnificent as it had always been since the day of creation, stretched from Syria, through the

Middle East, and the Red Sea, to Ethiopia. As he thoughtfully observed the grand basin, a sense of belonging crept upon him that soon transformed into a distressing feeling of misfortune. Suddenly, a question crossed his mind. Could the cause of the bloody conflict of this region be the natural wealth that lay beneath this valley? "What sort of wealth is there?" Looking to the east, towards the Middle East's petroleum empires, he wondered if the answer to his questions might be "Oil!"

As the plane entered the heart of the Eritrea air space, Ermias' glance drifted at the passengers. Very few Europeans, a couple of Orientals, a dozen or so Arabs, the rest were, of course, Ethiopians. Tourism had collapsed since the change of regime. Many of the Ethiopians were diplomats on their way home to be briefed about the Revolution. Some were radical scholars summoned by the ruling Dergue to replace the officials of the former regime.

Ermias exchanged friendly glances and smiles with a couple of passengers and then resumed looking out through the window. It was about 2 p.m. the sky was as translucent as the water of the ocean. One could see from one end of the horizon to the other clearly. Ermias watched as the stony mountainous desert of the Sahel came into view.

Then came the barren Barka pasture, frighteningly naked, no grass, and no vegetation. A stranger observing Eritrea from the sky would hardly believe that there was an eighteen-year-old war of liberation going on. One would tend to discard the very notion that there could be any living soul who would wage war to liberate and preserve that barren land. There was nothing to fight for, one would say.

"Hi! How is the journey?"

Ermias turned to see the speaker. A tall, dark-skinned man who looked like a prize-fighter was staggering down the aisle between the seats, greeting everybody with a smile as he passed by.

"It's fine," Ermias was brief.

The tall man walked past Ermias to the rear end of the aircraft, presumably to the toilet. A few minutes later, the man returned. As he lowered himself to occupy his aisle seat, the aircraft's front tilted upward to gain altitude. As the man staggered off balance and fell on the floor, Ermias saw a pistol on the man belt.

"Anti-hijacker," Ermias assumed.

Realizing that the aircraft was gaining altitude, Ermias shifted his gaze to the outside. He reached for the binoculars and peered at the country below. He didn't like what he saw on the ground. A small village was burning, thick black smoke spreading over it. His heart suddenly pounded hard. Withdrawing his handkerchief from his pocket, he first wiped his eyes and then the binoculars. Overwhelmed by sudden emotion, he looked down again; it was the village of Awgaro. He had information that it was under siege but had not known that fighting had broken out.

He saw the killing machines darting through the sky like rockets, two F-5 bombers spitting death over the village below them. The Ethiopian Air Force in the line of duty! Ermias' heart erupted with concern as he envisioned the poor villagers, the children caught in fire, women ripped apart, old people reduced to ashes.

As an undercover operator for Eritrean Liberation Front, he had been able to bear witness to numerous atrocities committed by the Ethiopian forces at various times. He had seen villages blown to ashes; innocent people mowed down in marketplaces and other public places. He had seen enough of the Ethiopian rule in which young men were arbitrarily arrested and summarily executed as suspected supporters of the liberation movement. Those images flooded his thoughts, raising his rage and repressing his reason.

A strange and powerful feeling surged through him and urged him to make a move, like to grab the pistol from the anti-hijacker and force the pilot to fly at the bomber's altitude. He pondered if those bombers would stop their deadly operations to avoid a collision with a civilian aircraft. His mind was filled with a frenzy of thoughts.

Ermias was a spymaster, diligent and unafraid, but he was not trained for such an encounter. Nor was he a skilled fighter type to overpower the anti-hijacker. He was tall and gangly, with stooping shoulders, a not muscular but firm body. However, he did not doubt that he could snatch the gun if he could move to the security man undetected.

As his heart pounded faster with anxiety, the plane reached the heart of the village. Just before he made up his mind to storm over the security man, Ermias gazed out again. He couldn't see the village; it was right under him. Instead, he saw a thick smoke of a rapidly descending fireball filling the space below the aircraft. Once again, he could not trust his eyes. It appeared like one of the machines of destruction had been blown up. He almost stood to applaud, forgetting that he was in the enemy's territory. Thrilled with what he had just witnessed, he observed the other bomber rushing further to the west for safety.

The bombing had ceased.

Ermias' eyes darted toward the anti-hijacker whose seat was now vacant. He looked right and left but could not spot the man. Though thrilled by his compatriots' success blowing a fighter jet, he was still high on adrenaline. But soon, his emotions subsided, and he began thinking of the consequences had it gone his way.

"Terrible," he thought.

He waved to a hostess and ordered coffee. Ethiopian coffee tasted good; it was probably the best in the world. Ermias liked it. Sipping the coffee, he tried to relax. The plane was now deep into Ethiopia, the country that held many memories for Ermias. He suddenly felt isolated and withdrew into himself, no longer conscious of the other passengers or the lush green country below. Both sad and happy memories unfolded in his mind

Ermias was born into a middle-class family in the city of Asmara where he went to the Italian school that had been established in 1903. His childhood life was noticeably well compared to the other children in the neighbourhood. Despite his mother's death at an early, he was not deprived of a parent's love. His warden, a close relative to his father had been able to cover the gap and make him feel comfortable, but the death of Ermias' father was so sudden that Ermias still had difficulty accepting it after so many years. It had been such a tragic incident that he had felt almost demented when he heard about it.

During the period of the Ethio-Eritrean federation, Ermias' father, Tesfay Kahsay, had been a member of the Eritrean political party. He advocated the idea of maintaining the federal arrangement as some encouraged complete unification, and others promoted total independence. At times, these internal conflicts had led to violent undertakings.

Taking advantage of that situation, the Ethiopian government had begun supporting the Unionist party that favoured unification, as it repressed the federalists and the separatists. Thus, the idea of complete unification begun to pick momentum. With the Eritrean Orthodox community's support, the unionists pushed to pass legislation that facilitated the erosion of Eritrean autonomy. In 1958, they voted to discard the blue-coloured Eritrean flag, replacing it with the tricolour Ethiopian flag. A year later, they replaced the Eritrean Penal Laws with the Ethiopian Penal Code. Then in 1960, it resolved to call the designation "Eritrean Government" as "Eritrean Administration" and the "Chief Executive" as "Chief Administrator."

Now that all preparations had been made, the Ethiopian regime could take the last step to the final goal. On November 15, 1962, Emperor Hailesilassie issued Order No. 27, declaring the termination of Eritrea's federal statutes. Eritrea "hereby wholly integrated into the unitary system of the Ethiopian Empire."

That angered some Eritreans and exhausted their patience. Ermias' father was among the first to make up his mind against the Ethiopian government's actions. Even before the formal dissolution of the federation, anti-Ethiopian sentiment had grown in Eritrea. Demonstrations, strikes, and other overt forms of protest had given way to clandestine political movements. By 1961, these movements had already created the setting for the emergence of an armed struggle. Equipped with obsolete Italian rifles, the Eritrean Liberation Army's earliest unit fired the first shot in September 1961, marking the beginning of a long, tragic war.

Ermias' father had been one of the leaders who organized themselves to liberate Eritrea from Ethiopian rule and make it a sovereign state. As there was an aggressive drive to prepare the people for liberation, he had been sent to Addis with the mission to organize Eritreans living in the heartland of Ethiopia. He had worked day and night and succeeded in organizing several people. Eritreans who lived in Ethiopia began to make material, moral, and financial contributions to the cause. Tesfay had been able to assemble hundreds of people in less than six months and collect a significant amount of money.

The Ethiopian government soon realized the danger posed by the liberation movement and devised ways of curbing those disruptive activities. The authorities arrested Eritrean activists, and covert assassinations became a common occurrence. As suspected Eritreans were persecuted both in Asmara and Addis Ababa, many disappeared, some went into exile, and few were found dead. Tesfay spared himself from the atrocities of the state by disguising and hiding until he accomplished his mission. He had almost made it back to Eritrea had he not stayed in Addis one day longer than he should have. He had been found dead in the middle of the city the day he was supposed to leave Addis, with no trace of the money collected to support the Eritrean movement.

The news of the death of his father had been a shocking blow to Ermias. It was so stunning that he could not cry or weep as though the grief had been like a fire that dried up every drop of fluid in him. Since his mother died few weeks after his birth, his love for his father had been twice more than any child could have for a father. With both his parents deceased, he had come to Addis to stay with his aunt, Abinet Kahsay and her husband, Goytom Gobezay. Back in Eritrea, there had been no one to look after of him.

After his father's death, Ermias had transformed from the cheerful child he had been once into a sad, mistrustful, and lonesome boy. He walled himself off from the world, retreating silently into some remote and lonely shadows of his mind. He had begun to look at the humanity around him with a suspicious eye, afraid of the forces of evil that had deprived him of a father. Some malignant fate had snuffed out the warmth and the light in his life. For Ermias, the world had changed forever; it had become full of menace and danger.

It had been under such circumstances that he went to school. Not surprisingly, Ermias' school performance had been inadequate. Neither was his behaviour pleasant. He did not play with his peers as children of his age should do. He spent most of his time thinking about his father's death and the cruelty of the world.

Shortly after Ermias' father died, Goytom Gobezay had bought the three-room house in Kera where Abinet resided now, and the family moved to the new house. Ermias and Goytom's children, who then had reached school age, joined the Shimelis-Habte-School, the nearest around.

However, Ermias' condition had not improved. Worst of all, he began to skip classes, and he failed his exams. As the years went by, Goytom Gobezay prospered more and more. At the same pace, Ermias grew and developed a striking resemblance to his father, which seemed to trouble Goytom. If Goytom had been having fun playing with his children, he would stop as soon as Ermias joined them. When Ermias would talk directly to him, Goytom would just pretend as if he had not heard. When Ermias would repeat what he said, he would yell at him. Most of the time, Goytom shouted at him for no reason. Using Ermias' failures as a pretext, Goytom had made it a habit to abuse the boy, often insulted him and beat him. When things got tense, Goytom's rage often spread to the rest of the family. His mistreatment would befall almost everyone except Daniel and Biniam, who were not at school age at the time. Abinet had been the one who had to suffer the most as she tended to protect her nephew from her husband's wrath. The agony his aunt had to experience because of him had been a distressing pain Ermias had to cope with.

At the age of seventeen, Ermias showed some changes. He began examining the documents he inherited from his father: letters, articles, memorandums. He also began to touch on Eritrean history in his quest for knowledge of the past. Deeply impressed, he studied history from the ancient Axumite era up to the Italian colonization of ERITREA. He learned why the British ruled for ten years in Eritrea and the subsequent Ethio-Eritrea federal arrangement. He also examined the process that led to the Ethio-Eritrean unity, which helped him develop a pointed interest in the liberation struggle. He began to look at his father's death in light of the independence struggle in Eritrea. From the history of Eritrea, he realized that his father's death had not been in vain.

After his father's death, the liberation struggle had grown by leaps, and that proved to Ermias the righteousness of the cause. It was at that time in his life that he started to see the light again. The grief and pain he suffered in his boyhood began to give way to hope and a vision of the future. As he entertained the thought of joining the liberation struggle under the banner for which his father sacrificed his life, he had been able to soften the pain of loss and respond to the pleasure of life.

Subsequently, his appetite for education grew tremendously. He began to register impressive results in his studies. He made friends in and outside of school. He met a girl named Saba

Berhe and fell in love with her. Apart from the recurring quarrels with Goytom Gobezay at home, every other aspect of his life had taken a new turn.

As Goytom had used Ermias' learning problems as a pretext to beat him, his improvements had also begun to make Goytom uneasy and wary. Upset with his business, Goytom came home one day, and wanted to unload his frustration on Ermias. To his surprise, Goytom was stopped by the adult boy who planted himself squarely in front of him and, looking into his eyes, told him: "I'm grateful that you raised me like one of your children, but at times you have been beating me unfairly. I can't take it anymore. I'll leave this house soon. Until the day I leave, please be patient!"

From that day onwards, Goytom did not dare touch him; and Ermias didn't stay long. A new era had come when Ermias and Goytom could not live under the same roof as Eritrea and Ethiopia could no longer remain under the same crown. In the summer of 1970, at the age of 20, Ermias left to join the independence struggle.

As the plane came closer to landing, Ermias remembered his first love, Saba Berhe. Departing from Saba, whom he had shared with wonderful and innocent times, had been a painful ordeal he had to sustain. After six years, Saba still had her place in his heart. The memory of the joy he shared with her for a relatively short period was still vivid after those long years of separation.

"Where would she be now?" he thought.

At precisely 3 o'clock, the plane touched the ground at Bole Airport. A moment later, he was out of the airport, speaking with the man assigned to meet him.

"Any problem?" asked the host, a tall and diligent-looking young man of 25 named Jovani, born to an Italian father and Eritrean mother. He owned an Italian restaurant which he inherited from his father, a 5-room villa and a fiat 124 spider. Jovani was one of the few Eritreans who led quite a lavish lifestyle.

"Nothing," Ermias said, voice dripping with melancholy that caused his shoulders to droop low.

The two had met a few times before in Sudan, but their acquaintance remained remote due to their encounters' brevity. Except for the greeting they exchanged, they did not say much to each other until they were well in the middle of the city. Jovani was just as eager to hear news from the battlefront as Ermias wanted to find out about the changes in Ethiopia. He looked right and left to see if the marks of the Revolution could be detected on the dwarf buildings, the narrow boulevards, and the hidden villas. When he found nothing from the dull street, he turned to Jovani.

"It looks very calm, doesn't it?"

"But underneath, it's boiling," said Jovani.

"What we hear outside the country is exciting."

"This revolution is not ours. There is nothing for us in it," replied Jovani and began telling his story. He related the recent horror in which twenty-four Eritrean businessmen and workers had been secretly taken to Awash and summarily executed for allegedly being members of the Eritrean Liberation Front.

"We cannot live with these people," he said bitterly at last. "We have to continue the struggle. How is it? We heard that our fighters are gaining…" he left his speech suspended in mid-air, trying to incite Ermias into talking. When he did not hear a word from him, he went straight to the heart of the matter. "We heard that our fighters would soon capture Asmara. Isn't it true?"

"Our struggle is long," said Ermias, his eyes fixed on the outside, not looking at anything but on something much more remote than the life on the street, something abstract and intangible: victory.

Ermias had never had illusions about victory. As times passed, victory seemed to run farther and farther away, getting increasingly unattainable, partly because the Eritrean cause had virtually no support from the international community, mainly because the liberation fronts were uncompromisingly divided among rival factions. He had, unlike Jovani, no illusions of victory. "Our struggle won't be short," he said again and lapsed into vagueness

Jovani parked the car along the street side in front of Bar Tiku at Tekle Square, a crowded area full of beggars, prostitutes, unemployed youngsters and brokers.

"This car will be at your disposal as long as you're here," Jovani said and bent to pull something from a pocket under his seat, "And I have got a small gift for you." It was a 0.22 pistol in a shoulder harness of brown leather. He reminded Ermias to avoid wearing it but keep it in the car safe by day and sleep with it under his pillow by night.

Ermias searched the young man's face for any sign of mockery, but he found none. Jovani's final words were sober and appealing, "This is an assassin town where people get killed for teasing at a little cadre of the revolution."

As he climbed out of the car, Ermias observed the coolies walk past with baskets balanced on their skinny shoulders, poor countrymen with their donkeys crossing the street, fully packed shabby busses rolling. The area was filthy. It had a horrible smell, the air dense. Then his eyes fell on the grey Toyota and his thoughts on the little pistol, by which he would end himself if the situations compel him to do so.

Chapter 3

Inango was a small dusty village with a single gravel road passing through it. On the eastern side of the road were half a dozen dwarf brick buildings that housed the post office, the telephone office, and other government offices. On the opposite side of the road, several mud houses lined up like ragtag soldiers at attention. Then came a tea-room, a shop, and a barbershop.

Behind the houses, the village's poor inhabitants survived inside crumbling huts. The adults wore no shoes, and the children went half-naked. In that village, the Zemachs, with their uniforms, caps and leather shoes, were regarded as exceptionally privileged creatures.

Daniel sat in the barber's noisy wooden chair staring through the glass window while the barber worked on his hair. It was Friday; he had finished work an hour earlier than on regular days. The Zemecha compound lay a few blocks to the left of the post office.

"It looks peaceful," the barber said, staring at the compound across the road. A few Zemachs were playing volleyball on the field. The building, with its hangar-like houses, had primarily been planned to serve as a primary school. It consisted of several rooms, a large dining hall, three dormitories for some thirty Zemachs, and two other office rooms.

"Not as it used to be," Daniel said, referring to the first few weeks since Zemachs came to Inango. The villagers had welcomed them with open arms, eager to learn from the esteemed Zemachs. Now a weary cautiousness lined the faces of the same villagers. Peace hung in the air only because the opposing sides hid their distrust behind plastic smiles and sweet words masking the poison in their hearts.

"In just a few weeks, I have watched them accomplish much," said the barber as he finished cutting Daniel's hair. "I don't understand why some are complaining now."

Daniel heaved himself out of the chair. "Real changes take years, and some won't wait that long," said Daniel as he paid the barber.

Brushing off bits of hair, he stepped up to the long, cracked mirror on the wall, which held the reflection of his entire 172 cm lean frame. He searched his face, which appeared to have grown thinner since he came to Inango. Yet his black, curious eyes remained mature and purposeful. The brown complexion, which had had a boyish smoothness before, now looked bony and rugged. From the change in his face, one could see the hardship the Zemachs were experiencing.

The Zemachs had found living among the farmlands cumbersome and were ill-prepared for the work that accompanied such a lifestyle. The first few weeks were manageable since they were busy establishing farmer's associations and redistribution of the land. In Inango and its surrounding regions, thirty-five associations had been created, and land had been redistributed according to the new legislation. As that had been completed with insignificant resistance from the former landowners, preparing the land for the next harvest proceeded expeditiously. That had, however, been the most challenging part of their work.

As the rainy season approached, the Zemachs had to participate in the actual digging and tilling part of the fieldwork to contain every drop of rain. Many were injured as they return home in the evenings with bleeding hands or swollen feet from toiling in the land beside the farmworkers.

Everyone worked according to their abilities toward the completion of the job. The farmworkers were as happy as they had ever thought it possible to be. Of course, there were a few lazy Zemachs who rose from bed late each morning and left work early; however, most were diligent and learned quickly.

Despite the hardship, Daniel, too, worked from dawn to dusk and was always where the work was hardest.

Performance and perseverance could add eligibility for a government job or admittance to higher education in the future, but Daniel never thought of that; he was only driven by a sheer sense of obligation and the joy of seeing improvements. As a result, he learned to till the land, and he loved the smell of the earth.

The discussion sessions were held on Tuesdays and Fridays, which proved to be both motivating and educational. During these sessions, they discussed society, politics, the environment, human rights, and the changing role of women. Daniel never missed a single session and was unafraid to ask questions or to speak his mind.

He was thinking about this new life as he reached for his cap and put it on his head. When he turned, he saw his face in the mirror and flashed himself a smile, and stepped out of the barbershop. Outside, the sun had already made most of its way across the sky. It would drop behind the mountains in less than an hour, and darkness would fall over the un-electrified village. Their discussion session would proceed after dinner under the glowing light of a few lanterns. Today's discussion, Daniel had learned, would be on People's Right to Self-determination.

Just before he was about to cross to the post office, a truck passed westward on the road, followed by a horse-drawn cart, raising a cloud of dust behind it. Daniel received two letters at the post office. One from his younger brother, Biniam, and the other strangely was from Ghenet. He found that unusual because she had never written before; there had been no need to. She was not that far away. Besides, not a week had passed since he had met her in Gimbie, a small town where Ghenet was posted for her Zemecha duty.

He opened Ghenet's letter first. It was dated Tuesday, June 17, three days before. She wrote that she had planned to visit him on Saturday, the following day. When he folded the letter and stuffed it in his shirt's pocket, he felt his heart beating faster with a pleasant wave streaming through his body. He almost forgot his brother's letter.

As usual, Biniam's letter began with greetings, then continued, *'Mother is worried because of Kibrom's strange behaviour. He comes home very late. No one knows where he spends his days. He doesn't talk to me, nor does he listen to Mother. Mother is worried about him. When you write to him, try to make him understand what Mother is going through and why. I think he will listen to you. I suspect he has joined a certain political organization. I have observed unpleasant things around him, such as firearms. I'm still working in Nyala Transports. Father has decided to sell it. I don't know why? We are all fine except that we miss you...'*

With mixed feelings of concern and delight, Daniel walked to the Zemecha centre. He was worried about his brother who could end up in jail like many of the students involved in political activity. As he entered the Zemecha compound, Ghenet came in his thought and filled him with happiness He went on whistling the new national anthem, which had been introduced along with the change of government. Like many of his generation, Daniel enjoyed the tune and cherished the lyrics because it revived a unique feeling of love for one's country.

He entered the room, a kind of ward with a dozen beds in it and a long table and benches down the middle. The chamber still held the oppressive heat of the day. As his eyes adjusted to the darkness, he saw his roommates, Kirubel, changing clothes, and Kebedde, lying on his bed at the corner of the room. Kebedde was a student at Haile Selassie University in Addis Ababa who, since he came to Inango, had been agitating the Zemachs to quit the Zemecha. He was in mid 20s, but looked much older.

"Oh! Here comes another loyalist who refused to quit, ah," said Kebedde pointing at Daniel,

"If I ever start, I never quit," said Daniel solidly,

"You are misled."

"I am not. I believe in the cause. For almost a decade, the slogan was Land-to-the-Tiller, was it not? Now we have it, and when we need to implement it, you run away. How can you run away from what you know is right and just for the people? I don't understand you."

"Read these leaflets. It's all there if you can understand it."

"I have read it. I don't share its opinion. I'd rather say that this Zemecha would broaden our horizon."

"What's here in the countryside that would broaden you? It's in the city where our party is flourishing: in the factories and schools."

"What party?"

"You don't know? You are living in a different time, Daniel. You must wake up."

"I know what I need to know."

"Look, you have got to read this. It's all there," said Kebedde, pointing at a leaflet.

"I told you that I have read it and did not like the idea of quitting the Zemecha at this stage," said Daniel, with a clear indication to avoid the subject.

"That's because you don't know what is going on."

"What's going on? If I may ask?" Daniel shot back.

"A People's movement to overthrow the fascist government: the Derg," Kebedde replied.

"I may not know about fascism or Dergue or whatever, but I do know there are many less fortunate people around. I'm here to do something to improve their lives," Daniel responded.

"You sound righteous when you say that, but soon we shall find out your connection with the government."

Daniel was startled by the remark and turned to Kirubel, "What is he talking about?"

Kirubel was a high school student, very close to Daniel. He was a humble person who simply liked the company of his friends more than their opinions. If his friends had not joined this Zemecha, Kirubel would not have been here.

"One or two spies have already been discovered among us, Daniel," Kirubel answered.

"Kebedde, are you implying that I could be spying on my friends?" Daniel asked, surprised.

"Who knows?" Kebedde said menacingly, rising from his bed, and left the room briskly

Kirubel, feeling that he had offended his friend, stepped closer to Daniel. "Look, Daniel…"

Daniel interrupted, "I know you meant no malice towards me, Kirubel, but it surprises me that you, of all the people, should say that to me."

"Well, I meant to bring the rumour into the open so that you can defend yourself."

"I don't have to defend anything," Daniel replied defiantly.

"But you should join the student community, their struggle, and their party."

"Party? And what does the party say about this Zemecha: quit?"

"It criticizes the Zemecha for its poor preparations and has called on the youth to boycott."

"That's what I don't understand. There is nothing wrong with this Zemecha. We are helping the poor. Just look at what we have achieved so far. Until now, work had been done considering the existing reality, and isn't that okay? Central planning has not been crucial," Daniel said.

Kirubel seemed to lose ground. He was not Kebedde's type, who understood the politics and the teachings of Marxism. Kirubel was an individual who had no opinions of his own, always found holding the person's beliefs to whom he had last spoken.

"I didn't know much about this," explained Kirubel, "but if you read the EPRP, I am sure you will change your mind. I read it, and it changed me. It's a party struggling for genuine democracy. It calls on the Dergue to lift all restrictions on democratic rights and step down and allow the formation of a people's government."

"You stop preaching me EPRP," said Daniel, "now, let's go for a walk."

"What's going on in this place? Many of these guys are not as friendly as they used to be towards me," Daniel said as they walked down the gravel road.

"You are so fascinated by the work of the Zemecha that you haven't noticed what's going on around you," Kirubel pointed, "The division between the political organizations is growing."

"What does that have to do with me?"

"Kebedde says it's because of your social class; you have not joined the students…the EPRP."

"What class?" Daniel seemed puzzled.

"Your father owns the Nyala Transportation Company. He is regarded as a wealthy man—a bourgeoisie," Kirubel said with a shrug of his shoulders.

"If he only knew how I was raised."

"What do you mean, Daniel?" asked Kirubel, showing concern in his furrowed brow.

"My father may be one of the few fortunate men in this country, but I did not benefit from his fortune. He left the family years ago, and we saw very little of him, and his money," Daniel's contempt for his father flew from his lips as he spoke.

"I'm sorry. I didn't know that," said Kirubel.

"Anyway, it's not because of social class that I did not join the group. It's because I don't know anything about it. Whatever I hear about EPRP isn't different from what I hear about its rival, the socialist party," Daniel replied.

"But the majority is with the EPRP."

"Yes, but what exactly does the majority know about the EPRP?"

"Well, I don't know. I guess the majority is always right," Kirubel admitted.

Daniel smiled, "Not always, Kirubel. I think a majority tells the total number of people wishing the same thing, not the number of smart people."

The following day the Zemachs were ordered to interrupt their half-day work and assemble in the compound. The night before, security people had visited the place and detained a teacher called Bezabih Mazengia, a Zemecha leader, the students held in high esteem. Late in the evening, a session chaired by Mr. Bezabih had been conducted right after dinner. The topic at that time was Eritrea and the Liberation movement, a sensitive issue but interesting.

In the middle of the hot debate, Bezabih had boldly given his opinion that the Eritrean people had the right to self-determination and that their struggle against the Dergue was just. Someone had leaked to the security forces about the topic of discussion and Bezabih's speech, and they came late in the night to arrest Mr. Bezabih. Some Zemachs blamed his arrest on pro-Dergue students and retaliated by beating them and chasing them out of the compound. The Zemachs had expected that the Station Chief would say or do something about it.

The Station Chief stood on the porch of the so-called office facing the volleyball field where the Zemachs assembled. From there he could sense the division that had torn the Zemachs apart. On the face of every Zemach reflected mixed attitudes, some resentful and vengeful, others terrified and anxious but all calm.

The Station Chief began speaking to the Zemachs, criticizing the fight that had broken out in the dining hall the night before.

"Those anti-people elements among you who are striving to divide you and sabotage the Zemecha…," the chief's speech was suddenly interrupted.

"Release Bezabih!" someone shouted.

"Who betrayed him?" another one cried.

Daniel and Kirubel stood together, leaning on the volleyball pole. Daniel asked, "Where did they take Bezabih? Why?"

"You heard him yesterday, supporting the Eritrean question."

"But he has the right to speak his mind."

"Oh yeah! You gave him that right or what?"

"Without Bezabih, this place will never be the same," said Daniel; his eyes darted to the Chief, who was trying to make himself heard over the crowd. As the Chief attempted to continue his speech, the Zemachs screamed at him, demanding to know why the police arrested Bezabih. Once again, he relented to a verbal assault by the crowd.

When the outcry died down, he said, "Okay! We will see what we can do about Mr. Bezabih. I hope it's some misunderstanding. But we have to continue our work with or without him."

That afternoon, there was no work. Daniel and Kirubel sat on the roadside, waiting for Ghenet.

"How long have you known her?" asked Kirubel.

"Since childhood - the same neighbourhood, the same school. Our brothers were good friends; our families are well acquainted. She is a kind of a sister to me."

"When did you begin to see her differently?" Kirubel asked with a smile.

"I guess it all started quite a while ago, but I gave it more serious thought since the Zemecha began."

"That's when we all began to mature. You need to tell her about your feelings," Kirubel suggested.

"I couldn't do that. I tried the last time I was with her, but I couldn't speak out the words," Daniel said.

"What about her? What do you think she feels toward you?"

"I think she has the same feelings that I have for her, but she expects me to take the first step."

"Then take it, Daniel. What are you waiting for?"

"The right time," Daniel shot back.

"Time is always the same; it just passes. It's you who could make the time right," said Kirubel watching a van pull up, "She has to be in that car."

He was right. Ghenet jumped out of the van she had hitchhiked a ride. She had put on a worn-out jeans jacket over her Zemecha uniform and tied a red ribbon on her head. She looked happy.

Daniel met her with open arms halfway across the road. They hugged briefly and turned to Kirubel to wave good-bye. They walked westward alongside the gravel road. It was a beautiful sunny day; the weather so pleasant that one would wish to stop the passing of time and live in the moment forever.

Ghenet waved at a van heading west.

Everyone seemed to like the Zemachs, ready to give them a hand whenever they needed one. The driver pulled over and let them climb in. The Zemachs took the rear seat. Impulsively, Daniel reached down to hold her right hand with his left one. Their fingers threaded first slowly, then harder before they squeezed together. They did not exchange words; neither did the driver disturb their peace.

On the right side of the road lay bushes with sparsely scattered trees that were once part of the dense forest and home of several wild animals. Now only monkeys flung themselves through the trees. On the pathway, women carrying dry wood on their backs walked.

The van jolted as it pulled into the next left turn. It was approaching the Farm. As they unlaced their fingers, Daniel straightened a little and stared at Ghenet. This was his first time to have a girl so close physically.

"Coming to the farm, Zemachs?" the driver spoke politely.

"No, you can drop us around here," said Daniel.

"My name is Eshetu. I work for the Farm as a driver."

"Nice to have met you; hope we shall meet again," Daniel said with a smile, "how far is the farm from here?"

"Not that far from here, but about ten kilometres from the village of Inango," said Eshetu.

Before the van turned to left, the Zemachs thanked the driver, climbed out, and strolled toward the pasture. The sun was halfway to the western horizon, its pleasant rays shining over the grassland and the forest.

They walked past huts with conical thatched roofs and face-size windows, the people watching them with friendly eyes, the naked children waving hands, and giggling. They turned to the right, walked into the woods, then climbed up a hill. They stopped near a green meadow looking over a small upland plateau, which appeared blessed with everything from water to fertile ground, thick surrounding forests, and a healthy climate.

"I think the farm begins here," Daniel said, scanning the cattle grazing the green grass; a significant number of cattle scattered across the vast grassland that stretched to the hills far beyond.

"I think life began here," admired Ghenet, her eyes shining with delight. "It's gorgeous. It makes me feel like God created the world for us."

Daniel lifted her small chin with his left hand and beamed at her. He touched her coffee-brown face and moved closer to her with parted lips that seemed to plead for water to quench a thirsty soul. As his face came closer to her mouth, she grabbed him with passion, and their lips met. They hugged firmly and kissed. Their legs suddenly felt weak, and they slipped to the ground.

Oblivious of their surroundings, they sank into the ocean of romance. They held each other tightly and rolled over the grass, kissing with passion.

Daniel's wallet had dropped from his pocket; its contents - photographs and a few cards - were scattered. Gently, Daniel parted from Ghenet, and looking into her eyes, said, "I love you, Ghenet."

Ghenet smiled, and they kissed again and again. The kissing, the caressing, the touching seemed endless. It was like nourishment to their hungry souls and fulfilment to their spirit.

A moment later, Daniel reached to retrieve some of the things he dropped. As he lifted a photograph, Ghenet got a glimpse of the picture that attracted her attention. "Let me see that. Is that your picture?" she said, reaching to get it.

"It's not me. It's big brother, Samson. You remember him, don't you?" He handed it over to her and beamed at the picture from over her shoulder.

"Isn't that amazing? You could use his picture as yours," Ghenet said, astonished by the facial similarity. Ghenet might not recall his looks, but she could hardly forget Samson's intimacy with her brother.

"I remember when he used to come to our home with Gaushaw. Where is he now?"

"I don't know," said Daniel with a tone of sadness.

"He left a long time ago, isn't it?" Ghenet asked.

"Some seven years, I think," Daniel answered.

Seven years ago, Daniel recollected the year when his father, Goytom Gobezay, left home for good, leaving behind a marriage that had staggered to survive 15 years. A few years later, when Goytom got married to a younger lady, Daniel's mother, Abinet, filed a charge. She asserted that she had the right over half of whatever Goytom owned.

According to the law, all property considered "Common Property" was divided equally between the spouses. As a rule, such division would be made in kind, and money may set off any inequality in such divisions.

Goytom Gobezay had registered everything he owned in his name with no knowledge that the primary legal presumption was that all properties were common property even if it had been registered in one of the spouses' names. When Goytom received the court subpoena to answer Abinet's claim, he did not appear at the court; instead, he rushed furiously to Abinet, armed with a gun.

Unfortunately, none of their sons had been at home when Goytom arrived. He did not talk to her. He just whirled on her like a bull and begun punching her with all his might. The first blow that sent her to the ground was directed at her face, dislodging her front tooth. Then he used his feet and stomped her into the cement-floor over and over. All that time, Abinet begged him to stop, admitting her mistakes, imploring that she would denounce all her claim. Having won the battle, Goytom produced a gun and threateningly said, "Go and cancel the case. My lawyers will fix the paperwork. If you ever try anything like this again, I will …"

Samson had entered the room.

It was a horrific scene—his father with a gun in his hand, in a killer's mood; and his mother, almost lifeless on the floor.

A fistfight began. Father in his mid 40s, a country-grown man with no idea of boxing. Son, approaching 20, well-trained city boy, a champion of a youth boxing club. The gun had no use. It flew out of Goytom's grip with the first blow to his left jaw. Samson delivered the punishment for some five minutes and stopped when Goytom fainted. Finally, when Daniel came home, he found his father lying on the floor, gasping for air, face swollen.

"That day, Samson left and never returned," Daniel said.

"God! What a story." Ghenet was speechless, mouth agape and eyes flashing with red hot anger on behalf of Daniel's mother. "What happened to the case?"

"Mother gave up and closed the case, but she did not renounce her ownership right"

On Monday, Daniel appeared before the Zemecha staff. He knew what was at stake. Taking a Zemach-girl for a picnic outside the sight or knowledge of the Stations had been prohibited. The Zemecha staff could not be lenient on that.

"We have heard what you two did last Saturday. We had strictly instructed all the Zemachs to refrain from such thing," said the station chief.

"We did nothing wrong. Ghenet is like a sister to me," Daniel said, trying to sound as innocent as possible.

"The staff had discussed the incident and reached a decision."

Daniel's eyes popped out with anxiety.

"We were on the verge of firing you out of the program," the station chief continued, "but since you have been very diligent on the work of the Zemecha, we have softened the punishment. You will be posted at the Debella-farm, where you will run literacy classes for the children and the families of the farmers."

"Debella-farm? It's over ten kilometres from here."

"Yes. We want you and the girl to be far apart."

"But…"

"No buts now. We have already arranged with the farm manager, Mr. Debella, to provide provisions and lodging. You will move tomorrow. Name a partner who would work with you."

"In that case, I would prefer Kirubel to move with me."

"So, shall be done. You will take your things with you and lodge there, but you will maintain contact with this station. One of you shall come to report every week and get instructions at the same time."

Chapter 4

Daniel's father, Goytom Gobezay, received a couple of letters from the authorities. The first was an acknowledgement from the Zemecha headquarters of his involvement in the national cause. The other one that startled Goytom was the letter of appreciation with the official seal of the Derg. He read the letter over and over and studied the signatory's name, a name that seemed to tear him apart.

Nervously, Goytom searched for a key in his pocket, fished it out, inserted it into the lock in the drawer of his desk, and with eyes fixed on the signature on the letter, he pulled open the drawer.

The old document was there, enclosed in a folder. As he saw it, he remembered the young army officer whose signature had not changed much even after all the years. It was as curly and distinctive on the old document as it was in the letter. It was him: Mengistu. No doubt about it. Goytom Gobezay placed the old paper back in the drawer and locked it.

Although a letter of appreciation meant no payment in cash, it had other values that would have made many very happy. Business people would pay a fortune for this kind of letter since it would buy them state protection, but it seemed like a dead-end to Goytom. It was not the money lost, nor was it the contents of the letter that triggered his fear but the man who had signed it – one of the few most powerful men in the Derg, Major Mengistu, the vice-chairman of the Derg.

"Does he remember me?" Goytom wondered. "Could he have recognized my name when he signed the letter?"

He went to Beza's office, and for a few seconds, he watched her typing with her back half-naked. It pleased him to see her so composed, in her little brown leather mini-skirt. Beza was not a gorgeous lady like her sister but a simple attractive girl with full lips, a little straight nose and black eyes. She was a grade 12 student who should have been serving the Zemecha duty at this time but with the help of Goytom's financial muscle, she had secured her exemption from Zemecha obligations on the ground of ill health. Right after her return from the Zemecha she had to leave home. Beza's father, a retired army officer, had been furious about her deserting a national call and obligation. As a patriotic man he couldn't accept her reasoning and told her either to go back or leave. Beza chose the latter, and moved to elder her sister, Elsa. Right away, Beza joined the Nyala Transport Company. She had already spent almost a month working as a clerk for Goytom Gobezay.

Sensing someone's presence, she turned swiftly to catch the boss's gaze. "Would you please come to my office, Beza," he said and returned to his office, Beza following him immediately.

"Have a seat, Beza," he said as he handed her over the letter from the office of the Derg.

"… As recommended by the Zemecha Headquarters, the Provisional Military Administrative Council conveys its highest regard for your contribution to transporting the Zemachs to their destinations. We look forward to your further co-operation in the future," the letter read—official with the seal of the Dergue and the signature of Mengistu.

"That's great!" Beza said as she saw the name—Mengistu. But to Goytom, who knew the major's past, it meant nothing but demise.

"I have decided to sell the company," he announced, "today they pay bills with blank paper, tomorrow they will confiscate your property."

"What?" Beza seemed bewildered. "I think, nowadays, people die for this kind of letter, especially businessmen.

Forget the money." Beza held the paper up and said, "This is more important than money. Nobody can touch you now. You know what state protection means, don't you?"

"No! No! There are other reasons," Goytom said, his face showing that he had already made up his mind.

"Tell the accountant to settle all financial matters within the month."

When Beza left the office, he picked the telephone and dialed the number of a business broker to whom he imparted his decision to sell the company. The call was short and precise.

Not long after, he went out of his office and moved around the workshop, talked to some workers and supervisors, promising them an arrangement that would keep them employed in case the company went to another owner. He also went to the maintenance section where his youngest son, Benaim, worked.

"How are you doing?"

"It's all right. I'm used to it now," Benaim said, watching his father intently.

"This business is going bad. I'm selling it," Goytom said withholding the true reason; as he watched his son's face for any reaction.

Biniam was startled. "I don't think this branch is that bad. It certainly makes money. You must have some other reasons."

"Not anymore. No future, not with a government that pays with letters of empty appreciation."

"I see," said Biniam, looking in the direction of the office. The old Land-Rover, which he often used for work, was parked near the office entrance. Goytom's eyes followed Biniam's and rested at the car.

"You may have the car," he said, pointing at the Land-Rover with his chin. "Well, it's old but better than nothing."

Biniam expressed his acceptance with a brief smile of delight.

Goytom Gobezay used to be a hard-working family man who seldom drank and never smoked. He loved the simple pleasures of his home. When he married his wife, Abinet Kahsay, he had been a chauffeur who lived a miserable life in Asmara, Eritrea's capital. Despite his hard work, his meagre income had not been enough to make ends meet. The family was often slapped by starvation, as a result of which their first child, a son they worshipped as a god, died before he learned to walk.

The child's sudden death had repercussions that brought about significant changes in Goytom's life, mainly his attitude toward money. The one-time son of a priest who had genuinely believed in God changed into one of the most frugal men who worshipped money.

After the birth of the second child, Goytom Gobezay found a job as a truck driver earning a handsome monthly wage. A couple of years later, the third child was born when the British Protectorate came to an end, and Eritrea and Ethiopian governments signed federal arrangements. Observing the event as a day of liberation, they named the child Kibrom, which meant Honor.

Soon after the British left, life in Eritrea's cities became challenging, prices surged up, and a shortage of commodities slowed the market. Goytom's salary was hardly enough to keep pace with the galloping inflation. When life became unbearable, the family decided to move to Addis Ababa with their two children, Samson and Kibrom.

In Addis, Goytom had been able to find a job in a few days. This time too, as a truck driver in the Ministry of Mines and Resources. Decent salary, pleasant family life. A couple of years later, the fourth child, Daniel, came into the world, and a couple of years later, the fifth, Biniam.

As Goytom got used to the way of life in Addis Ababa, he had learned the means of business. He was able to make quick money by fraudulent use of government trucks for his benefit. He had been involved in various unlawful activities that paid off and enabled him to start a small transportation company, which grew steadily, making him far wealthier than he ever had dreamed.

With his increasing wealth, Goytom's hidden nature had begun to surface. He began to come home late and drunk and frequently slept around with young ladies. As a result, he had been at odds with his wife often. In turn, that had put him in a direct fight with his children, who always tried to protect their mother whenever Goytom got violent with her.

"How about that one? Must be dead somewhere. Any news?" By 'that one' Goytom meant his son, Samson. He had never called him by his name since their last fistfight seven years ago. Samson was then a full-grown man of 21. Even as a teenage boy, Samson and the other little brothers used to protect their mother to their last breath every time Goytom got to his feet to harm their mother. Samson would first stand fixed on the ground, trying to block his father from advancing. At the same time, Kibrom labored to cover his mother with his little body, in case Goytom overrun Samson as it often happened. Little Daniel had a peculiar and effective way of protecting his mother, which irritated Goytom most. He would run out of the yard and scream so loud that the neighbors would come out. Goytom did not want other people to know of his family problem and his mistreatments. He simply had to stop his advance towards Abinet, run to Daniel, slap him few times, and carry him back. Goytom seemed never to forget that, and he always felt miserable about those incidents. Privately he missed his family very much, particularly Daniel.

"How is Daniel? Does he scr…, I mean, does he write?"

"Yes, he does."

"Mamma's boy, I don't think he will make it - this Zemecha. I wonder how he dared go in the first place."

"He is doing well. I don't think he will ever quit."

"Looks like he's become tougher. He was a chicken. Always afraid to fight boys of his age."

"You know him as a child. He is a man now."

"And Kibrom?"

"He is okay," replied Biniam, and their conversation ended there.

Shortly after twelve, Goytom Gobezay and Beza came home for lunch. Goytom's wife, Elsa, was not around as it was expected of her lately. Though Goytom used to be worried by her frequent absences, he seemed not to care much, so long Beza was with him. In a way, he even liked Elsa's disappearance; he had begun to enjoy Beza's company more than Elsa's.

Beza lived with her elder sister, Elsa, and therefore with her boss. This arrangement had pleased everyone, especially Goytom Gobezay. While the maid served lunch, Beza changed to lighter clothes and came to the table, shinning like a star. She wore a short shirt covering only half of her upper body and a mini-skirt that exposed a good part of her legs. Her hair was undone and fell on her shoulders. She had no bra, and a vast area of her breast was uncovered.

Goytom watched her searching for a hint, but he couldn't detect anything approaching an invitation. She was skimming through an Italian fashion magazine and calmly munching her food. From her appearance, it seemed to him that God created her merely to provide enjoyment to men. He wanted to swallow her like the food before him.

"It's Saturday, isn't it?" A plan was taking form in his mind. "Would you go out somewhere with me?" It was a hoarse voice mixed with doubt and anxiety.

"I'm at your disposal," she was quick to reply, "I'm your employee, am I not?"

"What I have in mind has nothing to do with your employment… ," He wanted to add 'sweetheart,' but chose not to. Goytom was a successful womanizer but had never dared approach these new generations who went around without a bra.

"Whatever you have in mind can be regarded as a new assignment. That work should only take place in the offices, has not been proclaimed, not yet," she was joking at the politics of the day that was full of proclamations. "Where do you want to go?"

"Recreation," he answered.

"I like it," she laughed, her cheeks flushing with pleasure. As the maid served coffee to Goytom, Beza went to her room. A moment later, she came back shining like the sun outside. Goytom couldn't wait; they left immediately.

The tropical sun had almost incinerated the car. So, Beza opened her side of the window to release the heat, and turned some degrees towards Goytom, one arm on the edge of the window, the other almost touching his shoulder. At Beyene Street, Goytom turned the car northward and went past the gate of the Nyalas.

Beza glanced at the gateway of the company. "How much do you expect from the sale of the company?"

"Around a million birr," Goytom was brief. He hated discussing his money with anyone.

"Wow! Won't you buy me something?" said Beza impulsively. She was not after anything except joy.

"Name anything you want?"

"Anything?"

"It depends … within reason."

"A little car. Won't that be reasonable?"

"A car. That's fine."

"Thanks beforehand. I was dreaming of owning a car since I was a child."

After brief moments of touring in the city, Goytom brought the Chevrolet to a halt outside Bar Mexico. Sitting in the car, they ordered drinks. Goytom's choice was Gin tonic, and Beza ordered Coca. Goytom believed Gin would add some energy into his body, which he would need with this young lady.

"Gin is good for the body. Try one," Goytom insisted.

"I don't need it," Beza said, "you should not drink if you are behind the wheel either."

"Who cares? This is a city of drunks."

"The rules."

"Money can break rules; don't you worry."

Goytom ordered again. This time it was single, which he gulped in one shot as it came, and paid instantly before the waiter left. Soon the car was on the road, heading north. Beza sat relaxed with her face turned in his direction. She stretched and put one arm on the window and the other on Goytom's shoulder. As she parted her legs, her miniskirt moved up to expose more of her thighs. He cast a side-glance at the girl's body before moving his hand slowly from the wheel to her lap. She smiled invitingly and caressed his hand.

In a few minutes, they reached Hotel-Dé Afrique. Goytom began to imagine himself with her in bed. He had done it before with many women in the same hotel, but this time it was his wife's little sister, and the venture itself excited him.

Breathing laboriously, he swung the car into the hotel yard through the rear entrance, as many of those older men who want to hide from curious eyes would do. There were plenty of free parking places, but a plain-clothed man stopped him before he occupied one.

"I'm sorry, sir. Parking in this area is not allowed for the time being," the man said politely.

"Why? What?" Goytom looked around. Several fancy cars were parked, and on both sides of the parking lot stood what Goytom suspected to be security people.

The plain-clothed man went to his pocket and held out his ID to Goytom, who immediately understood and obeyed. He had to park on the front side of the Hotel.

"I guess some big *pigs* are in the hotel," whispered Goytom as he led Beza into the Hotel.

He took one of the tables on the entrance floor and politely offered Beza a seat near him.

"What's up today? We were not allowed to park in the backyard beside the fancy cars!" Goytom spoke to the waiter who served them drinks. Most of the waiters were familiar to him; he had been there often.

"Top officials are having a meeting… upstairs," the waiter whispered.

"What officials?" Goytom inquired in a low voice.

"There are some members of the Dergue too," the waiter said with caution.

"Derg?" Goytom hated to hear that word, the popular name of the Provisional Military Administrative Council. He hated everything about it: its work, and all that it stood for. Not for some political reasons but because he simply was uncomfortable with such a powerful institution; a power above wealth and the law, that could neither be befriended nor bought.

"Major Mengistu is also there!" the waiter added in a whisper.

When Goytom heard this, the drink in his throat reversed its route, and he coughed noisily.

"Are you alright?" Beza and the waiter inquired simultaneously.

"It's nothing," Goytom said, turning to Beza, he added, "Finish your drink, and let's get out of this place."

Beza was surprised at the sudden change in Goytom's attitude; he seemed to have completely forgotten why he came to this place. She surely knew why he had brought her here, and she was willing and ready to offer whatever he would have demanded of her.

Beza was a kind-hearted, young lady who loved her sister like her mother. But she was too adventurous to see consequences and too thoughtless to reconsider imminent risks. Beza believed that her incursion in her sister's marriage was inconsequential since Elsa had been neither faithful to Goytom nor interested in him anymore. She was quite prepared to give Goytom the pleasure he had never experienced before. The challenge of nabbing him out of her sister's grip had a feeling too sensational to be abandoned now.

"Why?" asked Beza nosily, surprised by the change of plan.

He pushed his chair back and stood, "I'll explain later. Now let's get out of here."

Beza's curiosity grew as she now realized that Goytom got uncomfortable whenever he heard Mengistu's name. She recalled what had happened that morning: his sudden decision to sell the company. Many a time, the widely spread rumor that the regime would confiscate private property had compelled Goytom to consider selling his company before anything like that happened, but he was always hesitant and distinctly against the very idea of selling his brainchild: the Nyla Transportation. But today, after he received that one letter on which Mengistu had put his signature, Goytom was firmly on a path to sell it. And now, hearing that man's name again, he had utterly suppressed his overwhelming desire and held back from her. She wanted to know why.

"Do you know him?" Beza asked as he started the car into motion.

"Who?"

"Major Mengistu."

Goytom's lips parted, but no words came out.

Beza could not read the expression on Goytom's face because it was getting dark. Yet she could feel he was troubled.

Chapter 5

Eyes wide open in the dark, he had rested on his pillow for hours thinking of his new life on the Farm. The Farm was not as bad as he had assumed it to be. It was a quiet place with about one hundred workers. Many of the workers lived in the farm compound, some with their families. Though most of them were poor, they seemed not to be that unhappy in life. They appeared to be satisfied with the food and shelter they earned from the Farm. Now their children have started going to literacy classes, which made the Farm a livelier place. As weeks passed, even the adults had begun to join the literacy classes after work.

Daniel was delighted with his new duties on the Farm. He also liked the farm-food that was made from fresh ingredients from the field. The green scenery with herds of cattle, was a great environment to be in. His problem was the Zemecha regulation that restricted boys and girls to have affairs, so he won't be able to meet Ghenet privately right now. If they ignored the reprimand, they got last time, they would be expelled. At first, he had been able to endure the restriction, but as weeks passed by, he began to be uneasy and feel unhappy. Lately, he was occupied solely by Ghenet that he could not concentrate on any other thing. And in his dreams, whenever he dreamed, there was always Ghenet. Most of the time, he dreamed of romantic picnics filled with lustful scenes. Yet, all ended with her vanishing in the air, awakening him with horror in the middle of the night. Other times she would become a wife and mother of three or four children living with him, happily married.

Last weekend he had sneaked to the town of Gimbie and met her secretly. There, Daniel had told Ghenet of his dreams.

Ghenet had laughed shyly, "Haven't you ever tried the real thing before?"

"Never had I kissed another woman, let alone make love to one. How about you?"

"Yes, Daniel. I have tried it a few times."

Daniel had felt his heart leap; an irresistible desire mounting in him. He had probably been jealous, but her frankness was so disarming that he kissed her tenderly.

That day they had looked at every possible place in Gimbie where they could find some privacy to nourish their desire for each other, but they had not been rewarded. Moreover, the rules that forbade Zemachs not to engage in romantic amusement had been nagging them to back off.

"My place at the farm is good," he told her.

"What about Kirubel?"

"I'll tell him to leave for a day."

They had agreed, and ever since that day, he had been thinking of little else. Even a few days later, when he heard the news about the coming of Ermias and the whereabouts of his brother, Samson, he was excited and eager to travel to Addis and see them, but shortly after, he forgot all about them, his mind back on Ghenet. He occasionally wondered how she had come to take over all the love he had for his family.

He jumped out of his bed and walked to the window. Gently he opened the window and let the morning air into the house. It was raining and had lately been thunderous stormy weather. The sky was covered with a thick grey cloud. It appeared like heavy rain was about to come. For a moment, Daniel, standing by the window, weighed it, thinking of his appointment with Ghenet. She would come on Sunday; two days later. Kirubel has agreed to leave the room at their disposal during her visit. Hoping the weather would not stand between him and Ghenet, he stared far away across the long pasture at the other end of the Farm.

Mr. Debella, a man in his early fifties, stood on a hill with an umbrella in his hand, surveying the farm compound. Mr. Debella was a highly regarded man in the region for his comments against wrongdoers. He lived in Inango since the state banished him for criticizing its failure to satisfactorily avoid the catastrophe of the drought that claimed the lives of tens of thousands of people in the province of Wollo. Daniel liked him for his simplicity and courage.

Kirubel had woken, and coming to the window, he yawned, "Can't you sleep, Daniel? I know what you are thinking. Ghenet… isn't it?"

"What else!"

"First-time experience."

"Now, don't start that."

"First time everybody screams like… like a fox."

"Stop it. I'm afraid Mr. Debella might not like Ghenet coming to my room. You know the rules—no female in our room."

"If he knows that she is your girlfriend, he won't be angry. I suggest you tell him that you are having a company."

"What if he disapproves?"

"He is a modern man. He will understand. If he disapproves, you would only be saved from screaming. That's all," Kirubel joked and laughed aloud.

"I heard he would travel to the capital today," Daniel said.

"If he is not around, no problem… we can work it out. Now let's prepare breakfast and get ready for the day's work."

The wind was blowing so violently that they had to retreat from the window. July had come with massive rains and windy weather. It rained non-stop day and night. The dusty village of Inango was transformed into a muddy hamlet, difficult for pedestrians to walk and slippery for motorists to drive. Life seemed to come to a standstill, but Daniel and Kirubel held the literacy classes, undisturbed by the weather. They were twelve adults and twenty children actively participating - four hours a day and four days a week. The lessons went very well. Many of the children could now identify the letters of the alphabet without difficulty. The adults were a bit awkward. Most of them were not at all convinced that literacy would ever change their lives other than relieving them from the embarrassment of signing by the thumbprint.

"If I can only write my name, then it would be enough with this thing," many were heard saying.

But Daniel was always against quitters. He used to tell them that they should not give up, that a new era had come for everyone, and reading and writing were the primary steps that would enable them for the opportunities that would come along.

"If you cannot read and write," Daniel used to tell them, "Someone will do it for you, and you would not know what was exactly written."

Though half-heartedly, they listened to him, and the classes went on. Nothing delighted Daniel as much as seeing a slow improvement that his students were making.

On Tuesdays and Fridays, he used to go to the Zemecha Center to attend the discussion sessions, which, since the arrest of Bezabih, seemed to have lost their way. The meetings were dominated by propaganda agitation of various political groups, making Daniel lose interest and drop everything. Lately, Daniel was not seen around those sessions.

Shortly after Daniel ceased showing up at the sessions, Kebedde began visiting the Farm. He had been secretly agitating the farmworkers to join the EPRP, a communist party fighting to overthrow the Derg. He held meetings during dark hours in one of the farmworker's huts. Kirubel attended those meetings, but Daniel kept his distance. However, the politics of the day were like a wildfire that could catch anyone from any direction. It was as though you could not hide from it.

Just as they finished breakfast, a knock came on the door. Kirubel opened it. A farmworker who looks like Carl Marx, the 19th-century German philosopher, with his face full of beard, stood in the rain and handed over a piece of paper to Kirubel.

"What is it, Marx? Come in," said Kirubel. Zemachs had baptized the beard-man with the name Marx

"A message from Kebedde," Marx said and left instantly, running.

Kirubel read it to himself and said, "Daniel, do you mind if we meet in this room for a few hours today after dark. We could not meet in the hut because the roof is leaking. You are also welcome at the meeting. What do you say?"

"I don't mind, Kirubel. You can use this room as much as I. Besides, I owe you a favor… you're allowing me to have my privacy."

"Can't you join us today? Just sit and listen to Kebedde."

"Okay. I will."

As the lights from the farm generator went out in the evening, the comrades began to show up. Kirubel had prepared the room for the meeting as it would suit Kebedde, who preferred to sit on a mattress laid on the floor, with his disciples surrounding him. The room was not big, but it could comfortably accommodate two beds, a table and two chairs, and a little tea table where few cups and a kettle were put. On one side of the room, right below the window, a mattress was laid. Waiting for the others, Kebedde was already on place chewing Tchat, the famous green leaf with a mildly narcotic effect. He had come with few books in a plastic bag. A few years older than Daniel, Kebedde looked much mature with the appearance of a purposeful man. There were rumors that he was jailed several times for anti-government activities and had been released on probations and bails. It appeared like he was hanging on his last rope; yet his conviction for the cause was tremendous that he was determined to take whatever would come.

A candle was lit and hung on a holder over him to give light to whatever he would be reading. Another candle flickered on the tea table in the middle of the room. Daniel sat on the edge of his bed, and Kirubel was taking care of the fire to keep the room warm, looking after the tea as well.

"Kebedde," Daniel called, "what did you find out of my spying for the government?" Daniel had not forgotten the accusing remark Kebedde had made several weeks ago at the Zemecha center.

"I wouldn't have been here if I believed that you were a spy."

"But you did not apologize."

"I do, now."

"Any news about Bezabih?" Kirubel asked Kebedde, intentionally breaking into their conversation."

"Nothing so far,"

Before long, the other cell-members began to arrive and make themselves comfortable on the mattress. First came the farm guard and sat next to Kebedde. The guard had been following Kebedde's teaching in the last three or four meetings and found it very inspiring. Tolcha, the cook, and Marx, the errand-boy, came together and sat next to the guard. Tolcha, 32, worked in Mr. Debella's home. At last, came, Eshetu, the driver, who had developed good friendship with Daniel since they met a couple of months ago.

Now that all members were present, Kirubel began serving tea, and Kebedde distributed a few bundles of Tchat to those who would care to chew. Only Eshetu helped himself to the Tchat, risking his job if the word came out of this room. Mr. Debella was strict on Tchat chewers; anyone found chewing would be fired right away.

Under the glow of the dim candlelight, Kebedde's face looked strained as he composed his thought into words; then, he cleared his throat and began, "Before I go to the day's lesson, comrades, I must first welcome all the new participants." He looked at Daniel, but Daniel did not seem to get the message. He had sipped the hot tea which burned his fingers, and was quickly putting the cup back on the table before dropping it.

"As those of you who were present in the last meeting recall, we had discussed the people's miserable life in length. We had also touched on how their struggle led to the overthrow of the emperor. In a moment, we will continue to discuss how and why the military hijacked the people's revolution; first, I have something to introduce to you: the worst enemy of the land tillers and the workers."

Assuming the enemy would be the usual Capitalism or Imperialism, Daniel was not particularly curious about the subject. He was vaguely watching the comrades: Kirubel, giving more tea to those who wanted it; Eshetu, solemnly chewing the Tchat, pretending to be interested; the guard who seemed to worship Kebedde, eagerly waiting for the next lesson; Marx, appearing tired, facing the window; Tolcha very close to Marx looking worried of the noisy weather conditions outside.

Kebedde reached his plastic bag and pulled out a weighty book that looked like an encyclopedia to Daniel. He opened the book in the middle, where a piece of paper had been laid to separate the pages. He said, "I am going to read few passages to you then I shall explain how that shabby carpenter made himself to be worshiped as God."

It was now that Daniel sharpened his attention. He wanted to ask Kebedde if what he had heard came from his mouth but chose not to interrupt now.

"Not only him," went on Kebedde, "I will also tell you stories about other liars."

Then he read from the large book. The phrases he read disrespected the dwarves, the misfits, and the slaves on the planet. He read clause after clause. It sounded like the devil himself wrote it. Then Kebedde raised his eyes and looked at his listeners. Everyone was moved and angered by the subject matter. Satisfied with the impression he created, he said, "What you heard, comrades, was the word of God."

"Did I hear that? What did you say?" asked Tolcha and glanced right and left.

"Comrades, this is what they call the Holy Bible—the enemy of the poor!" Kebedde said and slammed the book. It was at this moment that the candle he used for reading went out. A few seconds later, tremendous thunder that moved everyone from his seat cracked the sky over the Farm. Instantly, the other candle on the tea table fell, leaving the room in total darkness. When that happened, Tolcha jumped out of his seat and, fast as a rabbit, dashed to the door, opened it, and disappeared into the darkness.

Nervously, Kirubel searched for the matches; the others were quiet. A moment later, the matchbox was found, the candle was put back in place, and Kirubel struck a match which flashed but failed to light. He tried several matchsticks—all failed. It was as though some angry spirit was putting them out. Seeing this, Marx stood quietly and sneaked out through the door that was left ajar by Tolcha. Daniel walked to the door and closed it. Then the matches flared at every strike, and the candles came back to life.

Kebedde cleared his throat. "These things can happen. We don't have to take as a work of …"

"Kebedde," Kirubel broke in, "Can't you leave God and the Bible out of this?"

"We must first learn that religion …"

"Look, Kebedde," Daniel said, interrupting him, "I appreciate that you are trying to teach us something, but such lessons are out of context and deplorable. Can you leave now and never show up here again?"

"What do you mean?"

"I mean, exactly what I said. Never show up here, in the farm again," said Daniel firmly.

"You can't prevent me from reaching the people. No one can. Not even the Derg. Kirubel, doesn't he know what our party can do to those who dare cross its way."

"Tell your party that I don't need it here. Now just leave, okay!" said Daniel heatedly.

"You will regret this soon."

"Just leave, or I will make you leave!"

"Cool down, guys," Kirubel interfered. "Kebedde, it's okay for today. You go now."

"Yes, of course. Kirubel, keep this book for me—it's wet outside," Kebedde said and left with Eshetu and the guard.

"Oh! Kebedde, what a character!" Daniel said, way after they were gone, reaching for Kebedde's big book. He opened it in the middle, right at the page separator, and skimmed the verses Kebedde had read. Then he closed the book from which a handful of air rushed and blew out the candle again. The other candle stood safely on the tea-table. Daniel could see Kirubel turning and staring at him under the feeble candlelight. When their eyes met, they couldn't help but laugh.

The next day a terrible thing happened; all those present in the meeting except Daniel and Eshetu were arrested. Eshetu had left early before the police came. The others were picked one by one and taken to the district law enforcement station in the town of Gimbie for interrogation. Daniel was baffled as to why he had been ignored. He had expected that security men, sooner or later, would come for him too, but it appeared for the moment he was saved.

Late in the evening, Kirubel came with a swollen face and bruised hands. He had suffered a severe beating while he was under interrogation. Tolcha and Marx were released without injuries but were told to keep their distance from subversive activities. Kebedde was right away taken to Addis Ababa for further interrogation. The guard, who was considered Kebedde's staunch follower, remained under police custody.

"Are you all right, Kirubel? What's the crime?" asked Daniel as he met Kirubel at home, back from the police.

"You tell me. Wasn't it you who informed the security men?" Said Kirubel with anger in his voice.

"What!"

"Come on. Everybody knows it. It was only I, the fool, who trusted you."

"Do you seriously believe what you are saying?"

"How come they didn't arrest you then?"

Daniel had no answer. After that, the two friends did not talk to each other.

On Sunday, Kirubel left early in the morning to let Daniel have his privacy with Ghenet, but Ghenet did not show up. Word had gone around the Zemecha centers about what had happened to Kirubel and the others, and Daniel was blamed for that. He waited for her until four in the afternoon. When she did not show up, he went to Gimbie to see her.

It was rainy and windy in Gimbie. The Zemecha Center was situated on the outskirts of the town. Daniel walked to the center in the chilly weather, soaked by the rain. When he reached the center, he was met by angry Zemachs who did not want to see him around. Some threatened to beat him if he set foot in the compound.

"Would you tell me why?" protested Daniel.

"You know why, Mister informer," shouted one of them and dragged him from behind. As Daniel staggered, a forceful shove sent him to the ground. Before he got up to his feet, four or five Zemachs caged him in a ring and began punching him. He was too low for a good punch, so they used the feet. Daniel covered his head with his hands, feeling the shoe thud in his back, shoulder, and ribs choking on a wave of pain. A moment later, he managed to get up, broke through them, and fled with tremendous speed. The Zemachs howled behind him but did not follow after him. They had given him enough for a day.

From town, Daniel sent for Ghenet and waited for her in a tearoom. His back was aching, but no bruise on his face. An hour later, he learned that Ghenet was unwilling to see him anymore. It was inconceivable. It seemed to him as though the entire world stood against him.

Depressed as he was, Daniel stood by the roadside waiting for an automobile heading south, to Inango or the Farm. Not long after, he saw Eshetu on the road driving the farm van. Daniel smiled at seeing a friend at this very moment of need and waved a hand. Certainly, Eshetu had seen Daniel stepping forward, but he did not pull up, making it clear that he was no longer a friend. Daniel watched the van disappear into the mist, shivering in the cold. He waited more than an hour in the rain before he could get a ride back to the Farm.

That night, he could not fall asleep, thinking of what had conspired to ruin him in just one day. As far as he was concerned, he had done nothing that could have led to the arrest of his friends or to justify the rumors that were spreading against him. There seemed nothing he could do to restore his name.

The following days were the darkest in Daniel's life. He talked to almost no one, or no one spoke to him. Kirubel was not seen around the Farm as often as he used to be, so Daniel was always alone.

On July 26, 1975, the Dergue announced the nationalization of urban lands in a national radio broadcast outlawing ownership of houses that were rent out. It confiscated all of what it called *extra houses*, allowing private ownership of only personal dwellings.

In a bid to obtain public support, the Dergue announced a significant reduction of rent on the confiscated houses and promised a roof over those who needed. So, in Gimbie, the mood following the announcement was festive. People rejoiced, coming out into the streets to express their support for the government's action. Gimbie was overcrowded with students and Zemachs from the surrounding regions.

On that day, Daniel took an aimless ride to the town of Gimbie. He heard the announcement in the van on his way to Gimbie without any interest to whatever it meant.

Daniel would have felt happier had he not been distressed by the sudden loss of everything he had: his name, friends, and lover. He was feeling empty inside; he had, at that moment, no dream, no goal, nothing to look forward to, and the events outside seemed so meaningless that he was peculiarly indifferent to the announcement and the changes that it would bring.

As he watched the parading crowd on the roadside, nothing of the announcement was in his mind. He was thinking of Ghenet. It had been a week since she had abandoned him, and the separation now seemed to be so much real that he began to feel depressed anew. He tried to compose himself and to appear happier, but it did not work. Anyone could tell that he looked like his house had been confiscated by the day's proclamation.

"I was so happy! Could I feel like that again with any other girl?" He hated the thought that crossed his mind—another girl. Without Ghenet, he thought, he would never be happy again. All of a sudden, in his despair, he decided to quit the Zemecha and go home.

He returned to the Farm, and in the afternoon, he went directly to Mr. Debella's residence to inform him of his decision. Mr. Debella's residence was situated in the far end of the compound of the Farm. It was a beautiful little villa surrounded by eucalyptus trees and a lawn on the front side, which had overgrown. It needed to be pruned, but the flowers around appeared fresh. Passing the garden to the house, Daniel could not help but stop and relish the scent before he knocked at the front door.

"I want to talk to Mr. Debella," said Daniel as Tolcha opened the door.

"Come in, Daniel. Mr. Debella hasn't come back from Addis yet," said Tolcha, standing by the door.

"In that case, tell him that I am compelled to quit the Zemecha due to circumstances beyond my control. I'll leave in a few days."

"Why, Daniel? …"

"I'm sorry, Tolcha, I don't want to discuss that," Daniel said, with resignation

"Step inside, I have something to tell you."

"I got to go, just tell me here."

"Daniel, I don't feel good about what is going on," said Tolcha, avoiding Daniel's eyes. "I believe you are wrongly blamed."

Daniel was awakened by those words. He looked at Tolcha attentively and stepped closer. Here was one person who knew that he had been wrongly accused.

"I must take the blame," continued Tolcha looking at the floor shyly. He then scratched his head and said, "it was . . . it was me who disclosed the information about Kebedde's activities to the security forces."

"Wait a minute, what are you talking about? are you telling me that you ..." Daniel said in disbelief."

"Yes, Daniel. I couldn't take any more of Kebedde's wicked theories. He had to be stopped. He is poisonous. At first, his teachings about equality and social welfare were interesting, and I followed him sincerely. But disgracing the Holy book and God is intolerable. I may not be a good religious man, but I fear God. You saw what happened that evening—the lightning. I never saw anything like it in my life. Trust me, that's a warning."

Daniel simply nodded, weighing the incident in the light of Tolcha's beliefs, "How come the security forces didn't question me?"

"I told them you had nothing to do with it," Tolcha replied quickly. He appeared lightened by the confession. "You have never been to our meetings, Daniel."

"Everyone thinks I was the one who informed the police just because I wasn't arrested like the others ..."

"I wanted to take responsibility right away, but I was afraid I would lose my job and my life. You know I have a motherless child depending on this Farm and me," said Tolcha with his sad-looking eyes on the floor.

A few soundless minutes went by as Daniel tried to acclimatize himself with Tolcha's confession, what he should do about it; and Tolcha, waiting for the verdict. But nothing came from Daniel. He was angry and calm at the same time.

Then Tolcha raised his eyes and said, "Look at the damage I have caused. The torture our friends suffered, and you accused of it."

"I don't think Mr. Debella will fire you for this. I believe, he will understand why you did what you did."

"I'm not only afraid of losing my job but my life too."

Daniel's eye widened, "What are you talking about? Who would be after your life?"

"The party. When I joined the EPRP, Kebedde had told me in clear terms about the punishment for treason."

"My God!" Daniel shivered. He touched Tolcha's shoulder and stepped inside the house, "This is terrible. What can I do to help?"

"Nothing. I have decided to tell the truth… come what may."

"Don't do it, Tolcha," said Daniel, "the damage has already been done. Think of your kid. He needs you."

"What about you, Daniel. Aren't you quitting because of this? I hate to see this happening to you."

"I'll manage. Thanks for your confession; I feel better now that I know everything. I won't quit. But can I tell this to a few of my friends? So that some of these bad feelings will stop? Is Kirubel a member of the party?"

"Yes, he is. Everyone in our cell is a member with an obligation to reveal whatever endangers the party or its members. Can this stay between you and me for a while until I find my way out? It would be a great help."

"Trust me then, Tolcha. No one will ever know," Daniel's tone carried his determined intent, but the flames of anger were vividly seen in his eyes. His anger was not on Tolcha or any single individual but on the entire situation of society and politics.

"Thanks, Daniel."

Daniel did not say a word. He was overwhelmed by the change of expectation. He simply hastened out and ran miles into the woods until his lung couldn't take any more. When

he came back from the woods, he was seen carrying a
beautiful rabbit.

Chapter 6

Bar Tiku was established in the middle of Addis Ababa some fifteen years ago, and it had not changed much. Standing repellently on Tecle Street, it appeared as innocent and straightforward as the other scruffy bars in the city. Though it bore its former owner's name, it had virtually nothing to do with him, and its activities had not much to do with its name.

Since the beginning of the sixties, the bar was owned and used by the Eritrean Liberation Movement as the center of the intelligence network in Addis Ababa. Its former owner, Tiku, a member of the movement, acted as the official owner fulfilling all legal duties. The fact that it had been opened well before the Eritrean problem intensified to the present level helped it conceal itself from suspicious eyes. So far, it had survived undetected as it continued providing lodgings and other services to members of the movement.

Ermias had been given a room at the rear section of the bar compound where he peacefully spent the nights since he came, planning and organizing his thoughts. It was a clean, single room with a bed, a table and two chairs, and a sort of wardrobe. It suited his needs perfectly.

He had not yet started his main work since he had to get used to the people and the place. He had to identify friends and foes first. The first couple of weeks had gone-by quickly; he had immensely enjoyed the company of family members, old friends, and close relatives. He had spent most of the time with his aunt, Abinet Kahsay, with whom he had lived his teenage life.

He had been shocked to find the large family he left eight years ago reduced to only a mother and a son. The father,

Goytom Gobezay, married to another woman; the eldest son, Samson, in the Eritrean jungle, fighting for Eritrea's liberation; Kibrom, having joined the EPRP living an erratic life, mostly out of the home; and Daniel, on the Zemecha program in Inango. His aunt was left with her youngest son, Biniam, who worked and earned a meager income for their living. Ermias had to fight back the tears as he tried to reconcile his boyhood memories with the revolting reality of the time.

In the past few weeks, Ermias had also inquired about his girlfriend, Saba Berhe. He had been able to learn that she had moved to the province of Gondar to study nursing. After having completed her studies, Saba had moved back to Addis Ababa. Though she was untraceable for the moment, Ermias had not given up. He would give it a try as soon as he completed his mission: to set up a new intelligence network in Ethiopia.

As an initial step to set up the spy network, he had gathered information about the country's present situation. The Dergue was still enjoying massive support from the general public and the military. In the countryside, those who used to till somebody's land were now happy to be farmers owning land for the first time in history. The working people had great expectations, as they had believed the revolution would alleviate their hardship and improve their lives. The socialist party—a small group of intellectuals—was behind the Derg, advising and encouraging it to move forward on the socialist path. All that Ermias knew, but he had no idea about the secret meetings between the Socialist Party officials and few Dergue members. The only opposition against the Dergue was the communist party known as EPRP, the Ethiopian People's Revolutionary Party. By now, Ermias had good knowledge about the nature of the ruling Dergue and its friends and potential enemies. The Derg, he knew, was ruthless; any slight mistake meant a lifetime regret. He had to be vigilant.

Today, he was scheduled to meet some members of the shattered Eritrean intelligence service in Addis Ababa. He had not slept well, and it was already dawn. At about seven, there was a knock at the door that woke him from his brief slumber.

"Who is there?" he inquired, voice low but demanding. He never trusted anything or anyone until he got used to the new location and put it under complete surveillance. He would rest, probably, when information started to flow from various directions. The previous intelligence network had been crippled following the Derg's arbitrary repression. Fear and apprehension were the inevitable reflections of the situation until a new spy network would be set up.

"I'm a waiter. Breakfast is ready, sir."

The voice was not familiar. Ermias searched under his pillow and fished out the pistol, which Jovani gave him to be used in case of need, including destroying himself.

"Just a minute!" He wrapped the small metal in a newspaper and approached the door. He held the pistol in his right hand and opened the door with the left one. A short man stood by the door holding a tray with coffee, bread, and what appeared to be butter or cheese.

"Come in," said Ermias, observing for what might lurk behind the waiter.

"Good morning," the waiter said and stepped in to put the tray on the table. He then politely asked Ermias if he needed anything else.

"Nothing. Thank you," Ermias said, showing him to the door.

The waiter bowed respectfully and left the room. Ermias closed the door behind him and locked it properly.

It was an hour later that he entered the bar through the rear room. There was no one in the bar except the bartender to whom he had been introduced as a trusted member the day he came. Over the weeks, the two had already developed an easy comradeship with each other.

Ermias greeted him and walked across the room to the table at a corner.

As soon as Ermias took a seat, the bartender dried his hands and walked to Ermias. "Mr. Tiku said that he would be delayed by half an hour or so."

"That's okay?"

"What'd you like to drink?"

"Anything soft."

As the bartender turned away, Ermias picked a day-old newspaper from the table and browsed the pages. He often detested reading government papers. However, out of curiosity, he began to read a news report which commented on the work of the Zemecha, criticizing the elements sowing the seed of discord among the Zemachs.

In some regions, the paper related, the work had ceased totally because of fighting between rival groups. In Inango, a notorious anarchist named Kebedde had been arrested by security forces for inciting farmers and workers to mutiny and lawlessness. Previously a counter-revolutionary teacher called Bezabih Mazengia had also been arrested in that same region. The government was considering to take drastic measures to curb the counter-revolutionary activities of anti-people elements such as the EPRP and the likes… .

Half an hour later, Mr. Tiku showed up, and Ermias stood to receive him. They exchanged warm greetings and sat side by side at the table.

"No sign of aging. The same Tiku I knew!" he said, smiling at the old man. This encounter between the two was the first since their meeting in Sudan four years ago. Tiku was a short, bulky man with a plain face, and a head full of black hair that made him look younger than his real age. He was in his mid-fifties.

As they chatted, the bartender who was familiar with Tiku's taste, brought him a black coffee without sugar and then returned to work.

"How are things going?" Ermias was referring to the climate of terror hanging over their organization.

"No one can claim to be safe at this time. May God watch over us. It's only we who know about the covert operations going against us at present." He sipped from his coffee and fell silent.

"So, how come they didn't arrest you?"

"Ghirmay!" Tiku said as if it explained everything.

"What about him?"

"He was the one who had direct contact with me. He killed himself before they caught him to save me and the others!" he said with a lump in his throat.

Ermias shook his head sorrowfully, "A hero indeed."

"Our men are waiting for us," Tiku lifted his cup, drained it, and wiped his mouth with the palm of his hand. He then peered at his watch and stood up to go. "We have to be there at nine."

As they crossed the street, Ermias observed something unusual which had not been there yesterday. Building walls on both sides of the road were painted with slogans, red banners on cloth and paper hanging on electric poles and wires. They read:

EPRP IS THE VANGUARD OF THE PEOPLE!
DOWN WITH THE MILITARY GOVERNMENT

Walking down the narrow alley into the neighborhoods, they saw walls painted with similar slogans.

"They did all this at night," Tiku said. "The entire city is painted with these types of words."

"There won't be a problem as long as it's done with paint and paper only," Ermias said. When Tiku turned and stared at him, he added, "As long as they don't resort to violence."

"Do you think they will go that far?"

"It always begins this way and ends the other way," Ermias said with a tone of concern.

Tiku had his attention focused on the ground right under Ermias, his eyes shifting rapidly between the earth and Ermias. He had remembered the controversial crime that took place on that spot some sixteen years back. It was there that

Ermias' father, Tesfay Kahsay, had been found dead. Tiku pursed his lips and shook his head somberly. He was one of the few people who had taken care of the body.

"Anything wrong?" Ermias asked, looking at the sole of his shoes to see what he might have stepped on.

"It was here we found your father's body," Tiku said with a low voice and ashen face. "The place has not changed much, and it always reminds me of him and his good work. Tesfay was a personality so rare to be forgotten. He was a good friend to me, and a faithful leader to our organization."

Ermias was quiet for a moment. "I have doubts around the circumstances of my father's death," he then said. "I want to find out before I leave."

"What's there to find out? It's obvious; securities killed him."

"In my profession, we don't conclude like that. Not after what I saw in our organization. Members get eliminated just for having a different opinion."

"Do you suspect that such a thing could have happened to him?"

Ermias did not answer the question. "Could you somehow acquire the police investigation files for me? I think no one needs them, now?"

"Yes, I can try to get you the copies if you want. I have contacts."

They walked further into the neighborhood. A while later, they were in a house where their organization had its secluded office. There were two men in the room; Jovani, who was on the phone; and another person Ermias had never met before.

The man stood up to shake hands with Ermias, who gazed at the man's scarred face longer than necessary. The man had a typical Eritrean look that revealed not only his tribe but also that he could be a rebel. Ermias never liked to include these kinds of faces in his spy net. But this man was not directly engaged in intelligence work. By his employment in the

Telephone Company, he had been recruited and persuaded to serve the organization in radio communications.

Jovani finished his telephone conversation, and the four of them sat around the rectangular table. The door and the two windows had been closed, and the light turned on. Tiku began the introductory speech. Ermias listened, his eyes examining the room.

It was a room of about 30 square meters, surrounded by brick walls with a high ceiling. Facing Ermias, on the top of a cupboard, was an electronics device. Apparently, it was a transistor transmitter. The wires connected to it going over the wall to the roof. On his left was a short table leaning against the wall, on which were placed the telephone apparatus together with the coffee boiler.

Tiku gave the floor to Ermias, who conveyed brief comradeship greetings and went straight to the agenda at hand.

"Since the military government came to power," Ermias began, "our intelligence network was severely damaged because of the rampant arrests and killings. Many of our most useful undercover operatives in the government's highest echelon have been substituted or fired. The main reason for my presence in the country, at this very moment, is to establish a new intelligence network.

"Raising financial contributions, at this moment, is dangerous and has to be terminated. Our primary focus will be on intelligence gathering. We shall be engaged in the task of recruiting dissidents in the army and other government institutions. As you know, people betray their country for many reasons; resentment, ideology, lack of promotion, even hatred of a superior. In this country, we will indeed find many mercenaries who would sell vital information for money.

Following Ermias, Jovani presented some minor intelligence reports, and the Radioman talked about matters relevant to his technical duties. He said that he needed a new transmitter because the old one was faulty. Then Tiku brought up financial issues.

"We will have to open new businesses to back up our economy." He indicated the income gathered from gas stations and transportation services, from hotels and restaurants as examples.

"Financial contributions from members and sympathizers involve more perils than benefits. So many have perished for so little. I'm glad it's discontinued."

Silence reigned following Tiku's speech, seemingly in remembrance of their fallen compatriots.

Again, Tiku broke the silence, "Goytom Gobezay is selling his company—the Nyala Transports. I have already expressed my interest to buy it on behalf of the organization. I think this will be a very profitable step. What do you think about it?"

There was no one against the proposal, and thus the decision to buy the Nyala Transportation Company was made.

Chapter 7

The first anniversary of the Revolution had come and gone. It had been widely celebrated like Independence Day throughout the country. Yet, Goytom Gobezay had not noticed it. He had been busy getting rid of almost everything he owned, mainly the Nyala Transportation. He was determined to go into hiding and keep a lower profile to veil himself from the Revolution and Mengistu. Due to the nationalization of urban land and 'extra houses,' he had lost over 10 km square of land in the outskirts of Addis Ababa and several rent houses. But the sale of the Nyala Transportation Company had gone smoothly, providing him with more profit than he had expected. It almost compensated for his losses and paid a few debts. But his ordeal was just to begin. The watchful eyes of the Revolution seemed to follow him wherever he went. This time it was the National Revenue Department. It had come up with a bill for five years of retroactive taxes plus interest, pressing him to pay the outstanding debt immediately. It was as though the Revolution had come to destroy none other but him.

"Elsa, don't you know someone influential in this government?" Goytom asked, looking at his wife through the corner of his eyes. She was dressing up to go out. Lately, Elsa appeared to have changed much. She had become more conscious of her appearance and away from home. A rumor that she was seeing a particular Dergue member had reached Goytom's ears.

Nevertheless, Goytom was not so unwise to confront her at this time. Besides, he was as tired of her as she was of him, so he had chosen better. He knew the man could help with his tax problem if Elsa cooperated.

"What do you mean by someone influential? Are you suspecting me with somebody!?" Elsa barked. She was not frightened of him anymore, as she used to be before.

"Understand me. I am required to pay a considerable amount of money to the State. I was looking for means of going about this through personal contacts."

"I know nothing of such things. You better deal with the authorities the way you used to do."

"What exactly does that mean?"

"Bribe. Is that not the way you have been doing business all those years?"

"Who am I to bribe. Mengistu? I think you want me killed-ah? So that you can… Goytom did not wish to offend her. He knew that was not the right time.

But Elsa wanted it out, "So that I can… what? Say it! I know you never trusted me."

"I just wanted you to help me solve this tax problem. That's all. I did not say anything unless you wanted to confess something."

"Since when do you talk money matters with me," cried Elsa, her voice very loud that her sister Beza heard from her bedroom and showed up.

Angrily Goytom stepped closer to Elsa. He was tempted to slap her. His hands were shaking. It was the sight of Beza that calmed him.

"What do you know about money except getting hitched by men who have?"

"Oh!" Elsa picked her purse and ran to the door. "I hope you cool down before I come back. I'm tired of arguing with you." She went out and slammed the door behind her.

Goytom cursed her and returned to his desk, pulled a drawer, and extracted a folder from it. The documents in the folder were neat and orderly. Goytom was good at file keeping. However trivial they might be, documents of the distant past were well kept along with any essential ones of recent times. As he was looking for taxation documents through the papers, he casually came on the papers which carried Mengistu's signature. He stared at each of them briefly and laid them back where they had been.

"Who am I going to bribe? Mengistu?" he said to himself.

He picked a paper and put a call through to one of his business agents. After warm but pretentious greetings with the agent, Goytom got down to the matter.

"It's about taxes."

"What about it? Didn't we settle that?"

"I'm required to pay the taxes for the last five years. Can't you help to straighten out these?"

The agent understood what Goytom was implying. "That's impossible, nowadays. We have already tried and failed with other similar cases. We don't know what is happening in the government. The State is looking into every revenue source, allegedly to cover its urgent expenses—war preparations, I guess. Nothing is known. By the way, I don't advise you to try to bribe anyone these days. You know, they execute people for offering or receiving bribes."

Trembling with anger, Goytom put the phone down and swore, "Disgraceful!"

He walked across the living room, stared out through the window for a while and then threw himself on the brown sofa. He tried to calm himself so he could concentrate on the solutions to his immediate problems: Elsa's recent behavior and frequent absences, the unpredictability of the coming times, and the Derg. Well, Elsa could be substituted by Beza; Goytom had that all planned. The Derg, in his case Mengistu, could be avoided if he, Goytom, could only keep a lower profile. But the future that he had planned to enjoy with a substantial amount of money at hand remained unsecured after the taxation case came into his life.

As he began to devise a plan by which he could deceive the State and retire safely, he felt heavy in his head and physically tired of the pressure on him. Not long after, he sensed something soft on the back of his neck and behind his ears; his back was being massaged. Gradually his tension relaxed. Beza had come to his rescue. She worked on him expertly, releasing his anger and his aches with her fingers.

During the past months, Goytom had not had much time to spend with Beza because he had been busy with the selling of the company. However, he had enjoyed Beza's Company quite a few times. They had occasionally been out for dinner and had had very brief and hesitant love touches and kisses. No more. They had never gone as far as to fire love guns at each other. Now Beza seemed to be determined to stage an assault with heavy artillery.

She pulled him off the sofa and led him to the bedroom. She could have gone to her bedroom, but Beza preferred the bigger one, the one that belonged to Elsa.

"Not here… Elsa might come back…the maid might…" Goytom stammered submissively.

"I have told the maids not to disturb you during your naptime. And Elsa will only come back after seven. Don't you trust me? The woman wants nothing to do with you!" the words came with slow, sexy breathing. Then she pulled off her red sweater in one swift movement. She wore no brassiere; her breasts needed no support. She then opened three buttons at the side of the leather mini-skirt and again, with a swift, sexy movement, stepped out of it. She had no underwear at all. Goytom was watching her as he struggled to get rid of his trousers. Beza jumped on the bed naked. Timidly Goytom approached the bed in his large shorts.

Unlike many young Abyssinian women, Beza was amazingly open to the pleasures of life. Going to bed with her friend's boyfriends or with her teachers was not a matter of disgrace for her. Such adventure excited her so much that she indulged herself in several similar situations. For Beza, sex was a natural source of pleasure, and she accepted it wholeheartedly, but she had never overlooked the unpleasant consequences that might result from it: unplanned childbirth, illegal abortion, or sexually transmitted diseases. She always took precautions and kept herself clean and healthy. She extended a hand to give him a condom-like plastic.

It was arduous, but Goytom managed to open the cover.

"Which side goes first?" said Goytom trying to split the plastic open. Beza had jumped on the bed and was struggling not to laugh. Goytom tried both ends of the plastic and said, "What is this? Joke or what? Both sides are sealed. Can't we do it without this?

"No, just spread it out gently," said Beza smiling as she watched him struggling with the plastic.

At this moment, Elsa was on her way back home. She had left only to make a call from the public phone box to her new lover, Captain Zeleke, a member of the Derg. Unfortunately, her busy lover was not available now; many of the Dergue members were not as available as they once had been before coming to power. Especially Captain Zeleke, who was in charge of Palace security, was not so easily accessible. But Elsa, having his private line at hand, could reach him if he happened to be at his office.

Back at the home compound, she observed that the cars were not moved. That meant that Goytom and Beza were still at home, and the plan that she set up with her lover might have come about. She entered the living room, crossed to the rear room, and went to Beza's bedroom. Nothing. The trap had caught. She tiptoed to her bedroom. At the door, she stopped and focused on her senses of hearing.

"I don't really like this thing," she heard Goytom say and Beza laughing.

She opened the door. There she found her husband and her sister on her bed.

Elsa pretended as though she was distraught and mad about them. She played as if she wanted to tear them apart but chose not to. Without a word, she turned and hastened to the living room. In her purse was the telephone number of the captain. She fished out the paper, dashed to the telephone, and dialed the number. From the other end echoed the voice of Captain Zeleke, "What's up, sweetheart."

"I want to see you as soon as possible."

"Any problem?"

"Nothing you can't handle."

"Can't you tell me on the phone?"

"I prefer to meet you in person."

"I prefer to see you in bed."

"You will have the whole night for that."

"How about your husband?"

"We'll deal with the bastard—I think the set-up has worked. That's why I want to see you immediately."

"See you at Shebelle right away. Ciao!"

"Ciao!"

That evening Goytom Gobezay was arrested. That very day, Captain Zeleke Guetta spent the night with Elsa, at Goytom's home, in that same bed. The following morning Goytom was falsely charged with providing financial and material assistance to the Eritrean rebels and was sent to jail. After that, Captain Zeleke took up residence in Goytom's house to live with Goytom's wife.

The next day, Beza, who only acted as told by her sister, had questions.

"Did you do that for money? Or to avenge the lady?" Beza asked politely.

"Both, my little sister. I admit the money was irresistible, and I feel sorry for her as well. A man who rapes his bride and then denounces her as not-virgin is a monster; he has to be punished."

"How did you believe her?"

"I know a wounded soul when I see one. Besides, I have lived with the monster for two years. I know how he treats women. Look at Daniel's mother. After all those years, he left her without a penny. My fate would have been the same. He has sold all his properties, but I have no idea where he puts the cash. I had to act in time. So, what we did is not only for the lady but also for us."

"How about the condom? Where did you get that kind?" Beza laughed.

"That was to keep him busy so that he doesn't jump on you before I show up."

"Thanks, you came in time. Did you tell the lady that he is in jail now?"

"Yes, but she is not enough retaliated. She wants to see him dead. By the way, she has fixed your visa. You can go and get it any time."

"Oh! Thanks. What is her name?

"You don't need it. For now, we call her The Lady. She wants it that way."

Chapter 8

Daniel had just finished the morning class when Tolcha came and told him that Mr. Debella wanted to see him.

"He wants to talk to you over the meal," Tolcha said. Though he looked unhappy, he appeared proud, dressed in a beautifully cut brown khaki.

A day before, Daniel had written a letter requesting Mr. Debella to finance the children's sports club. He had been organizing the children into soccer teams. The new free-time activity with the farm children was so inspiring that Daniel practically could put the ruthless rejection of the adults out of his mind. The farm children were now his only friends. His "friend" and roommate, Kirubel, was absent most of the time and never came to his room since the conflict had occurred.

Led by Tolcha, Daniel entered the house, passed the narrow hallway, and into a carpeted room and furnished with a sofa and two armchairs around a coffee table. Placed on a bookshelf full of books along the wall were a radio and a couple of framed photographs, who appeared to be Debella's wife and daughter.

Standing in the middle of the room, Debella pointed at his daughter's photographs on the shelf and said that she was a Zemach in the province of Wollo.

"She wrote recently that the atmosphere of the Zemecha in Wollo was quite unpleasant. She was considering quitting. She might come anytime this week."

"Is it all over the country? I mean the situation of the Zemecha."

"It appears so, Daniel," Debella said, "when I was in Addis, I met some members of the Derg, old friends. I learned that the Dergue is divided in almost every political issue. Some are well aware that they have no right to sit in power and are willing to step aside. Some are too ambitious to stay in power and dictate over the people."

Debella stepped forward, leading Daniel to the dining room, "It's this division that is reflected down to the student community and the Zemecha centers."

"I can't understand those forces trying to sabotage the Zemecha," said Daniel. "This is supposed to be a program that has to go on for many years, like national service. It would provide the youth with more knowledge of the people and the country as it'd stimulate rural development."

Lunch was served—injera with Shiro-watt (a special Ethiopian sauce) and Tella, a lightly fermented barley.

"I like your idea of a sports club. How many children are involved?"

"They are children from ages 6 to 12, about 20, boys and girls. I'm in charge of the training, and I have some farmworkers helping in their free time."

"My response to your request is positive. I'll arrange the money you need. As for the playing field, we have plenty. All you have to do is choose the best, and then I'll tell the workers to level it. Don't hesitate to ask for anything when the need arises."

"Thank you, Mr. Debella."

When the meal was over, Debella led his guest to the front room, where they chatted while drinking tea. At two o'clock, Debella switched the transistor receiver on.

The radio boomed that the Dergue (Provisional Military Administrative Council) would read an announcement after the news. That was not unusual; the Dergue was known for its announcements and decrees.

The news was followed by marshal music, which gradually sank only to be overridden by the announcer's voice.

"Announcement from the Provisional Military Administrative Council!" Then followed a war song of ancient Abyssinian warriors:

"A worthless goat delivers nine kids
Merely to see that none of them survives
Finally, it too dies ..."
Daniel felt a chill go down his spine. He knew something terrible was coming up. Debella's eyes were fixed on the radio.

"The oppressed people of Ethiopia!" the announcer called out, "your revolution, as you have been following it, has been progressing at tremendous speed, gaining new achievements and more victories. In turn, the victories revealed new vicious enemies who had pretended to be your friends. . ."

"…This time, your enemy is an organization that disguised itself behind a beautiful name - the Ethiopian People's Revolutionary Party, the EPRP…"

"… This gang of anarchists and petty-bourgeois has caused you and the revolution more damage than any of your other enemies put together."

Now it was clear to everyone who was referred to as ANARCHIST. It was not long since the pro-Dergue Socialists baptized the EPRP by this name

The radio announcer went on piling on accusations against the EPRP, ranging from causing public rebellion and an increase in commodity prices to strikes by workers, the spread of prostitution, and the fall in agricultural production. The worsening of living standards of workers and a host of other problems were presented as the work of the EPRP. It went on portraying the party as a CIA agent, anti-people, and anti-revolution. No insult was deemed unworthy, and no accusation was left unsaid. [1]

"We have been extraordinarily patient, with this group. We were expecting maturity and reason from them, but this, unfortunately, was interpreted as weakness and fear on our part. They dared even commit crimes as vicious as murder. Recently, its members killed a militant student by throwing him from the top of a school building, killed a security officer on a line of duty, and wounded two farmworkers in a shootout…"

"The law is obliged to take appropriate action… for every single revolutionary they kill, we shall retaliate by killing them in thousands."

It was announced that twenty-three counter-revolutionaries, having been found guilty as charged, were executed. The names of the dead were read. According to the announcement, most of them were from wealthy families or sons of the former regime's dignitaries.

Finally, the war-song came, spreading a wave of shock and anguish.

Debella rose slowly and switched the radio off with a controlled anger and disappointment. Tolcha, who had been listening from the dining room, disappeared into the backroom to be by himself as he probably wept with nobody watching him. Daniel held his head with both hands in disbelief and grief. He buried his face between his thighs: among the twenty-three were Kebedde, a Zemach colleague, and Bezabih Mazengia, who had been his teacher in Addis and his leader here in Inango Zemecha center.

For Daniel, the announcement was a lie in its entirety. He knew his teacher too well to believe a single word of the Derg's accusation. Unlike the "information" in the indictment, Daniel knew that Bezabih came from an impoverished family, a family so poor that it, at times, had had to beg for a piece of bread to survive a day, a family that expected charity from the so-called working class itself. Beggars of a poor nation, a neglected class even Karl Marx himself might not have heard of. But Bezabih was intelligent and hardworking. He had gone to school against all the odds, completed his education, and became a teacher. He had a militant history of active participation in the Ethiopian student movement for democracy. He was kind, friendly, and never seemed to forget his past, for he always told his students about it. He was not ashamed of his ugly poverty, like many would be, but proud of his victory over it.

As Daniel thought of Kebedde and Bezabih, he felt the food he ate move in his stomach.

"Do you know any of them?" asked Mr. Debella in a low voice.

"Yes. I know two of the executed. Kebedde was a university student, and Bezabih was a leading staff member in the Inango Zemecha center. He was my teacher in grade ten. To me, he was just like a friend, a man of great ambition, and an example of successes for many." Tears crossed Daniel's face and dropped on his shirt.

An hour later, when Daniel was standing on the porch about to leave Debella's place, a car entered the farm compound, speeding up the gravel way, and pulled right before Debella's house. Daniel watched the man, who climbed out of the car and rushed toward him.

"Hi, Chief. What's the hurry," called Daniel, extending a hand in informal greeting

The Zemecha center Chief greeted Mr. Debella and Tolcha, who stood right behind Daniel. He said to Daniel, "I have got to take you out of here right now. They are going to kill you."

"Who? What are you talking about?"

"The Zemachs assume you are responsible for the death of Kebedde. They are after you now. There was terrible fighting right after the announcement of the execution."

Hearing this, Mr. Debella stepped forward and requested the chief to come into the house.

"Who is fighting who?" asked Mr. Debella, as all took seats except Tolcha, who stood in the hallway between the dining and the front rooms, listening.

"Over the months, The Zemachs have been divided into two main groups - one supporting the military government, the other opposing it…"

Daniel was well aware of these divisions and their effect on the work of the Zemecha. Since some political publications were distributed in the farm, he was able to form an opinion on the recent developments. DEMOCRACIA- the main EPRP pamphlet - and The Voice of The People - 'the

Socialist's' - leaflet were distributed and read across the country. Daniel used to read them, although not often. But he still had difficulty determining their differences since they had almost identical political programs and ideological doctrines.

The chief went on, "some stood with the Socialist Party, but the majority supported the EPRP."

"How bad is the fighting?" asked Debella again.

"Many are injured," the chief said. "It is the most horrible scene I have witnessed in my life as a teacher. Now the police have calmed it, but the Zemachs are looking for Daniel. I have got to take him to a safe place."

"He is safe here," Mr. Debella said, "but what has he done to cause such anger."

"I don't know what Daniel has done, but I swear they will kill him if they find him. The Zemachs who are out there looking for Daniel are not the same guys I once knew..."

Debella's gaze moved from the chief to Daniel. "What is it, Daniel? Can you tell us?

It was now that Tolcha cleared his throat and stepped forward. But before he opened his mouth, a knock came on the door. He walked across the room and opened the door, revealing the farm guard who appeared as though he had seen the devil.

The guard stared at Daniel first and then hastily back to Debella, "Sir, a mob of angry Zemachs are trying to storm the farm. We have managed to block them, but I suggest the police better be called."

Mr. Debella heaved himself from the seat. "No one ever set foot on my property without my permission. I'll see who they are," he muttered, and turning to Daniel, he said, "You stay here with the chief. I will handle this. He left the house, Tolcha and the guard following him.

In the house, Daniel and the chief remained quiet for a moment until Daniel broke the silence.

"How bad was the fighting? Are many injured? inquired Daniel.

"Thanks God, not life threatening," The chief sighed raising his hands high indicating Divine intervention to save lives. "Three were sent for medical treatment. The announcement will have undesired repercussions,"

"It is devastating! No one ever anticipated that the Dergue would declare war on EPRP. I hope it won't spread all over the country."

"It will, soon."

"I can't imagine the aftermath, this time it's going to be real rev0lution, a bloody one" said Daniel with concern.

"Hostility is building up," the chief said, now calmer that before. "New fighting can easily flare-up. The Zemecha work cannot proceed under such circumstances. We must close. We cannot go on like this."

"We ought not to give up so easily. This Zemach could really make much difference in many aspects. I can imagine what the long-term benefit could be in unifying the unsteady nation specially after the downfall of a thousand-year dynasty."

"I agree with you. It was the monarchy and the church that held this nation of many tribes and religions together for almost half a century peacefully. Now both these pillars are demolished. Communists have taken over everything. The Zemecha itself is invaded and divided by these elements. What makes the matter worse is that they themselves are not one. One is Bolshevik, the other is Menshevik. One quotes from Mao Zedong, the other reads from Josef Stalin, and then they fight furiously on terminologies and definitions like deadly enemies. They agree in one thing."

Daniel pointed his attention, "What?"

"They all agree in destroying our past. Our past history," said the chief, "according to them, has no good at all. Every ruler was an oppressor. Every religion, is an instrument of oppression. And about God, they say, Man created God." The chief laughed and added, "Women created the angels." The chief laughed again, paused briefly and assuming a concerned looks continued." They are crazy but at the same time they are real threat. And there is nothing we can do about that; we have lost the battle. Daniel."

"We may have lost the battle, sir, but the war is just beginning."

"What's in your mind?"

"Let's save the Zemecha first. If the Zemecha fail and the Zemachs disband, they will fall prey in the hands of the Commies. They will use them for their political agendas. They will put their lives at risk. So, let's try to maintain peace among the Zemachs and go on. Mr. Debella will sure help. The Zemachs respect him, and they will listen to him."

When Mr. Debella returned, they had no reason to ask him to talk to the Zemachs. He had already decided to speak to them the following morning in the presence of all the Zemachs and the staff.

In the capital, Ermias and Jovani were sitting in Bar Tiku, discussing their organization's intelligence activity. The radio was not on, so they heard nothing of the announcement. They had their priority: Information gathering. Ermias' spies were spread over the government institutions and communication organs of the State, but he was not satisfied yet with the network. Up in the structure of the government, he saw a large hole that had to be filled. There was no information coming from the office of the Dergue or its prominent members. He had tried almost everything to place a spy somewhere close to the Derg, but it proved very difficult. He had people within the army, but they were very far from the Derg. He needed someone in the decision-making body, inside the Dergue itself, someone reliable, who might have a little personal ambition or dissatisfaction with the Derg. And that seemed more impossible than challenging, but he had to find a means. Otherwise, the spy network won't be complete.

Just at a quarter past two, they left the bar, walked out, and found themselves on the main street where two military trucks were parked; around them stood a few watchful soldiers. No pedestrian dared go near them. They skirted the vicinity of the trucks as if an invisible force kept them from going close. Men walked faster; their countenances turned away the soldiers lest they be shoved into the trucks too.

Ermias observed some homeless young men being herded into the truck. The other truck was already full of scared-looking young men.

"There is something fishy going on," Ermias whispered to Jovani, who was not so attentive. "I am beginning to smell it. What could it be? You see, the network is not complete."

"Maybe they are taking the unemployed to the farm areas like they used to do before when unemployed people overcrowd the city," replied Jovani, playing it down.

"They have sent sixty thousand students to the countryside with whom they have enough problems. I don't think so, Jovani. We better find out."

Just as they were about to walk away, a soldier approached and stopped them.

"Identifications, please?"

Ermias reached his pocket, produced his wallet, and held out his ID. The soldier took it carelessly and looked at it without paying much attention. When he returned the ID, Ermias was fast enough to pass a ten Birr note to the soldier. The soldier looked at the note, revived, and was ready for almost any order to come.

"What is going on? Where are you taking these young men?" asked Ermias calmly.

"I don't know, sir. I heard they would be enlisted in the army… I don't know."

For Ermias, it was a Thousand-Birr information. It was clear that some military preparations were going on, but the details were needed. And details could only be found from a very high position in the government.

The soldier turned away, smiling shyly without bothering Jovani for identification, but a moment later, he turned. Ermias and Jovani had already climbed into the gray Toyota and were moving. The soldier quickly looked at the plate number and jotted it in his notebook.

Half an hour later, right after the Derg's announcement of execution was aired, Ermias arrived at Abinet's residence. It had been quite a time since he had seen his aunt. She had an unexpected guest sitting before her at the rear room's far side: her former husband, Goytom Gobezay.

Ermias was surprised to see him. "My God! You are free. Nice to see you," he said, embracing him. Goytom had lost considerable weight. The full beard has sunken cheeks and barely made room for his ashen and chapped lips. He had on a brown cotton jacket that looked over-sized, his lean frame swimming in the bulkiness of the jacket. Ermias couldn't lift his eyes from him for quite a while.

Driven by a sense of sheer jealousy, Captain Zeleke had decided to slaughter him right after the Beza scandal. It was Elsa's determined effort to spare his life that rescued him. However, there wasn't much left of Goytom. Zeleke had fixed Goytom and Elsa's formal divorce and kept the lion's share of the property. Sitting behind bars, Goytom had been told that the rest of his property was confiscated to pay his debts. Finally, just before he was released, Goytom was told not to reclaim any of his properties, not to be seen near Elsa or Beza, and not to collaborate with the Eritrea liberation movement with which he had no connection at all. Certainly, Zeleke was very much aware of that, but to make the message clearer, that had to be added.

Goytom had just come directly from prison. He had nowhere to go but to his old home. Abinet, though hesitant, did not turn him down. Seeing him so broken and run-down, she had made him feel comfortable, making sure that he would not mistake her hospitality for a change of heart. Goytom was not so stupid as to have any incorrect expectations, either. Right after he had been served whatever was available, the terrible announcement had come on the radio. It was then that he thanked God sincerely for setting him free and alive at this dreadful time when young men had to be executed for minor crimes.

"Why did they lock you up? Did they get anything incriminating?" asked Ermias staring vacantly before him in a manner that showed little real interest in the issue.

"What could they find on me!? It was just a pretext to confiscate my property and my wife. Don't you see he is living with my wife in my own house? That's why he jailed me."

"Who is he?"

"That fascist! The Derg's captain."

"What is his name?"

"What do they call him, wait ah … yeah, Zeleke something. Yes, Captain Zeleke Guetta. Someday I'll make him pay for all he did to me."

Goytom rose and stretched himself to leave. He smoothed his shrunken trousers and crossed the room to the front door. Then he made a sudden turn at the door, and his eyes scanned the passage leading to the bedroom. To the left, the wall contained a door leading to the dining room. Goytom stepped into it, watched its wall and ceiling, and walked out.

Abinet was following behind him as he went around the house, inspecting it thoroughly. The three-room house he built 15 years ago had never seen reparation; the walls were weather-beaten, and the chalk beneath eroded. Yet it looked satisfactory with the large lawn around it, surrounded by a wooden fence. The doorway with a double door and a window beside it appeared neat, and the wooden structures stood firm. Goytom narrowed his eyes, contemplating its value. It was quite an asset to own at this particular time when inflation had hit a record 40 percent.

A few minutes later, he left without even saying thanks or good-bye.

"I'm afraid his visit is ill-meant," Abinet said to Ermias. "The way he surveyed the house…"

"What harm can he inflict now? I think they have bumped him enough not to cause any problem to anyone," said

Ermias, and quietly he added, "Does the man…the captain… live with Elsa now?"

"Yes, he is living with her."

"What about the girl?"

"You mean Beza? Yes, she too lives with them."

Ermias' mind was suddenly thinking on a professional track, but he stopped it immediately because he hated to involve his relatives in his orbit. "How about Daniel?" he said, shifting the subject

"He is okay. His letters come every other week. I don't have any problems with him. My problem is the other one."

Ermias knew that she meant Kibrom. "If I could only find him just once…"

"Where can you find him? Nobody knows where he goes, what he does, or who he meets. He comes any time unexpectedly, changes his clothes, and disappears for weeks. Isn't that outrageous!"

Shortly after 3, Ermias left.

From the moment he heard that Captain Zeleke was living with Elsa in Goytom's house, his devious mind was restlessly searching for any link that would connect him to the captain. Zeleke was one of the top Dergue members, a key figure in the Derg, and very close to Mengistu, the vice-chairman of the Derg. If I could get to Captain Zeleke somehow, the Network would certainly be completed. Ermias thought.

He drove by Elsa's residence, and he observed three cars parked in the compound. The green Peugeot 504, which was State property, must be Zeleke's, Ermias guessed, and made a mental note of the plate number. When he passed the Shimeis School, he slowed his car and wrote down the figures. Then he sped west, heading to the Nyala Transport Company, which now belonged to his organization. At the gate, he found Biniam chatting with a young man. He pulled the car and parked it alongside the gate.

He strode to them and threw a hand to the stranger.

"Gaushaw is the name," the young man introduced himself as Ermias stared at him with narrowing eyes trying to recall the familiar face.

"Don't you two remember each other? He is Gaushaw, Samson's friend. And he is Ermias, our cousin," Biniam helped their memories, and the two embraced as they recognized each other.

"He has been in the Ogaden," Biniam added.

"Soldiering? What are you doing in Addis? Transfer?" Ermias asked humbly, hoping to create a belief that he had asked it merely to say something.

"It's a whole bunch of armies moving, probably to the north. We will know soon," answered Gaushaw frankly.

Ermias didn't want to ask any further. It was vital information that indicated troop movement to Eritrea. He turned to Biniam, held his elbow, and said, "Excuse me, Gaushaw. I'd like to have a word with him." He pushed Biniam a few steps away and said, "Biniam, Tiku wants to hire a clerk for this company, and I have suggested that Beza be employed back. Can you ask her if she is interested?"

Biniam appeared puzzled. If Tiku wanted to hire someone, he has his ways. He had met Tiku in the morning, and he had not mentioned this.

"Yes, I can ask her," said Biniam, "As a matter of fact, she was around looking for me today. I was not here; I'll tell her."

"Please do. See you, you two." Ermias went back to his car and drove north.

"OK, what were we talking about?" asked Gaushaw, resuming the chat they had before Ermias came. "How is my friend, Samson?"

"We have found out that he is with the rebels in Eritrea. He is said to be alive so far." Biniam didn't mind telling the soldier about a rebel in the family, for he considered Gaushaw as one member of the family and believed he could count on his silence.

Gaushaw nodded gently, "I always thought that he might, somehow, make it to Europe or the States. He was not a man of the gun. He hated to see blood or wounds. When I decided to join the army, he was strongly against it and persuasively advised me not to. He tried whatever he could to make me change my mind: he applied to various jobs in my name, even tried to fix me a job in this company, but it didn't work out. Finally, he begged me to quit. He never liked the killing profession; neither did I, but I had to. After my father fell ill, our family had no means of income. We could barely make it for a day. Mother had become desperate. I was left with no choice except to quit school and join the army—the only job around at that time. But now you tell me, Samson is in it too. It's sad that our fate had to be guns."

Gaushaw talked about the childhood times of joy, innocence, and adventure. "From Kera down to Mekanisa far to Furi," he said, pointing south. "We roamed the lanes, explored the woods. All those areas were under our control. Nobody ever touched us when we went down to the farms to eat cherries, strawberries, and grapes and take home as much as we could carry. The farmers never complained. They loved us. In those times, people were kinder, and places were greener. Now, it's all memory." Gaushaw's eyes focused on Biniam and the present.

"Yes, the good old days! I hear people always talk positively about the past. Maybe, in the future, we will have some good things to tell of these days too."

Gaushaw smiled on the irony, thinking of the announcement of the execution an hour ago.

"Yes. Of course, there is a lot to tell of these days." Gaushaw tilted his head briefly and stared at Biniam with a peculiar smile that Biniam indeed could not mistake for anything close to a smile. "I hate to serve a lie, lying for liars. It's all a lie. I wonder if I have got to die or kill for a lie!"

After a moment of silence, Biniam asked if Gaushaw would go to Gimbie to see his sister, Ghenet.

"No, I wish I could. I miss her very much. But I can't. I'm supposed to report every day because orders can be issued at any time. Nobody knows when or where we would move—damned top secret! I have got to go now; my regards to your mother. Tell her that I'll drop by to see her before I leave."

The next day in the morning, Ermias and Jovani came, and they heard from Biniam that Beza had rejected the job.

"Why? I thought everybody wants a job these days," Ermias said in disbelief.

"There are plenty who need a job—this kind of job," said Biniam suspiciously. "Why her?"

"She had the experience. That's why," replied Ermias.

"She wants to sell her car and leave the country."

"She wants to sell her car? Good. Tell her, I'll buy it," said Jovani in a more serious manner than Biniam had ever known him to assume, which made Biniam more suspicious than before.

"Okay," shrugged Biniam, watching them out of the corner of his eye. "I'll tell her that too."

"She can call me on this number." Jovani produced a paper and held it out to Biniam. "Call her as soon as you can."

"I'll do that."

Right at this moment, in Inango, Daniel was watching the huge audience that had come to receive Mr. Debella in the Zemecha compound. Standing on the elevated platform, he wondered about the response Debella was able to draw. Word had spread that Debella would come to speak, so apart from the Zemachs, farmworkers and many of their children and passersby had come and filled the compound. Farmers from the surrounding area, who were enrolled for some military training, had also come to hear what Debella had to say. Even ragged, skinny people, who had come from the drought-hit regions and settled in the outskirts of Inango village, had made their way to the compound. For them, the Zemachs were angels of God as they were helping them in their resettlement. Daniel was taken by surprise when he saw them. Their presence was beyond his expectation, and the misery he saw on their faces was terrifying; hopelessness and desolation had overtaken them. Yet, they showed up to find some explanation for their suffering. He hoped Debella would give them some answers, and hope to endure the next day.

The Zemachs, on the other hand, appeared unforgiving. They were staring threateningly at him. A small unit of four or five police officers stood nearby, watching them. Daniel did not count on the police though they carried rifles; on the contrary, his real guards were those skinny farm children. They had come to defend him from any conceivable harm. They stood on guard at the front row, holding hand in hand as though to make a fence. Daniel looked at them and smiled.

A step before him was Mr. Debella facing the crowd. Next to Debella stood Tolcha and the Chief of the Zemecha. Mr. Debella cleared his throat seeking attention. As he moved a step forward, Daniel cast a sidelong glance and sensed the aura of dignity about the man.

Tall and broad-shouldered, Mr. Debella was a man known for his straightforward critics against any wrongdoer, be he an individual or a government. He was put under regional confinement because he had criticized the Monocratic administration's disregard of justice. But his voice was not confined; it rather echoed louder than ever since he had come to Inango some four years ago.

"As you see," Mr. Debella began, "I have come here with Daniel, one of your friends, and Tolcha Ragasa, one of my workers because I have to reveal to you an amazing mystery from which we all shall learn what humanity and kindness mean in the real sense."

"No forgiving, Sir. We won't forgive or forget what Daniel did!" someone said from far behind, where some newcomers were pushing through the crowd to come closer. Daniel looked at the newcomers and identified them as Zemachs from Gimbie. Briefly, he thought of Ghenet. He wished she was here to hear the truth from Debella himself.

"Wait a minute," Mr. Debella said calmly, scanning the crowd before him "I'll come to that, but before that, I want to tell you what I thought as I watched the crowd build-up. I was taken aback by a scene I had witnessed during the famine in the province of Wollo, just four years ago.

"The road between Addis and Dessie was lined with starving people, hundreds of them, begging for a bowl of grain, a scrap of cloth, pleading for their lives. I stopped at many villages on my way to investigate the famine. I saw horrible things wherever I stopped. Every village was full of suffering and death. Everywhere I saw people carrying corpses, digging graves, grieving, wailing, and praying. Wherever I stopped, hundreds of them rushed to my cars, pressing up against the glass, faces twisted with the pain of hunger, crying for help. It was like being in hell with swarms of the damned shrieking in pain, imploring me for relief from the torments. Yet, there was nothing I could do to alleviate their suffering. It was very difficult to take, especially when I had eaten well that morning.

"People who had not eaten for days, very weak and deathly ill, were climbing the mountains in an endless, winding stream of suffering. As my cars passed them, I saw their strength failing; I saw them collapse and die before my eyes, their lives slipping away where they dropped. I saw the terrible agony of people forced to choose between leaving behind their dying wives, husbands, or children and staying to die with them. Nothing can describe that anguish.

"There was nowhere to turn, nowhere to look. Each scene seemed more heart-wrenching, more frightening than the one before. The image that haunts me to this day is that of a young mother with three dead children around her, and at her empty breast; her face convulsed in anguish, rocking back and forth, tears streaming down her face, murmuring in a voice so weak that it was barely audible: "Please God, let me die and join my children …, please let me die…" [II]

"There is nothing as painful as to see your child starve to death. Can you imagine now the pain of that mother?" Mr. Debella paused and surveyed the Zemachs, and then he said, "That mother is this motherland, and those children are its people, and the question is what would you do to help her! Fight one another? I believe that is not what your poor mother expects from you. Seeing you, you, the one last hope left, destroy each other would hurt her far more than the natural catastrophe she endured."

Again, he paused briefly and said, "Yesterday, some of you Zemachs came to my farm to kill Daniel, a young man I came to admire not only for his benevolence but also for his depth of character. I understand you have a reason to be infuriated. But your methods are unethical, and your judgment of your friend Daniel is wrong."

As Debella said this, Daniel observed many Zemachs murmuring, not in protest but in a sort of disbelief.

"You have been gravely mistaken about him." Debella went on. "He was not the one who informed the police.

The Zemachs were listening attentively with their eyes wide open and mouths gaping as Debella told the truth of the mystery that had led to the arrest of Kebedde.

"…Daniel has been carrying another man's sin and has endured the consequences. He was unfairly accused of betraying his friends and paying dearly for that. Here comes the man Daniel has been protecting for so long at the cost of his name, at the loss of his friends, and at the risk of his life." Debella turned to Tolcha and encouraged him to step forward.

Tolcha stood erect, his hands shaking and his lips trembling. He stared at Daniel for what seemed a long time before he turned to the public.

"I know how sorry you are for what has happened to Kebedde. Kebedde was my friend too. He taught me my rights, and helped me restore my self-confidence. Suppose anyone of you asks me why I informed on him. Here is my answer: I informed on him not because I disliked him but because he went off the rails and began disgracing the holy bible and God.

"I may not frequent the church, but as a son of a priest, I have a great fear of God and respect for the holy book from which our religion originated. I'm not educated as most of you are. Six months ago, I had no idea how the letters of our Alphabet looked."

"I had no intention to harm Kebedde or anyone when I went to the police. I thought they would only stop him from spreading evil," Tolcha's mouth went sidewise, his lips trembled, and tears began running. Mr. Debella held on to his elbow and showed him to the side.

"You heard the truth," Mr. Debella said. "You heard the cause. There may be some misunderstanding, but I fail to see any crime here…"

Debella continued speaking about peace and love for some time. His speech was filled with mounting idealism, references to history, and pleasant dreams for the future. When he finished, the Zemachs were so moved that many of them began hugging each other, with tears on their eyes. Then one of the Zemachs from Gimbie approached Daniel and asked him for forgiveness. Daniel accepted the apology and gave the young man a hug.

Next came Kirubel and said, "It's all my mistake. I should have known better. I owe you an apology, Daniel." Daniel just stared at him shaking his head. At this moment, the children burst into applause, cheering Daniel's name again and again. Daniel flashed a big smile at the children and hugged Kirubel. When they parted, Kirubeal's eyes fell on the ground as Daniel's surveyed the public, shining like a star.

The other Zemachs came one by one and shook hands with Daniel as the children cheered and sang, praising their hero. It would have been the most significant moment of happiness for Daniel had Ghenet been around to rejoice with him. All these hands shaking him could never add up to make the soft touch of Ghenet's fingers. He was pleased by the salutation of the Zemachs who had once turned their back on him, but his heart had not rested its quest for the girl who had once reigned in it.

Ghenet was not around, not nearby, not in Gimbie. She had left for the capital with most of the Zemachs in Gimbie. In Gimbie, Daniel learned later; almost everyone had abandoned the Zemecha, after setting the compound afire, in a show of protest against the execution. Now he could only reach her by mail. And that would take weeks.

Chapter 9

The weeks following the execution showed distinct changes in the conduct of the people. The student community was infuriated by the government action, and the general public horror-struck. Many Zemecha stations were abandoned in protest against the Derg's injustice. The government's move was aimed at teaching a lesson, from which any opposition might learn not to play with fire. It was meant to terrify the living. The iron fist of the State had to be felt. It did not work; instead, it incited the youth to line up with the EPRP, and the EPRP to strike back in retribution.

EPRP staged an intensive inquiry to find out those responsible for killing its members. Promptly its supporters inside the Dergue revealed that Major Mengistu and Dr. Menkir, a scholar who was believed to have taught the Dergue Socialism, were the ones to account for the execution. Mengistu, it was found, had called the Dergue members for a quick meeting on the pretext of discussing serious state affairs. He then presented the executed as counter-revolutionaries and criminals who deserve to be punished—no charges in the legal sense, no lawyers, and no counter-arguments. The accused were not present. Mengistu just read a list of charges against the twenty-three. Dr. Menkir explained the motive and the damage inflicted, and both demanded the death sentence. A vote was taken—45 voted for and 40 against execution. The accused, some of them lifeless from torture, were thus executed; among them, a fourteen years old boy named Babile Haile Selassie.[*] (Not related to the royal family.)

Based on that information, the executive committee of the EPRP decided to pay back in kind—an eye for an eye. Right after the decision was made, the party dispatched a hit squad of seven men to kill Mengistu and Dr. Menkir Alemu.

Ermias and Jovani were sitting at the Post Rendezvous discussing current affairs and other intelligence-gathering issues. Having come first, Ermias had been sitting on the outdoor seats facing the Black Lion Hospital, observing the slogans painted on the wall.

> *Death to the collaborators!*
> *The Dergue shall be destroyed!*
> *We shall avenge our Comrades!*
> *EPRP shall overcome!*

Ermias had seen EPRP slogans before, painted on every place available in the city, but none were as violently tuned as these. They indicated that the party method of resistance had entered into a new phase.

"What are they up to?" whispered Ermias.

"They are out to avenge their compatriots. I heard a killer squad is dispatched to liquidate Mengistu," replied Jovani in a low voice.

Ermias was startled. Though killing was a day-to-day fact in his profession, he had a strong aversion toward the act of cold-blooded killing. To him, it counted as committing murder. It could be from the fact that his father was murdered in cold blood that he still felt traumatized when someone's life was to be taken away.

"Are they not bluffing?"

"Not after the execution," Jovani said. "If they take out Mengistu—with their support in the Derg, they can come to power."

"Eliminating one man doesn't change much."

"What's EPRP's policy toward Eritrea?" asked Jovani

---

[*] Babile is not related to the royal family.

"They don't have a clear stand on the Eritrean question. But they are far better than this military junta, I assume." Ermias didn't want to continue discussing the subject. "What will happen is already in its way. Now tell me about Beza. Have you succeeded?

"Yes! I can say I have."

Jovani said that Beza had called him on Monday. The next day they met at the Shebelle, drank tea, and talked about her car. Without bargaining, he had agreed to buy it. Ownership transfer and payments were made the day after. The same day he had taken her to dinner, where they chatted about almost everything. On the third day, she had been even more open, telling him about her life and plans to leave the country.

"I asked her if she could work for me as a detective. She was indifferent at first, because she thought I was joking. But when she knew I was serious, she said she would consider, as long as the job was less risky and paid fair."

"Did you tell her that she would be spying on Zeleke?"

"No, I did not. I need to be very sure first. I will spy more on her before I ask her to spy for us… got to find out her relation with the captain," said Jovani. "I'll meet her later today. I have learned that she is an honest girl. To start with, I 'll tell her that I work for an American news agency. And that I only need news materials."

Ermias nodded, his attention now drawn towards the traffic in the street. A white Volkswagen zigzagging between cars at high speed as though not to be delayed by the traffic pack. When the vehicle passed abreast of him, he had a side view of the face behind the wheel. The distance was too far to capture the picture of the face to be instantly identified, but as the image replayed in his mind, he straightened himself: the face he had seen was none other than his cousin, Kibrom's.

"Crazy!" he muttered for himself.

Not long after, Jovani peered at his watch that indicted five to three. He seemed to be restless as his appointment with

Beza came closer. "I have got to go," he said and excused himself to leave. Ermias rose with him and walked to his car.

Driving south on Churchill Road, Ermias slowed before he went into the intersection. He watched vehicles behind him through the rearview mirror before pulling the car to a full stop at the intersection to let the traffic on the left proceed. In front of him, a black limousine that came from the left circled the square and headed south. Three cars behind the limo came a shabby Fiat, which headed west to Ras Makonnen Street. Right after the Fiat, Ermias rolled his Toyota and turned right in the same direction.

A moment later, a white Volkswagen emerged behind him. Ermias watched it drifting to the overrunning lane, Kibrom behind the wheel, now a large sunglass on his face, and a young man next to him. He wanted to wave a hand, but Kibrom was looking straightforward. He touched the horn briefly, but Kibrom's attention was fixed elsewhere.

At the Sengaterra intersection, the traffic light changed from green to yellow. Ahead of Ermias, the Fiat accelerated to beat the light that changed red, so it stopped—the white Volkswagen by its side on the other lane. Suddenly homeless children stormed the street and scattered around the cars to beg for pennies. A couple of kids came to Ermias. Curiously none went to the tattered Fiat.

Ermias searched his pockets for coins. While he was offering coins to the kids, he heard two shots that jolted him from his seat and made him stare before him. A young man with a gun in his hand stood beside the fiat.

"My God!" Ermias said in disbelief. The gunman turned the gun in every direction and ran back to the Volkswagen, shoving the children aside. Before he entered the car, he pointed the gun at random menacingly—A-Mind-your-own-business warning to everybody who might dare to follow him.

The lights turned green, but the man in the shabby Fiat did not move. The killer jumped into the Volkswagen, and in seconds, the car was launched to top speed and disappeared into the traffic.

Nothing of this sort had ever happened in the city of Addis Ababa. Shooting a man in broad daylight in the middle of the city was an act people watch in the movies or something they heard happened on the other side of the globe. Some assumed at first that a tire had gone off or a faulty engine had misfired. But when the kids cried in horror, a curious crowd began to build around the Fiat.

Ermias didn't want to be drawn. He knew this was a political killing. He had discussed with Jovani that EPRP out for vengence. He rolled his car from the rear of the Fiat, and as he went past the car, he got a glimpse of the victim behind the shattered glass; the head was blown out and face covered in blood.

He drove the same direction Kibrom took. He was hit by an alarming thought: Kibrom's engagement in subversive activities and the possible peril that could befall the family. He knew how the security forces worked. If one family member were a suspect, the others, especially the young ones, would also suffer interrogation and torture. Kibrom must be told to leave town. Half an hour later, he found the white Volkswagen abandoned on the roadside at Lideta neighborhood, not a mile from the crime scene.

At this moment, in Inango, a similar crime was about to take place. Disguised as a farmworker, a gunman had entered the farm and had been looking for Tolcha. Daniel, who was scheduled to leave for the capital tomorrow, roamed around the farm, biding goodbye to everyone.

Lastly, Daniel went to meet Tolcha. Tolcha lived in one of the service rooms in the farm with his son. When Daniel came closer to Tolcha's residence, he smelled the aroma of roasting meat and wood smoke. Tolcha was having outdoor meal with his son and the neighbors. That was what the farm workers used to do on Fridays.

"You came at the right time before we finished," said Tolcha as he saw Daniel approaching.

"This outdoor feast is what I will always miss," said Daniel as he sat on a Borchuma, a three-legged stool made up of a wood root. A few meters away were children who, having eaten their share, began playing loudly despite their mothers hushing them.

As Daniel was served, Tolcha called his son and instructed him to bring an aerogram from home. Tolcha's son did not wait until his father finished, he just fled like a rabbit and came back with the mail in a couple of minutes

"This came today, Daniel" said Tolcha handing over the mail to Daniel.

Daniel had been expecting a letter from Ghenet but this was from his brother Biniam. He stuffed the Aerogram in his pocket and attended his meal—superbly steaked beef, onion, tomato, green pepper with homemade bread. Daniel loved the farm food, as they were always fresh, hot and tasty. He was also served a big glass of Tella.

Half an hour later, Daniel stood up to bid his farm friends goodbye. Tolcha knew this was a time of separation and raised himself.

Daniel scanned all and cleared his throat, "Today is the last day; I am living tomorrow. So, I want to say few things now.

"I stand before you with a lot of emotion, similar to those I had the first day I entered this farm. I loved the people and the place from that day. Over the months I had come to call this place a home. These ten months seem like such a long journey and you wake up one day and realize that suddenly, it's all over. You have been kind to me and my friend, Kirubel. You gave us not only your food and shelter, but also love, hope and protection.

"We might not meet again for ever, but I will never forget you. Thank you."

Tolcha had no words; he was overwhelmed by emotion. He stepped forward and hugged Daniel firmly. The others came one after the other and hugged him goodbye.

On his way to the other workers, Daniel spotted a nervous young man he vaguely knew to be a Zemach from Gimbie Station. "Hi, brother, what're you looking for," Daniel called.

Without turning, the young man strode forward as if he had not heard a word. Daniel studied the man from behind and felt uneasy as he thought of the bulge on the man's waist side.

"Hi, you!" Daniel called again. The young man stopped, stared briefly at Daniel, and then continued in the direction of Tolcha's residence. He was as tall as Daniel but looked more youthful, not older than eighteen. The EPRP seemed to earn greater obedience among the very young ones.

"Just a minute," Daniel approached him with long strides, "I want to talk to you. I think I have seen you before. You are a Zemach in Gimbie. Gimbie has closed. What are you doing here?'

"I don't have time to talk," the young man said nervously, looking right and left. "I have got a message to deliver urgently."

"To whom? To Mr. Debella? He is not at home."

"Not to Mr. Debella."

"Who else then?"

"Look, it's none of your business, and I don't have to answer your questions," the young man said and turned away from Daniel.

"You don't have the right to be in the compound without permission, and you don't look like you are up to something good."

The young man turned around and barked at Daniel. "You don't seem to read our leaflets, man. Anyone obstructing the work of the EPRP would be severely punished. Haven't you heard?"

"What work has the EPRP told you to do here?"

"You will find out soon. Now mind only your business."

Daniel looked at the young man's eyes but could not tell what he saw in them. There was a mixture of fear and loyalty in them.

"You are here to kill Tolcha," Daniel said almost in a whisper.

"I said, mind your business!"

Daniel relapsed into silence, his body now shivering. The young man turned and walked. Daniel could see his steps were unsteady, revealing uncertainty.

"May I ask you just one question?" Daniel said in a voice that could not go beyond the distance between them. The young man stopped, and Daniel came closer. "Did you join the Zemecha to kill poor people?"

"No, but my party believes that traitors should be punished whether they are poor or rich."

"Party? Party is not a human being. Party doesn't have a heart or a brain but you do. Use your brain; did you come here to kill people?"

"I believe my party stands for the good of the people."

"Have you ever killed before, young man?"

"No, I have not."

"You want to see what it's like?"

"What do you mean?"

"I want to show you what it's like before you commit one."

The young man appeared curious. "What are you talking about?"

"Come and see for yourself what taking a life is like. It will prepare you for your mission."

The young man weighed Daniel's proposal and said, "what's in your mind?"

"Come on. It's an experience you need."

"Don't try to be smart," the young man warned, showing the butt of the revolver he carried under his waist.

"Don't worry. I won't take the risk. Follow me." Daniel took the lead. The young man followed anxiously.

On the other side of the farm, down the waterway running across the field, past the large barn were thick bushes. Not far away in the bushes, there was a white rabbit which Daniel had tamed some time ago. Its baby was jumping around.

"Last week," Daniel said, "I stepped on a newly hatched chicken accidentally and crashed it to the ground. I still feel bad about it. Now I want you to kill that mother rabbit and experience the feeling."

"Why should I kill it? I have nothing against it."

"You kill it, or else I'll crash its head before your eyes so that you can see how it suffers."

"You must be crazy," said the young man as Daniel went into the bush and picked the mother rabbit. The child rabbit gave out a piercing sound and retreated. Then it stood in alert as if to defend itself. When Daniel stepped out of the bush, the little one followed behind him—determined to follow wherever he took her mother.

The young man watched the scene inquisitively. "What the hell are you trying to prove?"

"I'm going to crush its head before your eyes, and you will see little one going crazy." Daniel stooped to put the rabbit under his foot.

"I won't let you do that," the young man rushed at Daniel and shoved him. Daniel lost balance and fell, letting the rabbit lose. Both watched the mother and the little one running back into the bushes.

Daniel rose, dusted his trousers, rubbed his hand, and said, "Tolcha has a five-year-old motherless child. Now you can go and kill him in front of his son if you can live haunted by a parentless child for the rest of your life."

Thoughtfully the young man stared at Daniel, and then his eyes fell on the ground for a moment. When Daniel began to walk away, he said, "Wait a minute. I have something to tell you. It's not the rabbits; I wasn't decided at all from the beginning. Rabbit or no rabbit, others would carry out this mission. Please tell Tolcha to leave this place immediately."

It was now five o'clock. The farmworkers were finishing for the day. The young man mingled with them and left undetected without wasting anyone's life.

Later in the evening, the news of the assassination in the capital was aired by the state radio. Daniel was by himself in his room packing while he listened to the report. After the news, a brief obituary of Dr. Menkir Alemu's life was read. Sadly, Menkir, too, had a child.

'Doctor Menkir Alemu had returned to his motherland to serve at this challenging time of the revolution, sacrificing the better life he had in Europe,' the radio said.

The assassination was attributed to the EPRP. The report made it clear that the government would do all to bring the culprits to justice and penalize them appropriately.

'A single drop of a revolutionary would be avenged by the life of a thousand counter-revolutionaries,' the radio declared.

Daniel went to bed, but he could not fall asleep, wondering about the tragedies that were taking place in the country. The Zemecha was falling apart before it made its full span of eighteen months as planned. Gimbie had closed weeks ago. Inango was disintegrating. His friend, Kirubel, gone.

This month of March was the eleventh month since he came to Inango to serve in the Zemecha. Seven months to go in order to get hold of the certificate of completion and thereby the privileges promised: job and scholarship, etc. His dreams of a better future were vanishing.

He thought of Ghenet. He had written her twice, but a reply had not yet come. He didn't know why. Had she received his letters, he was sure she would have replied and he would have received it by now.

Laying on his bad he opened the Aerogram. It was from Biniam, his younger brother. Right after the greeting lines Biniam wrote mostly about Ghenet.

'I have received the letter you sent to Ghenet but I wasn't able to give her right away. Ghenet and many of the Zemachs from Wolega region were rounded up by security people right on arrival in Addis Ababa, and taken to the Karchele detention center.

'I have been able to pass your letter to her while I visited. All the Zemachs are charged for deserting the Zemecha, vandalizing state properties and disturbing the peace. I don't know how long she will be there. Efforts made to secure their freedom by bail has failed. Otherwise, she is in good condition. Nothing to worry about. I hope we will see her soon.'

Daniel was not particularly shocked by the news of Ghenet's arrest. The rumor about the arrest of the Zemachs had reached every ear. Besides he had expected that the government would take punitive measures on Zemachs who vandalized and deserted the Zemecha centers. In Gimbie, the situation had been worse. There was fighting among pro Dergue and Anti Dergue Zemachs in which some were injured.

Daniel placed the Aerogram contemplating what could befall Ghenet. The Dergue was unpredictable. The verdict could be anything from full pardon, to many years of hard labor, to Capital punishment. It all depends on Derg's mood of the day. If they lose a battle in Eritrea or a prominent supporter get killed, the verdict could be harsh. Daniel couldn't sleep for hours. He prayed longer than he has ever prayed before. With the prayers giving him hope, he finally began to think of good things in life, job, marriage, children and family. With the pleasant thoughts of Ghenet, he fell asleep.

Chapter 10

On Monday afternoon, Ermias received two messages left in Bar Tiku, one from Jovani, the other from the bartender. Jovani's note was a ciphered message written on a piece of shabby paper, warning him that he should watch his back. The other was a verbal message from his aunt, Abinet who desired to see him.

Driving to Abinet's dwelling, he looked around but saw nothing unusual. To find out if he had grown a tail, he made an idle tour around the city. And then he went into bar Mexico for a cup of coffee. In the bar, he made a few calls, and at around 3 o'clock, he left the bar.

On the road that takes to Abinet's residence, he observed a red Opel behind him. He didn't give it a thought initially, but he became suspicious when he noticed it following him for a while. He wanted to test by gradually reducing his speed. He then slowed to a little more than a crawl, studying the car behind. The car came very close and slowed, showing clearly an intention to stay behind his car.

He did not like the idea of driving to Abinet being tailed by strangers; it would be dragging trouble to his aunt. He chose to sort matters out somewhere rather than on his aunt's doorstep. Right after Guenet Hotel, he turned left towards Shemelis School, accelerated a bit, and stopped. He watched his followers drive past him slowly without looking at him. In the car were two men.

He opened the glove compartment, pulled out the small BB pistol, and checked its ammunition. It was fully loaded, but its size disappointed him. The effective penetrating range of a BB gun was approximately 18m (60 ft.). A person wearing jeans at this distance would not sustain serious injury. He knew he could not do much with this weapon, but at a distance of an arm he was certain that it could blow his brains out. 'No one shall take me alive; he vowed and stuck the pistol in his jacket's pocket.

Soon a thought crossed his mind—what if they searched for a weapon? Possession of a firearm, at this time of social turmoil, could lead to trouble. He took it out, placed it in the door pocket of the car, and stepped out. Before entering a bar on the corner, Ermias looked far ahead and observed the Opel making a U-turn at the school's main gate,

An hour later, he came out of the bar only to find the Opel next to his car. The two middle-aged men, in plain clothes, sat in it, looking very peaceful, yet purposeful. Ermias started his car, rolled it slowly up to the intersection, then swung it left on the Kera road and gained speed.

His heart pounding like a drum, planning how to encounter the eminent danger, he drove past the Nyala Transportation Company, turned to the right, continued westward in the direction of the City Prison, and parked the car in a quiet place to wait for whatever might come. A moment later, he slipped out of the car, but just before he could close the door, his followers showed up and parked five cars away from his. *Who the hell are they?* he thought. *Security people who have found out about my activities or opposition parties who wanted to talk?* If it proved to be the former, he had to do what is required of him to save his spy network and the people involved.

His eyes dropped to the pistol in the door pocket, and he made his right hand free, just in case. Sometimes it could be difficult even to take one's own life. So, he had to make sure that nothing stood between him and his decision to waste himself.

The door of the driver's side of the red Opel opened, and a gray-haired man with a square face emerged and walked straight towards him. The other one climbed out of the car but stayed leaning against it.

Ermias felt surrounded. 'I won't let them take me alive,' he said to himself. He thought of the spy net he had organized, neat, and flawless. He must save all the dedicated people working in it—and the time has come. He had always known that this was part of the game, and the rule was *thou shall not allow the enemy to take you alive.'*

It had never occurred to him that it would be as sudden and unescapable as it seemed now. He had always reckoned that he would somehow know or feel when such a moment came closer and be ready for it. This was unexpected and too sudden to reconsider. He opened the door a little wider and bent to its pocket to grab the pistol.

"Pardon me, sir. We want to talk to you," said the man, with a slightly stretched mouth that could hardly be taken for a smile, the voice low.

"What about? Who are you?" asked Ermias turning back just before his hand went to the pistol, playing simple.

The man produced an ID, stepped closer, and showed it to Ermias. He was from the Armed Forces Intelligence Service.

To Ermias, it was a dead-end, just like that killer was to the man in the shabby Fiat. There was no time to waste. He must terminate himself now before it would be late and presumably too difficult or even impossible. The cyanide tablet might have been better to buy some time. He would not have to use it right away. But he had preferred the pistol for the mere reason that it could be used as a defensive weapon as well. He wished he had a powerful gun or the merciful tablet.

"Please come with us, sir. We don't have the slightest idea of what it's all about," the man said, raising his voice just enough to make it sound like an order to be obeyed.

"I would like to make a call if I am allowed."

"That's not a problem," the man babbled and added, "you can follow us in your car if that suits you. You're wanted at the Ministry of Defense."

What had seemed sealed and incarcerating was now loose and relaxed but still so puzzling that Ermias almost wanted to ask the man to repeat what he had just said. "Okay! I will follow you, but I'll stop somewhere to make a call."

"Go ahead. We will follow you," the man agreed and went back to the car.

Ermias took the lead, and they followed loosely, circumventing the City Prison and uphill to Mexico Square. Ermias repressed the notion to escape that dwelt in him since he had been permitted to take his car. He thought it would be a futile attempt to even try it with his older car and the worthless little pistol he had.

What could this be? Ermias thought. *What do they want from me? Probably some interrogation. Certainly, they don't know who I'm. Or do they? Do they want to ask me to work for them? Do they know about the new Net?*

At the intersection, he swung the car left and approached the bar. Then he spun the wheel toward the curb and brought it to a halt alongside Bar Mexico. He lifted himself out of the car swiftly. For a moment, he stood on the sidewalk, observing the security people parking behind him. They didn't show any interest in following him into the bar.

He entered the bar, walked past the counter, and planted himself before the public telephone box. Thinking of some way to run away, he lifted the handset, inserted a coin, and dialed Jovani's number. There was no answer. Jovani was with Beza, he recalled. He dialed the number to Tiku's bar. The bartender answered. He briefed him on the situation and advised him to take certain precautions if he didn't call before eight.

Now that he was liberated from the heavy concern of saving his compatriots, he felt more able to face whatever might come boldly. In the bar, he lingered, thinking of any way out. The bar had no other exit. Minutes went by in a deliberate act of wasting time, waiting, and thinking. Finally, his curiosity grew larger than his fear, and he went out with firm determination to find out what it was all about.

The security men were waiting patiently in their car. As soon as Ermias came out, they started their car and led the way. At the Ministry of Defense's rear gate stood a guard who swung the grille open as they drove into the compound. Ermias and the security men parked side by side: showing no desire to hurry. The grey-haired man clambered out and came to Ermias.

"Follow me," the man said and led Ermias into the building.

Ermias was overwhelmed by a nagging curiosity to know and by recurring fear of the unknown. He followed quietly. They climbed a flight of stairs to the second floor of the building and walked the long, dim, and quiet corridor. There was a guard at the far end, standing motionless beside a door. Ermias read the inscription on the plate that was hooked on the door: EDF67. He knew what it meant—Section 67.

"Is the colonel inside?" the grey-haired man asked the guard.

The guard straightened, "Yes, sir. He is in a session with Dergue members—might finish soon, hopefully. They have been in for almost the entire afternoon.

"We can wait in the waiting-room," the secret service man said to Ermias and walked forward into the next room. The room was furnished with a leather sofa and armchairs surrounding a little glass table and an expensive carpet on the floor. *"The house of guns can buy fine things for itself,"* Ermias said to himself.

The man produced a packet and flipped it expertly to push out some cigarettes. "Cigarettes?"

"No, I don't smoke," said Ermias.

"Make yourself comfortable." The man lit a cigarette and sucked deeply from it. Ermias took a seat and concentrated on the face before him, trying to read in it any hint of information. There was nothing in the man's rectangular face and widely placed eyes that betrayed nothing except the signs of tremendous experience behind it.

Feeling he had nothing to lose, Ermias decided to try with words. "Who is he, who wants to see me?"

"It's the Chief, Colonel Assefa."

"Will he keep me long?"

"Maybe."

"It's ten to six. Don't you close?" asked Ermias showing no concern to the intentionally short answers of the man.

"We work around the clock."

"In peacetime?"

"Seven days a week, Sir," the man replied, watching the smoke from his cigarette diminish into space above him. Ermias knew he would not get anything from this man, so he gave up.

The room became almost silent, and he began to make a calm account of the last twenty-four hours: if there was anything that could have led him into this situation. He couldn't figure out anything. He couldn't know that the soldier to whom he slipped ten Birr for some information had jotted his car number and submitted his suspicion to his superiors. Since then, he had been under the surveillance of the Armed Forces Intelligence Section.

Half an hour later, the Chief himself appeared and introduced himself to Ermias as Colonel Assefa Zerihun. He was dressed in civilian clothes and wore no hat. He had a frank and open face. His grey hair was denser on the sides.

"How are you two getting along? I am sorry I kept you so long," Assefa said to Ermias, who was expecting an overnight interrogation.

Assefa glanced at his man. "That's a terrific job. You can leave us now."

Ermias' inquisitive eyes peered at the colonel, who, unlike many Ethiopian army officers, looked ready to ignore formalities and appeared easy to get down to business. Ermias was relieved by the colonel's simplicity but more curious than ever.

"You follow me, Ermias."

Ermias was startled as he heard his real name. He felt too exposed. "Can you tell me what this is all about, Colonel?"

"All in due time. Let's get into my office first." Colonel Assefa smiled at Ermias as he opened his office door. He let Ermias first, drew the door behind himself, and locked it properly from the inside. "Make yourself at home."

"I can't. I can't feel at home here," said Ermias stretching both hands open, indicating the entire house, his eyes moving quickly left and right, lowering himself into the armchair in front of the Chief's large desk at the center of the large room. Right behind was the portrait of the Head of State, General Teferi. The national flag and the armed force's emblem were hoisted, magnifying the office's high status. A little to the right was a wide window from which Haileselassie Square and Ras Makonnen Avenue could be seen.

"Permit me to explain to you what this office is," said Assefa pouring the whisky for Ermias and then for himself. "Cheers." He raised the glass and sipped a little.

"This office is," he went on, sitting on his armchair behind his desk, "the center of the Armed Forces Intelligence Service. Military Information from every corner of the world is gathered and processed here. I'm in charge here, and I have considerable autonomy in running this section."

Ermias listened attentively. He was looking at his counterpart on the enemy side.

"I know who you are. That's why I wanted to see you," the colonel said and sipped from the glass, watching Ermias, whose face expressed a combination of fear, curiosity, and suspicion. "You can call yourself whatever you like, but the fact that you work for the intelligence service of the Eritrean Front remains unchanged. I know that you're here to scout for some spies. I even have the information that you almost have completed your part of the job."

Ermias looked as if he was hit by a shotgun but he remained calm. "Why didn't you arrest me at the beginning, before several others got involved. Don't you people feel content unless you slaughter many?"

The colonel noted the expression and said, "Do not misunderstand me, Ermias. This meeting of ours is purely personal. It has nothing to do with my government or your engagement in an illegal organization. Besides, I have no animosity about the fact that you are a member of the Eritrean front. As for what you said, 'slaughtering many' you're right, but that has nothing to do with my office. It's the work of the government's security men."

"Who is the government, and who are you?" interrupted Ermias, puzzled.

"Dergue is the government. And it doesn't listen to us. We have constantly opposed the arbitrary killings against your people, member or non-member. We are only advisers with no final word in the conduct of operations. There is no one to whom you can talk sense in this government. This country is in the hands of people who are led not by reason but by wild emotions. Only God knows where we are heading. Now let's get to business. A personal matter."

Ermias straightened and opened his mind.

"I assume you have a recollection of the battle between our troops and yours at a place called Awgaro last year.

Ermias nodded in agreement, and Assefa continued, "Casualties were reported to be excessively high on both sides. Our Air force was involved that day."

When Ermias heard this, that day came vividly to his eyes. His mind was like a movie camera that captured scenes and events, storing in memory, never to be forgotten. He was now seeing Awgaro burning, as he had seen it then, from a passenger plane flying over the village.

"At this battle, one of our bombers was blown up."

"Yes," Ermias assented as though to himself.

"You know? Did you keep a record of this too?"

"As a matter of coincidence, I happened to witness the event with my own eyes."

"Did you participate in the combat?"

"No. I was in a passenger plane flying over the region. Don't you warn the civil aviation before your bombers start tearing up the skies!"

"That would count as informing you of our intentions in advance. Isn't the aviation in your hands?" Assefa said with a little smile that vanished before it developed.

"Ermias, nowadays, there is nobody who cares for human life. Don't you see we live in a time in which human lives or human rights are no longer anybody's concern? Political and military victories are the priorities of the time."

It was clear that Assefa was disappointed with the government, which was a positive sign to Ermias to recruit informers who have their reasons. They were reliable, trustworthy, and often preferable to those paid or blackmailed.

"Now, let's get back to our own business," said Assefa and paused as if to make a distinctive break between this issue and the next. He stared at Ermias with a clear indication that the important issue was to come now.

"My younger brother," said Assefa in a lower voice, "was the pilot whose jet was blown at the battle of Awgaro. He was safely captured and is under the custody of the Front. I want you to secure his release." His eyes were serious and watery, words dry, but they came from a wounded heart.

A moment of silence.

Ermias was surprised but didn't say a word. He was shocked by the sudden change of expectation, but he managed to suppress it. He was good at controlling his emotions. He was an excellent listener when he wanted to be, with an accurate instinct for how other people felt and an understanding of why they behaved as they did. As he stretched his hand to his glass, a thought struck him. He thought it was silly, but at heart, secretly, he entertained it, wondering whether he could not somehow turn Assefa's misfortune to his advantage. Who or what could be exchanged for the colonel's brother?

"You look surprised?" Assefa broke the brief silence as Ermias was immersed in his thought.

"I am rather shocked," Ermias replied honestly. "What do you expect me to do? Are you proposing an exchange of prisoners?"

"Not exactly. This is personal—between you and me. If you can set my brother free, provide him with a safe passage to Sudan, then …"

"That's not a problem," said Ermias cutting across the words of the colonel. "We can put him anywhere in the world safely. That's not…"

"The problem is what you get in exchange. Isn't it?" Assefa pulled a drawer, picked a file folder, and slid it across the table to Ermias. "This is what you get in exchange."

Ermias turned the cover of the file on the top of which read: CONFIDENTIAL in red. The next page was what shocked him; the code name, OPERATION RAZA, also in red. Below it, the words: "Orders and Directives of the Defense Sub-committee Of the Provisional Military Administration Council."

Ermias was breathing heavily as he turned to the following page, which displayed northern Ethiopia's map with details mostly on Eritrea and the northern part of Tigray and Gondar. He glanced at Assefa and returned to the papers. What had fallen into his hands was not as simple as the way it had come to him. The folder contained war strategy in detail: names, timing, and places. Moreover, the number of troops and armaments, in quality and quantity, was specified clearly, along with the order of marching, posting, and operation. Hands sweating, Ermias closed the file, vowing to himself to study it thoroughly some other place, later but soon.

"You might have information on the recent troop movements from the Ogaden to the north, but the details came just yesterday. This will not only save my brother but the lives of thousands of poor countrymen and other innocent people on both sides. I believe this is not the right way to conduct war. I hope I'm doing some good."

"I believe this is very significant," said Ermias looking very thoughtful. "I give you, my word. Your brother will be released soon. As you wish, we will see to it that he enters Sudan safely."

Assefa held out a piece of paper on which his brother's full name, rank, and soldier ID-number were written. Grabbing the note and the precious folder, Ermias tossed the rest of his whisky and rose slowly, extending his hand as he apologized for any discomfort the pilot might be experiencing. He assured Assefa no harm whatsoever would befall his brother anymore.

"The occasion calls for a handshake. Would I have the pleasure of meeting you again?" Ermias asked with a mood of complete satisfaction

"Of course. We shall meet. You can call on my private line," Assefa said, shaking Ermias' hand and giving him his number.

Before 7 PM, Ermias was out of the compound of the Ministry. It was then that the impact of the confidential file hit him fully as if from behind, shoving him forward, urging him to double his speed and alert his senses with the significance of his immediate mission: transmitting the information to the headquarters of the Liberation Front in Nakfa, Eritrea. Operation Raza was to be launched in the first week of April: three months from now, not much time to prepare an effective defense against the massive number as specified on the file but better late than never.

Chapter 11

At the beginning of April 76, the Dergue launched Operation Raza as its first major military assault to crush the Eritrean independence movement. More than 50,000 militiamen were given Portuguese and Czech rifles to storm into Eritrea, some of them over 50 years old, with no logistics support, virtually no ration, no clothes, or blankets. Backed by some units of the regular army, they were assigned to various officers and scattered into four major groups.[III]

In line with the strategy of operation Raza, two of the groups were to march from the region of Tigray across the town of Zal'anbessa. The other from the region of Gonder across Omahajer while the better equipped one, nicknamed Leblib which means steak, had already penetrated deep into Eritrea and camped a few kilometers north of Badme, in the southwestern region. Leblib was a two-thousand strong militia reinforced by two brigades of the regular army and well trained than the others.

It didn't take long for Leblib to acquaint itself with the surrounding area and terrorize the population. Within a few days of its arrival, it had already burglarized cattle and other properties worth thousands of Birrs from the local community. Leblib had expanded its invasion area the following days and had conquered more cattle, crops, money, and other valuables.

The treasure and joy Leblib enjoyed at the outset was so inspiring and encouraging that the militia could not stay another day waiting for the order to march. It was during this moment of joy, when they were feasting, eating raw meat and drinking fresh Tella, singing war songs, and dancing the

Iskista, that their leader—a non-commissioned officer and a Dergue member—came out and stood on the top of a hill with a loudspeaker in his hand.

"Comrades!" the officer called, "this region, as you see it, is prosperous. When you march forward, you will find more as you have never seen before. It's yours. You can take as much as you can, eat whatever you find, and kill whoever crossed your path."

Those closest to the officer could hear what he was saying, while most of the farmers were still singing and dancing without minding the speaker. Presumably, most of them, coming from Ethiopia's southern region where Amharic was not spoken, did not understand the language.

"The rebels of this region," the officer went on, "are traitors who demeaned our religion and collaborated with the Arabs to sell our country. We have repeatedly warned them, advised them, and even tried to talk sense to them with the help of the leaders of friendly countries. But they have stubbornly declined to listen and make peace. What else can our motherland do? There was no other option left for us except to let you show them your merciless, strong arm that would teach them unforgettable lessons."

Now that the farmers who heard the speech were touched, they started to sing loudly as some of them took their rifles and opened fire in the air.

"Hold your fire," the officer roared. "Tomorrow, you will have a target to hit. We shall march at dawn, exactly at six. You hear me! Tomorrow at six. We shall win!"

"Yes! We shall win! We shall destroy the rebels! We shall win!" shouted the farmers courageously and continued the feast, singing and dancing as they never did before.

Half a kilometer south of Leblib's encampment, a similar instruction was presented to the regular army troops. These troops were the ones who recently moved from the Ogaden. As a matter of fact, these troops had no idea why they had been ordered to withdraw from the Ogaden, where their presence was vital, and move to the north where their deployment would not make a difference. They were not trained to engage in guerrilla warfare, but the Dergue had reasons; most of the officers were considered to be hostile to it. Though restrained later, the Third Army Division, which these troops came from, had repeatedly called for the removal of the Dergue from power. It gave as its standpoint that the Dergue was primarily not meant to depose the emperor and assume government power, but to present their grievances to the emperor. And it had particularly called for Mengistu's expulsion from the Dergue because the majority of the soldiers, having been stationed on the Ethio-Somalia border, had had no part in his election to represent them. The idea behind Operation Raza was deliberately kept secret from these troublemakers to avert probable sabotage.

The officer in charge, a major who commanded considerable respect among the rank and file, was briefing the soldiers about the operation only twelve hours before take-off. Curiously, a sergeant who joined them in Addis Ababa attended him.

Gaushaw, one of the soldiers assigned to take part in this operation, stood in the first row of crowd closer to the major, listening to the commander attentively. Since he joined the army, Gaushaw had served most of his time under this same officer, for whom he had great respect and unshakeable loyalty. But he was suspicious of the Sergeant who stood beside the major. He never liked the man since he joined them a couple of weeks ago.

"This operation is unique not only in character but also in structure," the major asserted after having explained the plans of the operation. "It has incorporated tens of thousands of militias who have volunteered to sacrifice their lives for the unity of our country. We shall march with them across Eritrea to destroy the rebels conclusively. The operation's goal is to hinder secessionist activity, to frighten and disperse the rebels, and send a message that the whole nation is determined to destroy them. Meanwhile, the militia will settle in Eritrea, watching the activities of the population. I'll not go into the problems that this region has caused our country, but I remind you that we, as soldiers, always have the prime obligation to defend the unity and integrity of our nation.

"As I have mentioned to you, the militia commits itself to this operation only out of love of the motherland, and they are courageous enough to march before us. Tomorrow morning at six, they will set off. We will commence following them at the same time. to give them cover them in case they face strong resistance."

Casting a suspicious eye on the major, Gaushaw reviewed the order of the march in his mind and came up with a nagging question: knowing the enemy to be well-armed, why should the regular troops march behind the untrained and ill-equipped militia? The so-called militia was no more than a random collection of unemployed laborers and poor farmers rounded up from the streets and the countryside. Gaushaw wondered why the major, whom he had known for so long as a man of integrity, was not himself today. The major, Gaushaw had noticed, appeared to be under the pressure of the sergeant who was rumored to have been assigned by Major Mengistu himself to see that orders were carried out according to the procedures of Operation Raza.

"As you clearly understand," the major continued, "the militia is not used to gun fighting, so they could easily be dispersed under heavy fighting. Some of them might even retreat or flee. Our orders are," the major paused, looked to the sergeant, and then to the crowd of soldiers. With the air of having something important to say, he uttered, "Our orders are to shoot and kill those who run away."

A sound of protest came from the crowd. Gaushaw stepped forward and lifted his right hand for permission to put a question. The major nodded to Gaushaw, permitting him.

"How could we fire at our people, sir?" There were anger and disappointment in Gaushaw's voice.

The major weighed that this was not only Gaushaw's question but almost everyone's. And he had a simple question that could answer their questions. "Are we not marching on our own people as well! Gaushaw."

Then came other questions from several soldiers to which the major gave a comprehensive answer. "The revolutionary government could not have taken this course hadn't the situation asked for it. I'm sure there has to be quite convincing development that has provoked the government to take this action. We are soldiers, not politicians. Our duty is to carry out orders. We shall march tomorrow. Get ready for tomorrow morning. We shall move at 0600 hours," the major ordered and rushed to his tent, the sergeant following him.

A few kilometers south of this army, behind the hills and bushes, a small commando unit of the rebels was waiting patiently for their order to move. They had watched the militia intimidating their people, robing their cattle, and killing those who resisted. They had recorded every movement the army and the militia had made since they set foot on the territory. They were angry but still patient, waiting for the final order.

Since they received Assefa's Operation-Raza file, the rebels had been planning and reviewing a counter operation to paralyze the advance. They had planned to apply a decisive surprise attack at the army's Command and Control Center six hours before the march commenced. That would be at midnight tonight.

Twenty young men of the front's commando unit had been picked out to stage the counter operation. Daniel's big brother, Samson, was among them. He was listening attentively to the leader's final instruction. After the battle of Awgaro, from which he came out relatively unhurt, he had been immediately sent to a training center for special commandos. Three months were enough to qualify him as one of the best in the field. His physique had changed— grown tougher, but psyche, however, had shown some flaws, unnoticeable to the outside world. His conscience had never rested, reminding him of the innocent lives that perished in the bombing raid. He still believed, he could have saved lives had he forwarded his idea of evacuation. This thought depressed him all the time. The only time he was at peace was when he was at war. When he was engaged in fighting, he forgot his accusatory conscience and performed his duty as expected of him. When everyday field life resumed after fighting, Samson got upset easily and became unfriendly with his compatriots. There were reports of him having fought almost everyone in his group, including the unit leader. After the battle of Awgaro, Samson was a different person who enjoyed fighting merely to keep himself busy by killing someone.

Now that fighting was not far; the prospect filled him with a sense of purpose. Dutifully, he listened to every word that streamed out of the leader. At first, hearing the atrocities committed by the soldiers, he felt a gob of anger rising in his chest. Later, when the details of the counter-attack were revised, he calmed because the time of judgment under the law of the Eritrean desert was at hand. In this God-forsaken desert, there is no Geneva or UN convention that would restrict the flood of one's anger. The punishment applied was steered by the amount of blood required to quench one's rage.

The leader, holding a piece of paper and a pencil in his hand, pointed at a dot that represented the militia encampment, "From the north, our regular fighters will attack the militia with automatic weapons and heavy guns. Another artillery unit of our fighters is ready to attack the regular army from the west too. Now, you move from here at a quarter to midnight to arrive there at exactly midnight. Remember, no shooting unless the situation requires it. Destroy whatever is around as quietly as possible for as long as possible. When a gunshot is heard, your time starts ticking; meaning you got only a quarter of an hour left to blow the vehicles and the ammunition depot. Twenty minutes after the first gunshot is heard, our fighters from the east will set off heavy weapons.

So, you must leave five minutes earlier. Don't engage yourself in combat that you can't terminate in time. Did I make myself clear, comrades?"

"Yes, Chief," all answered simultaneously, but Samson had a question. He raised a hand.

The leader glanced at Samson, "Yes, Samson."

"Chief, why don't we continue northward to attack the militia after we evacuated the army camp?"

"Samson, you know quite well that we don't waste our time and energy fighting militias. Our regular fighters will do that job. Besides, we have to give the militia a route to escape. The idea is not to destroy but to disperse them. We expect them to run away southwards to the regular army in search of cover." The leader pointed at the map and went on, "so, we keep this area free for them. Don't shoot at them unless the situation is threatening. We know what they did to our people yet we are not here for vengeance. These are just a bunch of farmers who don't even know where they are, why they came, who they are fighting for or against.

"If we succeeded in destroying the Command-and-Control center of the regular army, our mission is accomplished. Leave the rest to our regular fighters. Understood?"

"Yes," many replied in word, and Samson just nodded in conformity, eagerly.

"Report in Barentu. See you there. Good luck. You have got a few hours to eat and rest."

They ate what they called 'the last supper' in the dark; and just before eight, they scattered in the bushes. The assault was to be charged at midnight, so they had four full hours to relax.

Samson laid his sub-machine gun on the ground and undid the holster; inside the holster he carried a handgun, several hand grenades and a knife. There, behind the bushes, he slumped against a trunk of a tree to rest.

He had enjoyed the meal, and his spirit was calmer. He slept easily. Unlike the time before the battle of Awgaro, with critical fighting less than four hours away, it had not been that easy to sleep. Even eating had been difficult, but nowadays the prospect of fighting seemed to give him an appetite for food and calmness for sleep.

Three hours later, he woke up and found himself staring at the sparkling starry sky. It was a night of deepest dark with a clear tropical sky that distinctly exposed every heavenly body—no moon, only a multitude of stars whirling and twinkling. They seemed to have appeared to witness the earthly drama of this part of the world, to which the human eyes were blind to see, ears deaf to hear.

As he usually did when he passed the night outdoor, Samson marveled about the very existence of the stars, wondered about their number and enormous distance. The nights held no fear for him. Starlight, darkness, and the mysterious and remote cosmos was the stage for vision and dreams. In high school, he had learned about the theory of the Big Bang, the relation of time and space, and galaxies and black holes.

As he contemplated the vastness of the universe, wondering about the purpose of life and nature, his eyes moved from a star congregation to another. Then, a question crossed his mind: *Could there be life up there in any one of those star-systems? Our solar system, our planet is filled with an abundance of life. How could it not be possible for other systems to develop life? There must be some sort of life, for sure. There must be. What kind? Plants? Animals? Humans? Yes, humans or something like that. Why not? What would they be doing? Would they be fighting? Killing each other? Yes, why not? How could we be different in the universe! We can't be alone or different.*

Just as he was observing the sky from the ground, he began to perceive the earth and its inhabitants from the sky, from an imaginary sky perspective. The panorama was wonderful, the earth magnificent, the atmosphere lively, and life—a source of endless exhilaration. No mark of boundaries that divided the countries, no indication of the different cultures and religions—just life and nature. Animals, plants and people. Beautiful people—humans, all alike. The similarities among humans overwhelmed their differences that the racial, ideological, and religious differences seemed trivial. Samson felt sad for the lives that were wasted in human conflicts.

"Why couldn't people try to solve their differences in peaceful ways?" he asked himself. But the answer that came to his mind was as mysterious as the stars: survival. It has to be the law of nature. Life has always been the history of the struggle for survival. When the strong was not just, and the weak unsecured, a rebellion would be inevitable.

As he arrived at this conclusion, the whistle to wake up went off. It was quarter to midnight, time to advance. Immediately the commandos gathered and moved to raid the camp of the regular army. It was so dark, difficult to see who was next to who, but for these commandos, who were well trained for attacks in darkness, the hurdle was not impenetrable. Right on time, they were near the army encampment, where they could see some flickering rays of light from the tents. They assorted into categories of two and spread widely in ten lines of advance. Samson and his partner were on the middle right line.

As they came closer, Samson heard a faint sound whose source he couldn't spot. The horror of death was approaching. He began breathing faster and heavily, his heart pounding harder. It was a sign of fear that would soon transform him into an apathetic killer. Suddenly, a hard-hearted, merciless monster evolved out of the kind-hearted young man who swiftly unsecured his machine gun and trained its muzzle on human height.

Samson's partner drew his knife out. He was good with knives and the best to strike a target with a knife than any other weapon. If the situation allowed, he preferred to cut the enemy's throat with his knife. For that, he earned a nickname: Knife. In the massacre of Omahajer, shortly after the Dergue took power, government soldiers had shot Knife's elder brother while he and his mother watched. It was then that he fled to join the rebels. His mission had nothing to do with liberating Eritrea. He was driven by sheer vengeance that frequently revived by a wild search of a beloved brother. His war would certainly continue even after Eritrea's liberation until he retrieved his brother from the blood of endless Ethiopians he sought to slaughter.

From a distance of about a hundred meters, a flashlight flickered briefly. Observing the twinkle that seemed not to be far away, Samson instantly took to the ground and crawled towards the direction of the light. His partner, Knife, did the same.

Few meters away stood two guards whose silhouette cast a darker form of their structure against the encampment behind. That made it easier for the attackers to share one man each. Samson jumped over the one to his side like a tiger and broke his neck right away while Knife enjoyed cutting his victim's throat with his knife.

They changed into the overcoats of the victims rapidly and proceeded towards the tents. In some of the tents, flickered lantern light that drew their attention. They strode to them. Samson went past a napping guard with whom Knife had a good time doing his awful things.

Further away, two soldiers patrolled the large tent, evidently the Command Center. Samson had already decided to visit it first. He reached to his knife, drew it slowly, and asked the soldiers if they had a match. His Amharic, the language many of the soldiers spoke or understood, was so perfect that it did not incite any suspicion. One of the soldiers searched his pockets while the other, with his rifle on his shoulder, relaxed. A sudden, simultaneous attack was necessary here, and the fighters accomplished it satisfactorily with minimum noise, without awakening anyone around or inside the tent.

As Samson stepped closer to the tent and peered inside through an opening, warmer air blew over his face. He examined the inside that appeared more of a settled headquarters than a temporary one, with two lanterns giving adequate light, one portable bed, a table, a couple of chairs, and radio equipment. The lantern hanging over the table illuminated the two soldiers discussing over a map-like paper laid open on a table. Then an amazing sight met his eyes, a young soldier of about his age, with a kettle and some coffee cups. He appeared from the opposite end of the tent and walked to the table to serve tea or coffee. As the soldier stood right behind the lantern and turned his face, Samson got a glimpse of the face and startled. He swore to himself that it couldn't be what he assumed it was, so he scrutinized it thoroughly. All the traces were there. The face had matured and darkened but not changed much. It was round and stained with the sun; the eyes fast twinkling and kin.

The face smiled but soon before it developed to its full size, it died slowly as if the remembrance of some sad events blocked it. *No, this can't be real … can't be Gaushaw.* he thought.

Gaushaw had a distinct smile that displayed both the happy and the tragic parts of his life, a smile so peculiar that no one except Gaushaw offered. Samson was now doubtless that the young man in a green army uniform, a handgun on his waist, was his friend, Gaushaw Metaferia.

Just as Samson acknowledged and was caught in a dilemma of what to do, a gun went off signaling the beginning of the count down. The first second of the fifteen minutes had gone. There were only fifteen or fewer minutes to go now.

Samson entered the tent and ordered the soldiers to surrender. The major, who was the man in charge of the encampment, obeyed instantly and raised his hand over his head as though he was expecting or wanting it. The Sergeant didn't move but stared at the major threateningly for surrendering so fast and easily.

The mission, as Knife understood it, was to kill and destroy who and whatever was around, no prisoner or no mercy. So, what Samson did was a mistake that he corrected by opening fire at the soldiers.

Samson was still hesitant to fire, but fast to take cover on the floor.

"Take cover! Gaushaw," he shouted. "I'm Samson. Do you hear me, Gaushaw?" Gaushaw jumped to take cover, but he seemed to be a second late, for he screamed in agony. Knife had caught him in midair.

"Hold your fire!" Samson roared at Knife.

"Are you okay, Gaushaw?" Samson called again, slightly lifting his head.

Gaushaw drew his gun and aimed, first at Samson, then hesitated, shifted his aim, and fired at the lunatic Knife who was violently pouring bullets in the tent. Knife got shot and fell. At this moment, the Sergeant turned to the major and shot him from a close distance. Then he turned to Samson but was chopped on the head before he made a full turn. The gunfire drama was over.

There was silence in the tent for some seconds but was broken by a sound of agony. Samson threw his machine gun and stood, "Gaushaw?" No response.

He walked fast to Knife, who was nearby—motionless, then hurried to Gaushaw, who was crawling to the major but, seeing a man coming toward him, rolled for cover.

"This can't be true," Gaushaw swore in disbelief, overwhelmed by the most dramatic and yet tragic rendezvous that could only take place in movies. "Is it you, Samson? Or am I dreaming?"

"Gaushaw, yes, it's me. You're bleeding. I must get you some help. Where are the medics? Where can I get them?"

"Just check for me if the major is alive."

Samson leapt over Gaushaw and kneeled to examine the major. "He is dead, Gaushaw," Samson declared. "I must do something; I can't just stand here and watch you bleed to death." Hurriedly he went out of the tent to look for help.

As he ran here and there, desperately searching for some medical help, he heard the first artillery drop in the middle of the camp, marking the end of the evacuation time. The last second of the twenty minutes' evacuation time had gone. The guerrilla fighters were now shelling the encampment. Bombs dropped one after another. Nearly half of the shelling hit targets. The ammunition depot was on fire, and the tents shattered. The army was terrified. The commanding officers must have been injured or killed because no commanding officer was there to get things under control. The fire in the forward part of the camp burned, giving an illuminated brilliancy to everything in the area. The vehicles exploded one after another, and soldiers were running to take cover. The scene was chaotic and cluttered.

Samson rushed back to Gaushaw, leaned down, and held his head. Gaushaw's condition was deteriorating by the loss of blood from his chest.

"Just hold on, Gaushaw," Samson whispered to his dying friend.

"There is nothing you can do. I just happened to be in the wrong place at the wrong time. I had to keep an eye on that sergeant; he was assigned by the Dergue to spy on us. He has got what he deserved. It's over…" Gaushaw paused.

"Drink some water," Samson held his water canteen on Gaushaw's mouth and helped him drink a few drops.

"I'm delighted…to see you, Samson. You, you better run away now. Save yourself. There is nothing you can do for me," Gaushaw uttered worriedly as his chest smarted painfully.

"No, I won't go. I'll rather die here with you than leave you alone."

"But … you have to. What … what good will it do. My … my case is hopeless."

"Not for me. Gaushaw. I got new hope from you. I saw whom I am fighting. All these times, we… you and I, brothers, were fighting each other."

The turbulent sound of guns and artilleries, the blast and the explosions, and the tumult in the encampment were so much that they had difficulty hearing each other. However, they were so intimate that they understood their minds by seeing each other's eyes. But they were not fortunate for that either. A casual bullet burst one of the lanterns putting them in half-darkness. Bomb splinters began hitting the tent. And the tent was no safer anymore.

Samson carried Gaushaw to a corner beside the table for a cover. High up on the pole, the other lantern flickered, giving them some light that enabled them to see each other. Gaushaw's teeth chattered. Samson reached to the blanket on the table and wrapped him with it. A moment later, the other half of the tent was shelled apart, filling the remaining with debris and smoke.

Gaushaw began to cough. His chest heaved and shuddered, and blood-flecked his lips.

"Hold on, Gaushaw," Samson's voice dripped with hopelessness, but Gaushaw summoned all his strength and lifted his head as though to live one more good time with his friend. A friend with whom he grew up from childhood to adolescence and shared the joy and excitement of juvenile life. Together they had walked to school and exercised and revised their studies. Together they had fought other boys and protected one another, tried smoking, and quitted; they had sneaked into the stadium without a ticket and cheered the winners until their throats soared; they had learned about girls and walked with them cautiously. They were like brothers, but although they had similar ages, Samson led, and Gaushaw followed.

Looking at Samson, Gaushaw was reliving that life of joy. Weakly he reached out and took Samson's hand. He held it for a moment, and a sweet smile suffused his face, as he, in Samson's face, saw a pure, golden light that calmed his soul.

"Samson," called Gaushaw.

Samson moved closer and hugged him caringly. "Yes, Gaushaw."

"Samson, I lived in this miserable world as one of the poorest men who never owned anything… nothing, no land, no money, no wife, no children, nothing. Isn't that tragic?" He paused and inhaled air for more strength, "But I don't see it that way… for I had one thing that many never have." Again, he paused and gathered enough energy to say a single word in the best way it could be uttered to imply its exact sense, "A friend." Then his body relaxed, and he was gone.

But the word reverberated and echoed in Samson's ear long after, reviving the long-forgotten memories that they shared from the early times of their lives to maturity. It was an honest word that came from a sincere heart in a moment when one had nothing to pretend for.

Samson looked at Gaushaw through the tears on his eyes and observed the face that had smiled to its full extent for the first time since he knew it. A smile that seemed to travel beyond the realm of death that Gaushaw endured in grace. Solemnly, he closed the eyes and the mouth. He watched Gaushaw for what seemed like an eternity, fighting back gallons of tears that were pushing to stream.

As Samson sat watching Gaushaw, a deep and abiding sense of humanity swept over him. The stupidity of war from which he could deduce the remaining time of his life was put on display before him.

Half an hour or so later, the bombing calmed. The heavy artilleries from the rebel fighters stopped. It was more or less quiet except for the noise of angry soldiers outside. But it didn't last long. A combined sound of light gun shooting and the screaming crowd was heard approaching from the north. Minutes later, a huge crowd broke into the encampment and took shelter in anything they could lay their hands on. Soon the encampment was pack by the members of the militia who were on the run.

A horde of militiamen entered the battered tent, which Samson and his dead friends occupied. As the farmer's tramping feet became unbearable, Samson changed place to the other corner where many farmers had already begun snoring. He wondered about some of the farmer's ability to sleep so instantly under this circumstance.

It was quiet now. Mission accomplished, the guerrilla fighters had pulled, and the night slipped out slowly to let the day count its toll of damage and death. The material loss on the part of the army was immense, but human causality was relatively less.

Samson got to his feet as the first rays of light reached his eyes. He had not slept. He had been thinking of his life, of the war, and the endless misery of killing and dying. He had been thinking of abandoning the liberation struggle. The way he understood it was all futile—a waste of time and life with nothing to achieve; whatever could be achieved would never change the lives of the people.

He dropped his eyes on Gaushaw's body, watched it for quite a while, and when tears filled his eyes, he turned and walked out of the tent, pledging to himself not to carry a gun again.

Outside, it was chilling. The sun was far behind the horizon to feel its warmth. He pulled the collars of the overcoat and proceeded right across the encampment. He did not look right or left but walked through the shelled tents and armored vehicles, some still smoldering. Stretcher-bearers were carrying out wounded victims of the shelling.

Regular soldiers and the militia were commingled. In the overcoat, Samson appeared like one of them, not that he cared much about his identity, but that there were hundreds of farmers who put on various types of military coats like him. Many were dressed in their ragged clothes. Some had shabby boots, while others had sandals and others were barefooted. The militia lucked uniformity.

Nobody asked Samson who he was, for nobody knew who anyone else was either. Samson was in no mood to hide his identity if he would be asked. He walked head upright, resolved. Direction south. Freeing himself from the organization that had led his life for seven years.

Many of the militia had taken the same direction—to where they came from. The other three militia army had fallen into traps set by the rebels at the borders. They were dispersed long before they had set foot in the rebel territory. Operation Raza ended in total humiliation.

Chapter 12

It was Friday, the busiest day of the week. The rainy season had come but there was no sign of rain. the air was dry and the wind appeared to be still. Daniel hoped that it was not a sign of drought. Drought seasons were scary in Ethiopia; they had left deep scars no one forgot.

Daniel had boarded a van heading to Gimbie on his way back to Addis. In Gimbie, he changed to a bus that would go all the way to Merkato, Addis Ababa. The journey on the highway would take some eight hours. As the bus drove past Nekemte, the biggest town of Wolega, a nagging thoughts crossed his mind. The bus was unusually half full and the road so quiet for the day. On Friday's, the number of passengers used to be high that it forced the busses to carry extra people and loads. The roads used to be overcrowded with trucks and busses. These were signs of a healthy economy. Roads were the arteries through which the economy pulses. Just as one could measure human health by checking the pressure on the artery, so could one weigh the nation's health from the traffic density on the road. Daniel guessed that the economy was slumping faster instead of rising as promised by the Derg.

The Dergue had nationalised the rural land, and confiscated private-owned houses and urban land. It had promised quick economic recovery, jobs to the youth and shelter to the needy when it seized power. Daniel was not that naïve to assume these promises could be accomplished within a couple of years or more, yet he had not expected that the economy would fall so fast.

Daniel recollected how it had been a couple of years ago before the revolution exploded. Ethiopia was right on the economic take-off runway. Private construction companies were flourishing and mechanised farming had begun. Telecommunications upgrading, shipping and airlines were expanding. An American Oil company had begun drilling in the Ogaden. Amidst the dreadful drought that claimed the lives of thousands, the economy had been on the verge of breaking through the suffocating grip. One could say the emperor had successfully achieved his goal in modernising the country. He had led the poor nation peacefully for four decades and ushered it into the modern world. It was at this critical period of economic advancement that the student revolution broke out spontaneously. Lurking behind the student movement, the military junta staged a coup only to disrupt the flourishing economic recovery.

As the bus approached the capital, Daniel begun to observe the people on the side roads; a huge number of young people walked aimlessly. Many were Zemachs who had abandoned their mission earlier, still wore the Zemecha outfits, or only the hats. Some stood idlily, leaning against street poles, barbershops, and tearooms. This was another sign of increasing unemployment. The revolution seemed to fail from the outset.

Finally came Mercato, the largest and busiest marketplace in Addis Ababa, covering a large area and employing an estimated 10,000 people in 5,000 business entities. Here was sold everything from a single left foot sandal to a pair of Kentucky's cowboy shoes, from the tiniest transistor to the largest television set.

Daniel felt at home when he saw the film posters on the walls of Cinema Addis, his favourite theatre place since childhood. Shortly after, the bus halted with a sigh inside the compound of the bus station. The door opened, and with the rest of the passengers, Daniel stepped out of the bus holding his luggage.

Mercato smelled like everything; gas, smoke, food, and life. You could hear all the world's languages and songs. You could see every kind of people from beggars to gold diggers. Daniel stood beside the bus for a while and just before he moved, he spotted his brother, Biniam, among a crowd of moving people.

Located a few miles west of the East African Rift, which splits Ethiopia into two—between the Nubian Plate and the Somali Plate—Addis Ababa, home to the Organisation of African Unity (OAU), was the largest city in Ethiopia with a population of nearly one million inhabitants in 1975. It also hosted the headquarters of the United Nations Economic Commission for Africa (ECA), as well as various other continental and international organisations. Addis Ababa was, therefore, often referred to as the political capital of Africa for its historical, diplomatic, and political significance in the world.

Addis Ababa was also home to the Kerchele, Ethiopia's central prison. Kerchele Prison possibly existed as early as 1923, under the reign of Empress Zewditu, but became notorious after Second Italo-Ethiopian War as the site where Ethiopian intellectuals were detained and killed by Italian Fascists in the Yekatit 12 massacre. After the restoration of Emperor Haile Selassie, the prison remained in use to house criminals and political activists. The Derg, too, found it to be utterly useful and expanded its size to meet the increasing number of prisoners.

Once in a week, on Sundays, the prison was open for families and relatives who needed to visit prisoners. Daniel lived not far from Kerchele. As a teenager, he had played soccer on a playground situated a few hundred meters away from the prison. But he had never thought of it as a site of mass killing, torture and execution; it was in this innocent-looking prison that the Dergue secretly massacred sixty-three officials of the Hailesilassie administration. What he knew of the prison until now was that it had been a locality where the polices locked only thieves and criminals.

Daniel went to see Ghenet on Sunday, a day after his return. No family members or relatives were with him when he walked past a pair of the iron gate and entered the prison compound for the first time. Not long after he entered the compound, he was ordered to line up and wait for his turn to proceed. The guards seemed to be humane although they carried rifles. Far ahead, Daniel could see concrete walls overlain with barbed wire. On the other side, he observed wooden houses and barracks behind a barbed-wire fence. In this section of the prison, most of the detainees were on their Zemecha uniforms watched over by guards with wooden clubs in their hands.

Half an hour later, a guard came and searched Daniel. He was then led in through buildings that appeared to be administrative area. Finally, at a small sentry box, a prison warden asked him, who he wanted to see.

"Ghenet Metaferia, a Zemach."

"What's your relation?" the warden asked without much interest to know.

"She was my friend for a long time."

Daniel had a Zemecha cap on his head and that could tell much of Daniel's profession and ease the situation.

"Your ID?"

Daniel handed over his identification card and was told to wait until they call Ghenet. Few meters from the sentry-box lay a broad concrete wall that separated visitors and prisoners. Visitors could see prisoners through their respective face-sized windows—twenty people at a time. Daniel could hear the mumble of voices modulated as one indistinct sound.

A moment later, Daniel saw a visitor leave a window at the far end of the wall and he was told to approach that same window. Coming closer to the window, he saw hands holding the bar. His heart pounding faster, he walked to the window faster. He touched the hand and peered through the window.

There she was with a frank smile on her face, shaved hair, and tiny body

"You look different," said Daniel after a long pause of reckoning.

"The place is different and makes you different."

"I don't mean physically "

"I know what you mean, Daniel. This place is not like what we used to believe, a house for murders, rapists, and robbers. Well, there are such people; it's still a prison, but they too change and be fine people. If you want to meet real saints, join Kerchele," said Ghenet then stared at his eyes. "I heard all about what happened in Inango.

"I heard what happened in Gimbie as well."

"Yes, Gimbie. It all happened suddenly. Everybody got crazy when we heard the execution."

"It could have gone worse."

"Yes, no human life was lost. We are in here for the material damage incurred, sentenced to serve three months. I think it is fair."

"Half the time to go. How would you tackle the time?"

"We are all the time busy working. We prepare prison food, wash clothes, water the plantation and clean cells day in, day out. It's more like the Zemecha but different. Here, we meet not farmers but doctors and engineers, scientists, and philosophers. We are learning a great deal from them. I have also met members of the royal family, probably the kindest people in the country. Daniel, what we were told about them was all lies."

"Which ones are they?"

"Princess Sara Gizaw and her three sons are here. I meet them every day. They don't deserve to be jailed; they are harmless. When I come out, I will tell you an amazing story nobody knows."

"You have become small, what do they feed you?"

"I told you; here we build not muscles but brains."

"I miss you."

"This is a 'miss' country. We will manage, Daniel. Hold on!" said Ghenet and laughed.

They chatted uninterrupted for a quarter of an hour more, joking and laughing, all the time touching each other's fingers.

While Daniel and Ghenet chatted, Jovani and Beza stood behind the sentry-box waiting for their turn. Beza came to see Ghenet; Jovani was simply a company. Although Beza and Ghenet were not that close friends, they knew each other so long enough as to pay a visit when one would end up in prison or hospital.

When his time was over, Daniel met the couple near the sentry-box, and chatted with them until they were told to proceed. Daniel and Beza were close friends. Their friendship began since they were kids of single digit age. They had gone in the same school, and at times shared the same classes. They had sported together, sang school songs, and marched together in protest demonstrations as students called for land reform.

Having heard the failure of Operation Raza, Ermias was in his happier frame of mind when he received a file that Mustafa, the policeman, had retrieved from the police archive and left at bar Tiku the day before. Sitting at a corner with his back toward the wall, he read the first part of the police report on his father's case. The file was worn out, and the handwritten text had faded out. He was anxious and nervous to make any sense out of the words. But somehow, he managed to read it through twice before Jovani arrived. The witness hearing that Corporal Beyene had conducted on Tuesday, March 20, 1962, covered five pages, and the report of investigation led by Lieutenant Alemayo covered seven pages.

According to an eyewitness account, the suspect was a short, Tigrigna-speaking man, probably from Eritrea. The witness, a night guard in the neighborhood who claimed to have seen the crime taking place, had asserted that the perpetrator and the victim seemed intimate with each other. They walked together in the darkness, chatting and laughing.

It was at this point that an outrageous thought crossed Ermias' mind. He hated it, but he couldn't help contemplating it. In his life with the Eritrean Liberation movement, he had many times encountered scandalous intrigues. There had been corruption and power struggles within the leadership. People had been killed in the battle to go up the power ladder. In the early years of the struggle for independence, Ermias' father, Tesfay, had gained fame and recognition among the people and the fighters. He had been on his way to become the topmost leader of the liberation movement, and his contenders wouldn't like that.

"Could those slayers have done it?" Ermias attended back to the file and examined the report. There was a passage that told his father's life history briefly elaborating that:

- *he was a secessionist who agitated the Eritrean people to rebel against the unification with Ethiopia,*
- *the was organizing Eritreans who lived in Ethiopia and collecting contributions to support the struggle.*

The report conceded that the suspect could not be found; presumably, had left the country. After exhausting its resources for the search, the homicide section had decided to discontinue the investigation.

Once again, Ermias' former belief was restored. He believed that the State, to curb his father's activity, had secretly liquidated him as it always did to its enemies. When he closed the file, he had no suspect other than the Ethiopian government. But he had to be sure.

In the afternoon, Ermias went to the Fifth Police Station to meet Mustafa again. The station was quieter and not crowded now.

"I wanted to see Private Mustafa, maddam," said Ermias to the receptionist.

"At your service, sir." words came from behind. Ermias turned to see Mustafa's smiling face.

They exchanged words of greeting, smiled at each other, joked a little, and then Ermias' face turned into a businessman's face.

"I'll like to have a word with you, Mustafa?"

Co-operatively Mustafa led Ermias to the exit. They went out of the station yard and stood at the far corner leaning against the compound's high wall.

"The file… was it helpful?" Mustafa rubbed his hands as though reminding Ermias that he owed him a service.

"That was a file of immense importance, Mustafa." Ermias held out an envelope and passed it to Mustafa. "I want you to do me another favor. I want to meet the policemen who were assigned on the case."

"Who were they? Do you have the names?" Mustafa felt the amount in the envelope before he put it in his pocket.

"Do you know these men?" Ermias unfolded another piece of paper and showed him.

"Beyene, Beyene …Alemayo, Alemayo… never heard of them. It's a long time ago, long before I was employed. I have only five years in the police. None of them were here at the time."

"You can certainly find out where they are now, can't you?"

"It won't be difficult."

"Let me know as soon as you find out."

"I'll surely do that."

Chapter 13

During months following the collapse of Operation Raza, the Dergue was undergoing some changes. Its attitude towards its opponents was marked by significant improvement. Abashed by the defeat in Eritrea, Dergue members who had opted for a military solution were caught naked in front of their opponents. As a result, the balance of power within the Dergue had rapidly shifted from the hard-liners to the liberals who were ready to talk peace and share power with the civilian oppositions.

Quickly, the liberals set up a 17-odd man commission, the objective of which was to examine the excess of the Revolution and to restructure the Dergue itself. They had to make a clear and public gesture to invite the opposition into a friendly negotiation and redress whatever grievances they had. Promptly, the commission recommended measures to strengthen the democratic and collective working of the Derg. Thus, Major Mengistu, the hard-liner's leader, was shunted aside and his power and ambition were curbed. He was still the chairman of the Steering Committee, but it was a hallow position. The plan was to strip him of power, tarnish his image, and finally remove him from office. A young man named Alemayo, a major from the police, was granted a secretary-general position with broad power.[IV]

A few weeks later, the entire socio-political situation of the country begun changing. Revolutionary indoctrination that had regularly dominated the radio and television programs reduced dramatically. Sights of armored vehicles in the street, armed soldiers, and civilians carrying weapons in public places began to diminish. Police and security inspection at the gates of government buildings, banks, and big institutions eased. In some places, political prisoners were pardoned and released.

Hoping that Ghenet would soon be set free, Daniel began planning his future again, looking for a job. In his possession was his high school certificate carrying average marks and a paper of acclamation from Inango farm verifying his work as a teacher. Before the rainy seasons came, he sent job applications to a dozen different government and private institutions. Many didn't even bother to reply to his applications. Nevertheless, there had been few responses. The one that interested Daniel most was a private school where he appeared for an interview and was told to start right away. A salary of 150 Birr a month was barely enough to cover a single person's necessities for a month. But Daniel didn't see it in terms of money. He was rather pleased to be busy doing something he enjoyed at this time of political uncertainties and social unrest.

In the last week of June, apparently in commemoration of its birth, the Dergue ordered the release of several hundred political prisoners, mainly Zemachs and students considered to be supporters or members of the EPRP.

Ghenet was set free on Tuesday, 28 June. Her mother, Askale; Daniel, Abinet, Biniam, and few relatives were at the city detention center's main gate to welcome her. It was another emotional moment of tears and laughter, hugging, and kissing.

"I told you, it won't take long," Daniel said as he embraced her at his turn after her folks.

"I never doubted it."

The crowd around was building every minute as new prisoners came out of the jail. A prison guard ordered that the public had to clear the gateway

"We have got to get out of this place before they turn you in again, Ghenet, get into the car with your family. I'll arrange a little party for you on Saturday. You go home with your folks now, rest, and come to the party, Saturday at noon."

"A party! What party, Daniel?"

"A welcome party and more."

"I can't wait to be there."

Later in the evening, Daniel told his plan behind the party to his mother.

"Are you telling me that you are going to propose to her at the party?"

"Yes, mother. What's wrong?"

"You should have given us more time, Daniel."

"It's only a family get-together."

Abinet had no objection to his plan except that it was sudden. She was overjoyed. Daniel was the first son who came close to formal marriage, with her eldest son lost in the Eritrean desert, the other lost in the city's turmoil. The preparation went on for the next two days.

On Friday, something awful struck again. A letter from Samson came and disclosed the final fate of Gaushaw, Ghenet's brother. The party had to be canceled and postponed to the future.

Ghenet's family was severely hit by Gaushaw's death. It was unbearable not only to the mother but to Ghenet as well. Despite Daniel's consistent effort to comfort Ghenet, it took her several days to overcome the grief and come out of the depression. Daniel's objectivity and his words of love always calmed her and had the effect of soothing her. On the other hand, Ghenet's mother, Askale, was not strong enough to take the blow. When she heard her son's death, she lost her sense and had to be observed by a doctor. Though she recovered from the shock, she had other health complications that aggravated the miserable life they already had.

Life, as usual, had to go on. Ghenet had to move on and do something before the family was struck by another adversary: starvation. She began to look for a job.

As it turned out to be, her effort to get one was depressingly fruitless. It made her hate she was born female, for she thought she could have a better chance had been born male. She had similar qualifications and experience as that of

Daniel's, but in a man-dominated society, with a long tradition of negligence for women, a woman's beauty and availability as an object of sex had more merit than talent and experience.

The condition at home, aging mother with poor health, three children who seemed to have stopped growing at all, was urgent. Virtually, the family had no means of income. Ghenet had to come up with something before starvation struck: some job or business. She had gone to every possible employer in the city, sent tens of applications, and phoned as much, but the response was annoying. Most of the employers she talked to were interested in seeing her for reasons far different from what she expected. Some government bureaucrats were unashamed to openly ask for sexual amusement before they even consider employment. When every interesting job seemed impossible than difficult, Ghenet began looking for less attractive and low-paid jobs like waitresses, kitchen maids, etc. Surprisingly, these jobs were not less complicated as she thought they would be because employers preferred uneducated country-girls whom they could exploit than city-bred girls who knew their rights.

Some taxing weeks passed. Ghenet did not give up; she went on looking for anything that paid, and Daniel was always beside her with encouraging words. There was no place she did not walk to, and no door she did not knock in the city. At last, an offer came from the Ras Hotel, and she accepted it. A job as a waitress—not bad for the time being. A hundred- and Ten-Birr salary was enough to make sure that there is a piece of bread in the bellies of her little siblings. Besides, she would not have transportation cost because it was only an hour walk.

"It may not help the kids to grow," Ghenet said when she told Daniel about the job, "but it could keep their heart to beat and their lungs to breathe."

"Better times will soon come, Ghenet. We are now in a time of peace. And in peace, there is little we cannot do," was all Daniel had to say.

Time went on. Weeks passed and the Ethiopian Yew Year came. With its secessionist adversaries in the north, violent opponents in the middle and aggressive enemies in the east, Ethiopia celebrated the New Year, On Sept. 11, 1976, as a year of hope, peace, and prosperity. The following day, Sept 12, was the second anniversary of the Revolution. On this day, it was officially announced that the Head of State, General Teferi Bante, would make a nationwide speech from the Revolution Square, a vast arena for a mass rally. It was called Mesqel Square[V] before the Revolution, in contempt of the church and the people, robbed its name. The festival known as Feast of the Holy Cross's Exaltation used to be celebrated by the Ethiopian Orthodox church on this sacred square every year in September. Located at the center of the city, a few hundred meters from the palace, the square was reconstructed and decorated after the Dergue assumed power. Government officials and senior military officials had a secured an elevated platform from where they could make speeches, watch processions and study the miserable faces of the poor masses.

It was Sunday, 12 September. The sky was gray, but the weather was pleasant. Daniel and Ghenet went to Revolution Square to listen to the speech of the Head of State, hoping there would be some policy change since Major Mengistu had been stripped of his power,

The square was crowded to capacity. Tens of thousands of people had come to hear the New Year promise; not to celebrate the Revolution but to listen to words of peace from the army officials who held the country's future in the palm of their hands.

"I feel like something good is to come," Daniel said as he scanned the crowd.

Ghenet, standing on her toes so as to get better view, looked at Daniel, "What did you see to feel like that?"

"I can smell it in the air, Ghenet. Don't you."

"The Dergue has a hundred and twenty different odors—too many to distinguish one from the other. The chief is on the floor now. Let's listen to the lies he has to tell."

The voice of the Head of State, General Teferi Banti, exploded:

"My fellow countrymen, let me first express my deepest feeling for this particular occasion and the ideals we have been striving to realize in the past two years. Since the overthrow of the monarchy, we have come a long way towards freedom and equality. As the Revolution gained momentum, we have achieved certain goals that benefited the mass. The nationalization of land, *extra houses* and private enterprise, the formation of the Urban Dwellers Association, and Farmworker's Associations are some of our outstanding achievements that required our utmost energy and time."

"The next phase of our progress would be to improve the lives of the masses, and that would require our commitment to sacrifice more of our time, resources, and workforce. The goal might seem far, tiresome, and difficult, but it's achievable. We may not see its fruits tomorrow or next year, but it will come for all of us to reap. I say all of us for I'm calling all to compromise differences and come to join a national salvation front which is open to all citizen…."

At this point, the message was clear. It was a call for tolerance, reconciliation, and compromise, just as many wanted and few expected.

"At this time," the General went on, "our beloved country is bleeding from within as well as from without. Our unity as one nation and our diversity as many cultures are threatened. Hostile neighbors are taking advantage of this time of transition. Assuming that we are weakened at this time of change, our enemies are lining up to launch their attack. Their first step was wearying us by dividing the people into numerous political groups who fight and kill each other. Indeed, they seem to have succeeded in that because that's what we see today in our country. Their next step, undoubtedly, is to resort to naked aggression. Are we prepared for that now? No, we are not. We are divided; hopelessly divided and severely vulnerable to foreign aggretion."

"The time has come now for us to respond accordingly. We have to undermine our differences and strengthen our unity. Therefore, I call all democrats and socialists, nationalists, and all peace-loving people to join hands and come to one democratic salivation front and defend the motherland."

This is a change of policy," said Ghenet.

"Indeed."

Following the Head of State, other Dergue officials also made prepared speeches, some supporting the need for unity and reconciliation, others arrogantly criticizing the very idea of forming a united front with all political groups. In their remarks, some indicated that the political organizations like the EPRP were enemies of the Revolution and the people, and no united front could be formed with groups that have opposing ideas.

"Can we fight and win foreign invaders while we have collaborators amongst us. The EPRP is a foreign agent working to topple the government and weaken the nation. We ought not to fight an enemy many miles away while we have one here next door."

"I gather that the leadership is divided. I don't understand," Daniel muttered in a voice so low that only Ghenet could hear.

"I think the policy delivered by the Head of State has to be the policy of the government. And that's what counts," Ghenet said.

"I agree. But some of the ones that opposed the Head of State are prominent Dergue members. This shows that Dergue doesn't have one stand on the issue. A divided Dergue is a divided army, and that's dangerous, Ghenet."

"The majority of the Dergue must have endorsed the Head of State."

"That remains to be seen. I would like to hear what Major Mengistu has to say on this." Daniel looked at the platform. He watched the last speaker finish, but there was no one after him. No Mengistu.

However, the following days marked an evident change of policy on the part of the government. The state radio frequently propagated peace and harmony, along with the news that the new policy of peace had got landslide support from the entire population. The EPRP, too, showed restraint on its violent form of resistance; tts retaliatory killings ceased completely. Streets, schools, and market places became calmer again. Subsequently, students and teachers, who had boycotted classes in a clear protest against the Derg's arbitrary arrests, began to go to schools. Business people commenced to buy more and sell more. There was a slight improvement in the stagnant economy. Slowly, imperceptibly life had began to normalize.

Chapter 14

The city of Gonder, which had been Ethiopia's capital city in the 16th century, had never been entirely tranquil. The ceaseless tides of the dispute between the political organizations, the Derg's repression and EPRP's retaliation that had plagued the nation, prevented that. Yet, since the government's new policy took effect, life had returned to its normal status again. Like the other parts of the country, the town enjoyed a period of peace and harmony. One thing distinctly strange was the growing number of new young faces that no one seemed to notice. The young had come out from the hiding, one could say.

Samson was the first to feel the sudden influx of young immigrants in Gonder. It had directly affected his job in the tea-room, where he had begun to work shortly after entering the town. He earned a few Birrs with free lodging and meal— no complaint on his part. After Operation Raza, Samson was decidedly against any form of violence, and in Gonder, he found a relatively stable environment where he could calm himself and sort out a plan for his future until his family motioned for him to come home.

The tea-room stood in the center of the ancient town overlooking the main square. From the square branched the main streets and alleyways, reaching in every direction to the high walls that circled the city. Now, these streets were filled with young people who frequently visited the tea-room. Samson was working twice as much as he usually did before the peace, to cope with the increasingly demanding job.

In a way, Samson liked the exacting job since he wanted to be in motion throughout the day to be able to forget the past, forget blood, death, and the human agony in the Eritrean desert. It was like another type of war that kept him sane and sober. In keeping himself busy, he managed to pacify the accusing conscience that would otherwise torment him by reminding him of the innocent people bombed in the village of Awgaro; he still believed many would have been saved if he had suggested evacuation.

The nights were not that peaceful. The life he lived as a guerrilla fighter in Eritrea; the battle, the killings, and the suffering used to come and distract his peace of mind. Then the accusing conscience would be transformed into a vicious prosecutor asking a single question, "why didn't you forward your opinion?" making the night sleepless and jittery.

In the middle of the first week of November, Samson noticed three young fellows enter the tea-room and take a corner table. This time he had an assistant, so the job wasn't as stressful. Indifferently, he followed behind the guests and waited until they made themselves comfortable to order.

"Three cups of tea," ordered the taller one with short kinky hair, narrow black eyes, and a big nose. He was dressed neatly, a sports jacket and a red and white striped shirt. Samson turned swiftly as soon as he heard the order. A few minutes later, he came back with the cups of tea and put them before each person. As he did so, his glance shifted from the taller to the one next, and his eyes narrowed in puzzlement and then widened in recognition. It was six long years; the 19-year-old boy was now 25, taller, the face broader.

"Kibrom!" Samson placed the tray on the table and threw himself at the perplexed young man who seemed to have just recognized his brother, and raised himself from the chair. Kibrom had heard that Samson was in Gonder but hadn't the slightest expectation to find him serving him a cup of tea. They embraced each other firmly.

"Look at you… you have grown up," Samson exclaimed.

"I heard you were in Gonder, but I never anticipated meeting you here. I thought it would take me some time to find you." Kibrom turned to his friends and said, "My brother, Samson."

Samson stepped forward and stretched a hand.

"Rashid," said the taller man hesitantly and shook Samson's hand with the tip of his fingers, distinctly showing contempt. Samson's shabby cloth and skinny body were not impressive to Rashid's type of people. The other younger fellow who appeared to have withdrawn inward shook Samson's hand politely and sunk into his seat.

Samson pulled a chair from the nearest table and sat next to Kibrom. He was flushed and excited, but Rashid was not welcoming. Fixing hostile eyes, Rashid watched him through the spiraling smoke of his cigarette.

"You're in the middle of our business. Can you leave us alone?" said Rashid sinisterly.

"I'm sorry if I have intruded. I was …"

"I know. You can talk to your brother later when we are through."

"I'll join you in a few minutes, Samson," said Kibrom, tabbing his brother on the shoulder.

Samson's lips twitched into a thin smile as he calmly left the table. He was bewildered. Leaning against the counter, he watched Kibrom and his friends talking and wondered what their secret business could be. Rashid was making most of the talking. Kibrom also was making some talks, but he seemed to be constantly interrupted by the big guy. The other young man was quiet all the time and appeared frightened. He didn't touch his cup of tea. He seemed to nod in agreement for everything Rashid came up.

"What are they up to?" he turned and asked the owner of the tearoom at the counter.

"Who?"

"These new faces? Haven't you noticed?"

"Yes, I have. I have never had my counter as full as these days, and that's all I care about. Anything bothering you?"

"Not that I can't handle. You see…" Samson pointed at Kibrom, "that guy is my brother, my younger brother"

"I see," the man said, pretending to be interested. "Whatever they take is on the house."

Half an hour later, Rashid and the other young man rose while Kibrom remained seated, waiting for Samson, who, on seeing the others leave, strode towards the table.

"Make it short," whispered Rashid in Samson's ear as he went past him. It sounded like an order, but Samson chose to ignore it.

"Sorry, you had to wait," apologized Kibrom.

"What is all this? What are you up to?" asked Samson, brows ripping down with concern.

"These are private things, Samson."

"Even between us?"

"Well, it's the time, brother… it's better not to know about somethings. I hope you understand what I mean."

"I'm not sure." Samson searched his brother's face and saw a hint of mischief. "I demand to know."

"I'm on the run, Samson. I can't stay in Addis."

"What have you done?"

"I have been in action. You know this EPRP thing."

"But I heard peace is declared."

"If it holds, then I won't be away for long."

There was a moment of silence and thinking. They looked at each other with eyes betraying the softness of their hearts. Through Kibrom, Samson saw the family.

"Come on, let's go out for fresh air and tell me about our family."

Outside, standing on the porch, overlooking the Royal Enclosure of Emperor Fasillades of the 16th century, Kibrom began narrating about their family. Few steps away, Rashid was waiting impatiently, the other young man with him.

Kibrom went on: "…Daniel and Ghenet are planning to marry. You have got to be there for the wedding."

"That's a nice thing to hear."

"I heard about what happened to Gaushaw. I'm sorry," Kibrom said. "In fact, the army reputed that he had deserted. So believed the family until your letter came."

Samson felt a combined wave of anger and sorrow pass across his body as he heard the name, Gaushaw, with the word desertion."

"War is a cruel thing, Kibrom," he said in a low voice. "We are killing each other for ideals worth nothing—much less human life."

"Hurry up, boys!" Rashid shouted.

"Who are these friends of yours?" Samson asked, staring at Rashid.

"They are members of the EPRP, the underground party. Rashid is supposed to take us to our sanctuary," Kibrom refrained from telling his brother that the EPRP had made themselves a fortress up in the mountain of Assimba. "The other one is like me, on the run."

"And all these new young people are going to the same place? You must be organizing an army!"

Kibrom smiled and said, "I suppose we don't have much time, but I'm delighted to have seen you."

"How long will you be in Gondar?" Samson asked.

"Not long. Maybe we will leave in the evening, and you? When will you travel to Addis?'

"I am waiting for a signal from home. When I know it's safe, I will move."

"Convey my regards to Mother. I feel I have wronged her. I hope she will forgive me."

Samson fumbled in his pocket and fished some twenty Birr. "It's not much, but… might help. I saved it for my transportation."

"I appreciate your kindness, Samson, but I can't accept the offer. You will need it."

"Not as much as you do. I work, eat, and live here in the tea-room. I don't have expenses. As for my transportation, I'll work a few more months. That's all."

Reluctantly Kibrom accepted the money and hugged his big brother firmly.

"You remember that Mother used to call you the guardian angel, and you have always been one."

"Goodbye, may God be with you, Kibrom."

"Goodbye, Samson. Don't forget to attend Daniel's wedding for both of us. Besides, he wants you to be his best man," Kibrom said as they parted.

"You bet, I shall be there. Good luck, brother," said Samson watching Kibrom go with slow footsteps. He knew his brother was going to join a rebel group like the one he had left some six months ago.

Chapter 15

The new peaceful environment had also inspired Goytom Gobezay to see the opportunities in business. He was able to consider the possibilities of making both legal and illegal businesses. According to what Goytom had come up with, the unlawful branch was the easiest and fastest way to prosper.

This peace, the State bragged about, was only in the cities between students and security forces. The rural areas were still under tension. The eastern territory was being torn apart by Western Somalia Liberation Front, the North Eastern region of Afar was at war with the regime, EPRP and the TPLF were establishing armed resistance in the north. Apart from that, corrupt officials could also make the way easy for the business in his mind to flourish. Could there be a better condition for the business of weapon smuggling and dealing! Goytom needed only a little money to start with, and he knew where to get it.

Last year when his hope to reclaim one of his confiscated villas died out, he had the urge to request his share of the house in which his former wife, Abinet, resided now. Considering the consequence of the conflict with his family, he had dropped the impulse and had tried searched for other means. But there had been nothing for Goytom to turn to, so he resorted to his former idea, and sent delegates of relatives to Abinet to pursue her into selling the house and give him what he was entitled to; half of the house's price i.e., over fifteen thousand Birr. Enough to start the business he intended.

Abinet was not the type to talk such madness with anyone. She had chased the delegates out of the house before they uttered a word. Hence, Goytom had to take the case to the court of law. And Abinet had been summoned to appear and present her objection, but she was so upset that she ignored the court. Another subpoena was issued to her.

Praying not to meet any of his sons, Goytom, accompanied by his lawyer, went to deliver the subpoena to Abinet. It was at this time that he met his son, Daniel, for the first time since his return from the Zemecha.

"How are you, father?" Daniel uttered, shocked by how much his father had aged. The deep lines were gorged across his forehead and down his cheek. He could tell that he had crashed head-on with the high-speed Revolution.

Goytom opened his arms, embraced Daniel and kissed him on his cheeks, "Welcome son, you have changed much."

"It's been long time."

"Is your mother in the house?" asked Goytom, casting a long glance deep into the compound, his voice quivering. Obviously Goytom hated what he was doing now. He wished there were other options to find money.

"Yes, she is inside," answered Daniel politely.

Goytom turned to his attorney and said, "You go in and give her.'

"May I ask what you're up to?" inquired Daniel when the attorney went into the compound.

"Some legal matters between your mother and me," Goytom said with an effort to avoid Daniel's eyes that were fixed on him.

"I don't think you're doing the right thing, Father"

"The Law will decide that."

"This is a family matter; what is right in the eyes of the law is not always right in the eyes of justice."

"Don't you preach that to me? Didn't I try to solve this dispute in the traditional way? Where were you then? Why didn't you talk sense to your mother then?"

"This will make worse the already shaky relation you have with the family," warned Daniel politely.

"What is left of me now. It can't be worse than it already is. I have lost everything, my property, my houses, and my families…" cried Goytom. When the lawyer came back, he stopped, and Daniel went back to see his mother.

"How did she take it?" Goytom asked his lawyer.

"Calmly."

"Don't you think the court would rule in favor of me if she doesn't appear this time?"

"Possibly."

At the Beyene street, Goytom hailed a taxi. When he was about to get in it, his eyes caught another familiar automobile behind the cab. He cast a side-glance at the occupant in the back seat, whom he identified as Captain Zeleke. The car flunked by security guards turned left, obviously to his old dwelling, where the captain now resided.

Goytom breathed heavily and jumped in the taxi front seat. As the lawyer took the rear seat, he turned sidewise and uttered a question.

"How is this new policy of the Derg? They seem to be tired of governing. Will they relinquish power?"

"That's the rumor going around," the lawyer said in uncertain manner.

"Don't you think so, yourself?"

"I believe only half of what I see, Goytom. And none of what I hear."

"Bunch of thieves!" grumbled Goytom.

Chapter 16

Ermias and Jovani met at Bar Tiku early in the morning when there was none in the bar beside the bartender, who was drying glasses. So, they openly talked about intelligence gathering that showed secret meetings between Soviet Embassy officials and senior Dergue officials.

"That could be a devastating blow to our struggle." Jovani said.

"The soviet plan is to enfeeble and put us out of negotiating position and then force us to swallow whatever solution they come up with," Ermias said.

"How can they have one foot in Somalia and the other in Ethiopia?" asked Jovani.

"The Soviets know what would serve their best interest. There is increasing evidence indicating their objective to form a Confederation of Eritrea, Somalia, and Ethiopia. This would put the entire Horn and part of the Red Sea in their control. Somalia had rejected the very idea of a confederation with Ethiopia. That has put her at odds with the Soviets."

"These are illusions. It will never work," stated Jovani.

"Superpowers think they can do anything on this planet," Ermias said and asked if there was anything from the local intelligence gathering.

"That's all for today, but I have minor things if you want to see."

"Minor things? Let me see them."

Jovani fumbled in his pocket and came out with a folded sheet of paper, "This is a list of names Beza copied from Captain Zeleke's papers. She gave me yesterday."

"I thought she wouldn't accept the job. How much are we supposed to pay her? said Ermias skimming over the list of names.

"Five hundred per month, that's twice as much as what she used to earn from the Nyalas. She needs money for her travel. She won't be around long."

"What are the signs supposed to mean?" inquired Ermias without attaching any particular attention to the names, and frowned at the signs beside each name: signs of the arrow, the question mark, and the cross.

"I don't know… could be some military code. You can ask the colonel," Jovani suggested and shifted his eyes at the policeman who just entered the bar.

"Here!" called Ermias as he saw Mustafa, the policeman.

Mustafa approached and introduced himself to Jovani.

"I hope I'm not interrupting," Mustafa said, smiling.

"Not at all. Have a seat"

"Yes," Mustafa licked his lips, "I just came from work to tell you what I found out.

"I can't wait to hear."

"Well," Mustafa went right to the point, "Sergeant Beyene has retired… very long time ago. Nobody knows whether he is dead or alive. But the other one, Lieutenant Alemayo, is an interesting character. He is a member of the Derg."

"Member of the Derg?

"Yes, isn't that amazing?"

"Tell me more about him."

"Well, he studied law in the United States and came back to join the Police Force, where he worked until June 1974. In 1974, he was elected to represent the Police Force in the Derg. Now he has the rank of a major and is a prominent figure in the military government. His friends talk about him as a man of exceptional intelligence and determination."

When Mustafa finished, Ermias hastily looked at the list of names in his hand. There it stood right up, number one, the name Major Alemayo with the sign of an arrow beside it. The coincidence surprised him, but the mystery was overwhelming.

"Thanks, Mustafa. That was a great job." Ermias slipped a note of a fifty Birr across the table to Mustafa, who grabbed it swiftly and stood.

"I have got to go. If you need me, don't hesitate to contact me," said Mustafa and left.

Ermias peered at the paper in his hand and counted the names on the list. There were seventeen names; General Teferi Banti, the Head of State, was one of them. He then folded the paper in four and kept it in his wallet.

"Well, your job seemed to be completed. When will you be going?" Jovani asked

"I have got a personal case to take care of. As soon as I finished that, I'll be ready to leave."

"Anything I can help?"

"Not much… I am looking for Major Alemayo. He was the officer who investigated my father's case. I have some questions to ask him. That's all. Assefa might help to set a meeting between Alemayo and me."

The following day in the afternoon at 4 o'clock, Ermias and Colonel Assefa met in Ethiopia Hotel. Sitting at the entrance floor they ordered coffee and fell into one of those desultory conversations that relieved high affairs tension. They talked about food and drinks, joked about soldiering and spy affairs, and laughed. Half an hour later, Ermias came to his point.

"I guess you know Major Alemayo, the Dergue member, don't you?"

"Yes, he is my friend," replied Assefa. "What about him?"

"Alemayo was the police officer who investigated my father's case. I want to ask him a couple of questions. I need you to help me meet him."

"I guess that is not much to ask. I can fix it any time except today. The Dergue is having an emergency meeting today. It's in session now. I hope it goes well."

"What is special this time?"

"There was considerable removal and transfer within the Armed forces recently. Troops of special force are stationed on the outskirts of the city. Don't ask me why, because I don't know. My section is almost paralyzed now. Many of my loyal agents are transferred."

"Wait a minute," Ermias fumbled swiftly in his pockets, took out his wallet, and pulled out a piece of paper.

"Here," he said and held out the paper to the colonel.

"What is this now?" inquired Assefa skimming over the list of names. A moment later, he had his fingers on his chin pulling hairs, a sign of deep concentration. Then his eyes widened, his neck stiffened. He seemed to come to what he had suspected but not believed. "Where did you get this? When did you get it?"

"We got it from Captain Zeleke himself," said Ermias and leaned back in his chair.

"My God!" Assefa rose to his feet suddenly. His suspicion of an assault against the liberal Dergue members became a firm conviction now. "Come on, follow me. I smell a conspiracy. Don't you see it? We have got to move fast."

"I don't understand," said Ermias, following behind Assefa.

"I'll explain later," uttered Assefa and moved fast. He went down the stairs two at a time. As he rushed outside, he spotted armored military vehicles cross past the street to the palace direction. Now half running, he arrived at the alley behind the hotel and leaped into his car. He opened the door to the Ermias and started the car. In seconds he was out of the alley and on the street heading to the Palace.

He drove fast, as fast as he could, jumping light, beating the changing signals, weaving in and out of traffic. He must be there before the Wolves strike. If a policeman stopped him down, he'd have to flash his badge and bellow emergency. He drove on the brink of recklessness, ignoring the angry horns. Halfway to the palace, the road was crowded with vehicular traffic—far ahead, a blockade.

"What's going on?" inquired Ermias as they approached the picket.

"The people on the list are liberals, who advocated for the formation of people's government. If we don't warn them in time, I am pretty convinced they will perish. Mengistu is up to no good."

"Do you believe he will harm them?"

"Definitely. If we can get to the Palace, it's not only them we save today but the country as well.

Assefa slowed the car and stopped right beside the guarding soldier, where he must show papers. The soldier checked the paper, showed his regards, and allowed him to proceed. But not far, at the intersection of Yohannes Street and Menelik Avenue, the road was blocked, forcing the traffic almost to a standstill. Assefa had to swing the car on the sidewalk. Pedestrians seemed to have smelled the feast earlier, so there were no many of them in the area. Without many hindrances, Assefa was able to drive further. At the blockade, he was stopped again. Armored vehicles and heavily armed soldiers had reinforced the barricade. No vehicular traffic was allowed to pass. Assefa showed his papers, but this time to no avail.

"It's a matter of national security," he asserted to the soldiers.

"But orders are orders, sir. You know, of course," the soldier said politely.

"What are the orders?" asked Assefa suppressing his anger and looking afar at the Palace yard, which appeared to be peaceful.

"That nobody should pass to this area until further notice. Strictly nobody."

"Whose orders are they, if I may ask?"

"Captain Zeleke's, sir," answered the soldier.

"Where is he now?"

"In the palace."

There was no need to waste time. Assefa started the car, backed up, shifted gears, and revved it angrily.

In the great hall of the Palace of Menelik, a emergency meeting of the Dergue was held. Some eighty-five Dergue members were present to discuss the country's national security, the current political situation, and the future of the Dergue itself.

Tense but not as tense as a person who would stage a coup in a few minutes, Major Mengistu was sitting at the far end of the front row, facing the podium. Since he was stripped of his powers, he had come to lesser contact with most of the Dergue members, but he pretended to hold no grudge and was cunningly showing a humble, smiling face to avert suspicion.

On the stage was General Teferi Banti, sitting at the center of a long table with honorary Dergue officials on each side of him; on his left Major Alemayo. He had been so preoccupied with the work to prepare for a smooth transfer of power that he had not noticed that the guards at his office had been changed when he went to his office in the morning. He was too pressed by the burden of responsibility as a Head of State of a nation in turmoil. There was no one present as eager as him to get relieved of that burden. Next, to his right, sat the vise chairman of the Dergue who still trusted his friend, Mengistu.

Among the audience was Captain Zeleke dressed full military, back at the far end, a strategically excellent position enabling him to survey the entire chamber. As the minutes ticked by, he was noticeably behaving nervously, chewing a gum and smoking continuously in the chamber.

In less than an hour, the first two Agendas had been discussed without raising any significant arguments. The last and the most controversial debate was to come: The future of the Derg.

Major Alemayo, a tall, handsome police officer who was an outspoken Democrat known for his advocacy to end the Derg's rule, was the first to speak on the subject. As he walked over to the floor, Mengistu's eyes were fixed on him all the way.

Bending his head to organize his thoughts, Alemayo took a few seconds before he opened his mouth. Then he lifted his head to confront the audience.

"Comrade Chairman and members of the Derg," addressed Alemayo, his voice loud and clear, "the Provisional Military Administrative Council has been in power for more than two years. Two years ago, we were ordinary soldiers and policemen with relatively lesser responsibilities. It was historical events that dwelt the ultimate responsibility of ruling the country upon us. At the time when the Revolution broke out, there was no organized political body to guide the turn of events or to enforce law and order. The armed forces and the police had to come in. And we did. Since then, we have executed various reforms that have gained public support and international admiration…"

After reiterating the gains of the Revolution, Major Alemayo cited the damages that the Revolution inflicted on the country extensively. As he explained the incompetence of the Dergue and demanded its urgent dismissal, many members of the Dergue fell to putting their heads together and consulting in whispers.

"Two and half years ago," went on Alemayo, "we swore before God and the people to relinquish power as soon as the socio-political situation normalized. We have arrived at a time when those words of honor should be respected and applied in deeds. Since we, at the beginning of this year, declared peace with all political groups, our cities have once again become calm and stable now. I believe this is the right time to hand over government power to the people.

"Members of the Council, I call you to endorse this motion and work to its end. Thank you."

The applause he received was tremendous that he had to wait on the floor for some seconds to entertain it. Then he, too, clapped and walked to his seat.

Chairman Teferi Bante lifted a heavy gavel and struck it once to end the applause.

"The floor is open to anyone having a different or opposing opinion," said Chairman Teferi.

Mengistu had declared himself against disbanding the Dergue from the start, so all eyes were turned on him, expecting him to fight to the end. Even now, members of the Dergue were equally divided in their sympathies. If Mengistu had prepared to say some words, he would have won the vote not only because he was a good speaker but also because he was well respected for his dedication to the Derg. Besides, most of the Dergue members relished the comfort and sweets of their present positions to be concerned with honoring their promise. Secretly they despised Alemayo's noble idea in support of Mengistu's lust for power. To vote for Alemayo, they knew, was to vote against themselves. But somebody had to dare to say it. And Mengistu seemed not to care.

"I assume," the Chairman said, "there is no opposition to Major Alemayo's proposal. In that case, the major shall proceed to explain the procedures of handing over power to an elected government."

Major Alemayo was again on the podium, now more resolved than before.

"As you can see, the copies before you," he bent to turn the first page of his document on the desk. "This is the first draft of the procedure. It was arranged and discussed thoroughly by prominent Dergue members and civilian intellectuals. It consists of sixty-two articles on forty-seven pages. We shall discuss them article by article to grasp the whole point and avoid misunderstanding. We shall cancel whatever we see unfit to the prevailing situation and mend or add whatever seemed necessary.

As Alemayo began to read the first Article, Mengistu skimmed over the pages of his copies. As he did so, he grinned. Then he lifted his face and surveyed the audience, who seemed to have been carried away by Alemayo. Few were reading the draft, while many had chosen to listen intently to the words direct from the speaker. Mengistu scanned the entire chamber, and his eyes caught the twinkling eyes of his right-hand-man, Captain Zeleke. In the speed of sight, messages were exchanged. With the order issued, Zeleke heaved himself out of his chair and sneaked out through the back door unnoticed. Mengistu sucked in his breath, drew back his shoulder, and waited vigilantly.

"Article 4," read Alemayo, "election of representatives of the people shall be held throughout the country... to constitute the parliament."

"Article 5, as soon as a civilian government responsible to the parliament is established, the Dergue shall be disbanded..."

There was minor applause that gradually grew louder. Even Mengistu joined cunningly, clapping and smiling. A moment later, he rose suddenly and left without excusing himself. Unsuspectingly the chairman had given him a sidelong look but darted his eyes to the chamber.

A few minutes later, when the clock on the wall ticked six o'clock, the main door of the great hall opened wide and revealed a horrifying scene that shocked the entire humanity in the hall. The conspiracy had come to the open now, naked, ugly for the entire Dergue to see. Led by Captain Zeleke, some forty soldiers armed with machine guns stormed the hall in two files.

Zeleke, attended by four guards, stepped forward as the soldiers spread left and right in half circle, pointing their machine gun at the members of the Derg. The Head of the State, General Tafari was numb in disbelief. Alemayo froze with his mouth half-open. The rest of the Dergue remained seated, confused, eyes staring at Zeleke.

"What's going on! Can anyone tell me!" shouted the vise chairman, a man of boyish frankness in his manner, known for his bold but selfish remarks against the Derg. After him came more protest, but Zeleke instantly hushed them down.

"Keep quiet! And be seated!" roared Zeleke. "Comrade Mengistu shall explain. Until then, I'm in charge, so do as I say!" Though he pretended to be tough, there were signs of indecisiveness in Zeleke's articulation and manner.

Nevertheless, the tumult died. Zeleke's trembling hands held a paper with a list of names, and he began calling from it. The first on the list was Major Alemayo. He was handcuffed immediately and dragged out of the chamber by three soldiers. Then the head of state General Tafari and five others were slated as Zeleke called their names. They were grabbed one by one, handcuffed, and shoved out of the chamber by snarling soldiers who seemed to have just forgotten that General Tafari Banti was the Head of State until this very minute. Finally, eight names; and the eight were seized, handcuffed, and hustled away.

Mengistu was in his office with a couple of his civilian supporters following the situation with the various army divisions in the provinces, giving instructions. The arrests began at six in the capital, carried out by a shock troop of the special Regiment under Captain Zeleke. In a single, brilliant strike carried out after darkness had fallen, some seventy men of the army and the police force were arrested without a shot fired.

By 8 o'clock, it was over.

"Comrades, we have won," declared Mengistu. "It's over now; only a few officers in the provinces had escaped the round-up."

As the civilians smiled in congratulation, Mengistu frowned and added. "We have minor things to do, Comrades. We have to do away with our enemies quickly. We will keep Alemayo for interrogation. He is too valuable to lose now. But the other six, along with Tafari Banti, shall be executed immediately. The other eight are less important. They will remain under arrest. What do you say?"

One of the civilians gave him a long, thoughtful stare, as though he were about to say something else, and then thought better of it. The other came with an idea, but he put it as a question, "What about that bull, the vice-chairman? Isn't he a risk to live with?"

"What do you suggest?" asked Mengistu.

"The same treatment," answered the civilian resolvedly.

"So shall be done," reassured Mengistu.

Having slept a peaceful night, the people of Ethiopia had to wake and rub their eyes when they found a new government in the formation of which they had no part or any knowledge of. What had happened in the palace yesterday was not yet clear to the ordinary citizen. Nobody seemed to connect the sporadic gunfire that characterized the city at night with anything bloody, lest with the putsch that was completed almost noiselessly.

Yesterday, when the Dergue had been going through its worst moments, Daniel and Ghenet were together enjoying each other's company. Having had a peaceful evening which consisted of a nice dinner and sensational music at an inn in the neighborhood, they had gone home before it was 8 p.m. By that time, the coup d'état in the palace was successfully carried through.

In the morning, Daniel switched the radio on as he paced to the breakfast table. Abinet was serving breakfast, and Biniam, sitting at his usual place. It was already seven, and the national radio broadcast had begun.

"The oppressed people of Ethiopia," boomed the announcer, broadcasting the statement of the new 'Derg' which still used the Military Administrative Council's name. *"Your enemies who oppressed you for ages are still striving to restore their rule of injustice even after you have discarded them off your shoulder. As they have always been conspiring to snatch away the revolutionary gains you have so far achieved, today, too, they were caught red-handed hatching similar anti-people plot. We have chopped their heads off with the blade of the Revolution, this time at the very top."*

At once, each in the room seemed to realize what that meant and they all at once turned their gaze upon the radio receiver. In each person's eye, there was registered a look of horror. Daniel stared at the radio with wide eyes as though he found it difficult to believe what he heard.

"My God! Did I hear that correctly?" he whispered to himself.

The radio continued, "… *As you have been preoccupied fighting against your enemies in a bid to preserve the victories of the revolution, few anti-people elements disguised as democrats had managed to secure positions of influence in the Revolution. Using their position, they devised a plan to dissolve the revolutionary Dergue and replace it with a reactionary civilian government.*" The radio then announced that Major Alemayo and other Dergue members were caught red-handed with a 47—page document on which the procedure of overthrowing the Military Administrative Council was drafted.

It further noted that the plotters were destroyed because they refused to surrender to the forces of law and order. Finally, it called the people to celebrate the victory at the Revolution square, where Major Mengistu would address the public. Government employees and private workers were permitted to stay out of work for the occasion.

In the afternoon, mass demonstrations supporting Major Mengistu's revolutionary measures were held in all the big cities across the country. Daniel and Ghenet did not go to the square but listened to Mengistu's speech that came on air live from Revolution Square.

In his speech, Mengistu indicated that the Revolution had progressed forward.

"*As a result of the decisive step taken yesterday against the internal enemies, our revolution has advanced from the defensive to the offensive. Henceforth we will tackle our enemies in all directions. We will not be stabbed from behind by internal foes anymore. To this end, we will arm all our allies without giving respite to reactionaries. We shall avenge the blood of our Comrades in double and triple- fold."*

"We shall illuminate all reactionaries," Mengistu vowed.

"Death to the EPRP!" Mengistu declared.

"Death to the EPRP!" the public cried.

It was an open call for the escalation of violence and repression.

Listening to Mengistu's speech, weighing its appeal and the response it received, Daniel felt a profound sense of shock coupled with an even greater feeling of pity. He envisioned Ethiopia bleeding of the deepest cut caused by its children; its people divided into opposing camps engaged in bloody conflicts. The bright days he had looked forward to at the beginning of the year were once again clouded with apprehension.

The following days, Mengistu gave the socialists and his supporters in the army full power to search and arrest suspected enemies. A curfew was imposed, and total censorship of internal and external publications was put.

Chapter 17

Major Mengistu waited for three long weeks before assuming the post of the Head of the State. He had to pretend that when he executed the six top Dergue members, he was not driven by blind ambition of power as his enemies often imputed, but by the love of country as his friends often liked to explain. Meanwhile, he had to watch the reaction of the people and the armed forces. As expected, some minor unrest in the military needed to be settled, and the security had been fast to put it down before it spread.

When every potential danger had been eliminated, and a relatively stable situation was realized, Mengistu called a general assembly of the Dergue on the 28th of February. The objectives were to replace the Dergue members who had removed from the political scene, and restructure the Dergue itself.

Carefully selected loyal soldiers from various army divisions were summoned to attend the convention and become Dergue members, filling the vacancies left by the dead ones. At this meeting, Mengistu who, right after the coup, was promoted to the rank of Lieutenant Colonel, elevated himself to the post of the Head of State as the Chairman of the Military Administrative Council. He also became Chairman of the Council of ministers and Commander in Chief of the Armed forces. The Derg, too, was reorganized in the way that suited him. Captain Zeleke become the chief of the Special Security Force.

Although there was no promotion he could give to his foreign friends as he did to the locals, Mengistu had not forgotten them. He knew what would make his Soviet friends happy: Americans! First, Mengistu opened a verbal war of slogans and condemnations against them, gloating monotonously over the victory of his Revolution, claiming triumph over internal and external enemies. When that seemed not to annoy the Americans, he suddenly ordered the reduction of the American embassy staff, expelled the American mapping mission, the United States Information Service, and other agencies related to the US government. Furthermore, Comrade Chairman Mengistu ordered the immediate closure of the Kagnew, American Military Station in Asmara.

Chairman Mengistu had not forgotten the importance of the Military co-operation pact between Ethiopia and the Soviet Union. Before the putsch, Mengistu had met Soviet diplomats in Addis Ababa, and they promised to help him in everything necessary to consolidate his power. After the putsch, the Soviet government, through its ambassador, had expressed its support to the new Derg, and had formally told Mengistu to visit Moscow.

Chairman Mengistu had decided to follow up the Soviet issue personally. He was scheduled to travel to Moscow after Labor Day. And Moscow, he was told, wanted a clean house; no EPRP, no counter-revolution. As a measure to clean its house and move the Revolution from the defensive to the offensive, Mengistu's security forces and his civilian cadres intensified secret executions.

In retaliation, the EPRP resorted to extreme violence. It carried out terrorizing attacks in Addis Ababa and other major towns, killing active supporters of the Dergue and members of the rival socialist party. The impact of EPRP's armed offensive was felt from its stronghold; Assimba, in the north, right to the capital, down to towns of Harare and Bale, in the south.

Mengistu was doing everything in his capacity to do away with this group. But the opposition seemed to become stronger as the government repression became harsher. The Socialists, who were EPRP's target, had to request Chairman

Mengistu to declare Free-Measure which gave them the right to kill freely, unobstructed by getting arrested, proof of guilt, or any other legal procedures. This Free-Measure policy would give the socialists squads the right to kill on sight anyone they suspected to be an EPRP militant.

As the head of the government, Mengistu could well realize the potentially devastating consequences the policy might have as it allowed ordinary people to kill freely in the name of liquidating the opposition. Mengistu, to the dismay of his supporters, chose to wait and see.

Labor Day came.

Organized by their respective districts and trade unions, tens of thousands of residents of the capital converged at the Revolution Square to celebrate the Day in a communist-style. Security was extensively tight. The chief of Special Security Force, Captain Zeleke, had deployed his security operatives among the population. Soldiers guarded the main avenues and government institutions. Motorized brigades kept watching over the radio station, the airport, power installation, and similar other potential targets of attack.

When Chairman Mengistu appeared on the platform at the Revolution Square, members of the security force and cadres took the lead in welcoming him with thunderous applause.

"Forward with the leadership of Comrade Chairman Mengistu!" cried someone; not many bellowed the slogan for the voice was swallowed by the mass.

"Revolutionary motherland or death!" a slogan came from another direction. Although many echoed it, the magnitude was weak to reach Chairman Mengistu's ears.

Mengistu's supporters went on roaring different slogans. The number of slogans one could come up with was the measure of a good revolutionary, since he would be considered genuine. Harsh, grim, and cruel slogans were the measure of courage and determination.

Chairman Mengistu appeared at the podium right when the people had had enough of slogans for a Labor Day.

"Comrades!" addressed Mengistu, surveying the mass as he reassured himself that his amplified voice was reaching all ears. He was dressed in military uniform. He looked like a boy from a distance, his dark brawn face shining against the sun overhead. The people preferred to sharpen their ears than to strain their eyes to focus on him. His voice was more persuasive than his body language.

The Chairman's speech began with a brief history of the international labor movement. He then continued explaining the similarities between the Ethiopian and the Soviet Revolutions. "In its early stage," he said, "the Russian revolution, just like that of ours, was faced by many internal and external enemies, but through the relentless struggle of the broad mass, it emerged victorious at last."

He also spoke about the prevailing situation in the country, the achievements, and the remaining struggle ahead. The crowd was absorbed by his speech, digesting every word of it.

"Although the Revolution has made the transition from the defensive to the offensive," Mengistu went on, "the process could not be exhaustive because revolutionaries were denied the appropriate means to fight the enemy as well as the bureaucracy of the law enforcement. It was indispensable to grant Free-Measure to help them overcome these problems."

The socialists received the chairman's speech with cheers and loud applause. The Chairman received the ovation with a smile, and when the tumult died down, he went on, "Comrades! We can only defend ourselves from the EPRP killers by killing them back; by destroying them."

Again, socialist revolutionaries expressed their support with loud clapping, some chanting his name, and raising their left arms. The people around had to imitate them, more out of fear than conviction.

Raising his hand, Mengistu called for silence and went on accusing the Eritrean Movements and the EPRP for the state of terror prevailing in the cities. While the crowd watched in alarm, Chairman Mengistu began to perform an unexpected show that occupied many in anxiety. He brought out a bottle filled with red-colored liquid and made a special bodily gesture to show that it represented a unique enemy. He looked left and right at his supporters, and then raised the bottle high over his head for everybody to see.

"Death to Imperialism! Death to Eritrean separatists! Death to the EPRP!" he shouted three times and hurled the bottle under his feet to show what the Revolution would do to these enemies. His supporters responded with more applause and more slogans.

"EPRP's terror," the chairman blared, "will be destroyed by our Red terror!" Officials and security personnel standing behind him reverberated the slogan in a loud voice.

"Red Terror!" demanded the cadres.

"Red Terror! Yes, Red Terror!" declared Mengistu.

A storm of applause broke out with new force as Mengistu roared those words. Hence, the Red Terror was officially declared by Chairman Mengistu himself on that Labor Day of 1977. Whether or not he realized that he had declared anarchy in the country, no one knew. That he publicly instigated one group of the population to take arms against the other was a record in history.

In the following weeks, bloodthirsty killers were recruited and assigned to destroy the so-called enemies of the Revolution. Mengistu's supporters were given carte blanche. With the free rein they were granted they caused atrocities including assassinating anyone they suspected as their enemy. Since the EPRP was stronger in Addis Ababa, the task to destroy its supporters were given to Captain Zeleke, who was quick to organize killer squads of civilians in a short time. Within weeks he was able to unleash them in the capital city and the surrounding suburbs.

The Red Terror had begun.

It was gang warfare with arbitrary execution, lynching, and street massacres. During the first wave of the Red Terror, anyone suspected of being an EPRP member or supporter was a target; if an individual were young and even slightly educated, that was often enough evidence to prove that they were involved in counterrevolutionary activities. No one was spared. Men and women, young or old, were gunned down in broad daylight or dragged out of their homes at night and killed. A band of men attacked anyone they suspected of holding opinions different than their own.

The Red Terror was not only an open call to outright carnage, but an extensive unchecked orgy of violence. Parents were executed for blunders of their children; children were punished for the crimes of their elders.

Mengistu had a list of hundreds of people to be eliminated in Red Terror. Others close to Mengistu had lists of their own. During a-house to-house search in Addis Ababa, a notorious Socialist cadre by the name of Girma Kebede personally liquidated some 30 people, including a nine-month pregnant woman. She was bayoneted to death after being tortured brutally. There were several Girmas.

Ensuring that the Red Terror was adequately doing its job, Chairman Mengistu traveled to Moscow, leading a delegation of officials purely from the Dergue members. Surprisingly, and for reasons only known to him, not a single civilian official among his supporters was slated to accompany him to Moscow.

Chapter 18

The Red Terror was grim. The arrests and killings conducted by the security forces were indiscriminate and ruthless. Virtually no youth was safe as they were summarily considered counter-revolutionary. As a result, it was evident that the party enjoyed considerable sympathy from the relatively conscious sector of the society. On Friday, 3 June 1977, the EPRP staged one of the largest public demonstrations against Mengistu since the Dergue ascended on power. On that fateful afternoon, nearly fifteen thousand university and high school youngsters turned out in Janmeda supporting the call for a people's government. They were to march to the Palace of Menelik, the headquarters of the Derg.

The demonstrators lined in eight files, the armed members of the EPRP occupying the front rows. Behind were young protesters carrying the Ethiopian flags and different placards, which called for the immediate establishment of an elected government, and condemned Mengistu's visit to Moscow. Daniel and Ghenet, too, had come out to join the protesters; they were somewhere in the middle of the huge gathering.

The demonstrators shouted, "Down with the Mengistu's regime! People's government! Democracy now!" their voice reverberating against the hills surrounding the city, echoing the message to the world.

Around half-past six, right before the demonstrators commenced marching, armored vehicles blocked the road leading to the Derg's headquarters. Mounted on the back of the jeeps were heavy machine-guns, behind them soldiers wearing black goggles.

A few minutes later, troops that were not the army, but a specially trained branch, recruited from impoverished, unemployed, illiterate immigrants in the city, prone to follow any order, arrived on the scene of the demonstration and encircled the protesters. In front of them stood Captain Zeleke on a jeep, towering over his troops. He held a gun in one hand and a loud-speaker in the other.

As the demonstrators watched the soldiers taking a position, Captain Zeleke's voice reverberated in the air, "This is an illegal demonstration, and you must disperse immediately!"

From a distance, Daniel could figure out Zeleke's silhouette against the headlight of the vehicles. He heard Zeleke once again ordering the protesters to disperse.

Then the soldiers began to advance, ready to shoot. Military vehicles turned and pointed their guns at the demonstrators. It appeared that EPRP leaders underestimated Derg's potential. Certainly, they had entertained the illusion that a determined political and military struggle in the cities could debilitate the government. Now that they observed the beginning of a potentially ominous development, the leaders ordered the demonstrators to return to their homes peacefully.

"The rally," they explained, "has already drawn satisfactory public attention, which was the main goal."

The demonstration had initiated the government response, which seemed to resort to violence. It was pointless to march to the Dergue headquarters, for the Dergue had come to them with its ugly nails and sharp teeth to eat them row. Daniel was quick to understand the new situation; something dangerous was to come. He held Ghenet's hand and searched for the shortest and safest way out. Soon a chaotic situation developed as everyone looked for a way out.

Although it proved difficult, Daniel and Ghenet somehow managed to get closer to the less dense part of the crowd and plan an escape route. It was now that a deafening gunshot went off.

"Are you crazy! You want to put us in trouble!" Daniel barked at the man who fired the gun. Again, another gunshot. Instantly some youngsters hastened to disarm the man who had fired in the air. At first, Daniel thought these shootings were provocative steps taken by the EPRP. But then, seeing the youngsters subduing those who were firing, he realized that it was instead a tactic used by the security agents to excuse themselves to open fire.

Then followed the thunderous automatic gunfire. The soldiers had begun firing at the demonstrators. The shooting continued. The sound of heavy gunfire echoed through the darkness. The machine guns tore between the demonstrators, as rifles picked one by one. The demonstrators trying to escape from the whizzing bullets fell one over the other. There were cries and screams. Daniel and Ghenet fled like antelopes chased by a tiger. It was chaotic. Soldiers were bayoneting anyone who happened to be near them while bullets claimed the lives of those in the distance.

Hysterically, Daniel and Ghenet ran in no specific direction. It was difficult to find an escape route. Everybody was running on everybody in a desperate search for cover. Under such circumstances, the soldiers simply had to shoot without aiming to score a successful result. As this went on, unarmed young men were seen jumping on the soldiers and capturing weapons stage a counterattack that helped to retard their advances. Few EPRP supporters too, took to their light weapons and shot back at the government forces and scored amazing results.

The soldiers were surprised by the speed and ferocity of the counter-attack. For a moment, the protesters seemed to outmaneuver them. As a result, several demonstrators managed to escape and save their lives. But soon, the troops recovered their wits and fought back. The protesters had to retreat.

Daniel and Ghenet were able to break out from the compressed embattled area and ran into what they considered a safer direction—a weakly lighted alley leading to the main road. Many took this direction, as it was a shortcut to the main road. But the soldiers didn't make it safer; they began pouring bullets on the fleeing protesters. Many were caught here, dropped dead or wounded.

As Daniel just slowed to help a fallen youth, Ghenet propelled up in the air and crashed against the ground. She was caught in a random crossfire. Before Daniel turned to Ghenet, he observed a soldier finish the fallen youth with bayonets. Seeing this brutal act of barbarism, Daniel immediately lifted Ghenet, carried her on his shoulders, and fled with enormous speed.

The battle of Janmeda lasted for almost half an hour. Zeleke's force finally defeated the demonstrators and liberated the arena from the EPRP. Ironically this was the very place the Dergue launched the Zemecha a years and half ago. In this place, Zemachs received the blessing of the people and the supreme commander of this killer army, Mengistu himself. A year and a half ago, to secretly contemplate that this would happen could have been considered as a sinister thought that would certainly put one under mental care.

Carrying Ghenet, Daniel run a great deal that he had to halt for air. Way up the alley, he relieved himself of her weight and laid her on the ground under the dim light of the neighborhood, and searched her body. A bullet had dug across the chest, spurting blood from the opening. He tore a part of her dress and wrapped her wound. He could only hope for the better.

"Hold on, my dear. It's going to be all right," whispered Daniel, thinking of the nearest hospital. Yekatit 12 Memorial Hospital was a few blocks away.

Carrying her, he staggered through the narrow alleys. A few minutes later, he emerged at the Yekatit 12 Square. The street lamps illuminated the square with the monument of the martyrs of Yekatit 12[VI] at the center. From there, he could see the hospital on the other side of the street, but it was difficult to cross. Soldiers were still hunting the dispersed demonstrators. Sporadic rifle shots whistled as they tore the air.

On the sideways, he saw several youngsters lying dead or wounded. Far at the square, he spotted Captain Zeleke standing upright on a jeep, surveying the area. Daniel looked to the left, and seeing a couple of military vehicles rush past him, he almost fainted. Then he stepped into the street, walked faster, stopped again at the middle to check from the right, after which he quickly crossed the rest of the broad avenue.

Exhausted as he was, his heart pounding heavily, he reached the gate of the hospital. It was unusually guarded by soldiers, evidently by Zeleke's men. A soldier stopped Daniel at the gate.

"Who are you?" the soldier inquired, "What do you want?"

"I have a wounded person, soldier," said Daniel as politely as he possibly could be with these soldiers after this incident, "she needs medical help urgently." He wanted to crash them all with all the rage inside him because Ghenet was becoming weaker with each passing minute.

"Where did she get hurt… at the demonstration?" the soldier inquired again.

"No, it wasn't there," Daniel had to lie.

The soldier consulted with his colleagues.

"Let them in," said one of them. "They are just kids. Don't you have a child!"

"Get in," said the one standing by the gate at last.

"Thank you, Sir." Daniel slipped through the gate, sighing with relief. The biggest hurdle was over.

Ghenet was still breathing. He walked up the stairs of the main entrance. Halfway on the stairs, he heard shouts from behind and turned. Captain Zeleke's jeep had just entered the hospital compound and was pulling.

"Didn't I instruct that nobody should be allowed in!" Zeleke snarled, pointing at Daniel and Ghenet, "Who ignored my orders?"

"Stop!" a soldier shouted at Daniel.

Daniel stopped, laid Ghenet on the stairs, and approached Captain Zeleke. "Sir, she has lost too much blood. Her life is in danger."

"That's not something I care about," Zeleke shouted, "reactionaries have no right to get treatment in people's hospitals."

Daniel was so desperate that he was about to lie by telling the captain that Ghenet was Elsa's relative. But before he opened his mouth, Zeleke hastily reaffirmed his order and dashed to his car. Hopelessly Daniel returned to Ghenet. She was weaker now, her body colder.

"Get the hell out of this place!" barked the soldier. Daniel did not seem to have heard the soldier's order. Having checked Ghenet's pulse, her deteriorating condition had disconcerted him. His head was on her chest, trying to listen to her heart that seemed to have stopped beating.

"I said… get out of this place," the soldier shouted once again, "don't you hear?"

No, Daniel didn't hear. He was desperately blowing air into Ghenet's body and massaging her chest just to ignite the heart to start beating. Helplessly he lifted his head and looked at the soldier.

"She is dying," Daniel implored. "For God's sake, would you please help?"

The soldier seemed to be moved by the situation. He turned to his friends and asked, "What the hell can I do with this fellow?"

It was at this moment that a nurse followed by assistants emerged from the hospital building. For Daniel, it seemed like Mother Mary herself had come to his rescue.

"Would you please help me, Sister? For Christ's sake, help me," cried Daniel, hands stretched up over his head.

The nurse did not waste much time. She did not come by accident but on purpose. She had been following the scene from inside the building and came just to render help. Her assistants laid Ghenet on a stretcher and carried her inside.

Some of the soldiers protested, but the nurse and her assistants were resolute. They ignored the angry warnings from the soldiers and proceeded into the hospital, Daniel following them. They took Ghenet to Intensive Care. Stunned and incapable of action, Daniel had to wait in the corridor.

He sat bent over on a bench drifting in and out of the thought of Ghenet's chance of survival. He blamed the soldiers for stopping him at the gate. Valuable time had been lost there. He hated the soldiers, particularly Captain Zeleke.

Not long after, the nurse emerged, and Daniel hastened in her direction. But she was in a hurry so she went past him without saying a word. Daniel was partly alarmed by the nurse's demeanor. Yet, he was also comforted by the concern; the effort to save Ghenet's life was going on in earnest, he believed. On her way back, he stood before her.

"How is she?" he asked, frowning at the nurse's face that appeared to look familiar now.

"We are doing our best to save her life. You will soon hear from the doctor," the nurse said and hurried away.

Daniel stepped to the window and looked out. There was no one in the area except a few patrol vehicles on the street. At the entrance of the hospital, the soldiers were doing something outrageous. A military lorry had come with many victims of the evening's tragedy. They were unloading dead bodies from the lorry into the hospital, pulling the bodies, and throwing them on a container.

As Daniel stood by the window watching the ghastly scene outside, someone in a white gown came and stood beside him. Sensing the presence, he turned to see a face that certainly had no good news to tell.

"My name is Ahmed, and she is sister Saba," said the man in a manner that showed no hint of what he had in mind. He was a surgery specialist and famous for his treatment of wounds inflicted by bullets and explosives. Doctor Ahmed had ten years of practicing his profession at the Armed Forces

Hospitals before he left the military and joined the Yekatit 12 Memorial Hospital.

As Daniel heard the name Saba his eyes went to the nurse's chest and, from the badge, read her full name: Saba Berhe. Now he remembered her—Ermias' girl a long time ago, but indifferently his glance shifted to the Physician.

"We have done everything we could to the best of our ability and resources to save her life. You came a little late. She has passed away," declared Dr. Ahmed.

Daniel was about to faint. His eyes seemed to come out of their sockets. He wanted to scream, but he could not open his mouth. His ears deafened of their own whistling. His body began shivering. Suddenly everything around him darkened, and his brain seemed to stand still. He could not think of anything as though all life had gone out of him.

Saba took him to the resting room and made him sit. She gave him water to drink and sat beside him.

"This has not happened only to you. Haven't you seen the dead bodies that were brought to the hospital—hundreds?" she said just to comfort him.

He sipped from the water, and his eyes clouded with tears. Through the tears, he saw Saba's refracted face, which slowly transformed into Ghenet's smiling face. Gradually the face faded out and reappeared as captain Zeleke's face. The captain's face, in turn, disappeared, and it was dark again.

Saba was still talking to him, but he was not listening to her. In his mind's eye were faces coming and going. Ghenet and Zeleke drifted in and out one after the other, and then both vanished, giving way to the dark emptiness. In that darkness, something glittering began to take shape slowly. A glittering metal. A gun. The gun. The gun at home. In his imagination, he touched the gun

Saba felt something was happening inside him. His face looked different now, not sad but resolved; eyes, not full of tears but radiating fire.

"You have got to move fast," advised Saba. "Unless you take her body immediately, the soldiers will take it. Hurry up. What was your name?"

"Do I have any name now! She was my name. I am nobody now," said Daniel and rose slowly.

"Change your jacket… they will arrest you if they find you with the blood all over you," she said and gave him a white overcoat to put on.

At around 10 o'cloak in the evening, the city seemed like it was in a state of siege. There was virtually no movement of life. The protesters who escaped from the massacre had taken shelter wherever they could get cover. The victorious soldiers had withdrawn to their barracks, except a few who were collecting the fallen youth from the streets. But, shortly after, the streets were filled with screaming parents and relatives, all running in the direction of Janmeda. Upset by Daniel's lateness, Abinet decided to go and find out.

"Where can we go and look for him now? The city is still in chaos. He might be with Ghenet," Biniam said unconvincingly.

"Let's check there first, and then we shall go to the place where the demonstration took place."

It was just when Biniam started the Land-Rover that a taxi appeared and pulled near their house. They saw a man in white gown climbing out of the taxicab and approaching them briskly.

"I am in trouble," said Daniel before they recognized him in the dark.

"What trouble? Abinet jumped out of the Rover and stood beside him. "What has happened to you, my son?"

"It's Ghenet," said Daniel.

"Ghenet? what about her? Oh! My dear, what happened to her?"

"She's dead, murdered!" Daniel broke the news and sat down on the ground. Shocked, Biniam held his head. Abinet screamed into the sky as though to call God. In a moment, the neighborhood transformed into a scene of violent screams. An organized Uo' Ota committee the EPRP had set up to urge the community to express their protests with shrieks whenever government forces launched an attack had reacted. It was like in hell.

"Where is she?" Biniam asked.

"At the hospital," said Daniel shivering out of anger.

When Abinet calmed, they drove to Ghenet's residence. They had to break the bad news to the family. How would Askale take it? No one knew; she had already been weakened by successive tragic misfortunes out of which she had not fully recovered.

At Askale's dwelling, standing by the door, Abinet felt like she would be executing her friend, not with bullets but with words of horror. She had to wait a few minutes to compose herself for the encounter. She adjusted her headscarf, wiped her face with her hand, and knocked on the door.

Ghenet's younger brother opened the door. Askale, who was suspicious and disturbed by her daughter's unusual lateness, seemed to have presumed what was in store for her.

"Where is Ghenet?" asked Askale instantly, "For God's sake, where is she?"

Who could say what! They only looked at each other as though frightened of the reaction to come.

"Sit down, Askale… Please sit down," Abinet pleaded.

"My daughter first," Askale insisted, her voice now stifled. She tightened her head wraps and stood erect with her hands on her waist. "Isn't she, all right? What has happened to her? Can't you tell me, Daniel?"

Daniel's head fell, and his eyes moistened. Then he raised his head and looked right at Askale's eyes. "Our beloved has gone forever!"

Askale didn't let him finish. She simply dashed to the door, dragged it open, and vanished into the darkness—Abinet and

Daniel behind her. Biniam called the neighbors to look after the kids, and ran after them.

It was not easy to catch a mother running to protect her child from imminent danger. Askale was running against time to bring back her daughter, who was unfairly taken out of her life. She had to run faster than time to go back a few hours into the past where Ghenet would be found alive, and there she would protect her daughter. In five minutes, she was exhausted that she fell near the gate of Shimeis School. When they helped her to the car, she had lost consciousness.

They drove to the hospital. The streets were filled with parents, and relatives looking for their dear ones. It was dark. For mothers, it was the darkest moment in their lives.

When they reached the hospital, Askale had lost all her faculties of speech.

"This is Ghenet's mother," Daniel told Saba, who immediately ordered her assistant to care for Askale.

"They have taken Ghenet's body to mortuary in the basement," Saba announced.

"Why?" Daniel asked.

"Orders from the soldiers."

As he heard this, Daniel rushed to the basement, and found parents queuing up to look for the bodies of their loved ones.

It was a long queue. Daniel waited.

When his turn came, he entered the room that looked like a human carnage house, an earthly hell. He was shocked by the number of the dead. There were hundreds, some not dead. Unspeakable! But for Daniel, the dead and the living were almost the same. Life and death seemed indistinguishable to him. All those bodies were living people just a few hours ago. The girl who played and laughed with him a moment ago was now reduced into a corpse. The borderline that divided life and death seemed so thin that he could not feel which was which.

Daniel lifted a body and put it over another. He pulled another from beneath and turned it over; young boys and girls, piled up one over the other, strewn in a blood pool. It was difficult to differentiate one from the other. After a long and painful search, Daniel found Ghenet's body and fell on it. He hugged her and kissed her and hugged her again.

"Dead or alive, I always love you, Ghenet. You will never be dead for me as long as I walked on earth."

He lifted the body, and carried it out of the mortuary. On the corridor, he saw a crowd of people who, with lifeless faces, looked like the corpses inside the mortuary, waiting for their turn to go in the death room. Others carried the dead to approach the special inspection desk, another equally outrageous place where the bullets in the dead were counted to specify the financial loss the state suffered.

Daniel had no idea what the inspection was all about, but he did what he saw others doing. As he reached the inspection desk, a soldier told him to put the body on the table.

The soldier examined Ghenet's body, turning it over and over, then inquired, "To whom does this thing belong?"

Sadly, Daniel shook his head at the rudeness of the soldier and said, "She is my love." His eyes were red with anger.

"Fifty Birr for the bullets," the soldier said.

"What is that for?" Daniel asked.

"Government losses. You have to pay that before collecting your thing," the soldier said.

Daniel could not believe what he just heard. He stared at the soldier. "What!"

The soldier repeated in a clear, loud voice for everyone to hear.

Daniel had no word to say. It was like a nightmare.

"I have no money now.'

"In that case, take the body back to where you brought it from," the soldier ordered and went on to inspect the next.

Saba who stood behind Daniel stepped forward and offered the money which the government owed Ghenet. Saba shook her head, tapped Daniel's shoulder, and handed him a blanket, "What else is there to do!"

"Thank you, Saba,"

Daniel wrapped Ghenet's body with the blanket and got out of the place of horror.

At the exit, he met Abinet and Biniam, helping Askale in the car. Askale did not react seeing Ghenet's wrapped body. She appeared to have checked out. Daniel placed the body in the vehicle and, sitting near the body, looked at the martyr's statue far in the middle of the square. His mind replayed the day's drama: soldiers killing unarmed students, bayoneting soft bodies of young girls. For a brief moment, he thought of those martyrs who sacrificed their lives during the struggle against Fascist Italy's occupation. He doubted if the Dergue barbarity was any less than that of the fascists of that time.

"Nobody ever imagined this to happen," Abinet said more to herself. Daniel did not respond, didn't even hear her remark. He was mourning his love, caressing her hair.

As Biniam started the car. Askale awakened out of her reverie and began screaming, "Where is my daughter? Show me. Where is she? Is this the girl I gave you, Daniel? Was she wrapped with a blanket when you took her?"

"I'm talking to you, Daniel. Is this the girl I gave you? Cold and inert. Where is my Ghenet? Ghenet, Ghenet! My Ghenet!" Askale was uncontrollable.

Her words moved Daniel. Every word that came out of her mouth knocked him hard in his heart like the bullet that struck Ghenet.

A few minutes later, Askale became quiet, and she appeared relaxed. Daniel looked at her. Her mouth was stretched to the sides, smiling. She seemed to be in a different world. She had withdrawn into her inner world, away from the real world of darkness and death. Her husband Metaferia, her daughter Ghenet, and her son Gaushaw, appeared alive in her inner world. It was a happy and safe world.

Daniel realized that Askale was suffering from a mental breakdown. He, too, had not yet recovered fully from the shock. The three images: Ghenet, an image of love; Zeleke, an image of hate; and the gun, an instrument of vengeance still drifted in and out of his mind, one after the other. Ghenet, Zeleke, and the Gun; until his mind was empty of every emotion but one: vengeance.

When they reached Askale's home, the neighbors had gathered, waiting for Ghenet to be mourned and the mother to be comforted. Askale was helped to sit on madras spread on the floor. Abinet sat next to her, relatives and friends of the family around. Amid this, Daniel sneaked out of the room, unnoticed.

He reached home as if carried and pushed by an invisible force. He was a peaceful person who never harmed anyone in his life. Even as a little boy, he had never been drawn into a fight or a situation in which he would harm another person. But now, he was put in a position he would take the law into his hands.

He changed into his jacket, went straight to the bedroom, and opened the closet. He searched for the key, and having found it, he reached for the wooden box and opened it. There it was, as peacefully as any piece of metal could be, wrapped in a plastic sheet. He removed the plastic, and the weapon glittered. He picked it, and felt its real weight for the first time. He opened the magazine and examined its contents. Two bullets, shining like pieces of gold, untouched since his father inserted them—enough for the purpose at hand.

As he stuck the gun under his belt, he heard a knock at the door of the front room. The door was not locked from inside. Sensing someone entering the house, Daniel stepped out to see who had come.

It was Ermias.

"How are you? I heard that there was some conflict in the city," Ermias said, taking off his coat

"We are okay."

"Where are the rest of you?"

"They are at the Askales," Daniel said.

"What are they doing there at this hour?" Ermias inquired again, making himself comfortable on a chair. He appeared as though he would not leave at all.

"They will come soon," Daniel said, devising a way he would get rid of Ermias. The curfew stands at midnight. Less than 30 minutes from now. Not much time. He remembered Saba.

"Hi, by the way—ah… that girl… lady…your girl, Saba.'

"What about her?" Ermias almost rose, eyes wide open.

"I met her today in Yekatit 12 Memorial Hospital."

"Ill?"

"No, she works there. She is a nurse. She was there this evening. I think she is still there now."

"You Devil," Ermias consulted his watch, rose, and picked his coat. "Have you any idea of what you just told me mean to me? I have been looking for that girl all over the country and never succeed. Now all of a sudden, you tell me she is here. Bye. See you, Danny."

Chairman Mengistu was strictly following the development at the demonstration scene from his office. Events were reported directly to him as they unfolded. He had no intention to leave his office before the situation was restored to normal. Late in the evening, he was waiting for the final closing report from the marshal of the field, Captain Zeleke himself. The evenings conflict had been the most challenging civilian threat the regime faced since the Dergue came to power. *'It has to be crushed by any means for his dreams to come true,"* Mengistu vowed.

Many of his plans were completed. The State was under his total control. The army was purged and restructured in the way he wanted it. Only this problem of the youth seemed to be irresolvable. He had even gone as far as to execrate the day he came to power as a day of misfortune.

He remembered, once, not very long ago, he had the admiration and support of all these young people, the very people who were now his bitter enemies. Had an election been held then, he would undoubtedly have emerged victorious. Sitting alone in his office, waiting for the final report of the Janmeda incident, Mengistu wondered where all that support vanished, what mistakes he might have committed to become the most detested man in the country. He blamed his civilian friends, the Socialist intellectuals.

I would not have gotten myself in such trouble had I ignored their advice. The nation might have been better off had we continued on the path of Bloodless Change as we had strived at the beginning. Damn Civilians! Damn intellectuals! He attributed every setback his regime encountered to the leaders of the Socialist party.

No! That's wrong, he argued with himself. *Without their advice, the Revolution would not have progressed, not even a single step. Besides, without their guidance, I would not have come to this position. What wrong have they done? What wrong have I done? All we did was what should be done in the time of revolution. It was done everywhere else. Every revolution has killed its enemies: we killed ours. If we hadn't, our enemies would have killed us. Yes, we had to do what we had. There is no redemption without blood; no revolution without killing.* When his thoughts came to this conclusion, the hero of Janmeda, Captain Zeleke, entered his office to report the day's event.

"From now onwards, there will be no more demonstration. We have given them a lesson they will never forget," Captain Zeleke said without even bothering to address the Chairman properly. He touched the butt of his gun, took off his cap, and threw his body on the sofa in front of Chairman Mengistu. But Mengistu, having been satisfied with Zeleke's success, was indifferent to Zeleke's manner.

"This is not the kind of lesson they understand, Zeleke. Tell me rather that you chased them away; they will come back tomorrow. That's not the solution," Mengistu said.

"No! We have dealt them properly. They will never rise again. We have knocked down hundreds of them," Zeleke said proudly.

"Hundreds? That's quite a number. But that's just punishment, not a solution. Zeleke, don't you remember that we smashed the reactionaries in the Dergue by crashing the head, by destroying the leading elements at the top. The EPRP will not give us peace unless we manage to smash the top leadership; we won't accomplish much by destroying the rank and file. Remember how many we have so far liquidated. What did we achieve? Nothing."

"So, what do you want me to do, Chairman?" asked Zeleke, staring at Mengistu as though questioning Mengistu's intelligence. "Is there anything better than gunning down spoiled people?"

"That's a good question. I was waiting for you to discuss this point. Now look, it was confirmed that Alemayo is an EPRP operative, probably a member of the central committee. You remember him telling us that he drafted his damned document with them. We have to who actually are the EPRP leaders from him, and this must be done today." His last word "today" was firm when he spoke it.

Zeleke stood to go almost before Mengistu finished. "That's right, Comrade Chairman. We will force him to confess," Zeleke said and left the office. He went to the basement where the Dergue kept important prisoners and called for the chief of the palace jail, to whom he told the Chairman's instruction and order.

"Alemayo? Alemayo can't breathe, sir," said the chief, "let alone talk. He is weakened and paralyzed that he is unable to feed himself or make the slightest movement."

"What do you mean he can't even breathe? What has happened to him?"

"I don't like the way the new interrogator is carrying out his job. Yesterday, he became frustrated and shot him in the thigh. Alemayo is bleeding, and there is no prospect that he would recover. He is dying, sir."

Zeleke hurried to the basement, the chief behind him. He paced along the corridor until he came to a heavily barred door. The Chief ran up and slid back the bolts. Zeleke slipped through the door.

There lay Major Alemayo in solitary confinement in a small room with a high ceiling and red brick walls. He was not allowed to see the sunlight since his captivity. Only a little daylight came in through a small barred window high up on the wall. The periods of his confinement were broken by visits to the toilet or the interrogation room.

Zeleke himself, in the brief presence of Mengistu, had conducted Alemayo's first interrogation. He had begun by demanding a confession; he had claimed that they knew from the other witnesses that he had been directly involved with the subversive activities of the EPRP and that he was a secret member of the Polit-biro of the party.

Alemayo had been sure that the securities knew very little of his activities and nothing of his contacts and connections. He had excellent knowledge of the methods used to extract information and the lies they would tell about their evidence; the forged documents they would put before him. He had persisted in his denials, and the security had changed its method to torture.

When Zeleke entered the cell now, he was assailed by a stench so overpowering that he took a step backward involuntarily. The ceiling light was on. The bulb was weak, but it showed him more than he wanted to see. The floor was covered with spatters of dried blood, and the stench of stale urine, vomit, and putrefying flesh was so powerful that Zeleke reeled. He had to grip the doorframe to steady himself. Then he peered down.

Huddled in the corner on the bare stone was Alemayo, half conscious, lying on the cold floor, socked in his blood. He had one of his eyes severed out of him under torture, and the other was covered by the swell of his face. His hand was swollen, most of their nails removed. From his nostril and mouth, thick whitish stuff mixed with blood leaked down. The torturer used to beat him with heavy clubs so that his body constantly fell forward with the full weight on the face and the head. In a desperate effort to break him, a shot was also fired merely to frighten him but unfortunately did not miss. The bullet had hit his thigh, inflicting excruciating pain and loss of a tremendous amount of blood. Although Major Alemayo was a strong man physically, he suffered from his wounds severely. He was deprived of medical care.

Despite himself, Zeleke was shocked when he saw the mutilated form, motionless. He put his finger on Alemayo's neck to feel the pulse.

"He is still alive," announced Zeleke. "Call the palace ambulance and see that he gets medical treatment as soon as possible. I need him alive. Quick! Take him to the hospital and see to it that he gets first-class treatment."

Zeleke hastened back to the Chairman.

Chairman Mengistu was disappointed when he heard Alemayo's condition. Alemayo was his only hope who would eventually reveal the leaders of the EPRP. He would not have any rest until he got them all.

"I don't like your methods," shouted Mengistu, "You have got to use systematic methods with such valuable information sources."

"We have used all the means at our disposal to force information out of him. We resorted to torture only when he became stubborn. How else can we make him talk?" responded Zeleke.

"You have to try to torture his soul instead of his body. That will surely work, Zeleke," the Chairman sounded philosophical. Although Zeleke did not understand what Mengistu meant, he listened attentively since he somehow sensed that there was an essential point in the remark.

"Doesn't he have a wife and children?" Mengistu asked.

"Yes, of course. He has two children." Zeleke was curious about the new idea.

"He will not resist when it comes to them. Let him recover first, and then we will show him we meant revolution. First, his wife and then the children…" Mengistu left the sentence hanging.

"Good! That's right," Zeleke had no difficulty grasping the rest of the idea.

"You follow up this case closely. We need a mature, systematic, and experienced interrogator. Cruelty alone will not do the job," the chairman said and rose.

At a quarter to midnight, the two victors finished their day's work and left the headquarters of the Derg. Zeleke drove to Elsa's house, followed, as he always did, by his bodyguards, this time several of them.

Daniel was seeing Ermias off by the time Zeleke left the palace; that was almost a quarter to midnight: curfew time. Zeleke had no problem with the curfew. He was a guardian of the law on whom the law did not apply; he was one of the few people who were above the law, who could do anything with the law and the people. They could harass, arrest, and kill fellow countrymen and not answer for their deeds.

People's patience is, nevertheless, bound to exhaust. They would one day say 'enough is enough' individually or in a group. They would be compelled to take the law into their hand and punish the offender by their conviction, for there was no law to prosecute the people above the law. Daniel's decision to take up his weapon emanated from this. He decided to take the law into his own hands because there was no law to deal with Captain Zeleke. Daniel had no option left. He prosecuted Zeleke, convicted him, and resolved to execute the punishment, all by himself

It was ten to midnight when Daniel entered Asmara Inn to call Beza from the phone box.

"Elsa's residence. Beza speaking," Beza replied.

"Beza, I'm Daniel. How are you?" said Daniel in a low voice.

"Hi, Daniel, are you all right. I mean, how come you call at this hour?'

"Beza, I would like you to do me a favor, please."

"What is it? I'll gladly help you if it's something I can. What's it?" Daniel was sure that she won't let him down, or betray him. Over the years, strong ties had grown between them for Daniel not to have confidence in her.

"Listen, Revo-guards are searching the neighborhood. I suspect they are after me. I want you to let me spend the night at your place since it's safer there."

"With pleasure," said Beza, "come as soon as possible. I will be waiting for you at the gate so that the guards won't give you a hard time."

This was all Daniel wanted; to pass the guards without being searched.

"Is Captain Zeleke in?"

"No, he has not come yet. Haven't you heard what happened in Janmeda today? He must be busy."

"I'm coming, right away. It won't take me long."

Daniel replaced the handset, tapped the gun under his waist, and inhaled air of strength and courage before he left the hotel. He crossed the street and walked straight north up to the Nyala Transport's gate, then turned to the right into the dark alley towards Elsa's residence.

Far ahead, Daniel saw members of the district Revo-guards—as they were called by the people—coming in his direction. He mingled with the people coming out of the pubs and hurrying to their homes before curfew time. He walked as calmly as he could pretend, and when the Revo-guards walked past him, he strode faster without looking back. It was now less than five minutes to midnight.

His heart started to beat faster as he saw the light from Elsa's compound at a distance. At the gate, among the wolves with black helmets guarding the perimeter, stood a thin, feminine figure dressed in white Gabi (thick cotton blanket), waiting for him.

"Hi, Beza, did I made you wait in the cold?" Daniel said, observing the guards behind Beza.

"Not at all. I just came out of the house," she said, "It's too chilly. I wonder how these wolves withstand the cold in the night."

"Do they spend the night here?" asked Daniel in a low voice, surveying the compound. The wall enclosing the house was high and topped by barbed wire. On the front side was a sentry box where an armed guard stood, dark and sinister against the sky. As they entered the compound, he observed two soldiers emerged from the backyard.

"There are also others who will come with him. An entire brigade of the army is following him wherever he is going," Beza said, with a tone of mock exaggeration.

"Do all of them stay here the whole night?"

"Some of them return, others stay here, one shift after the other."

A Brigade! Daniel thought. Exaggerated or not, he could only attack one person with one gun and few bullets. Zeleke had the entire army, the whole security force, the police, and the Revo-Guards behind him all the time. But none of them knew the anger, hatred, and vengeance he harbored. He has already managed to pass the guards unsuspected. Zeleke would not bring the whole brigade inside the house. He could not bring his tanks and launchers with him. Nor would his bodyguard come into the house. He would soon be alone inside the house, presumably, only with a gun, no more. Zeleke would be all by himself to face him. Just as Daniel wanted it: man to man. A student versus a soldier: a drama of a revolution that had gone mad!

As far as the battlefield and the surroundings were concerned, there was a relatively equal balance favoring each side. Both knew the house and its surrounding areas. Although Daniel knew the neighborhood better than Zeleke did, it was quite apparent that the Revo-Guards would take Zeleke's side. Inside the house, Beza would at least take Daniel's side because she liked Daniel as she hated Zeleke. For Beza, Zeleke was one of the perpetrators of the Massacre of the Sixty[VII] that took her uncle's live, on the night of 23 November 1974 when sixty-three former government officials were executed. Elsa would certainly favor her lover. Come what might, Daniel's plan was set as far as to punish Zeleke. No more. No escape, no backup plan, or defense plan.

At exactly midnight, Daniel entered the house. Elsa had gone to bed a bit earlier. The servants were not around. The place was quiet, worm, and reeked cologne.

"Will you go directly to bed, or do you want me to bring you something to drink?" Beza asked.

"I will stay a little. I would like to drink water if you can fix one," said Daniel.

"I, too, would like to have a chat. I have a problem sleeping these days. We will chat," said Beza and passed to the rear room.

Daniel's eyes followed Beza to the back door and remained there fixed, unaware of the precious artifacts, paintings, and precious decoration items that embellished the living room. On the floor was overlaid colorful Persian carpet, and the wall was concealed with curtains from the far east. Undoubtedly the sofa on which Daniel sat had been stolen from the Emperor's Palace or the like.

Daniel did not pay attention to all this. His heart was elsewhere. Even when Beza brought him a cup of water and sat in front of him, he was immersed in deep thought. Such an expression of sadness had never been seen on Daniel's face before. Beza observed him and somehow felt his sorrow

"What has happened to you, Daniel, aren't your folks all right?

"It's nothing. They are all right. I am disturbed by … what the Revo-guards might want me for," said Daniel struggling out of his depressive thought and forcing a smile.

"I heard the city was troubled today. Have you been there?"

"No, I have not. But I heard that there was a clash between security forces and students."

"It's high time to leave this country," Beza said. "When a priest runs a discothèque and a soldier rules a nation, morality diminishes, and the nation dies. It's hopeless."

Daniel held the cup, and as he gulped the water, tears diffused in his eyes. Within seconds they dried up as if the heat inside him dried up everything wet in him. Even his lips turned ashy soon after he licked it. As minutes ticked by, his heart pounded faster, giving more fire and energy to be dissipated any time now.

Beza was chatting about her plan to travel abroad.

"These days, it's easier to secure political asylum in Europe and America. Scandinavian countries are also generous in providing shelter to the exiled.

"Where do you intend to go?" Daniel asked Beza just to do away with the heavy silence that followed Beza's speech.

"Well, first, I'll go to Italy and see the condition of refugees. I'll see if the Americans can grant me asylum from there. If the process takes a long time, I will find a way to enter America.

"Do you have someone there?" He was not with her entirely, but he didn't miss the subject.

"I have relatives in Washington DC." Beza continued speaking about the lives of her relatives. She was so fascinated about America that there was no country in the entire world she loved more. "First, I will go to see them, and then I plan to settle in Los Angeles for my studies, and you? Why don't you try to look for some means to go out of this country?"

"Yes, I agree with you," Daniel replied. He then said to himself, *'Yes, I, too, have chosen exile, not to go out of the country but out of this world.'*

As Daniel was about to utter a word, his attention drifted to the sound of motor vehicles from outside.

"It's Zeleke," Beza said carelessly. Daniel lifted his head, and stared at the door, breathing heavily, his heart pounding harder. He heard the footsteps. Then came a knock on the door.

When Beza stood to open the door, Daniel remained seated, overwhelmed by impetuousness. The images that haunted him throughout the evening came again, faces of Ghenet and Zeleke, one after the other, faster than before.

Beza opened the door, and Captain Zeleke's huge body passed through it. Very slowly, Daniel raised himself from the sofa, hateful, flaring eyes fixed at Zeleke. Now Zeleke's imaginary form was replaced by the real, tangible body which could be hit or killed. Daniel followed the body with his eyes as it moved to the middle of the room.

"Sit down, for God's sake. You have got to forget the old tradition," the captain said, unaware of what was at stake for him.

"How are you? How are you, Beza?" Zeleke said, taking off his hat. He took off his overcoat and handed it over to Beza. "How are you? Sit down, please," he said, turning to Daniel. As he stooped to take a seat, suspicion flickered in his mind, and his eyes narrowed at Daniel.

"Do we know each other? Where have I seen you before?" asked Zeleke standing erect.

"Yes, we have seen each other today," Daniel blared between his teeth, revealing enormous anger.

The captain seemed to be confused and looked at Daniel and Beza in turn for an explanation. But Beza's innocent smile and Daniel's hateful gaze were ambiguous.

"I don't understand," Zeleke pretended as though to take the matter easy, "Where did we see each other?"

"I met you at the hospital today. You denied a wounded girl's medical care. She was my girl." Daniel shouted at the captain, who was now suspiciously watching him with the corner of his eyes.

"Yes, I remember you," Zeleke said, touching the holster of his gun on his waist, "how is she now?"

"She died. Because of you, she is dead now!" Daniel roared at the captain, throwing his hands in the air.

Beza was overwhelmed by the sudden turn of events. She stepped closer to Daniel and followed the scene with heightened curiosity. Zeleke seemed to be indifferent to what he heard.

"I guess she got what she deserved," Zeleke said, and pointing at Beza, he added, "Look, nice and decent girls stay at home."

Daniel felt a sudden surge of rage. He almost exploded out of anger. Ghenet's character was criticized by a monster of the lowest moral. Ghenet, who couldn't defend herself now, was accused of being not decent. He snatched his gun from under his belt, held it with both hands, and pointed it at Zeleke.

Beza cried sharply and then immediately fell silent, realizing the danger that could befall Daniel.

"How dare you talk like that! Do you know that you're responsible for her death?" Daniel blared furiously and retreated few steps as he held the gun pointed at Zeleke, his hands shaking.

Elsa emerged from her bedroom to find her soldier-boy standing stiff before Daniel. "What's wrong? For God's sake, be cool," she pleaded.

"Cool it, Daniel, for God's sake," Beza begged.

"Shut up!" Daniel shouted again, his forehead now covered with a film of perspiration. "This is between him and me. You have nothing to do with it. Get out of this!"

The women were silent now but very scared. Daniel had reached a point of no return, they knew. His choices were clear; killing or dying. There was no other option. Anyone who dared touch the princes of the Revolution knew what to await him. For Daniel, the appropriate course of action was to shoot and run, but he seemed to hesitate. He had never been put in such a situation where he would take the life of another human being.

The man who was responsible for the death of several hundred students, the lion of Janmeda, seemed to realize that he was in danger. This crazy young man could pull the trigger any time. At last, he whispered a lame answer.

"I am sorry for your girl. I had my orders."

Daniel was caught in a dilemma. He wanted not a man who crawls for his life but a strong and cruel killer to kill. He relaxed his grip on the gun and shifted his eyes to the woman. Having noticed Daniel's distraction, Zeleke stretched his hand to his gun suddenly. This was the small action Daniel needed to make him squeeze the trigger. He fired.

Daniel almost dropped the gun as a deafening shot went off. The officer staggered backward and fell on his back. Then followed Elsa's terrible scream. Daniel revived out of the brief perplexity that followed the shooting and rushed out through the rear door.

Alarmed by the gunshot and Elsa's screaming, the soldiers rushed to the front door and knocked it heavily. As Elsa opened the door, four soldiers burst in, and seeing Zeleke on the floor, two of them hurried to help him.

"I am all right. Just take care of that anarchist." Zeleke gasped with an uneven breath. With little help, he managed to raise himself.

Two of the soldiers put the wounded captain on the sofa and worked to check the bleeding, while the other two quickly turned to pass the order to the others.

The hunt had begun when Elsa put a call through to a retired dresser who arrived in less than half an hour and began administering first aid. The bullet that had dug across his right shoulder might have chipped a bone but did not put the captain in a critical condition.

"The bullet is stuck in your shoulder bone," the dresser said as he examined the wound. "I don't have the necessary equipment to pull it out now. You have got to go to a hospital before the infection spreads."

"Do you mean it can be treated here at home if one gets the equipment?" Zeleke asked. He was so egocentric that he wanted to bring the hospital to him to save himself the discomfort of going to it.

"Yes. But now you need an injection to avoid the risk of infection.'

"Elsa, call Dr. Ahmed and tell him to bring here a medical team. He must be at his work or home. Call him. He is an expert on such injuries," Zeleke said.

"Would it not be easier to go to the nearest hospital instead of calling him from such a distance?" Elsa suggested carefully, straining not to annoy him.

"I told you that he is an expert in treating bullet wounds. What has happened to you? Why don't you do as I tell you to do?"

As Elsa went to the phone to place a call to Dr. Ahmed, the dresser told Zeleke what to do until the doctor arrived. Then he gave him tranquilizing tablets, and before he left, he was strongly advised by Zeleke to forget all that he saw today.

"Any news of this incident would encourage the enemies of the people, and we don't want that to happen, do we?" Zeleke said.

"Don't worry about that, Captain," the dresser assured. "Good night."

Elsa came with what she got from her call.

"They say the doctor is very busy this night that he cannot come here."

"What? Who said that?" Zeleke shouted and made a painful effort to raise himself from the sofa. "Come on, give me the number."

Assisted by two of his bodyguards, he walked to the phone and dialed the number to Yekatit 12 Memorial Hospital. The call went through, and as soon as he mentioned Dr. Ahmed's name, the operator connected him to the surgery department, where Ahmed was supposed to be found.

"Sister Saba speaking. What can I help you?" a female voice said from the other end.

"I want to speak to Dr. Ahmed."

"He is busy with a patient."

"This is Captain Zeleke speaking…"

"So, what can I help you, sir," said Saba.

"I need him for an urgent medical case. I want him to come here."

"I don't think that's possible. The doctor is also working on an urgent case. It's a life-threatening operation, and I'm afraid he will not take a break under any circumstance," Saba said.

"How dare you speak to me like that. I'm Captain Zeleke, member of the Derg."

"Sir, we are dealing here with human life. I believe, you believe that all humans are equal," replied Saba with forced politeness.

"As a Dergue member, I order you to put me in direct contact with the doctor."

"We are also dealing with a wounded Dergue member, Captain," just as she said those words, the doctor came and stood beside her. "Here he is. You can talk to him now."

"This is Ahmed speaking," Ahmed's hoarse voice echoed in Zeleke's ear. "What can I help you, Captain?"

"How are you, Doc?"

"We are overflooded tonight, Captain. You left us a great deal of work. I am dealing with the patient you sent."

"Are you talking about Alemayo? How is he? Do you think he will recover soon?"

"I hope he might recover if he gets the necessary attention. I have rather found the torture applied to him to be contrary to the rules of treatment of prisoners, and alien to our culture." Ahmed was trying to coldly point out the illegality of their treatments because he knew other prisoners were being treated in the same way as Major Alemayo.

"Please, leave that to your Sheikhs to preach. Now, I want you to remove a bullet from my shoulder. I want you to come here with a medical team and the necessary equipment."

That was outrageous. Doctor Ahmed had never stumbled into such a situation in which he was ordered to abandon his patients in need, and give treatment to spoiled masters at their homes. He had no intention to start doing that today, not for Zeleke, not for anybody.

"Captain, would it not be more appropriate if you come here? I have to follow up on Alemayo's condition every fifteen minutes. Besides, new cases are coming every hour. The hospital is already working beyond its capacity. I don't think it would be right for me to leave the hospital at this critical time. That's professionally impossible."

"There is nothing impossible, Doctor. You can come if our Revolution ordered you to."

"If I could, I would have said so."

"Now, are you coming or not?"

Dr. Ahmed was infuriated that he didn't even give it a thought when he just said, "No, I'm not."

"Had it been your former masters, you would have come wagging your tail like a dog. You stupid! I'll show you who I am," barked Zeleke.

The doctor did not answer. He just replaced the handset before Zeleke finished.

Zeleke called one of his soldiers and gave the order to arrest the rebellious physician immediately.

"The name is Ahmed at Yekatit 12 Hospital. I'll teach him a lesson harsher than what Alemayo got. I'll make him crawl under my knees. Is this idiot a real Doctor!?"

A few minutes later, when he calmed, Zeleke decided to go to a hospital. As he left the house, with Elsa and his bodyguards, Beza was quick to run to the telephone set. In her hand, she had a piece of paper on which the telephone number of Yekatit 12 Hospital was written.

When the third call from Elsa's household rang, Saba and Ermias were together at the hospital. It had been only a quarter of an hour since Ermias arrived. He had soon found out that neither the time nor the place was conducive for him to chat with the girl he loved, and yearned to see so much. He couldn't tell how they met in the middle of the confusion and tragedy that marked the evening. What they had done in those exciting first minutes they met was vague. It was a moment of happiness amid sorrow and death. Yet, the atmosphere of anxiety that engulfed everything like a tempest did not allow it to flourish.

Watching Ermias with loving eyes, Saba lifted the telephone, "This is Sister Saba. What can I help you?"

"Hi! Listen. I'm calling from where Captain Zeleke just called a moment ago," notified the caller. "Soldiers are on the way to the hospital to arrest Doctor Ahmed, and I warn you to do something about it. I have heard his threats; what he would do to him. Act fast. Good luck."

"Thank you very much, indeed," Saba said, and the line went dead before she finished.

"Captain Zeleke has sent soldiers to arrest Doctor Ahmed," Saba told Ermias.

"So, let him know about it as soon as possible," Ermias said, privately impressed by Beza's concern for other people.

Saba rushed to the Intensive Care Section.

Dr. Ahmed was with Major Alemayo. For a brief moment, the major had regained consciousness but soon lapsed into a coma once again, and his temperature had risen. Dr. Ahmed and his colleagues were doing everything possible to help him recover. Saba could not interrupt the physician right away. She had to wait.

A moment later, when the doctor was available, Saba unfolded what was in store for him.

Dr. Ahmed gave instructions to his colleagues and hastened to the office. Earlier, he had met Ermias, so he just nodded to him.

"How much time do I have?" he asked, peering at his wristwatch. It was a quarter to one.

"If he sends his soldiers from Kera, it will not take them more than 30 minutes, the way they drive. If he sends from the Palace, you're finished, Doctor," Ermias said.

Dr. Ahmed's face turned white, and his eyes turned red. "I have to change. By the way, does anyone have a car?"

"I do," Ermias said.

"Can you take me home?"

"With pleasure," said Ermias, "go and change quickly.'

When Dr. Ahmed left, Ermias turned to Saba.

"You know, Saba," he said, his voice low, "this is a strange coincidence. I was desperately looking for Major Alemayo. He was the one who investigated my father's case." He paused, studied her reaction, and said, "I wish his life could be spared, and I could talk to him."

"Look, Ermias," Saba sighed, "You can't spend your entire life looking for your father's killer. You have to be able to forget the past. Crimes committed a long time ago should not steer your life today. Think of the lives of those young people who got killed today. It makes the past as though it has never existed and the future as though it would not come at all." She then pointed outside through the window and said, "Look."

Through the window, Ermias could see distressed and sad parents going home carrying the dead bodies of their loved ones.

"You're right, Saba. I only meant to use the opportunity. I didn't mean to follow up on the case anymore. Now that I'm so close, I merely wanted to grasp the chance."

The door opened, and Dr. Ahmed came in. He held a bag and an umbrella. Despite his attempt to appear different, he looked the same old Ahmed, his face ashen of fear, eyes red of exhaustion.

"Let's go out. Goodbye, Saba. Take care. I will not come back unless I have a full guarantee for my safety. Say goodbye to my colleagues on my behalf. I'll write from where I'll be; If I stay alive." He stepped closer to Saba, kissed her forehead, and rushed out.

"See you tomorrow, Saba," said Ermias, touched her shoulder, and left.

"Do you have papers for the curfew, doctor?" Ermias asked the doctor as they walked past the main door.

"Yes," the doctor said, "I'm not sure it would do any good today, but I do have one."

"No one knows that you're on the run until tomorrow. So, your papers are good for tonight."

"Look!" Ahmed pointed at the soldiers who jumped out of a jeep that just entered the hospital compound.

"They are the ones. Get in the car!" whispered Ermias.

"Just in time," the doctor sighed in relief as Ermias started the car.

Daniel was on the run, in a cat and mouse like chase. Running wildly and aimlessly through the rough, dark alley, he had managed to be at a comfortable distance from the soldiers behind him.

Earlier, when Zeleke's guards had been knocking on the front door to get in the house, the rear side of the yard was free for Daniel to escape. There was a barrel near the service house on which Daniel could climb and used to jump on the roof of the service house. From the roof, he had jumped down to the outside without seeing where he would land. Having landed safely, he had run blindly but very fast into the neighborhood. By the time Captain Zeleke left for the hospital, Daniel had sneaked out of the neighborhood was able to hid himself for some time.

He was now at the gate of Shimeis School, the school he had gone for twelve years. It was black dark; neither could he see anything, nor could he be seen by anyone, and there was only one way out, northward. At the school gate, he heard a familiar voice threatening him.

"Stop! Who are you!" It was the old school guard, Daniel knew.

"Live and let live. This is none of your business!" warned Daniel, tired and desperate. The gun was still in his hand. He had one more bullet to expended on who or what might cross him.

The guard who understood the message did not breathe a word again. Daniel continued northward, stumbling and falling. At the intersection, he turned left toward the neighborhood where Ghenet lived. A couple of blocks away, he heard the school guard telling someone the direction he took. Soon after that, a bullet whistled over his head, awakening the neighborhood. And more gunshots followed. The shooting roused the dogs in the community to bark as angrily and continuously as if in an earthquake. The Revolution-guards were out too, coming from the front, shouting and firing simultaneously.

Daniel had to lie on the ground to take cover because the shots were very close to blow his head off. Besides, he was exhausted that he wanted to ease and take a breath. Having accomplished his mission, he was in no mood to take a hide or to be on the run as a fugitive. He was ready to take the consequence, come what might.

It was a Revo-guard who came first and ordered him to surrender. Daniel dropped the gun and held his hands up over his head.

"Be careful," the Revo-guard warned, "if I see a slight movement, I'll blow your head off."

"You will blow it either way," Daniel said as he stood still.

"Well, well, look what we have here!" The Revo-guard came closer, turned his flashlight on, and picked up the gun. "This is the first time I see a real anarchist. What have you done with this gun?"

"He murdered Captain Zeleke in his home," said Zeleke's bodyguard, who just arrived and smashed Daniel with the butt of his rifle. As Daniel staggered, one of the Revo-guards punched him with a fist right at his nose. Again, Zeleke's guard used his leg to kick Daniel's belly. Another powerful blow came from behind that knocked him to the ground. As Daniel lay on the ground, they worked on him ruthlessly until he lost consciousness. Then they went through his pocket to look for his identity but found nothing, and none of them knew who he was.

"Why waste time for this anarchist? He has killed a revolutionary leader, and we must punish him by death right away," One of Zeleke's guards suggested. "That's what our revolution does with its enemies. Isn't it?'

"That's perfectly all right to us," replied the leader of the Revo-guards. "No anarchist has ever dared do such a crime in this neighborhood. This will be the first and the last. It'll be a lesson for the others who might dare to follow his example."

"So, let's finish him," the soldiers agreed and dragged Daniel to a wall. In no time, they established a five-man firing squad out of the soldiers and the Revo-guards. A short, round fellow who happened to be a Corporal was to lead the squad through the execution procedure. Soon the firing squad stood in a row, some five meters away from Daniel.

Seated on the ground, leaning against the wall, Daniel was not aware of what was going on. He had not woken from the state of unconsciousness when the corporal flashed a lamp at him, and the spotlight went down to his chest for the squad to aim at the heart.

"Attention!" the Corporal cried.

There was an awkward, disorganized movement on the part of the Revo-guards. Some were faster, the others slower, and one seemed to clumsily aim at the Corporal himself. He was corrected immediately by a colleague.

"Aim!" cried the corporal.

The members of the squad were now ready for the kill.

Daniel groaned out of physical agony, not fully aware of what was going on. He couldn't see clearly, nor could he hear what was said.

As the soldiers held their breath to pull the trigger, a sound of speech came from Daniel's direction, to which the Corporal responded instantly and drew himself closer to catch the words. When he couldn't grasp any of it, he stepped closer and bowed to listen.

Then he straightened and announced, "He is saying that he has valuable information to tell."

"Come on," said one of the Revo-guards. "He is just trying to fool us."

"He is trying to buy some time," added another one.

"He might be telling the truth. Why don't we hand him over to the experts," suggested the Corporal?

"Come on, Corporal, what about the lesson that the others have to learn from this feast. This is a school area we have many to teach, don't miss the chance," the Revo-guard leader said. "Now, let's get it over with."

"Good, back to your positions," the corporal ordered. The firing procedure was to continue from where it stopped.

The squads inhaled air and waited for the final killer word to come. Seconds passed. The Corporal composed himself and straightened to utter the word. A fraction of a second before his mouth opened, the entire area was illuminated by a car's headlight.

As the car came closer, Zeleke's soldiers recognized it and interrupted the firing to report the case to Captain Zeleke, who was on his way to a hospital. Zeleke disapproved the execution and ordered that the assassin should be handed over to the Special Crime Investigation Department for interrogation.

Daniel spent the night in the district confinement room. The next day, before noon, he was handed over to the Special Criminal Investigation Department in the Fifth police station, the district law enforcement office where he went through the formalities of detention. Thereafter he was brought to the registration section for a preliminary hearing.

Handcuffed, bare-footed, face swollen, blood all over him, Daniel looked like he had spent a night with a hungry leopard. He was exhausted when a policeman hustled him into the registration office.

"Take the cuffs off!" ordered the officer who was in charge of the section.

As soon as his hands were released, Daniel massaged his wrists, stretched himself, and peered at the officer: a middle-aged Lieutenant who had a light brown face with kind eyes that seemed to nurse some sympathy in them.

"You can leave," the officer dismissed the policemen and glanced at Daniel. "Have a seat, young man."

Daniel grinned and took the offer. He sat beside the officer's large desk and surveyed the room. The walls were covered with shelves and the shelves with dossiers. *This must be the busiest office in the country*, Daniel thought.

"Cigarette?" the officer held a packet out to Daniel. His method used to include offering cigarettes, seats, and trying to look sympathetic before he went to the real job. Daniel grinned again, and when his lips parted, a hoarse voice of suppressed anger and sorrow came out.

"I don't smoke, thanks."

"My name is Nigusie Bikila, Lieutenant," the officer announced, setting his cigarette afire and watching Daniel through the smoke. He stretched his left hand to the drawer and tugged it. Gently he grabbed the thing he wanted, lifted it, and laid it on the table. It was the gun covered with thin transparent plastic. Daniel was indifferent when he saw it.

"Is this yours?"

"Yes," replied Daniel instantly, with a look of disarming frankness.

Nigusie picked a pen and continued questioning, name, age, address, and occupation, to which Daniel gave the exact answers. When questions about his family were asked, Daniel gave all information as they were, without mentioning a word about his brother, Samson, and his cousin, Ermias.

Lt. Nigusie was very gentle with him. His manners appeared to be of a man of sympathy and kindness. Although he was an active member of the pro-government socialist party, deliberately placed in this section by the organization to interrogate political dissidents and anti-government activists, his methods had always been fair, never going out of the limits allowed by the law.

"Did you use this gun to shoot Captain Zeleke?"

"Yes, I did.'

"How many shots did you fire?'

"One."

"Did you aim to kill?'

"Sure."

"Have you ever killed a person before?"

"I have never touched a knife or a gun, nor have I used my fist to harm any other human being before."

"Are you a member of any political organization?'

"No, I'm not."

"Where did you get the gun from?"

"It was my father's."

"Are you aware of the fact that your father can be badly implicated," Nigusie pointed thoughtfully, "if he doesn't have the permission to possess a gun?"

"I'm telling the truth."

Nigusie put down all in writing and closed the file. He appeared to believe that Daniel was telling the truth.

"Why did you want to kill him?"

Daniel narrated the story, from the bloody demonstration to the death of Ghenet, and Nigusie listened all like a sympathetic friend.

"It's quite a tragedy," Nigusie said as Daniel finished. "I must say what you did was unprofessional."

"I am not a professional."

"If you touch people like Zeleke, you had to make sure that you finished them."

"Isn't he dead?"

It was shocking news that generated emotional anguish. Daniel had believed that he had avenged Ghenet, and was content and ready for the consequences.

"As a matter of fact, he is more alive than before to cause you a lot of trouble," Nigusie rang the little bell on his desk to call the escorts. "You're finished with me. I wish you all the strength to endure the rest of the interrogation."

The escorts came and led Daniel out. He had already been stripped of his belt, watch, and shoes when he was booked, so the policeman took him directly to his cell.

Special-crime-prisoners (as political prisoners were called) were treated specially and kept in special jail reserved for such people. It was located in the middle of a high-walled yard within the police station's compound. In this yard, there stood a grim and foreboding building, with a look of death, consisting of many cells for both female and male detainees.

Daniel surveyed the building briefly as he, escorted by the two policemen, passed through the iron-gate. The high wall was topped by barbed wires and broken glasses. Armed police officers stood guard at the corners.

For the first time, fear engulfed him, and he shivered. He had never been detained and never seen such a grim place before. He felt he would not come out of this place alive. The escort stopped in front of cell number 12.

"Here," shouted the policeman and stepped aside to open the rusty lock while the other stood in alert with his rifle cocked. It was, Daniel thought, a precaution to prevent being overwhelmed by prisoners rushing out desperately.

The rusty metal door opened and a terrible smell of suffering humanity diffused out of the dark cell. It smelt of urine, unwashed bodies, and there was a sickening stench of the rotting flesh of torture victims. The policeman pushed Daniel into the cell, and closed the door instantly.

"Come on, brother," a voice said, "nothing to be afraid of here. A thousand times better than where you have been unless, of course, you came from heaven, which you don't look like you did." The cell burst into brief laughter.

Gradually, darkness subsided as Daniel got used to it. Faces, young faces, unveiled to form out. Some twenty young men were confined in the cell. Built of massive, grey stones the cell, shaped itself as a room of 20 sq. meters wide with a small barred window high up near the roof. A toilet facility consisted of a small bucket at the corner was full. He stepped forward to occupy a narrow space he was offered by the inmates. He thanked for the hospitality and sat crammed on the cement floor. Then he began to observe and learn.

Right in front of him, on the right side of the door, there was a relatively comfortable place called the Tribune, which the inmates used to treat tortured inmates. Only two patients at a time could be treated in the Tribune. When they recovered, or a fresh torture victim came, they would move to section number two, where there was room to stretch legs. Section three, where Daniel sat now, had no place to lie or sit properly. Newcomers and inmates whose wounds have healed stay there in a condition of such close confinement that they were unable to move their limbs until they qualify for the Tribune again.

Daniel watched the two young men who were treating and comforting a groaning inmate who had severe injuries of torture. The patient, soaked in blood, lay on the floor over some clothes to relax his back. He seemed to have been paralyzed from the waist downward. Someone had to carry him to the bucket. It was a horrifying sight. He observed others feeding those who could not help themselves. The spirit in the cell was highly inspiring; it had nothing in common with the nature of the Revolution.

To Daniel's hopeless heart, the inmates appeared very determined to stay alive and so composed to face the interrogation, torture, and death to come. As he observed them, some sense of togetherness crept on him restoring his shattered strength in his tired and hungry body, reinstating hope of some sort in his sorrow-stricken heart. Here in the cell, there was a strange society, different morale that the people in the barbarous outside world of terror would envy. Brotherhood, in its best meaning, was practiced and applied in this horrible environment of prison.

Knowing that he was among those who would share the same misfortune and anticipate a similar fate, Daniel felt comfortable. Ghenet came in his thought. *She might be buried by now*, he thought. Instantly his eyes became wet. A moment later, he fell asleep.

Chapter 19

As revolutionaries with licenses to kill any suspect invaded the streets and began executing the Red Terror, the EPRP, in its effort to defend itself, intensified its urban guerrilla operations in all the big cities across the country. Its squads began assassinating supporters of the regime at a rate never witnessed before. The Dergue and its supporters were gripped by fear. They were going armed to their offices, changing their dwellings, afraid they might be killed by the EPRP.

As a measure to frighten the EPRP, the Red Terror was exceedingly intensified. The repression focused on the youth as they were considered in their majority to be supporters of the EPRP. The Terror also singled out worker's leaders, activists in the civil administration, and mass associations.

On the part of the regime, it was a deliberate policy to decapitate the EPRP by depriving it of leaders, by silencing its articulate voices and organizers. In this way, any youngster or intellectual was slated for execution unless he could prove loyal to Mengistu. Youngsters were so horrified that they fled in all directions. Many of them chose to leave for other countries. Others preferred to go to Assimba to join the armed wing of the EPRP. The town of Dessie and Gonder were filled with youngsters that were on the run. Gonder was set in turmoil since a notorious Dergue member named Melaku Tefera took charge of directing the Red Terror in the city.

For Samson, who needed a calm and peaceful atmosphere, the situation was not suitable. It stirred in him unpleasant memories of his life in the Eritrean desert and disturbed him. Gonder was no longer a sanctuary than Addis would be. Not only because it reminded him of the painful past but also because it began to impel him in violent encounters quite several times.

Today the tea-room was unusually quiet. Scared of Melaku Tefera and his men, the young regulars had abandoned the tea-room. Samson had some leisure time to do his affair. He was sat on the far end of the room, writing a letter to his family, unworried about his job because his colleague was satisfactorily able to take care of the guests as they showed up.

The three young guests who happened to sit two tables away were served. Had Samson paid a little more attention, or had he not been writing the letter, he would certainly have recognized Rashid. After he finished writing, he looked around and stared at the three. All of a sudden, he stood as he identified Rashid and stepped forward to greet him.

"How are you?" Samson said and extended his hand for a handshake. Rashid inhaled so much air that pumped up his upper body, looked at Samson in contempt, and stretched his hand lamely.

"How is Kibrom?" asked Samson, "Did you see him lately?"

"Who is Kibrom? What are you talking about?" Rashid sneered. "Who are you, yourself? Do I know you?"

"How is that? You must be kidding," said Samson smiling, but Rashid turned his face in disregard to ridicule him.

Samson studied the others who giggled at Rashid's performance. Realizing that he was not welcome, he turned around and walked to his chair. On his way, he picked a day-old copy of Zemen, the State-owned newspaper, and sat to read.

Most of the stories in the newspaper dealt with what the paper labeled as terrorism and anarchism promoted by the EPRP. On another page, there was a story about the search campaign conducted by government forces in Addis Ababa and about the weapons, typewriters, written materials, and duplication machines seized during the operations. It also featured a story about the capture of anti-people elements, anarchists and mercenaries, who the paper said, had been liquidated as they resisted arrest.

Samson turned to the next page and continued to read the comments. Soon, he got tired of the empty propaganda phrases intended only to brainwash the public and flung the paper away more in apathy than intent. A couple of ill-fated pages flew over and landed under Rashid's feet. Rashid stood and strode towards Samson.

"This is a State newspaper! How dare you disgrace it?" shouted Rashid, tall and heavy, towering over Samson.

"It's old, and I didn't mean to dishonor it or offend anyone," said Samson, slightly confused but cautious. Assuming Rashid to be an EPRP activist, he couldn't figure out why he would defend the state organ.

"Pick it up!" ordered Rashid, with both hands on his waist; the customers who sat in the tea-room watching the scenario.

"I'm telling you to pick up the paper! Or do I have to make you do that!" Rashid barked again.

Samson heaved himself from the chair and bent to pick up the papers. He preferred to avoid such unpleasant encounters and chose to suffer the humiliation now than to regret the consequence later, but then, a word slipped out of Rashid's lips.

"A son of a …!"

Big mistake. Rashid had transgressed the limits, and the tiger was offended. When the word entered his ear, Samson felt a painful punch at his heart. He abhorred this kind of slur. As he heaved himself from the bent position, he stiffened his neck and forcefully knocked Rashid on his left ribs with his head. Then he put his fist up straight away and delivered a quick jab to the stoker's belly before he resorted to his guard up. Rashid swore and took a swing that would have laid Samson out. But Samson had swayed to the side, feinted with his right, and landed two hard left punches. The big man winded and angrily came after Samson with his arms outstretched. He caught Samson in a hug that briefly squeezed his breath out of him. But Samson broke himself out and swiftly landed a blow to Rashid's jaw that sent him reeling backward. Rashid crashed into a table, sent the tea mugs flying, and landed on his back, bellowing and flailing his stocky legs. As he struggled to collect himself, the gun under his belt was slightly exposed, but Samson did not see it. With new force, Rashid charged against Samson. Again, Samson moved a few steps to the right and hit him twice, first on the belly the other right on the nose. Blood spurting from his nose, Rashid staggered but managed to keep his balance. He then hurled towards Samson with all his force. But Samson was fast to change his position and chop him on his cheek, cutting the skin. Rashid was now punch drunk and bleeding. He was certainly in no position to inflict any harm, nor was he able to take punches anymore. Mercifully, quite satisfied with the brief exercise, Samson retreated.

It would have ended there, but Rashid was to plunge himself into another deplorable mistake. As he regained clarity and saw his own blood all over himself, he drew his gun. Samson saw the gun, and anger flooded over him in a dark dizzying wave. His eyes opened widely; his veins puffed up. He began breathing faster. Instantly he was transformed into a killer guerrilla. Now nothing short of killing could calm him. Only blood, not drops but floods, could extinguish his rage.

Samson darted high in the air towards Rashid. Rashid saw him coming, leveled his pistol, and fired. The slug tore Samson's shirt, scoring burning streaks along his left arm. Samson now landed on top of Rashid, knocking him off balance, locked Rashid's neck between his legs, and took him down to the floor. He squeezed his leg harder to the point of almost crunching the neck. Rashid had no option left except to drop the gun or die.

Capturing the weapon, Samson jumped to his feet to face the others. He had noticed one of Rashid's colleagues slowly stretching his hand to his belt. Samson did not miss what the awkward movement meant.

"Come on! Get the gun!" he barked at the young man, "get the gun!" He appeared terrifyingly out of his mind. The youngsters couldn't dare move. They could see something from inside was pushing him into the killing.

"Come on, bring out your gun!" cried Samson like a lunatic. He took a step toward the youngsters and knocked one of them with the butt of the gun. He slapped the other on the face.

"Drop your guns now!'

Instantly both men laid their guns on the table and held their hands above their heads. As the customers in the tea-room stared at him with their mouths gapped in disbelief, Samson collected the guns and tucked them under his belt.

"Who are you people? Where did you get these guns? Do you have IDs?" shouted Samson.

The two showed him their identifications. He had expected that these people were members of the EPRP army, but he was wrong; their papers indicated that the two men were Revo-guards with licenses to carry weapons, and take any measure they considered appropriate against anyone they suspect to be anti-Revolution. In short, they were Mengistu's soldiers of the Red Terror.

"Yours?" Samson turned to Rashid.

Lying on the floor, Rashid showed his paper. It was an ordinary ID with no authorization to carry a weapon or search anyone. Samson returned Rashid's paper and kept the other two's in his pocket.

"Go ahead! Get up! Rashid and you two." He ordered the three to queue up and march forward with their hands on their heads. He followed behind them with a gun pointed at them. When they reached the counter, he asked the owner of the tea-room for the storeroom keys. "I'll lock them in because they have disturbed the house."

Excitedly the owner handed him the key, and Samson led the three to the rear room where kitchen materials were kept. He opened the storeroom and locked the two youngsters in there. Then, he turned to Rashid and drew him to a corner and began interrogating him.

"You lie, you die! Now, where is Kibrom?" asked Samson knocking him with the butt of the gun.

"Kibrom is in Assimba… cool down… I'll tell you whatever you want to know."

"What is Assimba… Where is it? What is going on there?"

"Assimba is a strategic place in the province of Tigray. EPRP's military base is there."

"Aren't you the one who took him there? Why did you pretend as if you don't know my brother and me?"

"Yes, I was with them," Rashid replied. "My job was to take youngsters to Assimba."

"And what are you doing with these people now?"

"It's a long story.

"I have the time to listen; just tell your story."

"I was arrested by the security, and now I'm forced to work with them. They told me they'd spare my life if I only do as they want me to."

"How did they trust you to carry a weapon?"

"I have been working with them for quite a while to be trusted. I'm a member of their organization now."

"Who are they?"

"The Socialist party."

"So, your job includes revealing the secrets you shared with your old friends… leading the security to your friends… the EPRP or whatever, is that right?"

"Well, I had to save my neck."

Samson shifted his eyes from Rashid to the floor, then to the roof, and back to Rashid, weighing what to do next. When he made up his mind, he said, "I'll throw all your weapons into the latrine and tear up your IDs. If I ever find you in similar circumstances again, I'll no more deal with you lightly. Do you understand me?"

"Yes, I do," answered Rashid, smiling mischievously.

"Get in there!"

Samson placed Rashid in the storeroom together with the others and locked the door from outside. He threw the three guns and the ID cards into the toilet pit and returned to the guestroom, where the customers were excitedly waiting to see the finale scene. When Samson appeared, they cheered and applauded. Although it was no laughing matter, he could not suppress a smile.

"You know how many lives they have on their hands!" One of the customers said.

"You're fearless!" said another one, "maybe you don't know who they are. They are the princes of the Revolution who can simply cut your tang for not saying their slogan or pull your eyes out for staring at them."

Samson didn't like much of the exaggeration. He waved a hand at them, but no sign of arrogance on his part was detected. He went to the owner to hand him the key.

"I'm leaving, Boss. I have enough of Gonder," he said, "you may release them two or three hours after my departure."

Understandingly, the owner nodded, and then he opened the counter from which he picked some twenty Birrs and slipped it in Samson's hand.

"You have been a nice boy," the man said and called a kitchen lad to help Samson with his baggage.

"I have only a small bundle. I'll carry it myself. Thank you for your courtesy," Samson said and left.

He went to the bus station in central Gonder and waited for the right bus, which was not due to leave until 5 o'clock. By that time, the Rashids would be free and begun searching for him. But the hours passed without event, and Samson boarded a bus bound south, to Addis Ababa.

When he entered the Capital, he had no idea of what had taken place in Addis Ababa the past weeks, lest to his brother. Over the weekend, there had been some clash between security people and the EPRP militants, as the securities tried to round up what they had suspected to be a hideout. In just overnight, more than 50 youngsters were reported to have been killed. Samson was numb with disbelief when he learned that. And his brother, Daniel, whom he loved more than anyone in the world, was in jail for shooting a prominent Dergue member.

Samson was not the type who would let anyone mess up with his family, and he was one of the best when it comes to the gun-game, which the Dergue had chosen to play with the unarmed.

Chapter 20

The prison in the Fifth police station was a ghastly place. Daniel had never imagined that there was such a place in the country where prisoners were treated in such a cruel manner. Once a day, early in the morning, they let the inmates out of the cell to empty their buckets and wash their faces at the running water pipe in the yard. Bread and a cup of water were the only food the station supplied, while families and relatives provided cooked meals almost daily. Those who fell ill or wounded under torture had no access to medication, though pain killer tablets were somehow smuggled in or bought by bribing the guards.

Daniel was disgusted by the situation in the cells as many of the inmates were sick and weakened by torture, but he was also toughened by their bravery and courage to hold on. He had found a few Zemachs he knew, and the others were kind to him. His job in the cell was to help victims of torture in any way he could. He had not been called for interrogation until now.

When he heard his name called from the outside today, he ceased treating an almost lifeless inmate and alerted himself. He heard the footsteps purposefully slamming the ground as they came closer. His eyes remained fixed at the rusty door as its handle moved. Then the door opened, and two armed policemen stepped in.

"Who is Daniel?" one of the policemen asked.

"Bring yourself together, Daniel," said an inmate, "you will make it."

Daniel rose slowly and stepped forward. He was neatly dressed and very awake. At noon Abinet had come and left food and clothes to him. He had eaten little and changed. He appeared ready for anything to come, but privately he was deadly scared of the interrogators. What they had done to the cell-mate he was helping! As he took another step forward, the policeman a policeman slapped a handcuff in his hands and hustled him out of the cell.

Outside, the daylight blinded him briefly, but the air was refreshing. Flanked by the escorts, he walked on the stone ground bare-feet. They went past the iron gate and continued to the main building.

The police station appeared calm. But he could sense the tight security around it. People were not allowed to enter the compound without special permission. Outside the compound, some relatives stood waiting with such a stance of extreme concern as though warning the state not to harm their loved ones. Daniel looked far beyond and searched if any of his were around, but before he scanned half the area, he was pushed to step into the main building.

The chief interrogator had his office at the left side of the main door, a few steps away. One of the escorts knocked at a shabby door. As he got permission to enter, he pushed Daniel into the room and remained behind.

A short, unhappy-looking man of around fifty was pacing the little room with both hands in his pocket. There were some strips tagged on his black police uniform. When Daniel entered, he slowed and stood behind the shabby old desk on which a file was laid open.

No time was wasted on formalities. The Sergeant barked instantly at Daniel. "Are you going to talk or not?"

"I'll talk. I take full responsibility for my actions," answered Daniel.

"I don't think you got my point. It's not your action or responsibility I need. For that, you will soon get what you deserve. Now, I want those behind you."

Daniel was alerted by the remark. He never expected this to come. He stared squarely at the Sergeant and said, "I don't quite understand. What do you mean by— those behind me?"

"Look," the Sergeant roared. "Don't waste my time and yours, if you have any. There are other ways of questioning, but before that, I want your co-operation. Just do yourself a favor. Tell me everything, and the merciful Revolution will see that you get fair treatment. You repent, and you will be reborn as a true son of the Revolution. Maybe you can qualify to be a cadre. With that, there is money; plenty of money to reap." He paused, sat on the chair, and studied Daniel, whose face showed no fear but confusion.

"On the other hand," the Sergeant went on, "we have other means of getting what we want. No one can stand it. So why you hurt your beautiful body."

Daniel understood what the Sergeant meant, yet he stood erect and spoke formally, "There is no one behind me. Honestly, I did it by myself, for myself. It was a personal matter. The man I shot was responsible for the death of my fiancé.

"The man? Who is the man?"

"Captain Zeleke."

"Hereafter, you refer to him as Comrade Captain Zeleke, do you get me!" the Sergeant shouted, "how is the Comrade responsible?"

Daniel explained briefly.

"What was the demonstration about?"

"Human rights."

"Who organized it?"

"The EPRP."

"So. That's what I want you to tell me. Who are they? Where are they?"

"I don't know them. They called the general public. Not only members. I joined the demonstration as a sympathizer."

"That's what you of all say. You offer yourself up and save your party. I have no further oral questions for you. Three meters below us, there is another section where interrogations are put in a different language, a language you people sure understand. You shall be taken there, but I'll give you one last chance. Are you going to talk or not?

"I have nothing to add to the truth," Daniel said with quivering lips.

The Sergeant rushed to the door and let the escorts in.

"Take him to the underground." Daniel had heard the word in the cell. It meant the place of torture.

The underground, a cold intentionally dimmed chamber, was some three meters below the ground. It had been newly rebuilt to accommodate recently imported equipment of torture. At the first glimpse, it looked to Daniel like a workout gym, the bed-like apparatus to confine legs and thighs, special chairs where the electric shock would be applied. There were knives and bayonets, wires and robs, burning liquids, hammering metals and plastics materials, and other equipment of torture, which he could not tell what they were used for or how. In a nation where more than a quarter of the population starved, and a quarter of the children died of malnutrition before they see their fifth birthday, the Peoples Revolution's primary need was to import pieces of torture equipment from East Germany and North Korea.

The chamber had been in action when Daniel was brought in it. It was filled with a crying sound of a young man who was suspended on a bar and the threatening torturers who were violently abusing him. As he stood to be handed over to his interrogator, Daniel saw the two torturers whispering to the young man, who then stopped crying and was soothed and taken down. The young man, Daniel thought, must have agreed to confess a crime or reveal his comrades.

Daniel's eyes darted to the other end of the chamber and spotted something wrapped by a dirty blanket. He asked himself, *'could it be a dead man?'* He doubted if he would come out of this place alive because he had nothing to reveal.

A pot-bellied man came out of a little room and approached the escorts. He held a bottle of Taj (locally brewed alcoholic drink) from which he sloshed twice before he looked at Daniel with his big eyes half-covered by the lids.

"Is this the anarchist who shot Captain Zeleke?" asked the man and belched noisily, his voice hoarse and whistling. "You can set loose his hands and leave."

A detachment of two armed men who stood a bit away stepped closer when the escorts left.

"If you want to confess, Mister Anarcho, this is the way," the interrogator pointed to the little office with his left hand, "if not," he pointed to the torture hall with his right hand. "I am sure you're not a fool. You will spare yourself and me a great deal of energy if you co-operate."

"I have nothing more to tell than what I have already told."

Daniel was slapped on the face for that answer, and ordered to take off his clothes. He complied quickly but hesitated to take off his underwear. A second blow from the torturer's clenched fist landed on his chest, and knocked him to the cement floor. Kneeling on the floor, he took out his underwear before he was kicked again.

"Prepare him!" the torturer ordered and poured all that was left in the bottle in himself. He belched rudely, tapped his belly, and went to the board where various types of whips and belts were hanged orderly. He scanned over them and picked a thick, long whip made of rough hide. He measured it mentally and contemplated the damage it would inflict on its victim in a short period if it would be used expertly.

The two guards tied Daniel's hands and legs and suspended him upside down on a wooden bar, supported by two poles that stood few meters apart. This was one of the barbarous methods of torture known as Wofe-Illala.

"This game has some rules," the totturer explained, "I'll apply them accordingly. I'll stop when you want to confess. I hope you understand I'm only doing my job. Are you listing to me?"

Daniel didn't hear a word of it. To him, the entire world seemed to have turned upside down like himself. His face was already inflating from the blood rushing to his head., His eyes puffed out, and veins swelled. As the first strike pounded over his naked body, he emitted a loud sound of agony and propelled around the bar as a pulsating current of pain diffused through his body. The whip made spiral scars all over the skin it touched. The second one that came from behind landed on his back, turned around, and ended at his buttock. New marks of removed skin appeared on his back. He cried with all his breath and dangled violently to break himself out, but to no avail. When he calmed, the torturer stepped to a different position and surveyed a new direction to inflict pain. He then gathered himself and lashed with tremendous power that the whip went deeper in the skin to cut flesh. Blood began to drop from the wounds.

Daniel arched his back and jerked convulsively. The pain was unlike anything he had ever felt. It came in three repeated waves of agony; first, the searing burn on his skin as the whip hit; then, the shock to his flesh and muscle as the blow cut into him; afterward, the terrible sickening sensation as the impact rippled through his body. Daniel screamed and howled of pain, upsetting the torture who seemed not able to tolerate it. To restrain the scream, the torturer brought a pair of dirty socks and forcefully stuffed it in Daniel's mouth.

"I can't stand your screams; you better confess than sing," said the torturer laughing at his own joke, "when you want to talk, you give me a sign. You hear me."

Daniel had almost no sense of hearing. All his sense system seemed to have slowed down to shunt the pain of the suffering body. His eyes were all the time closed. When he opened them, it was only to see the wrapped dead man whom he envied. Death, which was so surplus outside this station, was scarce in this chamber.

Now the whip landed fully on the bottom of the feet, tearing the skin brutally, but Daniel seemed to endure it. The defense mechanism of the human body was on guard now, shunting most of the pain of the body and comforting the soul. The beating went on without any result, and it stopped when

Daniel lost consciousness. When he was carried to his cell, even the escorts were horrified.

Chapter 21

The weeks following the bloody demonstration were marked by increasingly horrifying acts of terror. Socialist party cadres, government security forces, and Revo-guards were out hunting EPRP members and sympathizers. Terror had reigned in the city of Addis Ababa and other towns; parents were thrown into turmoil as they saw their offspring fall victim to arbitrary arrest and killing. It was hard, in any event, to plan for the future when everything revolved around only to survive the next twenty-four-hour.

For egoistic people like Goytom, it was business as usual. In this horrible social crisis, he did never flinch from his goal to win the court case against Abinet. And he did win. Since Abinet had ignored to appear at the court for the third time, the district court ruled by default that Goytom should get his share of the house. three weeks were given to Abinet to pay him his share, half the estimated amount of 30,000 Birr, or else the house would be sold in auction to pay him off.

Goytom would have settled for less to avoid the court mess and the embarrassment of evicting his family, but Abinet had nothing to offer. She was preoccupied with the misfortune of her son, Daniel. None in the family bothered much of losing the house at that moment of tragedy. But Ermias was not overwhelmed by emotions. A couple of weeks after the court's ruling, he met Goytom and talked to him to drop the case. Goytom was so stubborn to convince that Ermias had to beg him to wait until after Daniel's case ended in whatever way it went.

"I can't turn down the decision of the court. She had been given enough time to present her case. It's over now. I am only taking what the law grants me."

"Would you drop it if I pay you half of your share today?" suggested Ermias knowing full well that no one liked cash as Goytom did. Goytom always preferred half a sum in cash now than full in gold the next day.

"How much is half? Seven thousand five hundred? Today?" wondered Goytom, then he raised his head. "OK, I can take that."

"We meet at Asmara Inn this evening at eight. You come with your lawyer, and I'll come with a witness," Ermias said.

"Ermias, you have another important message," Tiku said, counting money out of the cash register of the Bar.

"Who might it be?'

"A lady by the name Saba Berhe. She said it was urgent… didn't say much. She only left a number."

Ermias went around the counter and picked the telephone. He dialed the number while Tiku still counted the money. In a moment, Saba was on the line.

"It's about Major Alemayo, Ermias," Saba announced, "he is to be moved soon. I thought you might want to talk to him."

"How would that be possible, dear."

"I have the night shift tomorrow. You just come tomorrow evening, and we'd figure out a plan. I have already one."

"Thanks, Saba," Ermias said, "I'll come."

At Seven o'clock, Ermias was with Abinet to tell her about his encounter with Goytom, but she wasn't in any mood to talk about Goytom or the house at the moment. She was absorbed by the thought of her son. Ermias understood.

"Where is Samson? Is he all right? I want him to be with me when I pay the money."

"He is in the backyard," answered Abinet quietly. Ermias could see that she was tired and weakened by clinging tragedies.

The backyard was some 70 square meter wide lawn where Abinet used to grow vegetables in the old good days. Now it was all gone. There was nothing green around. At the far end, stood the tattered service house, the traditional kitchen, Samson's favorite corner. In his young age, after school, he used to rush directly to the kitchen before he even laid his school bag, and claim his share of Mamma's bread. The kitchen still held that lovely fragrance of bread.

Sitting on the ground, leaning against the service house, and scratching the earth with a pebble, Samson was immersed in deep thought. His days were cold by the thought of Daniel, and his nights, burning fire by the nightmares of war. His appetite was so poor that he lost considerable weight since he came. The only lively organs in his body were his eyes; they still held their inquisitive glare.

When Ermias approached him, he blinked briefly at his appearance and then resumed scratching the earth. Ermias had pondered about Samson's emotional distress, which seemed to worsen from day to day. His behavior had nothing in common with those ex-guerrillas who suffer from post-war syndrome after returning to a peaceful life.

"I want to talk to you?" said Ermias in a low, firm voice.

"What about?" responded Samson in almost inaudible voice of a distressed soul, looking up to meet Ermias' eyes against the weak glow of light from the house.

"You."

"Me? You need all the time in the world to discuss me. And you don't seem to have that. Make yourself comfortable." Samson gestured to Ermias to sit on the ground like him.

Ermias sat on the greener part of the ground and took some time to formulate a question. Then he eyed his cousin and spoke, "I have seen fighters who experienced what you had been through and returned to normal life. But never have I seen anyone so depressed as you are. Fighters don't suffer war traumas as government soldiers do because they fight for a cause. They kill to save their people from murderers. So, tell me why yours is so different."

"Those fighters you saw might not have their brother in jail waiting to be slaughtered, or they might not feel responsible for the annihilation of a whole village, or they might not have seen their friend killed fighting on the other side. Each had so different experience and so unique encounters to deduce similarity," said Samson and threw the pebble in a spirit of anger: anger that had been tapped for a long time.

"Daniel is not a unique case. It's happening to every family in this country. But what innocent civilians are you talking about? What village are you talking about?" inquired Ermias curiously.

Samson began to tell the story. It was the story of the battle of Awgaro.

"As it occurred to me that the Air raid could follow, I should have forwarded the need to evacuate the civilians, but I didn't do that. I left the entire village to burn in a dreadful fire."

When he finished, Ermias moved his head sorrowfully in regret. "There is much thought that crosses our mind every day, and we don't forward them all the time. Things like that occur to some fighters. We are humans with flaws, hence we make mistakes from which we learn in order to become better people.

"A bomber was hit, and its pilot was captured alive at the battle of Awgaro. Recently we exchanged the pilot for a piece of information that helped us cripple Operation Raza. I know you blew the bomber. Imagine how many lives were saved by foiling Raza."

"What?"

"Yes, Samson," Ermias said coolly. "I took care of the deal. The information was beneficial. It saved many lives on both sides. You should get the credit for that."

"It was a matter of chance," Samson said, interrupting Ermias.

Samson began to recall the battle of Awgaro, concentrating on the final hours of the battle, the victory, and then the bombers. Everything came back to him vividly; that he had taken over of the anti-aircraft gun after the death of his compatriot; his desperate effort to blow the bombers, the fire and the smoke, the tumult, and finally the darkness as he lost consciousness.

"And Gaushaw is just a victim of war. In war, it's you or the enemy... no other choice. Whatsoever, you have saved a hundred times more lives than what you think you are responsible for the loss," Ermias tapped Samson and rose, straightening and brushing his trouser. He was sharp to notice the immediate changes in Samson whose face flickered a smile of a tormented soul that was set free.

"Listen, Samson," Ermias moved closer to Samson and laid a hand on his shoulder. In half an hour, I'm going to see your father. He has agreed to settle the dispute if I paid him half today."

"Half of his share?"

"Yes, I had to bargain half a day to come to that. Anyway, I want you to be with me to witness the settlement. This is a family matter, and I don't want outsiders to be in this."

Samson nodded.

"Let's go," Ermias led the way out, secretly cherishing the change on Samson. Before his eyes, the cheerful old Samson, that brave guardian angel, was being reborn.

Few minutes had passed eight when they arrived at Asmara Inn. Goytom had already come with his lawyer. They sat detached at the corner. Unlike the other customers whose eyes were fixed on the television set, Goytom seemed preoccupied with himself, fumbling with the glass on his table.

On the television was a government spokesman announcing Somali infiltration in Ethiopian soil and denouncing the military buildup of Somali regular forces along the Ethiopian border.

Samson greeted his father formally and sat at the next table. Ermias took a seat at the same table with Goytom. They waited until the television announcement, calling the people to be prepared for the Somali aggression, had finished.

Goytom made an awkward movement to start the talking, but his lawyer was quicker.

"Mr. Goytom will not go with the terms of agreement you reached earlier today. It was a mistake," said the lawyer flatly.

Confused about what he heard, Ermias looked at the lawyer and then at Goytom. "What do you mean. We have already talked and agreed about it."

"But…"

"You get yourself out of this. I'm not talking to you," coolly Ermias interrupted the lawyer.

"I'm his lawyer. I talk on his behalf."

"This is a family matter, Mister Lawyer. Would you please keep yourself out of this? We are not in court," Ermias warned the stubborn lawyer again.

"He is speaking my decision," said Goytom, "I want fifteen thousand. That house would sell for forty-Thousand-Birr— these days."

Sitting at the next table, Samson was following the argument without seeming to be interested in the issue. He was not surprised by what has come out. He knew his father very well; a cheat with no respect for word-of-honor. Slowly he rose and, without excusing himself, went out quietly.

Ermias wanted to argue more, but seeing Goytom's ignoring face, he gave up. When he rose, he knocked the table angrily that Goytom had to draw himself backward.

"I'll get you your money," Ermias said, "but you shall lose your family."

"You have the money; you make a family. Get the money, and we will work out the rest," Goytom answered back.

"There is no compassion left in the man," Ermias said as he met Samson outside.

"I thought you knew that."

"I assumed he has changed."

"Some people never learn. Forget the whole thing, Ermias. We will survive, somehow."

"I have got to go now. Good night, Samson."

"I'm sure I'll sleep well tonight." Samson crossed the road and went into the dark alley as Ermias got into the car and drove north.

Yekatit 12 Memorial Hospital was strictly guarded by armed soldiers and watched over by several plain-clothed security people. Major Alemayo was too important a person and too rare a source of information to ease the security around the hospital. Besides, EPRP's counter-attack was intensified in the city, and word had spread that there was a plan to rescue Alemayo.

Ermias, assisted by Saba, had somehow managed to pass the gate with less difficulty.

"Here I have all Ahmed's medical equipment," Saba said, showing what she had prepared in her office. "Here is his overcoat. I can see it fits you. You just try to look like a frustrated doctor."

"How do they look?"

"I'll make you look like one. Take off your coat."

In a few minutes, Ermias had changed. He had putting on the white overcoat with somebody's name tagged on it. It fitted well. He held a stethoscope around his neck and a patient journal in his hand. But he still felt like he has not changed much.

"What's left?" Ermias looked at himself and then waited for Saba's approval, "How do I look?"

"Try this glass." Saba produced a pair of eyeglasses, which fitted on Ermias' face. "That's okay. There is nobody around Alemayo now to reveal you... only the guards, and they don't know who is who. As long as you're with me, it's safe. This is supposed to be the last check-up for Alemayo."

Ermias stepped forward. "Let's move now," he whispered into her ears.

Saba held some items and led the way.

The two guards at the door stood to receive Ermias and Saba as the two approached the room where Alemayo was kept under strict security.

"Good evening," Saba addressed the guards, "The doctor shall make a final checkup now."

"Yes, Sister," one of the guards came closer to unlock the door, leaving his rifle to the other.

"Shall I unchain him?" the guard asked, pushing the door open.

"Yes, please," Saba said and pretended to look at her checking list.

Having unchained Alemayo's hand, which was tied to the bed, the guard quietly left the room, closing the door behind him.

The Major woke up, looked right and left with his single eye, which he then inquisitively fixed on Saba. His other eye was severed out of him under tortur.

"How are you, Major?" asked Saba in a low voice.

"Well enough to be tortured again, I guess," said Alemayo forcing a smile. "You're just preparing me to those cannibals to eat me alive," he added and turned to Ermias, "Doctor, why don't you give me an injection that could put me in eternal sleep than throw me to those wolves.

"I'm not a doctor, Major," Ermias said, sympathetically. "I came here to talk with you… private matters."

Alemayo lifted his head a bit, and his eye rotated between Ermias and Saba. For an instant, he suspected if this was a rescue mission, which would at least give him a little more time to see his wife and tell her the last precious words; to see his kids and tell them that they will somehow overcome the hardship of life without him. He was a man who worked to earn and struggled to achieve his position, but today he wished he could be free just to see nothing but his family.

"I needed a piece of information from you," Ermias added carefully.

The major's head sunk in the pillow.

"What information, may I ask?"

"It's an old homicide case, sir," Ermias began the story. "Back in 1962, a 38-year-old man named Tesfay Kahsay was murdered in central Addis Ababa. I gathered that you were the officer in charge of the investigation."

Alemayo tried to listen attentively. Saba was watching the reactions on his face.

"Do you remember?" Ermias asked.

Alemayo's eye narrowed as he drew inward to recall. But soon, his face shook sidewise.

"I'm sorry I couldn't help," apologized Alemayo, "what's it for you?"

"The victim was my father," Ermias said, his heart pounding, and his voice trembling. "He was a politician involved in the Eritrean movement.'

Suddenly Alemayo's upper body stiffened. "What did you say the name was?'

"Tesfay Kahsay."

"He has a sister who lives here in Addis, right?

"Yes," Ermias answered hastily, eyes narrowed, his heart pounding faster.

"I remember the case now. How can I forget it? It was my first criminal investigation I conducted. I can't forget it. Now, what is it you want from me?" said Alemayo, watching Ermias through the corner of his eye.

"The investigation was not completed. Why?"

"The State couldn't afford to investigate to the end," replied Alemayo. "Primarily," he went on, "the case was so complicated that we had no resource to go through the endless possibilities. Secondly, your father's activities were resented by the State that it rejoiced his elimination. So, nobody cared to find an enemy's killer."

"What about the State itself. I would have listed it as a first-degree suspect."

Alemayo smiled slightly, enough to expose that he had no front teeth left. "As a suspect, yes. But as a perpetrator, no. The State wouldn't investigate itself if it were involved."

"I guess that's why the investigation was halted. Didn't you assume that the State was involved?"

"I did. At first, everybody did," Alemayo appeared too enthusiastic to say more. "I'll tell you something, but you must promise before me, her, and God that you won't go after the murderer."

"You know who murdered my father?"

"I want just to know. I seek neither justice nor vengeance now. I promise," Ermias swore, his voice trembling, as he was about to hear a mystery that had turned his life upside down.

"When the official investigation was terminated," Alemayo went on, the words coming out of the one-time great speaker sounding like that of a child's now, his voice whistling through his toothless mouth. "I became angry, because they told me to discontinue in the middle of a suspenseful investigation. I was so engaged in the case that I couldn't leave it just like that. So, I continued the investigation unofficially to look for anything that could implicate the State or the Eritrean movement. I found out that none of them were involved. I began looking for a common robber—that too, proved to reach nowhere. Then I concentrated on his friends and family, including his sister and her husband. What was his name?"

"Goytom Gobezay," helped Ermias hoping the major's story would fall apart before it reached its conclusion. Not knowing exactly where it would lead, he was already besieged by a creeping horror.

"Yes, Goytom. Goytom had started running a small business, and he had a house under construction right after that incident. That added up to my suspicion. I intensified my follow-up on him. His salary was less than one-hundred Birrs, barely enough for a family with children. Where did he get the money? Your father was reported to have had some money to support the Eritrean Movement; that money was not found. I confronted Goytom, and threatened to open the case unless he confessed to me."

"Are you telling me that Goytom robbed and murdered my father," Ermias roared, his hands shaking. He had to strain to make every word as he said, "I can't believe this. This can't be true. Goytom, too, is my father."

"He confessed formally by signing a document," Alemayo went on, "He crawled on his knees, wept, and begged me not to take him to the court. I had to be rational. The case was officially closed. I continued it for my satisfaction. What is it for me, sending a father of small children to jail? So, the case was closed for the second time. If you want to convince yourself, the files of my investigation and his confession are available at my home. You can take them any time. They have no use for me but keep your promise—no vengeance.

"That's my word, Major," said Ermias with a tone of assurance, "I would like to see the files."

"My home is in Lideta, just a few hundred meters behind Bar Lideta. Ask anyone in the bar; they will show you. If you go," Alemayo's tones changed now, "please kiss my children for me. And tell my wife that I'm a soldier. She will understand." Then Alemayo broke into tears for the first time since his captivity.

The following day, at about 10 a.m., Ermias was awakened by gentle drumming on his door. He rolled out of bed naked and put on a light cotton robe. He knew it was the bar-tender whom he had told yesterday to wake him if he overslept. He had drunk quite a lot in an attempt to relieve the pressure of the heinous revelation he stumbled into yesterday. He could have accepted anyone as his father's killer, but Goytom Gobezay whom he, subtly, took for a father was a hot iron to swallow. The clash between this deeply held belief and the ugly reality had kindled a fire that seared in him and sickened him emotionally. His head throbbed from the tension.

He thanked the bartender and began preparing himself for the day. He had to visit Alemayo's family, fetch the confession file, face the murderer and comfort him with the discovery today. It was going to be a nerve-racking day.

He dressed and, without caring for breakfast, went to his car. He had no appetite. There was a fire in his stomach. In less than a quarter, he was in the heart of Lideta. He parked the car on the roadside, two blocks away from Bar Lideta. Unmindful of the surrounding, which appeared quieter than usual, he walked straight into the bar that also appeared deserted. Ermias' mind was so occupied that he didn't ask why.

In the bar, he ordered a bottle of cold mineral water and drained it in himself right away as if to quench the fire inside him. Before he got out of the bar, he made sure of the precise address of Alemayo's residence from the bartender.

"We heard some shooting near the neighborhoods." the bartender said.

"There is shooting all over the city," replied Ermias.

"Not at the these hours of the day. You take care anyways."

"Thanks." Said Ermias, and left.

It did not take him long to locate the residence, but the circumstance surprised him. Most by-passers, except few elderly people who had no idea of the situation seemed to avoid walking past the residence area. The grille was wide open, and no one seemed to be around. It was quiet. He wondered if the family have left the place or moved somewhere else.

He entered the yard with small lawn full of flowers on both side of the cobblestone pavement. On his left, he saw a dreadful scene; a huge dog, lying motionless, drops of blood still running out of its neck and shoulder. Ermias recalled what the bartender told about the shooting. *The Security must have visited the place and the brave dog might have given them a real hard time,* he thought.

Ermias stepped on the stairs of the parlor, and tapped the door first gently, and then, when he got no response, harder.

And harder. Still no response. Suspiciously he walked around the house. The backyard was clean and quiet.

"Anybody home?" Ermias called loudly,

Not long after, a disheveled girl appeared from the service house and stared at him with terrified eyes. Her dress was disrupted and torn. There were marks on her face, swelling next to her right eye.

"What are you looking for?" she inquired, her lips shivering.

"Isn't this Major Alemayo's residence?" asked Ermias politely, inducing a friendly atmosphere.

"Yes, it is," said the girl, her eyes narrowing.

"I came with the major's consent. Where is the rest of the family?"

"The major? Is he alive?"

"Yes, I met him yesterday. But where is the rest of the family?"

The girl wiped her eyes that soon became full of tears and said, "Soldiers were here. They took them."

"Why? Where?"

"I don't know."

"The kids too?"

"Yes, all. The mother and the two children."

"Assassins!" Ermias whispered between his teeth, thumping the palm of his left hand with his right fist.

He stepped closer to the girl. "I came with Major Alemayo's consent to collect some papers. Would you care to show me where he keeps his papers?"

"I'm only a housemaid." The girl somehow trusted him and co-operatively led him to the house. She limped as she walked over the stairs, Ermias noticed. It was now clear that the Red Terror had visited this place. The girl had received her share of the diabolic terror. She had been beaten and raped by the security people, Ermias suspected, and was shaken by this but remained calm.

Passing through the corridor, Ermias got a glimpse of the dining room. The table was not cleared; a kettle and teacups along with plates, spoons, and bread were spread over it. Some food staff had dropped on the floor..

"Here is his study," the girl opened a door and stepped aside to let Ermias through.

Alemayo's study was elegant, perfectly in order, and clean. Ermias turned to the shelves, scanned over the books, then shifted his eyes to the next shelve where folders were sorted in chronological order. Without touching a thing, he followed the order year by year. Down at the bottom, on the first folder from the left, was marked the year 1962. He extracted the folder, straightened, and stepped back a little. He struggled to compose himself, but he was shaking. He drew a deep breath as he pulled a bundle of documents out of the folder and leafed through. Suddenly he felt his own heart lift itself up under his chest. Perturbed as he was, he went over the papers faster and stopped at the document on which Goytom signed his confession.

Moved by that dry, cold crime reverberating through the years, Ermias stood transfixed as he read on the confession written fifteen years ago. All those years, he had convinced himself that his father was a martyr who had been murdered for a noble cause. He was addicted to this version of the story, a story that created an illusion of patriotic sacrifice, which made him proud of his father. By repeating and inflating his fabrications over and over, he had convinced himself that his theory was more trustworthy than the evidence before his own eyes. Now the illusion exploded in his face. His father's life was not sacrificed for a cause he was proud of but wasted by a greedy robber for a few thousand Birrs. How much demeaning it might be, the truth was stronger to overwhelm the illusion, and rationality was to take over emotion.

By the time he was out of Alemayo's residence, a dreadful silence had descended on the city. It appeared as though it was under siege. In the southern part of the city, the security forces were conducting a house-to-house search. All exits from the city were closed by armed troops. Bars were ordered to close, no public car heading south was allowed to move on the streets without permission. People were ordered to stay indoors, and open their houses to the searching teams. Ermias had to drop the idea to look for Goytom who lived in the southern part and headed north instead.

In the afternoon, he placed a call to Colonel Assefa.

"The hand of terror has struck again," Assefa jumped directly into the hot news, as soon as he realized the caller was Ermias, "Major Alemayo could not hold on any longer. He was forced to reveal the names of the EPRP leaders this morning. The security forces are now moving from house to house hunting them."

Ermias learned from Assefa that Zeleke had threatened to torment the major's family unless he co-operated. Alemayo was on the verge of a complete breakdown when he, to spare his family from the scourge of Mengistu, gave the names of a dozen central committee members of the EPRP. Consequently, others connected to the central committee were rounded up in a quick operation led by Captain Zeleke: many gave themselves up and denounced their associates under the simplest oral interrogation. In less than three hours, the security forces had managed to truck some 200 top EPRP leaders. Some were reported to have committed suicide when cornered by security forces. Many died in shoot-outs with soldiers. The death toll was high.

At 2 p.m., the State radio triumphantly announced that it dealt with the EPRP the final blow on its core. It bragged over the killing of several central committee members of the organization who resisted arrest. The organization, Ermias leaned, had been annihilated in one day.

How badly prepared they were, Ermias wondered, that one man's information could inflict such enormous damage to the entire organization, and hardship to its members. He thought of Alemayo. That man endured much more than any man could. He was a real hero. He upheld long enough that the EPRP could have found a way out…

Then the thought of Goytom crossed his mind, and his heart began to pound. He had already postponed the confrontation to take place tomorrow. Earlier, he had arranged with one of his spies to inform Goytom to meet him tomorrow, at 6 at Asmara Inn. How he would react, he did not know. Nor did he imagine how Goytom would take it. But he had worked out a scheme that might work for the time being. If Goytom agreed to his proposal, he would make it discreet and simple as it had always been with Alemayo. No vengeance, no suing. Goytom had taken one life and robbed 15000 Birr. He couldn't bring back the life, but he could pay back the money by disclaiming ownership of the house. *That would be a compromise,* Ermias thought; *I can settle for that. What else can one do, kill him?*

Ermias had come well before Goytom and was waiting unprepared for what would turn up if Goytom simply denied the crime and reject the proposal. At six o'clock, he looked at his watch and then at the entrance—no Goytom.

The security raid conducted yesterday had been intensified mainly in the neighborhood where Goytom lived now. Anything could have happened to him, just like it could happen to anyone.

As the minutes ticked by, Ermias became uneasy. He was half resolved to get up and leave when he, at last, saw Goytom enter the hotel briskly and spot him instantly. This time he had no lawyer with him.

Goytom looked eager to collect the money. His expectation was clear, nothing less than the 15000 Birr, his rightful share. He apologized for coming late and sat on the vacant chair in front of Ermias.

"You heard about the house to house searching they conducted yesterday. It was intensive and frightening. No one was allowed to go out or come into this part of the city. These murderers! They killed an awful lot of people," Goytom said.

"The world is full of murderers," said Ermias, fixing a hateful eye on Goytom. His eyes bore deep into Goytom to see the man behind the aging, innocent-looking face.

Goytom's eyes withdrew and fell on the floor where Ermias' black leather suitcase stood. He pursed his lips in the thought of his persistent struggle to this final. He had always believed that if he fought to the end, he would win. Nothing could stop him now to achieve his next goal, he thought. He would work his way up as he did before, fifteen years ago. He had enough knowledge on how to prosper in this community. All that he needed was a little start capital, just enough to be in the stream of business. And it was here a footstep and a few minutes away. From the briefcase, Goytom's eyes shifted back on Ermias, whose irritating stare still held on.

"What has happened to you? You look terrible," said Goytom with a slight look of confusion.

Ermias didn't answer, but his hand stretched to the briefcase, eyes still fixed at Goytom. He flipped the briefcase open, took out a folder, and slid it across the table to Goytom.

"What is this?" Goytom wondered, pulling himself away from the folder.

"There you have the money," said Ermias, staring squarely at Goytom, words firm and threatening.

Goytom's eyes dropped to the folder and his hands, shaking of fear and curiosity, opened the it. As his eyes narrowed to read some lines on the hand-written document, his mind woke to a frightening memory; a memory of a dreadful day in 1962 when he was cornered by a young police officer to confess to a crime he had committed or else go to jail. His lips stopped moving with the letters on the file as he understood what Ermias was up to. Without examining the text or even thinking about it, he flipped hastily to the last page to find what he dreaded. And it was there as fresh as it was signed yesterday, his confession of murder and robbery with his signature distinctly imprinted. The life of a man and an asset of 15, 413. 96 Birr in cash, on his hands.

He lifted his head and looked at Ermias. Goytom's face that had brightened by the prospect of hope had now darkened by an ugly reality. But the experienced cheat was not to be abashed; instead, he straightened to confront.

"What's this crap?" he said, pushing back the file.

"No one knows better than you," Ermias produced another paper from the briefcase. "You can't bring back my father, but the money you robbed him can be considered as a payment of your share of the house. You sign on this paper admitting that you have received the payment of 15000 Birrs, and I'll seek no justice or vengeance of any sort."

Goytom sighed, looked left and right, and stared back at Ermias. "I'll sign no paper." He rose and added, "You better tell your aunt to find a place to live because I'm selling my property. Time is running out of you." Unabashed by the shame of his crime, he walked out with his head high as a righteous man, resolved to win.

Suppressing his anger, Ermias remained seated, his eyes following Goytom to the exit, and they remained fixed there long after Goytom left.

Chapter 22

Somalia had long wished to annex the Ogaden region of Ethiopia in the Southeast, inhabited primarily by ethnic Somali with whom its people shared a common language, religion, and culture. The concept of Greater Somalia articulated in the 1940s by British strategists stands for the unity of all the Somali peoples adjacently found in Somalia, Kenya, Ethiopia, and Djibouti. Greater Somalia was symbolically accommodated in the five points of the white star in the center of Somalia's national flag. Over the years, Somalia had been building up a powerful military force to this single end.

At the beginning of the year, Somali intelligence reports had indicated considerable weakness on the part of the Ethiopian defense. They had known that Ethiopian troops were moved from the Ogaden to other parts of the country in huge numbers. Moreover, the Somalis had noted that internal unrest and purge had weakened the Ethiopian defense force. With the Eritrean rebel movement picking up momentum in the north and urban centers torn by the Red-Terror, Ethiopia had never been so vulnerable to aggression. The rainy season with its adverse weather conditions that could pose logistic restraint to the Ethiopian army was the right time to attack.

On July 23, Somalia invaded Ethiopia, while in Moscow delegates of the two nations held talks to solve their problems peacefully. Soviets and Cubans were pressing on the idea of Trade and economic cooperation in the Horn, but Somalia was not to be manipulated.

When the heavily armed, Soviet-trained Somali force crossed the border, the Ethiopian army in the Ogaden had all but to retreat further and further. It was a tragic moment for Ethiopian people in the region, resulting in terrible damage and loss of life, but for Mengistu, it became a blessing in disguise.

A day after the Somali invasion, Colonel Assefa and a general from the Third Army Division presented their identity at the reception desk in the palace and mentioned their appointment with Chairman Mengistu. In a few minutes, a young official appeared and led them to Mengistu's secretary at the headquarters of the Derg. The young official opened and entered the secretary's office, leaving the visitors at the door. In a moment, the secretary appeared and welcomed them.

The office was fairly somber and formal. The most dominant attraction of sight was Chairman Mengistu's extraordinary big picture hanged in the wall behind the secretary's desk. Mengistu's negroid nose and lips were smoothed, and the lines around his eyes that disfigured his face had been tactfully airbrushed out. Yet, it failed to fulfill its purpose; it reflected neither the militaristic elegance nor the leadership charisma that was desired.

"The Chairman is busy now, Comrades," said the secretary and told the visitors that they were an hour in advance of their appointment and that the Chairman, because of unusual pressure of work, was obliged to keep them waiting a little while. "I'm afraid you will have to wait longer, or tell me your case and go. I can present them to the Chairman later."

Assefa explained with pointed politeness that the Generals's early arrival was a special courtesy to the Chairman. Then he made it clear that they were not in any mood to wait any longer or talk to anyone except the Chairman himself.

"I was sent by the Commander of the 3rd Division to report directly to the Chairman," the general explained. "This is a matter of national security. Our country is invaded. Somali aggressors have broken into our territory and occupied border towns. This, I have to tell personally and hear his orders directly."

"In that case, wait and tell him," said the secretary and opened a folder as if ignoring the guests.

"How can we wait when every minute meant a hundred square meters of land to lose. Just mention to him that we have arrived," the General demanded.

"I can't!" the secretary shouted. "He's in a crucial meeting."

"Could there be anything more important than our national security!" the General shouted back.

"There are more important international matters too, comrade."

Assefa was about to say something but a green lamp, indicating Mengistu's call, blinked, attracting the secretary's attention.

"Now you can follow me, comrades," the secretary said and led the guests to Mengistu.

Mengistu's office was at the end of the corridor on the same floor, flanked by an office at the right containing two secretaries and another on the left containing two staff officers. Assefa observed the Soviet ambassador, Anatoly Rattanov, being escorted out of the staff offices. The secretary knocked on Mengistu's door, waited for the gruff command to enter, and then showed the visitors in.

The office was over-decorated and well furnished, containing a large desk facing the door with a set of four leather club chairs grouped around a low table near the windows, overlooking the vast green lawn of the western part of the palace compound. Mengistu was sitting on a special gold-painted chair that almost looked like a throne. He had become a little Emperor. Dressed in a brown suit with a grey silk tie and a golden pin, he stood to receive his guests. His face was darker, and his eyes were shifting and smiling. He greeted the officers formally and showed them to sit.

A servant appeared with coffee.

As they drank, Mengistu inquired after the General's health and expressed his hope that he had got used to the new post and its responsibilities. The General was moved from the Second Army Division in the north to the Third in the east during the purge.

Mengistu smiled as he talked, and his shrewd dark eyes searched the General's face for any flicker of emotion. He made brief compliments about the General's work in reorganizing the army, and then he turned to Assefa. "Your face is familiar…ah … have we met before?"

"Yes, years ago," Assefa answered

But the General wanted to come to his point. "Colonel Assefa is with me to report recent developments in the Ogaden. The Somali armed forces have crossed our lines and occupied some towns."

When the General finished, Mengistu was indifferent to the news. Astonished by Mengistu's emotionless posture, the General first doubted whether Mengistu had heard any of his words or had heard everything before. Slightly disappointed, the General invited Assefa to present the details.

Assefa cleared his throat and stared at Mengistu.

"Comrade Chairman," called Assefa formally, "we have received reports indicating that the town of Furfur has fallen into enemy hands yesterday. The invaders are heading towards Kalafo. Our force in Warder and Aware are retreating. The enemy is heavily armed."

Mengistu listened calmly, but astonishingly he showed no emotion. When Assefa finished, he said, "Comrades, in its early years, the soviet revolution, just like that of ours, was faced by harsh internal and external enemies. But finally, it emerged victoriously. I assure you, we will destroy all our enemies, be it the aggressor in the east or the secessionist in the north, or the collaborator in the center. Don't doubt it. We shall overcome!"

"Action, Comrade Chairman," said the General, his voice louder, "we have to take action. We have to reinforce our army and recruit new ones as fast as possible."

"I appreciate your concern, General," responded Mengistu, "we are not sleeping here. Diplomatic efforts are being undertaken. We will appeal to the UN and the OAU. That's the formality, but the action is here, Comrade." Mengistu pointed at the documents on the corner of his desk. "Look, General, when these things arrive, no force, in this part of the world, can stand my army."

The General studied the documents. 48 MIG 21 and 6 MIG 23 bombers, 150 T54 and T55 tanks, BM 21 rockets, 155 mm and 183 mm heavy artillery, air to ground and ground to air missiles, along with several Soviet military advisors. Another document showed that Cuba had pledged to send an army of 15000 strong at the time when Ethiopia would be invaded by any hostile force. The Chinese were to ship a substantial number of lite arms. North Koreans first installment of arms and military equipment was on the way. Yemen had expressed its concern for Ethiopia's security, pledging to stand by the Ethiopian side.

"This is it, Assefa," the General sighed in great admiration. "Didn't I tell you that this man is going to make history?" He smiled at Mengistu in satisfaction and passed the documents to Assefa.

Assefa weighed the size of armament and the commitment of socialist countries. But as a spymaster, he couldn't help to be skeptical. He felt his country was sold in some way. Foreign forces with no traditional ties with the country were to sweep across the poor nation to defend it. He knew there was a prize to pay.

"Isn't that great, Assefa," the General asked, "what do you think?"

"I gather we have to change to a completely different weaponry system while we fight the enemy," Assefa said. "Let the old army use the old American weapons while we build a new people's army and train them with the new weaponry. I have decided to raise a people's army of three-hundred thousand strong in three months. We have begun recruiting; the first fifty thousand shall be dispatched soon.

Until then, we defend with all we have, Comrades." Mengistu
rose, indicating that the session was over.

Chapter 23

Prisoners in cell number 12 were singing songs of strength and brotherhood when the door suddenly opened, and two policemen stepped in to take Daniel in that Friday afternoon of July 1977. It was daytime, so execution was not anticipated, but torture on a body burning of injury was no less than execution. It was only four days since he had been taken to the palace torture hall for interrogation, where he was strapped down on a frame-like bed with his head covered by a blanket; then, using screws, sharp points were driven into his limbs. Captain Zeleke himself administered the tortures, laughing and sneering as he did so. Daniel had received severe internal injuries from Zeleke's ill-treatment. When he was brought back to his cell, none of his cellmates had any prospect that he would recover.

With the resilience of naturally healthy youth, Daniel had recovered rapidly, but he still had piercing pain on his mutilated feet as his body weight pressed against them. He wished he was dead, and for the first time, his heart questioned the Creator, '*oh! How could You allow them to play on the lives of your creatures? Did You create some of us to be treated less than a child's toy by fellow humans? You must have a reason and a good one.*' Then he prayed for strength and endurance. The prisoners who had never learned to pray before had began to do so since Daniel joined them; and had found that prayer could bring comfort and that it gave a more than human endurance. They had also learned that the prayer of their friends and relatives could transmit a current of strength to them.

Daniel stood up and stepped forward. As the handcuffs were slapped on him, he scanned the miserable faces of his cell-mates who, as they used to do, didn't cheer and encourage him this time but followed him with that cold gaze of farewell. They seemed to believe that this time Daniel wouldn't hear the next church bell ring.

"I'll come back, friends," said Daniel forcing a smile, knowing that he won't come back breathing. "I always did. Didn't I? Come on… Cheer up."

Everyone loved Daniel, even the new ones, for his natural cheerfulness and his sense of humanity. His stories of strength and faith from books he read were sources of courage; His frequent references to the Bible were contrary to the Marxist teachings of the time, that many found themselves spiritually restored as they heard him talk through the nights. For them, he was too rare a person to lose. Some began to cheer him up.

"Yes, you will. We shall pray," responded one of them.

"Cannibalism shall be demolished!" cried another angry young man who had been force-fed his own brother's chopped flesh: as a result, he had repeatedly tried to commit suicide and persistently begged the cell-mates to kill him to end his agony.

Since Daniel came to this cell, several prisoners had come and gone. Many with whom he had developed intimacy with were gone. They had been called in the middle of the day or the night and never returned, for they died under torture or execution.

Daniel thought briefly of the missing ones and envied them. At least they had something to confess and end their ordeal. Those who confessed sooner were executed sooner; those who held up longer were passed to special torturers who applied harsher methods of various stages. At the last stage of torture, the victim would be either dead or confessing guilt. Either way, no part of his body, no organ of sense, would be functionary after the last stage of torture. What would be left of the young, energetic man was only mutilated meat with a suffering soul at the edge of death: a death that seemed to have refrained from visiting the cell. What wounded the inmates most was such sudden disappearance of a cell-mate, with whom, waiting for a similar fate, they shared whatever small they had and comforted each other in their times of trial.

Daniel had little to confess, which he had done the first time he was interrogated, but the interrogators were not content. He knew he had to go through all the stages or die under torture. He had made it through the fourth stage. As a result, his left ear was damaged, all his nails pulled out, and one of his testicles was smashed. Every part of his body was in burning pain.

He gathered himself and followed his escorts. Outside, he searched for the sun he missed like his dear mother. It was hidden behind the thick grey cloud. Limping on his bare feet, he proceeded through the iron gate, passed the corner that led to the torture hall, and stepped on the stairs of the main entrance of the police station. From there, he looked back far to the street beyond where relatives and friends stood in line to hand food and laundries to the prisoners. Before he entered the building, he spotted three people who stood detached from the others. They were Ermias, Mustafa, and another young man, whom Daniel presumed to be Samson. It was a revitalizing scene that lifted his spirit to survive.

Mustafa, who had proved to be a very good friend of the family, was enormously helpful. Lately, he had managed to secretly pass messages between Daniel and the family. That was how Daniel learned that Samson was back in town. There were also other policemen who sympathized with the prisoners. Through them, prisoners were able to follow new developments in the country. They had information about the crackdown of the EPRP, the Somali aggression, and the hostility between the Dergue and its supporters, the Socialists. Similarly, information was passed in between the cells too. What took place in one cell was known in the others, enabling them to take records of prison history.

When Daniel entered the building, there was a ridiculous court in session. Unknown to the people and the Law, the Red-Terror Court was making a mockery of justice. Prisoners were made to stand before that court, and their fate was decided in one day, in less than an hour. The court, of no authority to set a defendant free, had full power to sentence one to death. Daniel was brought to this court, but he had to wait in the corridor until the case at hand was settled.

A moment later, a handcuffed little man was hassled out of the Red-Terror court.

"I had to do away with you," the young man snarled back at the judges as he was thrown out, "I, Mokriya, am not chicken to beg for my life. I am the son of a hero, and I'll die like a hero."

Daniel wondered if this was the famous Mokriya whose revolutionary actions were highly admired by the youth in the cells. Mokriya had been honored as one of the best EPRP urban guerrillas who was responsible for the killing of several Dergue supporters. In the bloody demonstration of Janmeda, Mokriya was said to have fought courageously against the security forces and dropped many of them dead. He was arrested in line of duty on the night of the demonstration.

With great admiration for the skinny fellow, Daniel entered the courtroom, which was draped with a large banner that read: RED TERROR WITH REVOLUTIONARY DISCIPLINE. Right below the banners, paintings of Lenin and Mengistu frowned with hollow dignity on whoever looked at them. Daniel stared at the three officials who sat on the right side of the long table. One of them was Lieutenant Nigusie, the police officer who had interrogated him the first time he was booked in. Four civilians sat scattered in the room.

The presiding judge entered the room, his co-judges following, and both sat behind the long table. The defendant, Daniel, was placed immediately in front of the judge, still handcuffed. His trouser was unbelted that he had to constantly hitch them up or press them against his body with his tied hands.

Before the proceedings began, Lt. Nigusie walked to the Judge and whispered in his ear. Then the judge searched for a person and called a name that had a doctors tittle.

"Would you please approach the bench?"

A bald man, obviously one of the socialist intellectuals, Daniel assumed, hastened to the judge. He first listened, then whispered briefly to the judge and returned to the far end of the room. Another man walked across the room and sat on the chair beside Daniel. Then the judge told Daniel that the person who now sat beside him was his attorney. Daniel nodded but still puzzled by what was going on. *It must be a dream,* he said to himself.

The judge asked his name, age, and address and scribbled down as Daniel replied formally and correctly without betraying any emotion of the suffering he endured.

"Are you, in any way, related to any of the members of the Derg?" asked the judge.

"No."

"Do you have any relative among the cadres of the Revolution?"

"No, not that I know of."

"Any revolutionary relative?"

"Isn't it the people's revolution? I must have some."

"I'm not asking you about the people," the judge snarled.

"Are you related to any of the dignitaries of the old regime?"

"No."

"What's your opinion on Chairman Mengistu?"

Daniel thought about the relevance of the question. *What are these people up to?* He looked around to find an answer from the faces that turned on him. They had no answer but were waiting for him instead. He looked at the judge and said, "I don't know him." His voice firm, carrying all the resentment in him.

All laughed.

Then the indictment was read over. He was labeled as one of the notorious EPRP terrorists responsible for the death of half a dozen revolutionaries, including attempted murder on a senior Dergue officer.

A man from the far right side of the room stood and spoke of Daniels crime. *A prosecutor*, Danial guessed. The man spoke fast as if he had studied his words by heart. He piled up Daniel's crimes: counter-revolutionary activities, and the danger he could pose to society. When he finished, he demanded capital punishment.

The judge glanced at Daniel, who appeared indifferent, and nodded to the attorney.

"Your honor!" Daniel's attorney said, "My client has admitted all his crimes under fair police interrogation. I have no objection to make. The defendant is ready to accept the verdict."

"The defendant," the judge called, "do you have anything to say?"

"I have plenty to say, not to you but a real court of God," said Daniel, staring at the judge.

"God!" shouted somebody from behind. It was the bald man whose name had a doctor's tittle. "You shall meet Him soon."

The judge and a few of those present laughed. The the judge stared at Daniel, "If that's all you have to say, the court shall proceed," He began to deliberate on what had been said, and then consulted with the other judge in a low voice.

For Daniel, it looked like a kangaroo court of ancient times or some elementary school drama rehearsal; he couldn't accept its seriousness. Then his eyes met Nigusie's, and he read something that confirmed his doubt. In Nigusie's slightly smiling face flashed a sign that was meant to encourage him.

The judge cleared his throat.

"We have deliberated on the entire case adequately and found the defendant Daniel Goytom Gobezay guilty of all charges. The case as it is presented to us is of immense magnitude, which frustrated our good intention to find any possibility for correction and rehabilitation of the young man. In our deliberation, we tried to be as lenient as the Law allows us to be. We have gone as far as to consider the defendant's insignificant contribution to the community and the country. The only thing we can do for him is to shorten his miserable life in the cell and to order that no further interrogation shall be applied on him until the final day. Our obligation is to the people and the revolutionary government. We have sentenced the defendant to death by firing squad." The judge lifted the wooden gavel and slammed the table.

It was raining outside, and everybody had run for cover. Daniel looked afar and searched for his brothers as he walked down the stairs on his way back to his cell. They were gone.

In the cell, he wanted to be left alone for a moment to take a mental account of the courtroom scene. Though the entire procedure appeared to be inconceivable, it came to him not as a drama but as a real thing. Those people meant it all. The sentence would be carried out. A few days from now, he won't be around. He won't be able to see his brothers anymore, even from a distance.

Ermias and Samson had run for cover when it began raining, and entered the nearest pub around. Before they resumed the discussion, Mustafa fumbled in his pocket and held out a small ball of paper that he had unfolded several times.

"Here is what Daniel slipped through friendly guards," he said as he handed over the piece to Samson.

The writing was hard to read, but the message was clear. It read:

The interrogations are going on, and the torture is becoming unbearable. What I have to reckon with is obvious, unless a miracle happens. The misery all around me is so much that I sometimes think to take my own life. If it were not for you and for my friends here in the cells that made my will to live so strong, I believe I would not have survived for so long…' Dan.

Samson read the paper again, and as he finished, he turned to Mustafa.

"How is he physically? Have you seen him recently?" asked Samson with a thin film of tears in his eyes?

"The last time I saw him going for interrogation, I was astonished by his strong will to survive, but at the same time, I was shocked by his appearance. It was a young man weakened by harsh treatments who passed beside me, handcuffed, in the same light clothes he had on him two weeks ago, face thin and drawn, strangely different, but it was his eyes that shocked me most. They were once bright black eyes that held a light in them. Now there was no light in them; they were like eyes of a blind man, nothing like I had ever seen before. His looks seemed turned inward. What I beheld was a man with the weariness of death in his soul."

They were quiet for a moment, then Samson said, "We shall end his suffering."

Since Samson was set free of his mental distress, his brain was occupied by a single thought of rescuing Daniel from the imminent final fate. In his days with the Eritrean commando brigade, he had taken part in various operations where the guerrillas had succeeded rescuing prisoners out of a tight security situation. They had raided army encampments and ruined installations. They had ambushed garrisons to robbed rations and arms. They had sneaked into State prisons to help compatriots escape, in many cases with minimum loss of life.

Although the situation here was different, the possibility for a successful rescue operation appeared to be more challenging and realistic to abandon the idea. Once, he had thought of contacting the EPRP to join him. His idea was to charge a sudden raid on the police station, but the recent wave of terror to wipe them revealed that the EPRP had not been as strong and reliable as people believed it was. Its members had already given up the cause and began to denounce the party. So, he had to drop the EPRP and think of other means. Days had passed before he came up with what he and Ermias, now believed to be a feasible idea.

"You know what awaits our brother, Mustafa." Samson went on, disclosing the rescue plan to Mustafa, "Sooner or later, they are going to execute him. So, we want to do something about it."

"How can I help?" asked Mustafa, "I feel sorry for Daniel. Those few short times I came to visit him, I learned he is a man of peace. He is the one who gives hope to his cellmates. Everybody likes him. Allah! Help them all!"

"If we men help, Allah too will help," sighed Samson.

"If there is anything I can do to help, I won't hesitate," said Mustafa.

"I think you can contribute something. Can't you find out the place where executions are carried out?"

"What? Mustafa asked thoughtfully. "You mean… ah…no… you don't mean that …"

Samson let Mustafa come with the words.

"Are you suggesting to rescue the kids right at the execution spot?"

"That's right, Mustafa," reassured Samson and narrated his plan briefly.

When Samson finished, Mustafa was almost breathless from the suspense, then he managed to say, "It's a brilliant idea, but are you sure you can do it?" His eyes rapidly shifted between Ermias and Samson.

"We are serious, Mustafa." It was Ermias speaking now. "What we want to know first is the place and then the date of execution. You just find out that. We will take care of the rest."

"This is a hell of an idea," Mustafa said, as he began to digest the whole plan. "I think you people can make it. Why not! This is a marvelous idea. Sure, I can find out the place. It won't be that difficult, but the date of execution varies. In fact, no one knows when one would be executed. They just come by night whenever they get bloodthirsty and take those fine young people."

"We will try to work out some means of knowing the date of execution. Now let's find out the places," said Ermias. Here Ermias was thinking of the help Assefa had promised him.

"As soon as you come up with the information, contact me, Mustafa. You have been very helpful so far. Thank you for your time," said Ermias.

"I will do everything I can to find out, and I will not waste a second to contact you when I do," Mustafa said and paused to concentrate on the faint distant sound that distracted his attention. Samson and Ermias also gave their ears to catch the direction of the sound. When they knew it was coming from the police station, at once, they rose and walked quickly to the door.

It was still raining outside. Across the street, under the thunderous cloudy sky, the police station appeared darker for this hour of the afternoon. But the sound that came from it had an inspiring effect. The prisoners were singing a song of freedom. At first, it was weak that the three could hardly hear, but a moment later, it became forceful and was heard past four, five blocks.

The people in the neighborhood came out and watched. As passer-by vehicles stopped to listen. The shop workers, the prostitutes, and street people crowded around. Song after song continued. Songs that lifted the spirit to fight for justice and freedom. Songs of brotherhood that moved many into tears. It was such a movement of song that appealed to every human heart to rebel and repel dictatorship.

Suddenly, an armored band of the army arrived and surrounded the station. Some of the soldiers ordered the crowd to disperse as the others marched in the police station to silence the inmates by beating them.

"Okay, guys, I leave you here," said Mustafa fighting tears, and left.

Chapter 24

As the first week of August passed by, Daniel's mother, Abinet, was caught by indecisiveness. She had only a week to stay in the house, yet she had not fixed a place to move to. By the end of the week, she knew she would be evicted out of the house, but she still did not seem to think about it seriously. There were other things to worry about, mainly Daniel. Askale and her children were also her concerns. Since Askale had been put in a mental hospital, the responsibilities of the children had fallen on her. No relative was willing to take care of them. She was the one who cooked their food and took care of their laundry. It was demanding, but she held on.

What kept her largely sleepless was Daniel's misfortune. She had heard of the torture he had been put through, and she knew what to expect of his situation. All she could do was pray; and that, she did well. Not a single day had passed without her praying for him in the names of all the angels she could come up with. Not a single Sunday had passed without her paying a visit to the nearest church to render alms to the needy in the name of God Almighty.

The other day when Biniam had been at the police station to deliver food and outfits, he had succeeded in effecting an exchange of letters with Daniel through sympathetic police guards.

'*It seems,*' Daniel had written, '*we are standing at the end of our life. Here I am with many innocent young men who are waiting for the end. I hope our death shall be a sacrifice, which may bring peace and harmony to the living. I want you all to be strong enough to take whatever comes. Mother, I know they can't break you. Nobody can. You will make it through the hardships. May God bless you all.'*

This had almost broken down the strong woman. But she went on wrestling with humankind and God, searching for an answer to the fate that had befallen her. She felt she no longer understood the nature of God's will. *Where is the God of mercy in whom I always trusted?* She would say.

It was only through the constant encouragement and comfort of Samson that she began to come to terms with the realities of the situation. All there was for her was to wish for the good and pray for mercy. Every day she prayed: *"Lord of all mercy, oh listen to my plea for my son and send Michael, the chief of your angels, and the armies of your angel so that they may march against the evil Revolution to save my son."*

Like many mothers, she believed that the angels in heaven would soon come to topple the regime and save her son. Yet she had no idea what the guardian angel she gave birth twenty-eight years ago had in mind. Samson had intentionally kept the plan of the rescue operation secret from her. He was not sure how she would react; she might disapprove the plan since it could put the entire family at risk.

"Mother, don't worry. It's going to be all right," Samson would say to her whenever he saw her overwhelmed by sorrow. And in his words, she would sense aspiration that restored her strength to live and to bear the burden of the next day.

She had sensed Samson's preoccupation and had been aware of his preparations. But she could not connect it with Daniel. Cruelly saved money was used to buy spare parts for the Land-Rover. New tires, batteries, lamps, and spark plugs were purchased and changed. The engine and the gearbox were drained of the worn-out oil and refreshed. Biniam had accurately adjusted the electrical and mechanical systems of the engine.

By Saturday the 13th of August, when Mustafa and Ermias came to see him, the mission vehicle was mechanically as ready as Samson was physically and mentally prepared for the rescue mission. Weapon-wise, much has not been arranged. Two hand grenades were bought from the black market. The quest to procure a convenient machine gun was on the way.

Samson was in the sitting room when Ermias and Mustafa showed up. Abinet had left to look after Askale's children. He received them warmly and gestured them to a seat. Shortly after, Ermias broke the story of the verdict of the Red-Terror court. But it did not shock Samson. He had learned to expect the worst in such circumstances.

"We know they would do it sooner or later," said Samson. "What do you have, Mustafa?"

Mustafa laid a sketch on the table and started elaborating.

"I have some information, according to my source, executions are conducted in several places. A mass grave of 22 people was uncovered in Sebeta, a suburban district near the capital; hyenas had dug out the bodies from the shallow graves. A similar mass grave containing 20 bodies was also found in Kotobe, a district at the eastern end of the city. Prisoners from our part of the city, that's to say from central prison and the fifth police station, are usually executed here in Mekanisa." Mustafa pointed at a spot on his sketch and lifted his head. Mentally Samson visualized the area, a very familiar place. That was a plus.

"No one passes this area after midnight," Mustafa went on, "Even the district Revo-guards are not allowed to come any closer than here." He pointed at the southern end of the Mekanisa Tej Brewery, "The same from this side too." Now his finger was on Jimma Road.

"Here you have the narrow footpath that stretches into the woods. It has been broadened recently to allow vans to enter deep into the woods. The killers can drive up to here. Then they force the prisoners out and drag them into this field. Here, they shoot and bury them," said Mustafa and lifted his finger from the paper.

When Mustafa was elaborating on the sketch, Samson visualized the area in his mind's eye. He knew the place more than anyone in the world. He had enjoyed a good part of his childhood and teenage in this part of the district. On their way to Furi, Samson and Gaushaw had run through these woods. They had played on the green lawn and breathed the fresh air. He remembered that it had been a beautiful place then.

"So, you are sure that prisoners from the fifth are executed in Mekanisa?" inquired Samson.

"My source is reliable."

Samson pursed his lips and thought for a while, then suddenly he said, "I'll see the place tonight." Decidedly he picked the sketch, folded it, and thrust it in his pocket.

"I think you have given us adequate information we need for now," said Ermias. "Is there anything about the executioners? How they are with guns or what weapons they use and so on."

"Look, these killers are not from the police or the regular army. These are a bunch of civilian cadres and former criminals who couldn't acquire a job other than this. Some are armed with the old M1 rifle… others hold the new AK-47 Kalashnikov. It doesn't look organized either. Who gives orders, and who conducts the shooting is not clear. Sometimes orders are simply issued orally. Law enforcement institutions are not used to these types of procedures.

"How many executioners do usually come in one round," asked Samson.

"I have seen ten at one time and more at another… nevermore than fifteen, in any way. The number of victims used to be more or less the same. They never took more than fifteen at a time. Not from our station."

"Anything on how to know when an execution takes place?"

"Well, there are strange things we see. If their meager supper is given early and some of the Socialists cadres are seen around, we know there will be execution. Just before midnight, prison vans would enter the compound, and the man in charge would call the unfortunate names. Executions are always conducted after midnight," said Mustafa.

"Is there any way to find out when a certain prisoner would be executed?" asked Samson. "You see; we want to know the exact day of Daniel's execution."

"That's going to be very difficult. I'm not in a position to find out such things," said Mustafa thoughtfully.

"If we can't know Daniel's execution day," said Ermias, "the whole plan is not going to work."

"We have got to work out something," Samson glanced at Mustafa.

"If I were to attend the night shift on that day, I could warn you in time. I can also find some friends who would follow up on Daniel when I'm not around."

"I guess that's the only option we have," said Samson. "You know what to do? As from today on, I will be waiting at the office of the Nyalas. There are two telephones available for us. Here are the numbers." Samson wrote the two numbers on a piece of paper and passed it to Mustafa. "Whenever you're not around, inform your friends what to do."

"Daniel's execution might take place very soon," said Mustafa. "So, I will try to attend the night shift as much as I can; changing my shift with others whenever possible."

"That's very kind of you," appreciated Ermias and took out his wallet. "This is no much for what you're doing for us." Ermias produced a hundred Birr note.

"What are you implying, Ermias," Mustafa frowned, disappointment clouding on his face. "Do I look like a person who profits from the misfortune of fellow countrymen? Daniel is my brother too. I appreciate your generosity, but I can't accept the offer."

Samson couldn't help being impressed by the sheer conviction Mustafa spoke and said, "Mustafa, there are few people of very noble character like you. I am very proud to have known you. Take the money; it might help to buy some favor from others."

"Yes, in that case. Okay, it can help to persuade my colleagues and buy some services from them. I assure you; I'll never touch a single cent for my use." Mustafa took the money and added, "by the way, for some reason known only to the securities, Daniel is given fair treatment, and no more torture is applied to him. He looks much better now, healthy and fresh. Maybe he has confessed everything he knew."

"Daniel has nothing to confess. I think it's because they have torn down the EPRP and don't need to interrogate anyone anymore," commented Ermias.

"Yes, the EPRP is finished," agreed Mustafa. "The Derg's new enemies now are the Socialists. Securities are hunting them. There is a rumor that the chief of the Socialists is arrested and others on the run."

As they talked about the current situation, Mustafa suddenly remembered something, "I almost forgot, your father is wanted for interrogation. I advise he should go into hiding for the time being."

"What do they want him for?" asked Ermias with his vengeful emotion on his face.

"Daniel had confessed that the gun he used belonged to your father. That gun was the property of the army, and they want to find out how it came into his hands. They have reasons to believe that some army officials or Dergue members had armed Daniel to kill Zeleke. That's what made the interrogation on Daniel harsher," explained Mustafa. A moment later, Mustafa excused himself and left. He said he had to rest because he had the night shift today.

It was a long exacting day full of planning and preparations. Arrangements were made: from today on, the brothers will spend their nights in the Nyalas waiting for Mustafa's telephone call. Should his alert call come, Samson would be launched to the execution field before the tragic drama took place. Now he had to see how the stage looked like by night.

Late in the evening, at about 10 o'clock, Samson sat behind the wheels of the Land-Rover and rolled it out of the Nyalas. He could feel the improvement of the engine as he pressed the gas and gained speed instantly, the headlights illuminating brighter against the darkness. Biniam had done his part efficiently.

Beyene Street was very quiet. Tension reigned over the city, Samson could feel it. The test of strength between, the Mengistu and the Socialist, was felt all over. Having decremented the EPRP, Mengistu has now turned to the Socialists who had been his staunch supporters helping him all through putsch and the subsequent Red terror campaign. Cadres who served both masters, who died and killed for both the Mengistu and Socialists, were faced now with ugly choices to make. To choose one could be a devastating mistake if the other came out to be the winner.

The Socialists relied on the country people they claimed to have had organized and armed. They had worked hard to come closer to the goal. They had killed many lives and paid as much sacrifice to concede now. They were not going to let Mengistu expend them without a fight. They knew every hole in the government that they could use to stage a coup to topple Mengistu successfully. But the Mengistu was quick to close their offices, shunting them from all their branches and locking their top leaders, making sure they were in no position to issue any order. It appeared that Mengistu was after them, and they were on the run.

As Samson approached the bridge on Roosevelt Road, he saw cars lined up. He had the time and the space to make a U-turn to avoid what he presumed to be a picket of soldiers, but he chose to wait and continue. When he pulled the Rover behind the last car in the queue, he realized that only vehicles leaving the city were being searched.

He turned off the engine and waited for his turn patiently. There was nothing suspicious about him. He carried no weapon except the knife he hid behind the seat and the flash lamp he kept in the car's pocket. His ID was good, showing his employment in the Nyalas. Half an hour later, it was his turn.

"Identifications!" a soldier beamed a flashlight on his face.

Samson was quick to submit. The soldier checked and returned the paper.

"Get out of the car!"

Samson complied, and two soldiers inspected the car in and out. Nothing incriminating or counter-revolutionary or *Revisionist*, as the Socialists were labeled these days, was found. He was allowed to proceed.

An hour had gone, saving him just an hour before the curfew. He had to speed up. He drove past the Brewery, turned left, and in a few minutes, he was on the narrow dark trail that led to the woods of Mekanisa. As he got in deeper, it grew darker. No street light, no witness. The Dergue knew a perfect place to commit murder.

At the intersection of the street, Samson turned left to the woods, living Jimma Road to his right. A moment later, he was inside the woods. He turned off the engine, and the headlights went out. Impenetrable darkness. Here, he felt, death reigned.

He took out the sketch, flashed the hand lamp on it, and checked the map to establish the spot he stood on. He was right on the place where the execution vans would park. That was dangerous. He started the car again and turned around. Soon he found a safer place on which the Rover could not be seen from the place where the vans would park.

He stepped out of the car to find the killing field. He had to go deeper into the woods. Assisted by the flashlight, which he used sparingly, he staggered forward. Then came a sickening smell, which made his stomach clench up. Beaming light on the ground, he was met by a terrible sight: a human skull, a female with its long hair still on it, invaded by worms. Samson shifted his eyes aside only to see other bodies, half-eaten by hyenas.

He was used to the sight of dead bodies, bombed and dismembered in the battlefronts, but this gruesome scene shocked him to the core. The victims appeared so young and somehow innocent. These people were all other Daniel's, defenseless.

In a moment, he was inside the field that had once been the most beautiful place in the world. For a moment, it reminded him of his childhood times, when there had been so little conflict and so much hope. As children, his friend, Gaushaw and him used to hang around this area and cherish its fresh air under the shadows of the trees. Now it was only memory. The revolution had changed it into an appalling killing field, a graveyard of the worst kind. It smelled of death.

He observed several mass graves in the upper part of the field and a few open ones waiting for the next execution. They were wide and deep enough to dump some twenty people in one grave.

From the grave cavity, he counted his steps to the woods to devise an effective position of attack. He stepped into the woods and looked for a place that would be suitable for hiding and following the executioners.

Satisfied with what he obtained, he came out of the woods and sat on the ground leaning on the trunk of a tree. He was tired but more confident than he had been before he came here. This, he knew, was his place and no one on the other side knew the game better. He looked at the sky to recount the facts with the stars he loved, but tonight none of them dared to come out. They were all covered by a thick blanket of clouds.

He consulted his watch, which showed a quarter to midnight—quarter to curfew—not much time left. He bustled into the woods. He had to hurry up.

From somewhere in the middle of the woods, a few steps before he reached the Rover, his eyes were caught by a tiny flicker of light that made him stop instantly. He knew he saw a moving light and alerted himself to attend. Squinting through the trees, he tried to figure out what it could be. Then came the sound of roaring engines closer. Two vans. They pulled at the place where he had parked the Rover earlier and lined one behind the other, with their headlight illuminating on the killing field before them. He knew what it was: Execution.

He assumed that Daniel could not be among these ones. Or could he be? No, he couldn't because Mustafa was at the police station all through the evening. Had Mustafa seen strange things, he would have called and warned him. Nevertheless, he couldn't be sure.

As the sound of the two engines died out, a horrible sound of screaming people reverberated across the woods. Hand-tied people were pushed out of the first van down to the ground. Samson counted twelve prisoners. The army truck that carried the soldiers was behind the van, its lights directed to illuminate the field.

Cautiously, Samson moved towards the field, all the time watching the prisoners, young boys and girls, being pushed and butted into the field, some of them cursing the soldiers and the regime, others begging for mercy. Some had already fainted and had to be dragged. Then sensing, rather, seeing a shadow moving towards him, he ducked down and pressed himself flat against a tree, waiting and listening, his hands searching for something bulky. As he thoroughly scanned behind himself through the woods, he saw the silhouette of a man dragging something into the woods. He then heard a weak voice. It was coming from a woman, crying and begging.

"For Christ's sake. In the name of Mother Mary…, please don't hurt me. Please spare my life."

Up there in the field, the executioner had made advances. They had reached the grave cavity and was forcing the prisoners to jump into the opening. Samson observed them throwing a feinted prisoner into the mass grave, the other prisoners fighting back despite the heavy blow they received on their heads.

Here, some eight foot-steps behind him, Samson could hear the girl bravely resisting the a rapist's advance. She was not begging now but calling the man names, fighting like a tigress.

Suppressing his rage, Samson followed both scenes, his eye rapidly shifting here and there.

Right away, a cracking sound of the machine guns tore through the darkness. Samson jolted as if a bullet hit him. The execution had begun. Soldiers poured bullets into the grave cavity over the youngsters. It went on for several minutes. When it stopped, horrifying silence followed, and the scent of death carried by the smoke of the guns diffused over the field and in the wood. Samson's heart pounded harder and faster, his breath hot. His fury rose, and his head pulsated. He was transforming. The killer guerrilla spirit was taking over him.

Transformation completed, head upright and chest pumped up, he moved to the direction where the girl's sound was coming from. She was quiet now. She must have fainted after the shooting. The rapist must have misunderstood it. "Oh! You want it, too," Samson heard him saying, "You were just pretending, little girl. Come on now. I heard you're a virgin. We don't waste virgins, just like that. We show them what they are going to miss before we do away with them. Come on now! Be a nice girl."

Samson flashed the lamp for a fraction of a second just to capture a clear picture of the situation. The rapist had taken his overcoat and laid it on the ground, his machine gun on top of it. He was on top of the girl, between her widely opened legs. The girl appeared to have given up the fight, probably because she realized that she was under the devil's grip and her life was counted by minutes.

Samson acted instantly. He threw a stiff and swift foot to the man's face. The man spun backward and staggered. Samson then jumped over the girl and landed on top of the man, crushing the face with his elbow. It had to be quick and noiseless. In seconds he broke the man's neck and was back to the girl who was reviving to awareness.

"Just calm down," whispered Samson. "You're all right now, sister."

The girl seemed not to comprehend. She was not fully aware of herself and the circumstance. For a moment, she believed she was dead, and her guardian angel was leading her to heaven.

"You must be my guardian angel," the girl whispered, trembling of shock, her teeth shattering of fear and cold.

"You're all right, sister. Just be silent now." He lifted the girl's head and wormed it under his chest. He pulled the overcoat, wrapped the girl with it, and let her lean against the trunk of a tree while he examined the machine gun.

On the killing field, the soldiers had refilled the last earth on the mass grave and were returning to the vans. On their way back to the vehicles, they called the missing comrade by name as some of them pissed and smoked, waiting for the rapist to come back.

"The virgin is giving him a hard time," said one of them.

"Just give him all the time he needed."

"Let's get out of here. He will come by himself as he used to do."

With the machine gun in his hand, Samson watched the soldiers. They appeared to be impatient and angry about the delay. A moment later, he saw the vehicles roll back and forth to make their way out. When they left, Samson turned to the girl.

"Are you all right, sister?"

The girl mumbled some words and shrunk into herself.

"Try to stand up; we have to move." He said lifting her up. Supporting the girl who walked lamely, he somehow made the tough way in the darkness, through the woods to the Land-Rover and laid the girl inside the car. The time was well past midnight; they had to spend the night in the woods to evade the curfew.

Slowly the girl recovered and began to perceive the surrounding.

"Where am I?" she asked, lifting her head.

"Take it easy, girl. You have been in trouble. You're safe now. Just try to sleep. . . if you can."

"They killed them, didn't they?"

Samson didn't replay. He just touched her gently.

"Who are you? What are you doing here?"

"The name is Samson. I just happened to be around," said Samson, and to be sure that Daniel was not among the dead, he added, "Where did they bring you from?"

"From the State prison."

"How long have you been in prison?"

"I don't know… some three months?"

"Where do you live?"

"I live in Goffa' Sefer with my parents."

"We shall move at daybreak. I'll take you wherever you feel would be safe for you. Now try to sleep."

Chapter 25

Goytom was in a happier mood when he visited the 5th Police Station to request a police force that would evict Abinet from the house. Weirdly, it had not occurred to him that this was the very station that held his son under arrest. Over the weeks, he had been so preoccupied with his business plan that he even could not, for once, think of Daniel. He had made remarkable progress in his business plans. He had contacted the newly started liberation movement that operated in the northern province of Tigray and told them of the weapons he could procure. The rebels, who were in desperate need of arms and ammunition, had taken him seriously and promised him a good deal. So, using his contacts, Goytom had boldly contacted a couple of army officials and was working on a scheme to smuggle weapons out of the military warehouse. That was all. The business was fixed. What remained to be done on his part was to make a small payment to the officers to start the job.

As the police bureaucracy worked on his request, it stumbled into what Goytom never anticipated. Goytom himself was acutely wanted by the police for interrogation. So, they kept him under custody. The next day, he was summoned to Lieutenant Nigusie's office.

"Mr. Goytom, we were looking for you all over the city. I assume you're not living with your wife, are you?" inquired Nigusie, inducing a friendly atmosphere.

"Which wife do you mean, officer?" Goytom managed to stammer.

"How many wives do you have, sir? Are you not living with Daniel's mother?"

"She? Oh no! I left her a very long time ago." Goytom had some information of what Daniel had done but he did not anticipate that he would be sitting here for interrogation.

"Did you marry another after her?"

"Yes, I had another one."

"I had? Are you not living with the other one now?"

"No, sir. I'm not."

"Are you living with anyone now?"

"No, I am not."

"Okay, let's get to the case at hand. I believe you know why you're here."

"No, I don't."

"Don't you have any connection with your son, Daniel. He shot a prominent Dergue member?"

"I have heard, but … ?" said Goytom with shivering lips.

"You know the consequences of touching those type of people, the princes of the Revolution."

"I know." said Goytom, wondering about what could have impelled Daniel into this. "My son is a peaceful boy, the most peaceful person in the whole world. There must be some mistake."

"We will come to that soon, but now we wanted you on other criminal charges."

Goytom's eyes popped out. "What crime?"

"Rape, assault, and murder. Do you know a lady by the name Asmeret?"

"No, not really?"

"Try to remember from long past. A 16-year-old girl you married at your home town in Eritrea.'

Goytom made a mental journey to that long past. The scene of the wedding day was still vivid in his memory. "O! yes, I remember her."

"She is suing you for rape, assault, and murder."

"She is suing me? Where is she? Suing me for what?"

"You abused her like an animal."

Goytom was silent.

"I am talking to you!" the Lieutenant raised his voice.

"That was a long time ago."

"You age, crimes don't."

"She was not a virgin, and I had to turn her down. That's age-long tradition.'

"Mr. Goytom, you beat her cruelly. Disgraced her before her family and relatives, and then you took her little sister in exchange."

"Back then, that's what we do to brides who were not found intact on the first night."

"But the bride was a virgin. Why did you have to deplore her that way?"

Goytom stammered inaudibly.

Nigusie went on. "Mrs. Asmeret has also charged you for the murder of her brother."

"Murder? What murder?"

"You will have to tell me that. Now let's jump to the next case. I'll brief you. Your son has confessed that the gun he used to shoot Captain Zeleke belonged to you.

"I didn't give it to him. I don't know where he got it from."

Nigusie stretched a hand, pulled a drawer, and produced the gun, wrapped in a transparent cover.

"Is this not yours?"

Goytom leaned forward and peered at the gun without touching it. Nigusie took off the plastic cover and pushed the gun to Goytom, who instantly picked it and searched for some sign.

"It was mine. But I didn't give it to Daniel."

"How did it come into his hands?"

"As I told you when I left Daniel's mother, I left behind a lot of things. Among the things was this gun."

"Do you have a license to possesses or carry a weapon?"

"Yes, I have."

"Where did you get the weapon?"

"I bought it."

"Where?" It was a question of place, but Nigusie made it sound like "from whom?"

"It was a long time. I don't remember."

"You have to, Mr. Goytom. This case is not in the scope of this police station. The headquarters of the Dergue is behind this case. I advise you to tell the truth. When did you buy it?"

"Some seventeen years ago."

Better to put it this way, Goytom must have reasoned, than to name the fateful year of 1960. That year was marked by a bloody military turmoil when an army general, named Neway, staged an abortive coup against the Emperor. Mentioning the year might prompt other questions.

Nigusie was fast but not that smart, "In 1960? How much did you pay for it then?

"Not much."

"A hundred? Two hundred?" How much, Mr. Goytom?"

"Something like a hundred and fifty Birr for one."

A hundred and fifty Birr for one. Nigusie did not seem to have pointed attention to the significance of the answer.

"Do you have papers? Purchase receipts?" This was a simple question for Nigusie to ask, but for Goytom, it was the most difficult to answer. The whole thing hung on the answer to this question: his future, his life, everything.

"Papers?"

"Yes, purchase receipts."

Goytom was caught in a dilemma. "Yes" would be a catastrophe; "no" would mean more interrogation, which would include torture, not the type he had sustained before but this time a Red one. Terrified by the very thought of it, Goytom stammered.

"Yes, I do. I surely do have."

"You do? How come! The gun is registered as State property. It was identified as the property of the army. It had never been for sale. I think you're making a mistake. It's impossible that you could buy it, Mr. Goytom. Do yourself a favor. Please, tell the truth and face the consequences."

"Which truth?"

"There is always one truth and tell it, or they will make you tell the ugly way."

"I have purchase receipts, and I can show you if you insist, but I advise you not to."

Nigusie looked puzzled and threw an inquisitive eye on Goytom. "You advise me not to see the papers! You advise me not to do my job. My goodness, what is it! I want to see the papers." Nigusie rang the table bell.

Mustafa and another policeman entered the room.

"Mustafa, please escort Mr. Goytom to his home and bring all relevant papers of this case to me."

"Yes, Sir," Mustafa saluted the lieutenant, and turned to Goytom. "Please, follow me."

Goytom stood up, turned to Nigusie, and said, "I suggest the papers should only be seen by you."

Nigusie was bewildered, but then he took Goytom as a confused man and smiled at him out of pity. "Yes. Mustafa, you heard him. The papers should be wrapped and sealed until they reach my office."

Five minutes later, Nigusie's telephone rang.

"Number two calling," whispered the earpiece. "Nigusie, listen… our men will be coming on Saturday to fetch the tools. Make sure everything is ready. We can't afford to make any mistake now. Understood."

"Why is the rush?

"Time! Nigusie. We are running out of time. That monster is out with sharp teeth to eat us all. You know it. In a week, none of us will be alive to relish the flowers of September. We have to act fast to save our necks.

"When and where is the feast."

"At Sigameda. We will see to it that he doesn't come out alive. It's well planned and highly organized."

"Any news about Number one?" asked Nigusie. "Is he still alive?"

"He is okay but in a complicated situation. I'll tell you later. I have got to go now. Remember, Saturday is the day. It shall go as planned."

A couple of hours later, Goytom, escorted by Mustafa, entered Nigusie's office. When Mustafa delivered the envelope in which the documents were sealed, Nigusie was preoccupied by Number two's call. He knew, the Socialists were in an adventurous political gamble to get rid of Mengistu. If they failed, Nigusie knew, they will pay a heavy price.

Now less interested than he was before, Nigusie gestured Goytom to sit on the wooden bench at the wall as he opened the envelope. Some five sheets of paper of normal size were stuffed in it, neat and orderly, but Nigusie was not that eager to examine them. Absently he went over them, "What the hell are all these."

Goytom did not answer. He was busy with his nails, jaw clinched.

Nigusie picked a paper. "Is this the license?"

"Yes."

The license was proper. Nigusie put it aside and glanced on the other papers coldly. A lot of numbers, serial numbers. "Are these all guns? I assumed we were talking about one gun. Here I see, you were a professional weapon dealer!"

Goytom kept quiet. Nigusie flipped one page after another, shaking his head thoughtfully.

"Is the crime weapon among these?"

"Yes, it is. It's on page two, line ten."

Nigusie leafed to page two and focused on line ten. He held the gun and compared its serial number with the number on the paper. They were exact. He underlined the line and closed the sheet of papers.

"Whom did you buy these guns from?" A simple question for Nigusie to put but the most difficult for Goytom to answer, dry and burning, with a smell of death behind it. Anything could be answered, but this was heavy to the tongue to say.

"You see the name at the end of the document on the last page." That was somehow easier to say.

Nigusie flipped to the last page and looked at the last lines. The total number of guns was one hundred, and the sum of money added up to a total of fifteen thousand Birr. The date and dealer's name were clearly stated. And signatures under the name. But Nigusie's mind was not thoroughly focused on it, Goytom could observe.

"Where are all these guns now," he asked.

"I sold them long ago. I kept this one for myself."

"And now the people are gunning down each other with these guns! Where did he say he got the merchandise…? I mean the seller."

"I didn't ask. I gather you said it belonged to the army."

"The army? Where is the seller? Is he alive?" asked Nigusie and dropped his eyes on the name of the seller again. Now his face began to change; first, his eyes narrowed in puzzlement, then widened in recognition; at last, they almost popped out of their sockets in panic. He made as if to get up, but then he remained seated. His hands reached to the telephone but could not lift the handset. Then he remained seated for a while thinking, with his mouth gaped.

"How! … No! Wait a minute. Who is this man?"

Goytom didn't answer. He was grinding his teeth.

"I'm talking to you. Who is this person?" shouted Nigusie.

"My brother, you know who he is. This thing has damaged my life, and now yours. Whoever sees this document shall perish."

"No, I can't believe this …." Nigusie didn't dare finish his words. He just held his head and said, "Oh, my country! I cry for you!"

"At the time of military unrest in 1960," Goytom went on, "he was working in the army warehouse where he had the opportunity to lay his dirty hands on State property. He had contacts, and the circumstance was suitable for stealing. I bought only one hundred; others bought more. Now, many of them are dead, killed one by one because they knew his scandalous past."

"How did you survive?"

"I survived by keeping a low profile. I sold my company and went underground just to get rid of him. I know I won't live long after this."

"He won't live long either," Nigusie spoke between his teeth as though to himself, thinking of Number Two's call.

"Mr. Goytom, you seem to be in bad shape. You have a lot to answer for. You will stay under police custody until the court decides. You have real, tough people against you."

A lady and a gentleman entered the room. Lt. Nigusie stood up for the lady's courtesy and showed them to a seat on the right side of his desk. Goytom was far on the opposite side, sitting on a wooden bench, staring at the lady for what seemed like an eternity, and then dropped his eyes on the floor. He was not sure of what he saw. It was impossible; the little girl he almost killed could not resurrect and rise up. The little girl he ripped and raped and denounced as a whore on her wedding day could not walk with such elegance and confidence. That country-girl he flogged and disfigured could not possess such charm and beauty. No, she could not. He looked at her again and searched for scars on her smooth brown face. There were none. They were gone. Time had washed them out. But the scar in her heart was displayed on her eyes; the scar time could not wash.

"You remember me?" the lady asked, her voice soft but demanding, eyes piercing.

"Who are you?"

"Mr. Goytom," the Lt. Nigusie said. "I don't have to introduce to you the first person you chose to marry nearly three decades ago."

Goytom jerked as if he was hit by a bullet. His eyes popped out like he saw a ghost. He then held his head with both hands and screamed like a wounded hyena. "Oh, no!"

"Lieutenant, can you leave us alone just for a couple of minutes. I need to talk to him privately," the lady said.

"Yes, of course," said Nigusie and lifted himself. The gentleman who came with the lady also left the room.

The lady raised herself, moved to the other side of the desk, and opened a button in her red leather jacket. She wore a yellow skirt, and on her feet were average size red shoes. Her hair was formed in Marlyn Monroe's style.

"Look, I am not here for revenge; I only seek justice. I want to know what happened to you. What transformed you into a beast that night. I loved you. I worshiped you. I was a virgin. Everything was so perfect. It was my happiest day. Tell me, what made you change your mind?"

Goytom was withdrawn, his eyes looking inside, his mind traveling 30 years back to the wedding day. He remembered how the priests in the church laughed at them.

"What are they laughing at?" he had asked his best-man.

"Forget them?"

"How can I? Everybody is looking at us as if we are monkeys."

"It's nothing. It's just that you are shorter than her," his best-man had said, laughing uncontrollably.

Goytom remembered the embarrassment he had gone through in the church and then at the wedding feast. Then he woke up and looked at the lady. "You were taller than me. Everybody laughed at our disparity. So, I had to quit. I couldn't stand the thought of everybody laughing at me for the rest of my life."

"What?" the lady shouted, her eyes popping out. She strode closer to him, looked at his eyes and uttered, "Is that why you falsely denounced me and disgraced my family?"

Goytom had nothing to answer. His head fell and he fumbled with his fingers

"Do you know that my father died from the shock of that night?" The lady snarled at him like a tigress. "I had to flee from home due to your false accusation."

There was a pause. The lady continued, lowering her voice "The most disgusting of all your deeds was that you demanded to take my little sister in exchange." Now her eyes were filled with tears as her voice quivered. "You saw the gentleman who came with me. He is my husband, probably shorter than you. I never thought you were that short until you mentioned it now. We, women, see the strength, not the length. I guess you never had the strength either."

Goytom sat motionless on the bench; eyes fixed on the floor.

"Why did you kill my brother?" demanded the lady, now a bit louder.

"I did not kill your brother. Your brother started to talk about what I did to you. He flared up, and we fought. He fell on the ground, and something hit his head."

"You stole the money!"

"The money was at home. Who should I have given it to, then? I used it to raise his son. I raised Ermias like one of my children," said Goytom shyly.

The lady smiled at his response. "You kill the father and raise the son! Jesus!" said the lady and knocked on the desk. It was a signal indicating that she was finished with Goytom.

Nigusie came back with the gentleman and a cap who held handcuffs. As the lady spoke to Nigusie, the cap ordered Goytom to stand up. Goytom said something in protest to the handcuff.

"Shut up and turn around!" the cap snarled as he yanked Goytom's hand in place and slapped on the handcuffs.

Goytom turned slightly to the lady when he heard her mention Daniel's name to the Lieutenant, but the cap jostled him out of the room roughly.

Chapter 26

Mustafa was on his way home when he suddenly observed an unusual thing in the compound of the police station on that Saturday evening of August 20. A gang of soldiers, who claimed to have instructions from the Dergue, had rushed in the station with three vans and demand to take twelve prisoners. It was not 11 o'clock yet. Alarmed by the strange incident, Mustafa decided to stay longer to follow up the situation.

Hurriedly he left the station to make a call from one of the public boxes. He had to warn Samson. When he returned, the soldiers had already packed some prisoners in the first van, and it was moving forward to make room for the second van. Mustafa did not know what exactly was happening to the prisoners. Nobody was allowed to come to this part of the station until the vans left. Everything indicated that there would be an execution tonight, but he had no means to know whether Daniel would be taken.

Hearing the tumult outside, the prisoners did certainly know that there was execution, but no one had any inkling of whose turn it would be today. Everybody thought it was his turn, but the surest of them all was Daniel. When he heard the key on the rusty cell door crack, he did not doubt that today was his turn.

The door opened. Two soldiers entered the dark cell and beamed death-light in the room.

"Who is Daniel Goytom?" demanded one of them.

As Daniel raised himself, the spotlight came on his face.

"That's him."

"Out!"

Daniel stepped forward and tuned back to see his cellmates, whose faces under the glow of the flashlight looked darker than the death outside. They seemed not prepared for this. They were numb from the shock. They gazed at him with hollow eyes. For the several weeks, they have been his companions every minute of the day and night. The experiences in which they had been yoked together: the torture, the pain, the hunger, and exhaustion seemed to have welded them into a single being whose existence depended on one another. Now Daniel was being ripped away from them. Daniel wanted to say a word, a word of brotherhood, of gratitude, of grief, and of hope.

"I'm glad to have been one of you," spoke Daniel. "A thousand times better to be one of you and die, than to be one them and live. God bless you, brothers." I shall…" His mouth opened to shout something to his cell-mates, but before he could finish, he was hurled out of the cell. The prisoners were so stunned that none breathed a word as Daniel was shoved out of the cell.

It was cold and dark outside. Daniel looked around. There were three vans and armed men around them. He wished for something to happen, some miracle, something that could stop this nightmare. There was nothing; nothing to rescue him. His heart sunk in despair. When they tied his hands, he didn't resist. When they dragged him to the waiting van with its rear door open, he wasn't obstructive to jump in.

Inside the van, three young men whose face, in the darkness, looked alike sat at the corner. Daniel couldn't identify them. But just before the rear door was closed, a flashlight was beamed briefly which helped him to get a glimpse of the young men, and his brain registered one of the faces long enough to remember a name: Mokriya, the famous young man whom Daniel saw coming out of the Red-Terror Court the day he had been sentenced to death. As Daniel sat on the floor beside Mokriya, the rear door boomed shut, and everything darkened.

A couple of minutes later, the engines roared. Suddenly the entire prison was filled with cries and screams. The young men in the vans cried for help beating the vehicles from the inside and punching the floor. Inmates in the cells also screamed, all in one blustering sound: "Stop the killing! Stop the killing!"

Boarding crew and passengers, the journey to the killing field commenced at half-past eleven. The first van carrying the executioners led the way, and the other two carrying the prisoners followed. Daniel was in the third van, screaming for help and drumming the side of the van with all his power. The others did the same, but there was nothing that could stop the journey to death.

As soon as the last van was out of the compound of the police station, Mustafa rushed into cell number 12. Despite his anticipation, he was shocked to learn that Daniel was gone. He hastened out of the cell and discreetly ran to the nearest public telephone box across the street. Unfortunately, and to his surprise, it was occupied by his superior, Lt. Nigusie.

Mustafa had to make the call now. Time was running out. Every minute meant a life to save, and Nigusie was wasting them. Mustafa was so tense and disturbed that he wanted to knock the officer down. What the hell is he doing here! Can't he call from his office? Mustafa stepped closer to indicate that someone was waiting for the phone. But Nigusie appeared so nervous to notice him.

"They are out now. The four tools are in the last van. Good luck!" Nigusie said and hung up. Mustafa had overheard Nigusie's conversation. Obviously, Nigusie was talking about the prisoners. He wondered if Nigusie, too, was notifying Samson. Having relayed his message, Nigusie nervously left without observing Mustafa.

Mustafa put through the call

It was Biniam who answered.

"Did anyone call you a moment ago?" asked Mustafa hastily

"Yes," answered Biniam.

"What was it about?"

"It was a friend of Ermias. Needed to meet him urgently, and Ermias left right away."

"Did he say where?"

"Not exactly but something to do with Daniel, I assume."

"Where is Samson?"

"Waiting in the car. Ready."

"Yeah! Tell him to hurry up! Brother is gone. Good luck!" Mustafa placed the handset slowly and prayed briefly. Then as he thought of Daniel, his eyes became wet.

At that time, the vans had done a quarter of the journey to the execution field. Helplessly Daniel moved to the corner and sat alone. It was time to bid farewell to the world he lived in for twenty years and the people he loved for so long: his mother and his brothers, his father, Askale and her children, all his school and Zemecha friends. *How would they take this? How would they be after me?* The world carried, not only friends, but enemies too. Captain Zeleke, Mengistu, and their supporters. *How long would they go on killing people and destroying families? How many will perish before someone stops this madness?* He thought of the dead ones. *Would I meet my loved one that have passed? Would I meet Ghenet? Is this really the final moment of my life? How can it end this way? Is this all there is about life? What's life? I'm alive, so what am I? What's death? What is the difference between life and death? Isn't Death a part of life? Isn't Death, life. What about the other way around? Is life death. Death life. Life death.* Suddenly he was lost and confused. He couldn't tell which was which.

He had heard gunfire: a single shot; and the vehicle had come to a halt. Then came voices, someone threatening someone.

"Don't move. I will blow your head off!

"Hands up! Come on now. Move it.

"Where are the keys. Slowly…

"Open the door! Good! Now move."

A moment later, the rear door opened. Two men stood in the dark, casting their shadows in the van against the weak street light.

"You're safe, Comrades. Get up!"

"*Am I dreaming? This can't be true,*" Daniel thought.

"This is the EPRP!" announced one of the men.

"Long live the EPRP!" shouted Mokriya and jumped out of the van first.

Confused and in a way delighted, Daniel was the last person to jump out of the van. He looked around and discovered that they were on Roosevelt Road. The other vans were long gone.

"Harry up! We will untie you when we reach our hideout. Harry up now. Follow me."

A car was waiting a few meters away. One of the rescuers got a bit ahead and opened the doors. "Get in the car," he whispered.

The survivors, with their hands tied, were packed in the rear seat, thrilled, overwhelmed, and disoriented.

Mokriya was delirious. "I knew the EPRP would survive. I knew it wouldn't fail us," he said as the car started to roll south. Daniel looked right and left to take account of where they were heading.

In seconds the car was at its top speed. It rolled over the bridge, then turned left out of the street and into the dark neighborhood. Daniel had made out where they were. Not far from Kera: not far from his neighborhood either. After a few right and left turns on the crocked pavement, the driver announced their safe arrival as he drove the car through an open gate, which closed immediately behind them.

"Here we are, comrades," the driver said, "You're going to stay here until further notice. You will be safe here. Your contact person is Rashid." He pointed at the tall man beside him. "You can ask him whatever you want, and you should do as he tells you to do. Now follow him."

Rashid leaped out of the car and opened the side door for the survivors. "Sheesh!" he hashed one of the survivors who wanted to talk. "Not here. We can talk inside. I will untie your hands inside. Follow me."

At the front door, Rashid extracted a key, which he put in the lock, and the door swung open He reached the switch, and turned the light on, revealing an ordinary living room with a sofa, a table, a television set, a book-shelve, and a cupboard on the top of which was a telephone.

Rashid strode rapidly to the telephone, lifted it and dialed hurriedly.

"May I talk to the chief," Rashid spoke into the mouthpiece and waited. A moment later, he said, "Hallo Comrade. Rashid speaking." He paused to hear the words from the other end and continued, "The flight was excellent, and the landing is safe." He waited for the response, and when he finished, he returned to the survivors.

"Now, come on one by one." He took Mokriya's hand first and untied him. "Which one of you is Mokriya?"

"It's me," replied Mokriya stretching his free hands, looking eager to perform other duties for his party that always came to his rescue every time he needed it. Mokriya was one of the five militants who were rescued with Kibrom a year ago.

"Our mission was to rescue you. You're very important," said Rashid and turned to the next fellow. "And you?"

"My name is Mohammed from Marcato," said the short, bald young man whose hair was set afire under torture.

"And you?"

"I'm Aklilu," said the 16-year-old boy, who appeared to be oblivious to the situation.

"And you? Have we met before? Your face is familiar." That was a question people would put to Daniel after having encountered his big brother, Samson.

Daniel stared at the face with a big nose and narrow black eyes. "No, I don't think so. Ah… I thought the EPRP was destroyed. We heard so."

"Damned Alemayo, the traitor," Rashid swore, "yes, the central committee is blown. A stand-by committee has taken over the leadership. We will talk about the current situation in due time. Now, you shall rest."

In the next room, where they were ushered to, were two beds along the walls and a table with four chairs in the middle. On the bench, near the window, were the new camouflaged uniforms and four pairs of boots, evidently, from north Korea and beneath the bench, machine guns of the AK-47 type.

"You will stay in this room all the time. You sleep and eat here. When you want to go to the toilet, you call me. I'm always around to help you," Rashid said, scratching the scar on his face.

"Anything we can put in our stomach?" was everyone's question, but it was Mokriya who came with the words.

All eyes watched Rashid, who simply smiled and shook his head, "no food now, but water… we have plenty." He walked a few steps to the door and stopped to say, "You're lucky to have been rescued. Those young men in the other van shall not see the sun tomorrow. Now go to bed. Goodnight."

It was a night of deepest dark with a clumsy wind buffeting across the field. The vans had their headlights turned on, illuminating the field satisfactorily. Samson could see the prisoners being dragged out of a van and pushed into the field as they screamed and fought to get themselves free. Among the prisoner to be executed, Samson could hear, were women crying in such intensity that spanned well beyond the field and the woods.

Arriving well ahead of the executioners, he had first retrieved the machine gun he captured last Saturday from where he had hidden it in the woods. It was new and fully loaded. Carrying the machine gun, two hand grenades, a knife, and a flashlight he had spotted a strategic position from which he could watch over the execution field. This time he was sure, Daniel would be among the prisoner, a few minutes away from death. He knew he should be quick and cautious. His brother's life hung up on his performance. A slight mistake would be a lifetime regret.

As the executioners came nearer to the grave cavity, smashing and beating the retreating prisoners, he took few cautious steps closer. Now, he had a better view and a comfortable distance to use the hand grenades. There were seven executioners and eight prisoners, he counted.

Suddenly, one of the prisoners broke away from captivity and tried to run away. Following that, a machine gun exploded right away, cracked through the darkness. Samson saw a young man fall a few meters away from the grave cavity, hopping the fallen man was not Daniel. All of a sudden, the other prisoners jumped into the cavity seeking cover. This left the executioners exposed to Samson, who was now completely transformed into a killer guerrilla.

The fallen guy could be Daniel. Is he dead or wounded? A distracting thought crossed his mind, but there was no more time to contemplate it. The executioners had their guns pointed at the cavity. Instantly, he snatched out one of the hand grenades, pulled the safety out, and threw it at them. Then, just before the grenade exploded, he swiftly reached the machine gun and started pouring bullets on whoever was on his two feet in the middle of the death field. The hand grenade wiped half of the executioners, leaving the rest to the powerful machine gun and its holder, who did his part as expected from an experienced guerrilla fighter. He loved the sound of the weapon and its dynamic effect when it hit a target, the executioners being lifted in the air and crashing down on the ground. When all fell, he paused for a moment. With the sudden silence whistling sharply in his ear, he changed the machine gun to a single shot gear and stepped a little out of the woods. He began to shoot the fallen men one by one, the bullet bursting their heads into pieces, making sure that none was left breathing.

"Daniel!" he called. The youngsters in the grave cavity showed their heads up, some crawling out. Instantly a machine gun went off, its bullet whistling through the space over the field. It came from the direction of the vans. The drivers! Samson had forgotten.

"Get back into the grave hole!" He instructed and ducked back into the woods and zigzagged his way through the woods to the vans.

Samson approached the vans undetected, and from a comfortable range, he threw the second grenade at the nearest van. Retreating back to the woods, he waited for any move from the drivers as the van flamed up slowly. There was no reaction from the drivers; they might have skulked away from the place, or hid quietly. He then rushed to the other side of vans and aimed to shoot the fuel tanks. Not long after, an enormous explosion that moved the ground like an earthquake roared.

Elated with the quick result, Samson ran back to the youngsters. Once again, he called Daniel's name and hurried to the fallen guy. He turned on the flashlight on the young man's face. It was not Daniel's.

He returned to the survivors who now have come out of the grave hole and began untying each other.

"Daniel!" Samson called out loud, but no one responded as having that name. "Does any of you know a young man by the name Daniel?"

The survivors looked at each other but didn't answer. Samson's heart sunk, disappointment overwhelming him. "Weren't you in the fifth police station?"

"Yes, they brought us from there," said one of the survivors, "who are you?"

"That's our guardian angel. Who else could he be!" replied one of the girls, supporting another girl who had almost fainted.

"Are you all well?"

"Yes, we hope so," said one of the survivors.

"Those of you who can handle guns…take from the dead and follow me. Hurry up. We have got to get out of here.

Four of the young men hurried to the fallen soldiers and picked their rifles and followed Samson along with the other survivors, who appeared too overwhelmed to digest the miracle that just happened to them.

The woods were burning immensely, thick black smoke erupting as the fire caught tree after tree. Samson and the survivors made their way through the woods before the fire reached the Rover. Two of the armed ones sat beside Samson at the front seat while the others hurried to occupy the rear. When the Land-Rover began rolling, another explosion shocked the earth marking the destruction of the second van. As a result, a huge fireball and thick black smoke erupted into the sky. The entire area was illuminated by the fire.

Samson had to drive fast to elude the wildfire behind him and the subsequent government force that might appear to contain it. Driving at top speed, he put a question that was nagging him to the survivors.

"Were their others who were taken out for execution before you?"

"I saw three vans at the station, and now I see only two. I wonder where the other one vanished," said the guy beside him.

"You saw three vans?" asked Samson curiously.

"Yes, there were three vans," answered two or three of the young men simultaneously.

"Where the hell did it disappear to?" said Samson, angrily. Without caring to slow the car to a turning speed, he swung it to the right, drove past the Brewery, and in a few minutes, the Rover was on Roosevelt Road heading north. At the intersection, he turned right to enter into the very road his brother had been transported, less than a half-hour ago, under the custody of Rashid.

He speeded towards Kera. Soon they were on Beyene Street heading north. It was quarter to one, well past the curfew time. No life was supposed to be seen on the streets, but far ahead, Samson saw some armed men, and as if attracted by their guns, he pressed the gas pedal. The vehicle thrust forward with a new force.

"These are the Revo-Guards… turn back!" warned one of the guys.

Samson knew what he was doing. Ignoring the young man, he continued faster. It was apparent that he wanted some more fighting. More blood to feed his anger.

An armed man showed a stop sign with his hand, to which Samson gladly complied.

"Are you crazy! What are you up to! These people are murderers!" shouted the same guy again.

"Let's see what they can do," swore Samson between his teeth and pulled, his right hand reaching to the machine gun.

The Revo-guards cocked their rifles and approached the car. "Who are you people?" one of them asked, his breath reeking alcohol.

"Get out of the car and show your paper!" ordered another one with his gun pointing at Samson.

"You want papers… I give you this!" Samson dragged the machine gun and pointed it at the Revo-guard, clearly resolved to shoot at the slightest mistake any one of them might dare to commit. The armed youngsters beside him also had their rifles at hand.

"You want a paper or this, mister," Samson pushed the man with the muzzle of the gun provocatively, but the man was not the type to give him the fight that he was looking for. The Revo-guards were quick to understand guns. To Samson's dismay, they made no mistake.

"No problem, fellows. You can proceed. We saw nothing unlawful," a Revo-guard said and advised his colleagues to turn back.

At precisely 1 o'clock, Samson reached the gate of the Nyala Transports. Biniam opened the gate with high expectations to see Daniel. When he did not see him among the survivors who jumped out of the car, he simply cast an inquisitive eye at his big brother for an explanation.

"We will find out tomorrow, Biniam," said Samson. "Now, show these people a place to rest."

At daybreak, Daniel and the three others were awakened by Rashid, who came with breakfast and cigarettes. For security reasons, Rashid had made it clear, they were not allowed to see or talk to anyone except himself.

"What about our parents?" asked Daniel, who seemed to have no appetite for food. "Can't we inform them somehow so that they don't assume we are dead?"

"That's out of the questions," answered Rashid flatly. "Let them assume you're dead. That's safer." He reached for the packet of cigarette, flipped it open, and offered it to Daniel

"I don't smoke," said Daniel, retreating from the table. "I live not far from this area. Allow me to contact my family."

"You heard me, that's impossible!" Shouted Rashid back.

Daniel didn't want to say any more. He somehow felt that he was not in good hands.

After Breakfast was done, the plates and the mugs removed, Rashid approached them again with the air of having something important to say. He glanced at the weapons under the bench and cleared his throat.

"There is something I am instructed to tell you. The very reason you were rescued is to rescue this country. Our people are executed by the cruel hand of one man: Mengistu. Our party, the EPRP, has come with a plan to solve this problem. For the plan to work, your relentless effort and co-operation are absolutely necessary. Not as a gratitude you owe the party but as an obligation of a good citizen to save his people."

Rashid knew how to talk to youngsters. He was good at stirring their feelings. He had worked for the EPRP and had mastered the magic of words., He spoke eloquently of the misery of the people and the commitment required to liberate them.

Mokriya was already excited and very anxious to hear the order, his eyes shifting between Rashid and the machine guns.

Mohammed appeared to be in a hurry to avenge the injury the security people had inflicted to him. He was smoking nervously and not listening as attentively as he should, as though he knew what was to come. Aklilu, the youngest and the weakest, was not present mentally. He appeared to be not frightened but withdrawn. He had suffered much, both mentally and physically. To extract information from his big brother, he had been tortured in front of the brother. When the big brother held on, the mother had been brought in and beaten in front of her sons. The big brother still did not talk, the torturers had become mad that they broke his neck and killed him in front of the mother and little Aklilu. The mother was released afterward, but she became insane and killed herself a few days after. Aklilu's father, who already was an alcoholic, took to the bottles more destructively. Aklilu saw no meaning in this rescue. He was already half-dead. He was not listening to Rashid at all.

Daniel seemed to see some light at the end of the tunnel. Rashid's speech made some sense; Mengistu's removal could surely bring some change that would end the agony of the people and the suffering of his cellmates. The Zelekes would be brought to justice, which would be equivalent to killing Zeleke. There was a lot in Rashid's speech. He was listening attentively.

"The EPRP has planned to assassinate the monster. And the plan will be carried out by you," disclosed Rashid.

"Us? We don't even know how to use a gun," responded Daniel

"I gathered you were squad members of the EPRP," said Rashid and turned to Mokriya, "aren't you, Mokriya?"

"Yes, I am," replied Mokriya proudly. "Besides, I have a personal score to settle now."

"Me too," said Mohammed.

"Anyway, what we need in this operation is one good sniper like Mokriya. The rest of you will have a minor part."

"How well is it planned? What are the risks?" asked Daniel.

"It's well planned," said Rashid. "Mengistu's new army is taking military training in Sigameda. Tomorrow morning Mengistu is scheduled to pay a visit there. The plan is to assassinate him there. Mokriya will do the real job. The rest of you will put on those outfits to look like the army and mix up with them. As soon as you see Mokriya aiming at Mengistu, you start firing in the air to generate confusion and disorder. Afterward, a rescue team will come to take you out of the turmoil. Simple, clean, and effective.

"I have nothing against the plan," spoke Mohammed. "But, is there no other squads outside to do this job. Why take risks to rescue us?"

"There is no EPRP squad left now. The Red-Terror has wiped out them all. Besides, Mokriya was considered to be the best for the job, and you were found to be very strong under interrogation and torture that we believed you can still hold on if something should go wrong and you get caught." He paused, studied their faces, and continued, "We certainly believe that nothing will go wrong. We will talk about the details later on. Now listen to music and prepare yourself for the mission. I'll see you at lunchtime. After lunch, a comrade will come to show you how to use those machine guns, and you will rehearse the operation."

Chapter 27

Mengistu stood behind his office window and dropped his eyes on the ground below. It was a bright, clear morning, but his head was not that clear. He had not had a good night's sleep. He felt apprehensive and nervous not because he sensed that he was to be assassinated today; he was not a man bestowed of that sense of danger but because he was losing confidence in his security people. They seemed to have no clue of the cause of the Saturday night's fire incident, which had inflicted huge property damage and chattered the public belief that the nation was under Mengistu's total control.

Having destroyed the EPRP and chased the Socialists to hiding, Mengistu had assumed himself as an autocratic leader who was to lead the nation through the coming wars, and out to peace and prosperity. He was supposed to concentrate only on the Somali invaders, chase them out, topple Mohammed Said Barre, and set up a friendly government in Mogadishu; a government that would go along with the idea of the East African Socialist confederation.

Zeleke entered the office, but Mengistu remained unmoved until the captain uttered words.

"You don't look prepared for the day."

"What day?" Mengistu roared, his back to the captain.

"Graduation of the new army, Chairman"

"Oh! That, I almost forgot it," he said and turned slowly to the captain. "Anything from the Saturday night's incident?"

"Nothing," Zeleke's answer was intentionally brief.

"Nothing!" Mengistu imitated the word angrily and stabbed the desk furiously. He then paced the room, whirled around, and strode back, talking unceasingly in a half-whispered mixture of oath and insult until he came with the right words. Then he stared at Zeleke.

"Do you people know your job or not! Do you know that this job of yours is a twenty-four hours' job? I don't tolerate this negligence. You have got to find out who was behind the fire."

Zeleke was perturbed, "I don't think it was political. It could be an accident."

"I don't care what you think. I want facts. I authorized the execution of eight counter-revolutionaries, not twelve. Who added those four that day? And among these four is the guy who shot you. Did you include him?"

Frightened by Mengistu's restless fever-red eyes, Zeleke said, "No, I didn't. I won't do that before the investigation is over."

"Who else does have the authority to execute prisoners. The Socialists are shunted. Don't you see there is something fishy here? Somebody is playing a nasty game with me. Find out, Zeleke… Soon!"

The telephone rang.

It was a test call. The installation of the new Hot-Line communication, connecting Mengistu's office directly to the commander of the Air force in Debrezeit and the commander of the Third Army Division in the eastern region of Harar and Jigiga by microwave, was in progress. Mengistu was supposed to lead the coming war through the wires, merely sitting in his office. It was effective and safe; he thought and hung up after expressing his pleasure in the rapid accomplishment of the phone company.

He walked to his desk, and before he took his seat, he said, "I want a serious investigation to be carried out on what happened? Find out everything. Where did the four prisoners vanish?

Again, an intercom whistled, and Mengistu lifted it and said, "You can come in."

Not long after, the secretary entered.

"I just wanted to remind you of the day's schedule, particularly the inauguration of the new army."

"I have it in mind. I have a couple of hours to prepare." Mengistu ignored the secretary and turned to Zeleke, "I feel we are going to have similar sabotage in the future on every execution site. What's your solution to this problem?"

Zeleke's brain was not known for solutions; his brain was good only in executing orders. Zeleke appeared thoughtful but didn't come with any suggestions. Mengistu had one.

"I tell you a solution! From now on, every enemy of the Revolution shall be executed in the open, not by night but by daylight, not in the woods but on the streets. The bodies shall lie in the streets for everyone to see and learn a lesson. Nobody except our security people should pick the bodies. If the address of the person is known, throw the body near the neighborhood. No parent or relative shall be allowed to take the body or mourn the dead!"

The secretary listened when Mengistu gave the instructions. A minute before he was to leave the room, another call came through and he stood still to hear what would be said. Mengistu picked the handset. It was the palace operator.

"I'm sorry, Comrade Chairman, but it's urgent. Please allow me to talk to Comrade Captain Zeleke."

"It's for you," Mengistu gave the handset to Zeleke.

"Comrade Captain," said the operator, "someone by the name Rashid wants to talk to you. He says, it's of extreme importance."

"Who is Rashid? Would you please put him through?"

Zeleke waited impatiently for the man named Rashid to come into the line, and Mengistu's eyes were fixed on Zeleke, waiting to know what the urgent matter could be.

"What is it? Who are you?" Zeleke asked

The caller began explaining. Zeleke listened without interrupting, and then he drew a deep breath to ask only one question.

"Where can I meet you?"

Zeleke made a mental record of the information he heard and hung up. Hurriedly, he walked to the door, then turned to Mengistu to say, "Comrade Chairman. There is a plot to assassinate you. Cancel the inauguration."

"What are you talking about?" Mengistu roared, but Zeleke was already out of sight.

At the same time, when Rashid called Zeleke, Samson was on his way to the 5th police station to see Mustafa. He had paid a visit to the station yesterday, but he had not been able to meet Mustafa, who had also gone to the Nyala to see him. They had gone past each other on their way. Meanwhile, Samson had taken the opportunity to ask about Daniel and had been told that Daniel was not under the police custody any longer, that he could take his brother's belongings if he wished to. This always meant the prisoner was dead.

Until he knew the exact whereabouts of his brother, Samson wanted to keep what he knew to himself. He did not want his mother to have any suspicion at this time. So, he had kept all Daniel's belonging at the Nyala and spent another sleepless night at home.

In the morning, he expected Ermias to show up. The urgent call Ermias had received from Colonel Assefa could mean a lot of things. Had it been something good, Ermias would have let him know as soon as possible. Certainly, Samson thought, Ermias himself might have been exposed and arrested or killed. Samson became anxious, and quietly he left the house.

He drove to the police station with a spirit of a fighter who, at the slightest provocation, would set the city afire without hesitation. He had the machine gun beside him and the hunting knife holstered under his waist. He drove over seventy kilometers per hour, well over the speed limit in the city.

He was not the only one to the hustle and bustle today. At Mexico square, just before he cross-passed the intersection, a military vehicle just whirled into the junction at a much greater speed than his. Samson had to make a noisy stop to avoid a collision. With angry eyes, he watched the vehicle spin past the square. Sensing that the soldiers were as usual up to no good, he glanced at them again as they swung to Roosevelt Road heading south, the same way the Daniels took the night of the execution. Samson did not pay any particular attention to the leading vehicle, an open jeep on which Rashid and Zeleke sat side by side. They had driven past the intersection just a second before Samson reached there. Had he spotted them just in time and recognized Rashid, God knew what his instinct would tell him. Probably, something that would provoke a change in the course of events could have taken place. But that was not to be like in the movies. This was a real world, real-life where the good did not always win, and the bad did not always lose. Without any inkling that the soldiers were going to the four survivors, Samson proceeded north to the police station.

Mustafa had a shoeshine boy working on his shoes when Samson arrived. He paid the boy before he was finished and hurried to Samson. The news of the wildfire in Mekanisa had reached every ear in the city. And Mustafa knew that Samson had everything to do about it.

"I was at the Nyala yesterday looking for you." Mustafa began. "How did it go?"

"I, too, was here yesterday looking for you," Samson said. "Look, there is a problem. How many vans did you see the night of the execution?"

"Three. Two of them carried the prisoners, and the other one carried the soldiers. What about that?"

"There were only two vans. Where did the third one disappear? Daniel must have been in it."

"Two vans?"

"Yes. Those who came to the execution field are rescued. They are safe now."

"That's great, but what are you talking about?" Mustafa was bewildered and got lost in thought, for something was taking form in his mind, something vague as though from a distant memory. But it faded quickly, making him uneasy. He tried to recall, but it seemed to vanish further. He knew it was important, but his increasing uneasiness disturbed his memory.

"How can that be!" said Mustafa thoughtfully, in a very low voice. He then saw Lt. Nigusie walk past him to the station without saying the usual words of greetings. That was not like Nigusie. As Mustafa observed him, Nigusie seemed to be entirely absorbed to perceive his surroundings. It was now that Mustafa remembered the important thing: the conversation Nigusie had at the coin-phone the evening of the execution when he was to make the call to Samson.

"Listen, this is absurd. You're telling me that one of the vans disappeared in the night. Well, let me tell you something that was nagging me like a pebble in my shoe. This officer you see," Mustafa pointed a finger at Lt. Nigusie, "made an interesting phone call the evening Daniel was taken. To my surprise, the message he sent was exactly similar to the one I had to tell you."

"What did he say?"

"He said, 'there are out now. The tools are in the last van'," said Mustafa and looked at Samson absently. "He must have been talking about the van that disappeared with Daniel. Someone may have rescued them. Go, follow him into the office and ask him. He is a nice guy…"

Samson did not wait until Mustafa finished.

Lt. Nigusie opened the door of his office, stepped in, and when he tried to close the door behind him, it resisted and flung open. Samson was behind him, his head high, face frightening. Suddenly he shoved the Lieutenant to the wall, flattened him against it, and searched him quickly.

"Sit down!" Samson's voice was low but firm.

Startled, Nigusie walked to his desk and took his seat. He had not slept since Saturday, one could see. His mind was occupied with one thought: the assassination of Chairman

Mengistu. He automatically connected this sudden intrude with the plot of the assassination.

"Anything wrong?" he asked as Samson took the seat on the opposite side of his desk.

"That's what you will answer to me." Samson's eyes were fixed on the officer, suppressed anger behind them.

"Who are you? Do I know you? Your face is familiar."

"You never saw me before, but you have seen my brother, Daniel, who was under your custody. I want to know where he is now," demanded Samson showing precise determination to know by any means.

"Who are you to ask?"

"Daniel's brother."

"Just a brother?" Nigusie sighed in relief. His suspicion that this intruder could be Mengistu's agent subdued to compose himself as an authority. "You can't just come into my office and ask questions...

"Don't tell me that!" Samson's countenance was something sinister. "Where is he now?"

Nigusie took his eyes off Samson, turned his face sidewise to get rid of Samson's stare. But Samson did not soften his sight grip.

"I can't tell you."

Samson abruptly rose, threw his body over the desk, and grabbed the officer's throat with his left hand; the right hand held the big knife.

"Don't play games with me! I have had enough of you people!" The point of the knife touched Nigusie's soft skin under the ear.

"Easy...easy, I'll tell you." Nigusie shivered in apprehension. "Easy man."

"Not when you're playing with my brother's life." Samson squeezed harder before he softened his grip and let Nigusie free.

"Okay, what is that you want to know?"

"Is Daniel dead or alive?"

"As far as I know, he is not dead."

"Where is he now?"

Nigusie sat quietly for a moment contemplating the question. If he would tell Daniel's whereabouts, he thought he would endanger the assassination plan, which was a matter of higher priority. As for this intruder, he could call some help to get rid of him. He squinted down at his wristwatch. "I cannot tell you now. Maybe an hour later, not before."

"What's to happen in an hour?"

The phone came to Nigusie's rescue. He was expecting a call, but this one seemed a bit earlier.

"Maybe, I can tell you after this call." Nigusie lifted the phone. "Nigusie speaking,"

"This is Number Two."

"Anything wrong?"

"Everything is wrong. Rashid has sold us. He has betrayed us."

"Rashid what?"

Samson considered the name Rashid.

"Rashid has revealed our plans to the security forces. Now they are after us. Get lost immediately."

"What about the kids?"

"I don't know."

Hurriedly, Nigusie replaced the handset and rose.

"Get up," Nigusie muttered. "We have got to get out of here immediately." Hastily, he reached the drawer, pulled it open, and grasped some documents which he stuffed into his attaché case. "Follow me, hurry up!"

"What happened?" asked Samson, puzzled by Nigusie's reaction.

"Just get me a taxi."

"I have a car."

In a moment, they were in the car heading south. On the way, Nigusie began to talk.

"The Socialists had worked on a plan to assassinate Mengistu. To implement the plan, we needed reliable men with a strong commitment to remove Mengistu. The Socialists had few militants, but we didn't want to assign them because if the plan should somehow fail, the consequence would be devastating. So, we devised a tactic to use detained EPRP militants who were caught in an armed fighting. We knew of one militant who would do whatever his party ordered him to do. We added three more who would help him. I picked Daniel because a lady, presumably your aunt, appealed to me to save him by any means possible.

"We arranged a fake court and sentenced the Daniels to death. When we learned that the securities were to take out some prisoners to execute, we manage to include Daniel and the three young men on the list and transported them with a separate vehicle. The driver was well informed and generously paid to co-operate. On their way to the execution site, our people, disguised as the EPRP, intercepted. Daniel and the three were taken to a safe hideout. Today they were supposed to assassinate Mengistu and go home.

"Had everything gone as planned… had that fellow, Rashid, shut his big mouth, Mengistu would have been killed by now, and Daniel and the others would have made it. Daniel's part in the operation was relatively simple.

Samson's attention was not fully with Nigusie. He was thinking of any chance left to rescue Daniel. "You're going to take me to the hideout now," Samson said without looking at Nigusie.

"What? Are you crazy? Didn't you hear what I have been telling you?"

"Dead or alive, I have to see my brother. Now, which way?"

"I advise you to reconsider your decision. I told you… your brother is caught by now. You can't help him; you will only put yourself in danger.

"Which way!" shouted Samson, smashing the steering wheel.

"Right ahead."

In a few minutes, they were on Roosevelt Road. A few minutes later, on the bridge; after which they turned left. Few blocks away, they saw a crowd on the sideways watching something on the ground.

"Pull up here," whispered Nigusie. The car slowed and halted as Samson pressed the brake.

The centers of public attention were four bullet-ridden dead bodies thrown on the street like dead dogs. Young, naked bodies deprived of the simplest respect, left in the open for the people to see and learn not to play with Mengistu's revolution.

Samson broke through the crowd and kneeled beside Daniel's body. He looked at the tortured body of his brother, a thin film of tears on his eyes. Through the tears, he briefly visualized the one time jubilant, and loving little brother, embracing him as he welcomed him home. Then he sensed him say, 'Angel, you came a little late.'

He touched the mutilated face tenderly. '*For this, they shall pay heavily!*' vowed Samson by heart. He caressed the face and closed the eyes that still seemed to register the surrounding even after the life had gone out of them. Then, he took off his jacket covered the body and as he lifted it the crowd broke apart to make a way for him

'I'm sorry,' said Nigusie solemnly as Samson laid Daniel's body in the car. 'I hope you'll find the strength to overcome this tragedy.'

Samson did not look at Nigusie; neither did he say a word. When he started the car, there was no tear in his eyes but a flashing flame of rage. By the time he reached home, he had already made up his mind. *"To take up arms against a sea of troubles, and by opposing, end them."*

Epilogue

Despite Mengistu's successful obliteration of his political opposition, people's support for the Dergue government decreased as a result of economic and political disasters, conflict, and famine. In the Ogaden, an estimated 25,000 civilians were killed in 1980 following the defeat of the Somali army, and, in Eritrea, between 70,000 and 80,000 combatants and civilians were killed between 1978 and 1981.

In 1989, several long-standing liberation movements took the opportunity to consolidate forces, and the Tigrian People's Liberation Front (TPLF), the Ethiopian People's Democratic Movement (EPDM) formed a united front called the Ethiopian People's Revolutionary Democratic Front (EPRDF). In February 1991, the EPRDF and the Eritrean People's Liberation Front (EPLF) launched new offenses against Dergue forces and were able to overpower the army, which had become divided and frustrated with the brutality of Mengistu's rule. in May 1991 Mengistu fled to Zimbabwe and the Eritrean forces along with the EPRDF entered Addis Ababa and took control of the country.[VIII]

Dedication

We dedicate this book to the memory of His Majesty Haile Selassie Emperor of Ethiopia. We also publicly appeal to the parliament of Ethiopia to consider restoring the original name of Haile Selassie University in his commemoration. We ask students, teachers, scholar and government officials in Ethiopia and other countries to join us in our effort to achieve this goal. Certainly,, the Emperor deserves more; his contribution in the field of education was so immense that ignoring him would be a shameful ingratitude history will record.

Stifhab book club.

Stocholm,

March 12, 2021

Acknowledgment

Red Tears: **Dawit Woldegiorgis**
Killing a generation   **Babile Tola**
The Generation by   **Kiflu Tadesse**
Eritrea: Dynamics of National Question. **Medhane T/tsion**

These historical books were source of vital information to the author. As indicated on the end-note, some well written pose from these books were modified to fit in the story and used in the text of novel.

Endnote

[I] Ref: To Kill a Generation. Babile Tola.

[II] Except for a few restructurings of sentences to suit the novel, this passage is copied from RED TEARS/ Dawit W/Giorgis (It was his personal account of the situation.)

[III] RED TEARS/ Dawit W/Giorgis.

[IV] RED TEARS/ Dawit W/Giorgis

[V] Mesqel: The Cross. The square's name was changed to Revolution square by the communist military regime.

[VI] Martyr's of Yekatit 12 : Killers of armed *Blackshirts* and Fascist civilians were unleashed on the defenceless residents of Addis Ababa in Feb 17- Feb 21, 1937

[VII] On the morning of 23 November 1974, 60 imprisoned former government officials were extrajudicially executed by the Dergue.

[VIII] **U S Bureau of Citizenship and Immigration Services,** ***Ethiopia:***